KISSA

SENJA SUUTARI

Boilerplate Books, llc | Maine

For information contact us at www.boilerplatebooks.com
Book and Cover design by Boilerplate Books, LLC
ISBN: 9781734793420

Print Edition, 2020

10 9 8 7 6 5 4 3 2 1

For my daughter, Holly, who serves as my muse and posthypnotic suggestion

CONTENTS

CHAPTER 1

It was two o'clock in the afternoon in Stastas. Although it was only early August, the weather was rainy and raw. In Stastas there seemed to be two kinds of summer days — cold and wet, or hotter than hell. Kate Oksa hated the place. She hated the smoke from the pulp mill. She hated the dumpy little town with its dull, stupid people. She hated being poor. She hated living with her drunken father and her shrewish mother, so much so that a lot of her life was spent wherever she managed to find shelter. She'd hated school enough to drop out at sixteen to become, if not exactly a street kid, a kid of the streets. The town of Stastas was so small that just about everyone there knew who Kate was, although most of the townspeople ignored her (except the Old People) and Kate, in turn, barely tolerated them.

Kate burned with one ambition: to get out of Stastas, although she had no clear plan as to how she would do it. Too young and too uneducated to qualify for any but the most menial jobs, Kate had no money except the little she was able to earn running errands for the Old People.

It was to visit the Old People that Kate was headed, carrying a shopping bag and clutching her frayed denim jacket around her thin shoulders. Kate's Old People lived in the Stastas Retirement Village. While the name seemed to conjure up neat houses with flower beds and clipped lawns, the place, due to budget cuts in a flagging economy, was as run-down and as depressing as many of its inhabitants. It had been built forty years earlier as a retirement village/home/hospital complex, the divisions of which were now called the Village, the Lodge, and the ECU. It was designed so that the "residents" (the politically correct term — *not*, as Kate had been told, "inmates") had access to more intensive care as their age advanced and health deteriorated. Kate referred to the place as "a laundry chute to Ouijaland" and compared the inert elderly, sitting in wheelchairs in the Lodge lobby, to fruit rotting in a bowl.

Kate's visit was more mercenary than mercy. The Old People, at least some of them, had enough spending money so that Kate managed to make a few dollars performing services for them. To Kate it was strictly business. She wasted little time on affection or compassion. The Old People, to her, were just another example of how "life sucks," and she affected indifference to their plight, with only a dash of morbid interest in those who died and their manner of dying.

On the other hand, several of the Old People were crustily fond of Kate. Perhaps she was a sprig of youth in their dried bouquet — the one remaining filament connecting them to their fast-departing independence. After all, if Kate wrote a letter, carried a message, or did a bit of shopping, nobody else had to know about it, not the staff nor family members — if a resident's family were still anywhere in evidence, that is. Kate's abrasive personality was a change from patronizing jollity, in that you could count on her not to dress up in a clown suit and try to get everyone to sing "You Are My Sunshine." At Stastas Lodge, Kate was, if not universally embraced, at least so far, accepted.

Kate walked past a row of private dwellings, duplexes with faded paint and weathered woodwork. This was Stastas Retirement Village. Here the Old People, mostly couples who still had their faculties, lived in the shadow of the Lodge, and (Kate thought) in denial. They weren't the ones who needed Kate's services, at least not much. The ones on the other side of the Lodge, those in the hospital Extended Care Unit, were far beyond needing them. The Lodge stood in the middle. Purgatory: the halfway house between the quick and the veg.

Kate had several calls to make at the Lodge that day. Her first mission was to go see Mrs. Trachtenberg and help her write a letter. Mrs. Trachtenberg's eyesight no longer allowed her the luxury of private communication with her daughter, Miriam. She had a son, Saul, who lived in Stastas and visited her every second week. Saul would have also done her letter writing for her, except, as Mrs. Trachtenberg told Kate, "Every time I tell him what to write, he say, 'Mama, why you want to say *that* for?'"

"Say whatever you want, Mrs. T. It's no skin off my ass."

Mrs. Trachtenberg shifted her bulk in the antimacassared easy chair she'd brought from her home. She raised her right hand, the index and middle finger extended, punctuating her dictation with a double-pointed gesture toward Kate, who, without looking up, copied her words onto a piece of lined stationery in a notepad. "Listen, I tell you, Miriam, you gotta keep a clean house. And fix up the place. And don't spend so much money on shoes."

Kate looked up. Mrs. Trachtenberg spoke with an accent. "Excuse me, Mrs. T, was that *juice* or *shoes?*"

"Shoes. *Shoes.* On the feet. Shoes. Imelda Marcos she thinks she is!"

"Gotcha. Shoes."

"Look, Miriam. Everybody's got marriage troubles. Even your papa and me, we had our bad times. But we fix up the house, get new curtains, paint the place and we take a vacation in the Catskills, and everything works out okay." Mrs. Trachtenberg paused, directed her gaze out the window, then continued: "This girl at Marty's office. Just wait it out. Marty will come to his senses. But you gotta keep the house clean." Mrs. Trachtenberg sighed and stopped.

"Is that all?" Kate asked.

"Hah? Oh, yeah, that's all. Sign it 'your loving mama.' And hand me my purse from the table there, Katie." Mrs. Trachtenberg dug into her bag and handed Kate a couple of wadded-up bills and a dog-eared card with her daughter's address on it so Kate could copy it onto an envelope.

"Okay, Mrs. T. Anything else you need?"

Mrs. Trachtenberg took a couple more bills from her handbag and gave them to Kate. "You come see me again next week and bring me a carton of Lucky Strikes. And don't tell Saul about the letter and don't tell him about the cigarettes. He don't like me to smoke."

"Right, Mrs. T. No problema." Kate was too young to be buying cigarettes, but she had connections. When anyone at the Lodge wanted them, Kate would ask one of her friends at the Dump, usually Sumo, to buy them for her at the supermarket or drugstore.

Mrs. Trachtenberg looked at Kate and smiled. A long time ago, a *very* long time ago, Mrs. Trachtenberg had been a slip of a girl with brown hair and big brown eyes. Mrs. Trachtenberg mused that *she* had been pretty too — well, at least pretty enough. "You're a good girl, Katie, and you'd be nice-looking if you'd wear a dress and fix yourself up a little. Put a little curl in your hair. You got those big eyes and those cheekbones just like my sister Ida. We used to tell her, you could be a movie star and catch a prince with those cheek-bones." Mrs. Trachtenberg waved her hand dismissively. "So, instead she marries Bernie Finkelstein. But she didn't do *too* bad. Bernie's a lawyer. But, Katie, you're too skinny. You oughta eat more. You don't take drugs, do you?"

"No, Mrs. T."

"'Cause drugs'll kill you. You don't never wanna use drugs, you hear me? You use drugs and you wind up *dead* in the alley."

"Right, Mrs. T. See you next week. I gotta go." *And if I live clean and don't do drugs I may end up like you in a butt-sprung chair in a nine-by-twelve waiting room to hell.*

Actually, Kate didn't use drugs. She'd tried it once and the result had been weird, to say the least. Pot, which all of Kate's friends smoked, and which was even a "recreational drug" to their parents, had left Kate with a fever of 103°, out of her head for two days on the floor of a dirty room in what had once been a garage and gas station. Now the place was called the "the hippie house" by those old enough to remember the sixties. To Kate and her friends it was simply the Dump, short for What-a-Dump, the name they'd given it the night they'd broken into the abandoned building and made it their own. It had been there, with her then-boyfriend, Barry, that Kate had smoked her first and last joint. She didn't know what had happened. Barry had insisted that she must've had the flu or something, but Kate had awakened stiff and sore, as if she'd been beaten, terrified by her experience.

Not using drugs had made Kate even more of a loner. Several of the high school dropouts she knew were, by now, zombies and burn-outs — blown fuses. When things at home got so bad that she had to go spend the night at the Dump, Kate wasn't exactly "overstimmed" by their company. Even Barry Harwood, whose name was as beautiful as his body, was beginning to have trouble finishing sentences.

Drugs had driven the wedge between them. Kate didn't use them; Barry had become more and more dependent on them. It was clear too that Barry had other problems as well. They hadn't broken up so much as just drifted in different directions.

Kate wouldn't have admitted it, but these days she felt more comfortable with the Old People, even though she viewed them with a tinge of contempt. Old People had a past. They may not have any future (yeah, like her own was so bright?) but to Kate the past was fascinating. Whenever her old man was out cold and her mother had tired herself out yelling and gone to bed, Kate liked to watch old movies on TV. She wondered how it was that back in the 1940s *everybody* wore hats. Hats! Men wore hats. You'd see a crowd scene and every freakin' guy wore a fedora. And women wore hats — stupid-looking hats that made them all look like a bunch of dorks — but they all wore them. And everybody dressed the same. They all had the same haircut. Nobody had a beard. The women all wore high heels. All the skirts were the same length. It was spooky. People were like sheep back then. You couldn't *get* people today to dress alike. What would it have been like to be living in those times? And of all those people in the old movies — huge crowds of people — hardly anyone would be alive now. A few diehards, maybe, in places like the Lodge, but in a few more years they'd all be gone. Swept clean. Planted. *Kaput.*

As Kate crossed the Lodge lobby, she nodded perfunctorily at the Old People sitting there, some in wheelchairs. Had they really wanted to live this long? Kate tried to visualize seventy or eighty years into the future. Would *she* want to live that long? What would it be like to be old in a world that could be straight out of *Star Trek?* Nah, we'd have blown ourselves up by then or been poisoned by pollution. Or we'll all be dead of AIDS or cancer caused by plutonium leaks. Or we'll be living underground, or in glass bubbles, having to pay for air like we pay for water. God! Old people wouldn't even be allowed to *live.* There probably wouldn't be any animals either, except those raised for food. Nobody would have any pets. No dogs or cats. There'd probably be air cops who'd come busting in your house to make sure you didn't have a hamster stashed away — or a grandmother.

As if in answer to Kate's musings, a dark, furry form slithered past her ankles and continued on up the corridor. Moonrise, the Lodge cat, had moved in about the time that news reports began claiming that animals had a salutary effect upon the elderly and the mentally disturbed. She'd become a favorite of the wheelchair crowd, and such a welcome visitor in the psych ward, that the Powers That Be had decided she could stay. Sort of. No one had made an official declaration of welcome, but no one had called the Humane Society either to have her removed. As if aware of her ambiguous status, Moonrise would dart across the lobby, slink down hallways, and relax only in the rooms and laps of the Old People. She was apparently en route to visit one of them now, even as Kate was.

"Hey, Moonrise, you little flea hotel, cross in front of me a few more times. I could use more bad luck." The animal paused, threw Kate a glance from huge yellow eyes that had given the cat her name, then scuttled around a corner, out of sight. Kate noticed that there was something different about Moonrise. A solid black shorthaired female, the cat had always been rangy, but she seemed thinner than usual, more low-slung. *Dragging her tits. Getting old too, Kate guessed.*

And speaking of old, there's Mr. Anthony Reed. Mr. Reed usually left his door open, as if to maintain some contact with the world, even while he withdrew from it deep into the pages of his books. Kate approached the man in the wheelchair and knocked softly on the open door. The man raised his head from the volume he was reading, moved his eyeglasses to the top of his head and smiled. "Hey there, Kit-Kat."

"Hey, Doc. Called up any demons lately?"

The big black man chuckled. "A few, a few. There's one a-chewin' on my *bee*-hind right now."

"So how *is* the old rheumatiz, Doc? I mean, a man with your training ought to know how to cure it. A little frog juice, an eyeball or two, some chicken guts?"

"Sounds like my first wife's recipe for sausages."

"Well, if you can't magic yourself young again and out of here, is there anybody I can help you *nail*? Chicken blood and raven feathers delivered on request. Toenails and hair of the victim will cost extra.

Clay for dolls thrown in free."

"Where were you when I needed you? We'd have made a great team." Anthony Reed handed Kate the book he'd been holding. "Please, will you take that back to the library? Mrs. Murguia has some more books for me, and if you'll bring them back you'll earn my gratitude and ten bucks."

"Sure, Doc." Kate took the book. "Might even get there tonight before they close, if I hustle." She hefted the book and looked at the title: *Cosmic Consciousness and the Nature of Creation.* Whoa! The book must have weighed several pounds. Anthony Reed watched her, smiling faintly, as Kate opened the book at random, then closed it again as if she'd accidentally walked into the wrong room. "So, Doc, what's this all about anyway?"

"The power of the mind, Kit-Kat. It's about how we all create our own experiences in life."

"You think we do?"

"Yes. Absolutely."

"Then how come our lives are such a pile of crap?"

"I didn't say we were *good* at it."

"You mean if I walk out of here and get hit by a bus, I'm the one who caused it?"

"Not consciously, Kit-Kat. Nobody gets up and says I think I'll get sick today or I think I'll get mugged. But someone who is *afraid* of getting sick or *afraid* of getting mugged and thinks about it all the time will actually attract that sort of thing. That's what the book is about. You get what you expect in life, both good and bad. We all do."

Kate mulled that over. "Okay then, if you know all this, how come you're here? You should be living in a nice house someplace."

"Well, Kit-Kat, first of all, we'd have to assume that having a house is important. To me, right now, it isn't. Second, wherever I am, and wherever *you* are, is exactly where we should be."

"But I hate this crummy town. You mean this is where I should be all my life?"

"Not at all. Let's for a moment pretend we're playing a game."

"Like a computer game in the mall?"

"Yes, that's a good analogy. You've just fought your way, say, to Level Two. Now, to get to Level Three, you have to fight some monster who's out to zap you, right?"

"Yeah, well, okay, close enough."

"You don't want to stay on Level Two forever, do you? But that's where you are now. You had to do a lot of things to *get* to Level Two, so it was your own actions that got you there. You may not even *like* Level Two, but you have to pass through it to get on with the game. So what do you do?"

"I fight my way to Level Three?"

"Exactly. You don't say, well, Level Two sucks but I have to stay here forever. And that's the point, Kit-Kat. Where you are now is like a report card. This is the reality you've made so far. *And you always have the power to change it.*"

"And how do I do that?"

"You start by believing that you *can.*"

"Is that all?"

"No, that's just the beginning. And it's not that easy. For now, just start thinking about it, Kit-Kat. Try to picture the kind of life you *do* want. You're still very young. What would you like to happen in your life? Where do you want to be, for instance, two or three years from now?"

"Somewhere the hell away from Stastas."

"Ah, but *where?* If all you want is to be *away*, it leaves all kinds of open possibilities. Some of them may be a lot worse than being in Stastas."

"I don't know, Doc. I've never been anyplace else."

"Have you thought of going back to school? Knowledge is power. With an education, you'd have more choices. Life is all about choices,

Kit-Kat. You can make them yourself or they will be made for you."

"But how would I know what choices to make?"

"We don't always make the right ones, Kit, but it's still better to drive your own car than to hand the keys to someone else."

"So, Doc, have you ever made some bad choices yourself?"

"More than once. Some were worse than others."

"So what did you do? Gimme an example."

Anthony Reed sighed, took a moment before he answered. "Well, I once chose to do nothing when I should have done something. *I* gave the car keys of my life to someone else, and the results were disastrous. And I'd give anything to be able to undo what happened."

Kate's curiosity was piqued. "So what *did* happen, Doc?"

Mr. Reed hesitated again briefly. "An innocent person died."

"Oh, jeez, Doc. Friend of yours?"

"Yes, she was. I didn't know her well, but she was always kind to me."

"How did she die?"

"She was murdered during a botched burglary."

Kate's eyes widened. "Megabummer," she said softly, then waited, hoping Mr. Reed would elaborate, but Anthony Reed sat silent. Then the corners of his mouth twitched, and a laugh came bubbling out. "Yeah, Kit-Kat, it certainly was that. *Megabummer.*"

"Guess I should be going so I can get to the library before it closes."

"Run along then. By the way, Kit, you want a Mission Impossible?" Anthony Reed raised his large hands, the fingers knobby and deformed by arthritis, and placed his palms together. "I just got to thinking this morning that there's one thing in this world I'd like to have while I still have a pulse, and that's a good old-fashioned mess of collard greens! I don't know where you'd find 'em. Most white folks don't know about collards. Maybe someone with a home vegetable patch might have some. Anyway, there's nothin' in this world better than collard greens in the fall after the first frost has turned 'em sweet.

Fresh greens, not canned, cooked with a little salt pork like they do in the South. Won't be long before we start getting frosts. Twenty bucks in it for you. Thirty if you can get 'em to me while they're still hot!"

Kate nodded wordlessly and left, her mind doing a search of possible sources of collard greens, whatever *they* were. Something like cabbage? Her grandmother had grown kale and Swiss chard; she'd have probably known. Maybe Mrs. Murguia could tell her. Mrs. Murguia, the Stastas librarian, knew everything. She was the one who ordered books from all over the country for Anthony Reed on interlibrary loan. Kate put Mr. Reed's book in her shopping bag and headed for her next stop, Mrs. Niemi's room.

Kate did not like Elina Niemi who had only recently been admitted to the Lodge, and was, at least for the time being, living uneasily in a double room with another woman resident. Mrs. Niemi made no secret that she considered her roommate to be socially beneath her, and that she was prepared to tolerate her only until a single room became available. Kate had known Mrs. Niemi all her life as part of the Finnish community, as a pillar of the Finnish Lutheran Church, and as a woman who considered herself the line monitor of all Christians queuing up on the road to heaven. As far as Kate knew, no one in her own family was standing in that line; no one in Kate's family had even been given a number, although rumor had it that Mrs. Niemi's late husband and Kate's father had been related somehow. The original name had been Oksaniemi, shortened and split somewhere in the Americanization process.

Kate would have gladly passed Mrs. Niemi by, but her instincts told her that it would be bad for business. Mrs. Niemi was cheap, arbitrary, and demanding. And she was a troublemaker, spiteful enough to find some reason to complain about Kate and get her barred from the Lodge altogether. Kate did her best not to "dis the bitch" and tried to have as little to do with her as possible.

Mrs. Niemi's roommate must have felt the same way, because she was nowhere in sight. Elina Niemi was alone — a small, reedy woman with osteoporosis stoop who walked with the help of a cane whenever her arthritic knee was acting up. She spent most of her time doing cross-stitch with the aid of an illuminated magnifying glass she had clamped to a small worktable next to her glider rocker. "You're late, Katri!" (as if they'd had an appointment). "Did you get my floss?"

"Yes, Mrs. N." Kate pulled a handful of colored hanks of embroidery thread out of her shopping bag.

"I am *not* 'Mrs. N.' I am Mrs. *Niemi.* Now say it right."

"Mrs. Niemi." *And I am not Katri. I am Kate. Can you say 'Kate?' I* thought *you couldn't.*

"Not Mrs. Nee-mee, Katri. It's Mrs. Niemi. Nee-yem-ee. I must say it's a disgrace that you don't speak your own language, Katri. A disgrace and a sin." She walked to her magnifying glass and studied the floss under the light, fingering the threads. "This isn't the color I ordered, Katri. I wanted number 826, medium azure blue. This is 827, medium *sky* blue. It's not the same thing at all!"

"I'm sorry Mrs. — uh — Neeyummy. That's all they had. The clerk said to tell you that if the color wasn't close enough, they'll be getting another shipment of floss next week, and if the 826 doesn't come in, they can order it special next month."

Mrs. Niemi threw the floss on her worktable and, cane in hand, thumped across the room to stand in front of Kate. "The clerk said, *the clerk said.* You should have demanded to see the manager. The clerk is a *nobody.* A stupid *underling.* Why do I always have to deal with fools! I may be old and I may be ill, but *there was a time!* There was a time when people said 'yes, ma'am' and 'whatever you wish, ma'am.' There was a time when I had a house full of servants and I commanded respect. I *demanded* respect. I had a beautiful house by the sea — a house with thirty rooms — and that house was spotless. Never so much as a speck of dust. My servants knew I wouldn't tolerate it. But what would you know about such things, Katri? Medium sky blue indeed!" She indicated the floss on the table. "You can just take that back where you got it and don't expect me to pay you. Let that be a lesson."

Kate sighed, retrieved the floss, and turned to go. "Not so fast, Miss!" *Oh shit!* "Since you've ruined my day, you can just run down to the church library and bring me some books to read. Here's a list, and here's a dollar for your trouble, although you don't deserve it."

A dollar! A whole dollar to add to my getaway fund!

"Now what do you say?"

"Huh?"

"You say, 'Thank you, Mrs. Niemi.'"

"Thank you, Mrs. Niemi." *And may the issue of a thousand crab lice find real estate in your orifices.*

...

Kate had one more stop at the Lodge that day and she approached it with hesitation. Augustina Norland had, in her youth, been a great beauty. Throughout her life, she'd also been accorded a high degree of respect for her good works and her intellect. Senior citizenship had brought her, informally, the status of Village Wise Woman, consulted about such things as career choices, marriage problems, and by some (it was said) even financial investments. Mrs. Norland was a student of theosophy, and had a following of townspeople who felt that her mystical knowledge made her an oracle. When Mrs. Norland spoke, people listened, although her conversation tended to be sprinkled with references to nature spirits.

When Mrs. Norland had turned ninety, she'd sold her house on the edge of town and checked into the Lodge. There she'd established a court of sorts, with herself as queen. At ninety-two Mrs. Norland was still active, coming and going at will with a regal air, treated with deference by peers and staff alike. What Kate (and, so far, maybe no one else) knew was that, somewhere along the path to enlightenment,

Mrs. Norland's celebrated intellect had recently hung a sharp left into some strange territory.

Augustina Norland was sitting in an overstuffed high-backed chair as if on a throne. She was dressed in a Japanese kimono, her dyed jet-black hair piled in a topknot, *à la concierge*. She held in her hands a length of crochet. In earlier years, Mrs. Norland's needlework had won her many ribbons at county fairs. Now, her work had taken on an obsessive quality. The floor of her room was covered with crocheted rugs, her chair had a crocheted cover, her bed a crocheted spread — and all seemed to be made of the same red ombre wool yarn with the same J-size afghan hook. That and her red, undulating lava lamp gave Mrs. Norland's surround an other-worldly quality, like Madame Defarge in Hades, or in this case, with the cat, Moonrise, sitting on the arm of her chair, the look of a witch and her familiar in their milieu.

"Come in quickly, Katri, and close the door. Did anyone follow you?"

Kate smiled warily. "I don't think so."

"You can't be too careful. They want to kill me, you know, just like they killed President Kennedy."

"Now why would anyone want to kill you, Mrs. N?"

Mrs. Norland lowered her voice to a whisper. "Because I *know* too much. They follow me everywhere, but they don't know that I can see them. You don't believe me? Ha! They *count* on the fact that no one will believe me! But I have proof. Here, I'll show you." Mrs. Norland rummaged in her bag of yarn and pulled out a small stone. "See this? They left it for me as a sign. This was in the middle of the walk when I went out this morning. It means they're going to try to kill me."

"Aw, c'mon, Mrs. N! Hey, how's your yarn holding out? You want me to pick up some more? They're having a sale at Woolco."

"That's not why I asked you to come, Katri." Mrs. Norland got up and walked over to Kate. She glanced furtively around, then leaned over so that her face was inches from Kate's. "I'm going to have to trust you. There's nobody else. First of all, you have to promise not to speak of what I'm about to show you to anyone. *Anyone.* Do you understand? Do you promise?"

"Yeah, yeah, sure Mrs. Norland." *If I'd told anyone about you, you'd have been in the psych ward long ago.*

"I don't expect you to understand this Katri, but I've been entrusted with a very important task. I've been given a mission. It's vital that I complete it before I die, and I need you to help me."

Kate squirmed and wondered if she'd still be able to make it to the library before it closed.

"I see I'll have to show you." Mrs. Norland went over to her bed. She knelt down with surprising agility and pulled out a cardboard box from under it. Moonrise, who had followed her, jumped inside, and Kate, who hadn't known what to expect — certainly not *that* — saw that the box contained a litter of kittens. There were three of them, squeaking and squirming, searching for Moonrise's nipples. Once plugged in they began to nurse, kneading her belly with tiny, clawed front paws.

"You see, Katri? If they find them, they won't let me keep them."

Kate saw. Moonrise in the Lodge was one thing — hadn't that cat been spayed? Obviously not! Kittens were something else again. What Kate should do, of course, is to tell someone on the staff that wiggy old Mrs. Norland had a box of kittens in her room and — oh yeah, right. She, Kate Oksa, was going to fink on a 92-year-old lady who might have a heart attack any second. Besides, this was, after all, pretty funny. Kate wondered how Mrs. Norland had kept it secret so far. When the housekeeping staff came in to clean her room, were the kittens out for a walk in Mrs. Norland's yarn bag? Or had she paid off the maid?

"Just what is it you want me to do, Mrs. N?"

Mrs. Norland's eyes, like lasers, gazed into Kate's. "The kittens are safe now. They're still very young and their mother feeds them, but once they open their eyes they'll be harder to hide. *And that's when I want you to take them.*"

Kate looked at the old woman. She probably had been very beautiful when she was young. Broad forehead, high cheekbones, eyes so dark it was hard to tell where the iris ended and pupil began. Now the eyes had sunk back to glinting black holes, and she was wearing too much rouge, giving her the look of a circus clown. Kate suddenly felt sorry for her.

"Uh, Mrs. N, I dunno. I'm no good at taking care of pets. I've got no place — "

Mrs. Norland clutched Kate's arm tightly with long bony fingers. "*Please help me.* It's *very* important. These kittens *mustn't* get into the wrong hands. I can't explain right now, but you *must* help me. You're the only one who can!" Her voice was taking on greater urgency and her breathing was coming in irregular gasps.

"Calm down, Mrs. Norland. Yeah, sure, okay. I'll do what I can. If they're still here when they're too big for the box, you can give them to me." *And I can drop them off at the Humane Society and no one will be any the wiser. And I'll be saving your ass, Mrs. N, as well as ol' Moonrise's here from a fate worse than death.*

Mrs. Norland relaxed her grip. "Thank you, Katri," she whispered. Then, slowly, she smiled. "And don't worry, they'll still be here." To Kate, she looked altered, somehow alien, until Kate realized that in all the years she'd known Mrs. Norland, she couldn't remember ever having seen her smile.

CHAPTER 2

THE NEXT week things were going so smoothly for Kate that it made her a little uneasy. Life at home had been quiet: No drunken rages, no furniture hurled through windows, no threats of bodily injury, no neighbors calling the cops. Her father, normally the focus of such incidents, had hardly been seen all week. Furtive in his goings and comings, he'd appeared to be preoccupied by something — something he obviously didn't want to talk about. He would down a hasty cup of morning coffee, then leave, almost as if he had a job to go to, then appear again briefly at dinner, only to absent himself again for the evening. He gave no explanation, and when his wife asked, offhandedly, where he thought he was going, he mumbled something about it being a man's business and that women didn't have to know everything. Kate was just grateful that he seemed to be staying sober; she didn't question where or how he might be spending his time.

There had always been rare times of temporary calm in the Oksa household — times when her parents seemed to be almost companionable — times when Heikki and Helvi would linger at the kitchen table over a cup of coffee and chat. But Kate had noticed that the only common ground her mother and father seemed to have was seated in the past. Kate always listened with interest, as their conversations would involve family history, old gossip, and her parents' often-divergent memories of how things had been. It gave Kate a glimpse into a world she hadn't known, or been too young to remember: a time when her mother and father had been young and newly married. Had they ever been in love? Had they ever even *liked* each other? Whenever she'd asked her mother to tell her about their early times, Helvi had curtly said that there was nothing to tell. Kate concluded that Helvi meant there was nothing *good* to tell, as Helvi could recite her husband's transgressions with the fidelity of a tribal priest charged with preserving the oral history of his people.

But, sometimes, in an unguarded moment, Helvi and Heikki would recall some scene from the past:

"I ran into old Pete Grunenfelder's grandson today at the barber shop. You remember Pete? He used to have that dairy farm down the road from us."

"Oh? Do the Grunenfelders still own that old place?"

"No. Pete's in the county home now. He was a good twenty years older than me, so he just got old, I guess. His wife — what was her name? — died in Florida a couple of years ago while she was visiting their daughter."

"Heidi. His wife's name was Heidi. I never had much use for her. She was a hard woman. Always had her nose in the air. Thought she was better than the rest of us."

"Heidi. Yeah, that was her name all right. Good-looking woman, in her day, Heidi was. Pete got himself a good-looking young wife."

"Heidi? I remember she had thick legs and buckteeth. Snooty and stuck-up. And she wasn't all that young either. What did she die of? Old age?"

"Car accident. Shame. She was *years* younger than Pete. Lots of men had their eye on her, I'll tell you."

"You, too, I suppose. Well, Heikki, I'm telling you she'd never have looked at the likes of you, not even accidentally!"

"Wouldn't be too sure about that, woman. She had a liking for younger men. You remember the stories that went around about her and her husband's younger brother, what was his name?"

"Anton. Was he still living with them when you and I got married?"

"I think he was, but he moved out soon after. What was the name of their daughter? Agnes? Annie? She was still just a kid then."

"Alice. They all lived together, and folks said nobody knew who the father was, Pete or Anton. Probably Heidi herself didn't know."

"Well, if you're going to screw around, two brothers are a safe bet. Kids won't wind up looking like they don't belong in the family."

"Who owns the old farm now? The grandson?"

"I think it's up for sale. They need the money to pay for Pete's keep. That was a nice spread. If I'd had a place like that, I coulda made it into something, believe you me."

"You'd have boozed it away like you did the one we had."

"Christ, woman, doesn't your tongue ever get tired? You got nothing to complain about. I support you. You got a roof over your head and food on the table."

"Yes, and who puts it there? You? No, the only thing you support is every tavern in town. While I'm out working so hard that sparks of fire are flying out of my eyes, you're spending every dime we have on hooch."

"Well, maybe if I had a woman who showed me some respect — "

"And maybe if I had a man who *deserved* some — "

"And maybe if I had a woman who knew when to keep her damn mouth *shut* — "

Unfortunately, the sentimental journeys came with a round-trip ticket to the fractious present.

More surprising to Kate, that week, was her mother's

uncharacteristic silence. For a woman who communicated in a stream of criticism and complaint, it was as if suddenly the "cat got her tongue." She appeared distracted, her searchlight of attention turned off. Kate felt able to come and go without the need to show a passport.

Yes, the week was going well. Kate had even made a start at finding Mr. Reed's collard greens. Mrs. Murguia, the librarian, had not only known what they were, but had a sister who actually had collards growing in her vegetable garden in Stastas. Mrs. Murguia's sister, a woman who had lived in Florida and knew a lot about southern cooking, had said she'd be happy to fulfill the wishes of an old man in a wheelchair. In fact, after the first frost, she'd cook the collards and bring them to him herself. And perhaps Mr. Reed would also like some grits and ham hocks and sweet potato pie?

Yes, things were going very well. Kate had taken Mrs. Niemi her religious books, and slipped out before the old woman had a chance to harangue. Later, when Kate returned the embroidery floss, she found that the azure blue had indeed arrived, and she was able to exchange the floss for the correct color. A half-dozen skeins lay in the bottom of her shopping bag, awaiting delivery to Mrs. Niemi.

There had also been a few changes among the residents of the Lodge that week. Old Mr. Coombs had suffered a stroke and been admitted to hospital, and 88-year-old Editha Coffey had died quietly in her sleep. That left Ed Mingus and Lauralee Beatty without room-mates. As there was always a list of people waiting to enter the Lodge, the spaces had been quickly filled by two *new* Old People whom Kate had wasted no time in checking out.

She found she knew them already. One was Jock Ostriker, the Meanest Man in Town. Originally from somewhere in the East, Jock Ostriker had lived in Stastas longer than Kate had been alive. He had owned the Stastas Main Street News, a hybrid business that sold magazines (many of the outdoor type and those targeted at survival-ists), as well as firearms and ammunition. Kate's earliest encounter with Jock Ostriker had been the day he ordered 12-year-old Kate and two of her friends out of the shop, when he found them trying to get a peek at some of his adult magazines. Kate and her friends had fixated on the word "adult" as a synonym for "pornographic," and for several days afterwards they would double over with laughter when a teacher would refer to "adult education" or say, "Why don't you try acting more like adults?"

Ostriker had earned his "meanest man" title by being consistently belligerent. Women avoided him and his shop, referring to him as "that dreadful man." He in turn seemed to enjoy alienating them by treating any female customers with scarcely veiled contempt, and parading about with a gun visibly holstered on his hip. He was never without it and claimed he carried it for protection. Secretive, suspicious, and quick to take offense, Ostriker had few friends. He did have a couple of hunting buddies, men of his own stripe. No one was privy to their secret lives or what may have transpired on their hunting trips.

Kate had never been inside his home, but it was said that Ostriker had heads of animals mounted all over the walls. His photo regularly appeared in the *Stastas Courier* showing him with some beautiful animal he'd killed. Of course when you kill wild animals you call it a "harvest." It was just that sort of hypocrisy that Kate detested and Ostriker represented: the annual "deer harvest." Kate wondered why you never heard of a cattle, pig, or chicken harvest. Animals raised for food were okay to slaughter, but if an animal could make it through life on its own, you had to give it the status of a field of wheat before you could justify blowing it away.

Age and diabetes had caught up with Jock Ostriker. He'd never married and had no family to care for him; after he'd had a foot amputated, he'd ended up in the Lodge. There he spent his time roaring at other residents and taking swipes at household staff with the cane he always carried. Kate had little sympathy for him. After all the animals he'd killed, there was justice in Ostriker's having to relinquish a body part of his own. Kate decided to stay out of his way, at least until someone had taken the edge off him with medication. She did feel a little sorry for Ed Mingus — a harmless old coot — for having to share space with Ostriker, but since Mingus had never been a customer of hers (all he ever seemed to do was sit and stare at the wall and whistle), it wasn't going to make much difference to Kate.

Lauralee Beatty's roommate seemed to be a better match. Wilhelmiina Hill's husband, who had immigrated to North America in the early 1930s, had anglicized his name, "Mäki," to "Hill." Wilhelmiina, a first-generation North American Finn, born in British Columbia, clung to the Finnish spelling of her given name as if in protest, pronouncing the "W" as "V." Mrs. Hill had been a history teacher. Kate had never "had" her; she'd retired long before Kate entered and exited Stastas High. After retirement, Mrs. Hill had devoted herself to researching early settlers, native tribes, and genealogical histories of the families in the area. She was a slender woman with white hair and an erect carriage except for a small dowager's hump. She was friendly and chatty, with a good memory for anecdote; Lauralee Beatty, who never could get much conversation from Editha Coffey, might now have someone to talk to.

Mrs. Hill had greeted Kate cheerfully. "Of course, you're the Oksa girl — Katri, isn't it?" Kate nodded in mute resignation. She hated the name, but Finns invariably remembered to call her Katri. "And aren't you related to Aksel Oksaniemi who used to be a traveling minister of the gospel throughout this area? He used to go about on horseback, performing marriages and baptisms." Mrs. Hill chuckled. "Of course, in the mountain communities that were snowed-in all winter, it often turned out that he had to perform *both* services when the road cleared."

"I really don't know much about my dad's folks, Mrs. Hill. He never talks about them."

"What a shame, dear. It's such a colorful history."

"I don't think my dad knows much about it either."

"Most people here aren't that interested in their roots; it's all still so new in the West. But if there's ever anything you want to know, Katri, it'll be in a book somewhere. And as long as I'm around, I'll be glad to help you find it."

There's a switch, Kate thought. *And Old Person offering to do something for me. Maybe if she'd been my teacher I'd have finished high school.*

Kate had carefully avoided going anywhere near Mrs. Norland's room. She'd seen the cat, Moonrise, coming and going as usual, but nobody had made any mention of kittens. Maybe Mrs. Norland had been successful in keeping them hidden, or maybe she'd already gotten rid of them. Kate hoped that by now the old twit would've forgotten all about her, and that the whole thing would just quietly go away.

...

It was on Friday, the thirteenth of August, that Kate got the message. There was no way to ignore it; it came from everywhere. Her mother, who had hardly said two words to her all week, told her, in hushed tones, that Mrs. Norland had called from the Lodge and wanted to see her. Her manner was the same as if the Queen of England had called to invite Kate to tea.

Oh well, she had to take cigarettes to Mrs. Trachtenberg anyway, and embroidery floss to Mrs. Niemi. She might as well go and get it over with. She hopped on her bike and headed for town. When Kate got to the Lodge, it was as though there had been an APB out on her. Jane, the receptionist, said to be sure to go see Mrs. Norland. Every resident she encountered mentioned that Mrs. Norland wanted to see her. Mrs. Trachtenberg thanked her for the Lucky Strikes and said, "Don't forget to drop in on Mrs. Norland, dollink." It seemed as though the very wheelchairs hummed, "Kate, go see Mrs. Norland."

Reluctantly, Kate headed for Room 15, and met Moonrise in the corridor. "Yeah, Moonrise, I know. Go see Mrs. Norland, right?" The cat flashed her a baleful glance and bounded down the hall toward the lobby.

Mrs. Norland had been waiting. She literally yanked Kate into the room and shut the door. "It's *time!*"

Kate saw that Mrs. Norland showed none of her former queenly air. Her hair, usually piled and lacquered, sagged to one side with wisps straggling over her ears. Without her bright red lipstick and spots of rouge, she looked pale and ghastly. Mrs. Norland wasted no time in niceties. In one decisive move, she ripped Kate's shopping bag out of her hands and thrust her yarn bag into them. "Take them," she hissed. "Take them quickly — and *go!*"

"But Mrs. N — "

"*Go now!*" She shoved Kate out the door and slammed it shut. Kate found herself standing in the corridor, holding Mrs. Norland's yarn bag made of red ombre crochet. It was lined with scarlet taffeta and had wooden handles. Inside, there appeared to be a rolled-up piece of the familiar ombre woolen. Kate saw that it was faintly moving.

Oh great! Kate knocked gently on Mrs. Norland's door. No answer. She knocked again. "Mrs. Norland? Mrs. Norland, it's me, Kate — uh, Katri. I'm sorry, but you have my bag. Will you give it to me, please?" Still no reply. "Mrs. Norland, you have Mrs. Niemi's embroidery floss. Is it okay if I come in and get it?" No sound. She tried the door. It was locked. Doors to the residents' rooms *had* no locks, but this door was locked. Daffy Dame must've jammed it with a chair. Kate didn't want to attract attention, what with her bagful of contraband kittens. Her better judgment was telling her just to get out of there — fast. Grasping the crocheted bag, Kate started down the hall. She would've made it if Mrs. Niemi hadn't been standing by her open door.

"Katri, *come here!*"

Oh Christ! "Sorry, Mrs. Niemi, can't stop now." Kate kept on walking.

"Thief! Stop, thief!"

What the fuck?

"I see you stealing Mrs. Norland's bag! You just come over here and give it to me!"

Confused, Kate hesitated a fateful second, just long enough for Mrs. Niemi to reach her side, grab her by the arm and pull her into her room. "You thought you'd get away with it, didn't you? You people are all alike, thieves and liars — wallowing in sin and degradation. But what can you expect from the spawn of a drunk and a whore like your parents! You people have no breeding, no self-respect. Look at you, you're nothing but a slut and thief, and you belong in hell!"

Whoa! All this over a yarn bag? Kate realized that while Mrs. Niemi was shouting at her, she seemed to be addressing a larger audience, her eyes wide and glassy. Could this woman possibly be *on* something? Or has she just catapulted off into Macadamialand? Kate squirmed to loosen Mrs. Niemi's grip on her forearm and managed to wrench herself free, but Mrs. Niemi, in yanking the bag out of her hands, spilled the contents out onto the floor.

Kate, to her dismay, saw the crocheted mat unroll to display three kittens. Two of them seemed to be dead. One tottered around feebly. Mrs. Niemi screamed, then shouted, "Get those filthy animals out of here!" She seemed to recoil from, and at the same time *reach for* the living kitten. As her hand closed around it, Kate made a dive to retrieve it herself and their hands touched. For a moment, the three of them seemed to be freeze-framed into a *tableau vivant*, and then everything went black.

CHAPTER 3

A BREEZE blowing in through an open window stirred the net curtains, causing them to billow, then blow aside, releasing the smell of sea. The room was small, with just enough space for a cheap iron bed and a wooden dresser upon which stood a porcelain bowl with a plain white water pitcher. The faded wallpaper had once been a pattern of yellow flowers. A border of them marched around the room next to the ceiling, and to Kate, in her dizziness, appeared at first to be actually moving.

Kate felt terrible. Stiff. Sore. Sick to her stomach. She was lying on the bed, fully clothed, in — what? A dress? Kate hadn't worn a dress since her mother forced her into one for a grade school concert. This one looked as if it might be some sort of uniform. In trying to orient herself, she focused on the fabric of the sleeve — a pale gray cotton stripe — and she seemed (for chrissakes!) to be wearing an *apron*. The apron was large and white with shoulder straps and a bib that covered her chest. Kate forced herself carefully into a semi-sitting position on the saggy mattress, causing the bedsprings to creak, and saw that she was also wearing black cotton stockings and a pair of black leather shoes with laces. Had she passed out at a Halloween party? That must be it. There seemed to be a couple of other costumes hanging on hooks on the wall.

I wonder where the john is; I think I'm going to barf. Kate slid her legs over the edge of the bed and sat up. Then — *oh, God* — she saw the kitten. It was still alive, lying on its side on the shabby chenille bedspread, not moving, but looking at Kate through narrow, rheumy slits of eyes. Kate sighed. Okay, then it was a dream — no, a nightmare, but at least that explained it. Any minute now she could expect Hillary Clinton and Fred Flintstone to walk in and do the lambada.

Just as Kate was trying to get to her feet, there was a knock on the door. "Ellen? Ellen, are you in there? Are you all right?" The voice had an English accent.

Ellen? Who's Ellen? The door opened and a woman came in. She was dressed in the same type of clothing Kate wore (a maid's uniform of some sort?) the gray striped number with the big bib apron and also — Kate wanted to laugh — what looked like her mother's bouffant shower cap. Okay, so it wasn't Fred Flintstone, but. . . .

"Are you feeling any better, Ellen? Should I tell Hastings you're sick and need a doctor?"

"No! No — I — " Kate expelled a lungful of breath, grasped the iron rail at the foot of the bed for support, looked around and got another shock. Someone else was in the room — another uniform. No, it was a mirror! The dresser mirror! And the face was not her own! She almost fell, but the other woman caught her.

"You'd best not try to get up yet. I'll tell Hastings you're still under the weather."

"Thanks. Uh . . . I'll be okay. Just gimme a few minutes."

The woman raised her eyebrows in surprise. "All right, then, Ellen. But I think you should lie down again. Have a bit of a rest. I'll look in on you later and bring you a nice bowl of beef tea." She left and gently closed the door.

Nightmare? The *demo* for all nightmares! Kate gave herself a smart slap on the cheek. It didn't help; such things never do help in nightmares, and Kate had been prone to them all her life. She'd been chased by tigers, shot by gunmen, thrown off pinnacles, and pursued by giant crablike space creatures — but this was different. She felt like the hero in the old TV series, *Quantum Leap. Except I don't have anyone to tell me what to do. Unless* . . . Kate looked at the kitten that seemed to be barely breathing. *Yeah, you're a big help.*

Kate carefully got to her feet. There was a dull pain in her lower back. Wobbling a bit, she walked to the mirror and peered at her own image. She saw a blond young girl with blue eyes, her hair pulled back into a bun. The girl *was* looking rather unwell with gray smudges under her eyes. "I'll be damned," said Kate, and started at the sound of her own voice which was not her own.

Kate looked around. The room seemed to be in an attic. She went to the open window, looked out, and saw that she must be in the upper story of a very large house by the ocean. She gathered her thoughts. *I, that is, Ellen must work here. But who is Ellen and where is this place?* The room didn't offer many clues. In the dresser drawers, Kate found a meager wardrobe of clothing she'd never seen: more cotton stockings, cotton underwear, bulky looking cotton panties. Bloomers? Knickers? They were a far cry from lingerie, far cry from Fruit-of-the-Loom even. There was a strange-looking vest that could've been a bra if it had had cups, and which had four long elastic straps that hung down with stocking clips on the ends. On a hunch, Kate hiked up her skirt and saw that a similar wire loop over a rubber button held up her stockings: the generic version of the sexy garter belts of the nineties. "Golly, Toto," she said to the kitten, "I don't think we're in pantyhose anymore. Not that *I've* ever worn them."

The room and its contents seemed too impersonal for anyone to be living there. Maybe Ellen was here on a visit. Then, on another hunch, Kate knelt down and peered under the bed. There she found a suitcase. It looked cheap, made of some cardboardy material, the outside shabby and peeling. It wasn't locked. Kate opened it. *Bingo!* There were letters and papers. Kate tried to read a postmark but couldn't make it out. She opened a letter and saw that it was written in a foreign language. *Finnish.* For the first time, Kate cursed her inability to read her mother's tongue. The letter began, *Rakas Elina.* Elina? Ellen? Maybe she preferred to be called Ellen just like she, herself, preferred Kate to Katri. Elina would be her Finnish name. Or maybe Elina's employers found it easier to say. Kate's grandmother, whose name had been Tuulikki, had been called Julie in the workplace, because it was easier to pronounce.

The letter was dated 5/2/23. May 2, 1923? Seventy years ago? She looked again. More likely February 5, 1923. Finns put the day, month and year in that order, that much Kate knew. She looked at the signature: *Äiti.* Mother. Okay, this girl was an immigrant from Finland, working, she guessed, as a maid for a wealthy family, much as Kate's own grandmother had done. Kate riffled through the letters — March, March, April, June, July — so this might still be August, only seventy years earlier. The girl had probably been in the country only a short time. Her full name was Elina Saari, and she was working in — Kate looked at the envelope, trying to read the handwriting, which was neat and stylized, but was the word Block or Black? Something Point, Connecticut. Kate had never heard of it.

One thing was sure; Elina wouldn't be able to speak English very well. *Glad I didn't start doin' the dozens with Laurie when she was in here. Whoa! How do I know her name? I don't. Maybe it isn't Laurie. Or maybe I know her name because Ellen knows it. And maybe any second now this dream is going to run together like a Halloween window in the rain, and I'm outta here.* She looked at the kitten. It was lying on the bed, near eye level with Kate as she knelt by the suitcase. "You! You can stay, you miserable little fuzzball." The kitten blinked weakly.

Kate realized she'd have to get out. She had scarcely any information on who Ellen Saari was, and knew nothing of her job description. How could she possible pass herself off — suddenly she felt her stomach turn over. *What the bleep is the matter with me?*

Knock knock. Who's there? *Gotta be Laurie. We'll find out if her name* is *Laurie.*

"Are you feeling any better, Ellen?" The woman came in, carrying a bowl of soup on a tray. She had changed clothes; now she was wearing a black outfit with a smaller apron and a starched white cap.

"Jaa, much better. Tank you, Laurie." Kate was using her grandmother's accent.

"Well, that *is* good news. It's always worse in the mornings, luv."

"Hah?"

Laurie put the tray on the dresser and sat down on the edge of the bed, narrowly missing the kitten that she apparently hadn't noticed. "Oh, come on, Ellen. We all *know.* You've been vomiting and looking peaky. You won't be able to hide it for long."

Kate's mind raced like a gerbil in a wheel. *Hide* it? *Hide what?*

"Now don't look like that, luv. It's not as bad as it seems, and it happens to lots of girls." Laurie directed her gaze out the window and sighed. "It must be so lonely for you, so far away from your home and loved ones. Coming to a strange country. Not speaking the language." Her voice took on an edge. "And isn't there always some son of a . . . rich family ready to take advantage of a poor young girl!" She took Kate's hand. "You know, he wasn't even supposed to be here this summer. Why didn't he just stay in the city where he belongs!"

Laurie sighed and looked long at Kate. "You poor little thing. But it'll all work out, luv, you'll see. Life has a way of going on, and nothing's as bad as it looks at first. You'll have to leave here, of course, but if you go to the mistress, she'll have to give you some money. She's done it before. And then you'll go off and make a new start."

Kate put a hand on her abdomen.

"I've got to go now, luv. Hastings says you're to rest today. I'll look in on you later. Try to eat a little. It might settle your stomach."

I'm pregnant! Ellen's pregnant. She's been knocked up by a son-of-the-rich. Kate fought down a sudden flood of emotion and took a couple of deep breaths. Well, first of all, she had to find a bathroom. They *did* have indoor bathrooms in the twenties, didn't they? Kate opened the door and found herself in a narrow hallway. She tiptoed along the worn carpet runner, looking for a promising door. The trouble with dreams is, you can look for a bathroom all night long and never find one. But she did find one, a small room at the end of the hall. The door was ajar and Kate went in. She didn't feel nauseated anymore, but she emptied her bladder, noticing that toilet paper of the twenties had a shiny look and a slick feel. She held a sheet up to the light and saw what looked like little bits of wood imbedded in it. And the toilet tank was fastened up high on the wall. She pulled the chain. It flushed loudly.

Kate was making her way back to Ellen's room when one of the hall doors opened and a young girl came scurrying out. "Oh, Ellen, you're up. Glad to see you're in the land of the living. You'd best change though, before Madam sees you. You know what an old hag she is about proper uniforms for mornings and afternoons. You'd think we were in New York City instead of at the summer place." She scuttled on down the hall to what Kate saw was an opening that led to the floor below. Kate gathered that this was the servants' floor and the opening was to the servants' staircase.

Back in her room, Kate concluded that the black garment she'd mistaken for a Halloween costume must be Ellen's afternoon uniform. Apparently the stripes and shower caps were for mornings. Kate awkwardly changed into it, thinking she'd be less conspicuous if she tried to keep to the drill.

The kitten was still on the bed, tottering around on weak legs. "Here, have some soup, you little shitbag." Kate dipped a spoonful of cooled beef broth and held it under the kitten's chin. The animal dipped its nose in it and sneezed. "Sorry it's not your mother's milk, but it's the only bar open."

Kate was becoming aware of two aspects of her situation that were new. As with Laurie's name, she was beginning to *know things*. She was Kate, first and foremost, in somebody else's body, with Kate's mind and memories. However, she found that by letting herself go a bit, altering her state of consciousness, she could feel herself *being* this Ellen person. It wasn't that Ellen was inside her, trying to get out. It was more as though she, Kate, at moments, *was* Ellen — or in the process of *becoming* Ellen. It was weird. For instance, she found she could picture the layout of the house. She knew where the big staircase was, the parlor, the dining room. She knew that the servants' staircase was accessible from each floor and ultimately led into a hallway next to the kitchen.

The other thing was even stranger, and it had to do with her emotions. They seemed to be all over the place. She felt panic — and that was understandable — but she was also feeling Ellen's emotions — the strongest of which was *rage*. Not just anger, but a swelling fury that had so shocked her that she'd forced herself to emotionally change the subject. Kate, herself, had a sharp tongue and a bad temper, but she couldn't recall ever feeling homicidal. She'd first noticed it when Laurie had been talking about Ellen's pregnancy. Kate had never been pregnant, but *hey, if I'd been knocked up by some creep, maybe I'd want to kill him too.* Anyway, it seemed to Kate a good idea to try to get out before something really bad happened.

Kate looked at the nameless kitten, now sleeping. "Sorry I got you into this. Right now I gotta try to come up with a clever plan."

She tied on the dorky cap that looked like a headband, trying to get it to look like the way Laurie's had. For want of a better idea, she planned to check out her surroundings and, if nothing else, try to get a fix on the nearest exit. Laurie had called this the summer place. For all Kate knew, they could be miles from anywhere. So where would she go and how would she get there? Hike? Hop a freight? How do you plan to operate in yesteryear to the seventieth power? Kate's guess was that Ellen didn't have a dime. She probably sent her earnings to her mother in Finland like Kate's grandmother had done. *Okay, so what happens if I stay? Ellen's going to be out on her ass anyway. Yeah, but maybe she* will *get money from the mistress. If I could just wake up, I'd be glad to leave Ellen to her own problems. Meanwhile, nothing is solved by my sitting here, talking to wallpaper.*

Kate left the kitten asleep and slipped into the hall. No one was around. She headed for the servants' staircase. The stairs were steep and poorly lit, and in some places they curved, making the treads narrow toward the center. It made footing precarious, especially in the unfamiliar leather-soled shoes. Kate longed for her thrift-shop Reeboks.

Carefully, she inched her way down to a landing with a door, opened it, and saw she was now on the story below the servants' quarters. Before her lay an expanse of carpet. On her left were rooms, their doors shut; on her right, a railing. The gallery led to a large staircase descending to the main hall. She took a few steps along the Oriental carpeting, peered over the railing, and, for a moment, considered going down the big staircase. But there was someone there — a man — sitting on a carved wooden bench in the lower hall. Kate studied him for a moment. He looked elderly, with white hair, and was dressed in dark clothing. To Kate he looked like an undertaker. No, probably a salesman, cooling his heels, waiting for a chance to make his pitch. Kate didn't want to attract attention. She went back through the door, continued on down the servants' staircase, and found herself at the door to the kitchen. It was open and, a bit warily, she went in. A beefy woman in a large white apron was mixing batter in a bowl. "There you are, Ellen. Feeling better? Would you like a cup of tea?"

"Uh — no, ma'am."

"No, no, no, Ellen. You don't call *me* ma'am. You call the *mistress* ma'am or Madam. Me, you call Mrs. Trundle." The woman spoke slowly and loudly, as if to the deaf. She tapped her own ample breast. "Me — Mrs. Trundle. The mistress — Madam." She sighed loudly and rolled her eyes. "You immigrant girls. They get you to work for next to nothing and they expect *us* to train you and teach you the language as well. Anyway, since you're up and about, don't just stand there gawking. Nip on up to the dining room and help Laurie with the decorations for the dinner tonight. They'll be setting out the good china and filling the place with flowers. It's not every day that the young master announces his engagement."

Kate felt herself stiffen. *Young master? Engagement? Could this be the son-of-the-rich who'd gotten Ellen pregnant? Announcing his engagement? But not to Ellen, I'll bet!* Kate could feel anger rising — a spasm of fury that momentarily made her feel she had superhuman strength. She fought for self-control as Mrs. Trundle chatted, more to herself than to Kate, whom she wouldn't have expected to understand more than simple commands. "Well, run along, girl. Run along. Up to the di-ning room." She mouthed the words as if to a lip-reader.

Kate departed, leaving Mrs. Trundle head-shaking and tsk-tsking. She'd recovered her emotional equilibrium, at least somewhat. That last blast had left her breathless, and more puzzled than ever. Where did it come from? And worse, where was it going? It seemed to flare up like a wildfire leaving Kate feeling helpless in its grip. Kate leaned against the corridor wall. *If I could just get out of here! Out of this place, out of this body, out of this dream or whatever it is!*

"There you are, Ellen. I was just about to go up to see if you were well enough to come down. Madam wants to see you in the parlor."

Kate knew this to be Hastings, the butler, the guy in charge of all the help. She nodded. The less she spoke the better. She followed Hastings to the parlor door, waited outside while he went in to announce her presence, then came out again and motioned for Kate to go in. The door closed behind her.

The woman who had summoned her was seated on a flowered settee. She looked to be fortysomething, dressed in a light, floaty fabric that might have been flattering on a younger, slimmer figure. Her hair was carefully set in tight waves that reminded Kate of corrugated cardboard. She eyed Kate with open dislike, issued a command to "Come here, girl," but did not invite Kate to sit down. "I hear you're with child." It was a statement, drawled and dripping with contempt.

Kate said nothing and waited.

"You know my rules. You're to pack your bags and get out."

Actually, so far, this wasn't in conflict with Kate's own agenda. Getting out of the house had always seemed to be a necessary first step.

The woman seemed to become angrier under Kate's level gaze. "You people have no self-respect. You have no breeding. You and all your kind. You spend your lives in sin and degradation. But what could I expect from the spawn of ignorant peasants. Look at you, you're nothing but a slut!"

All this was sounding somehow familiar.

"I suppose you expect me to give you money. Well, I'm not going to finance any more bastards for you people. You all seem to thi— " The woman's eyes opened in surprise, then her face crumpled in horror and revulsion.

Kate had felt what she thought was rage rising in her throat, but this time, instead, it was a wave of nausea. She whitened, swayed, pitched forward, and spewed a gush of greenish vomit right into the lap of Ellen's biological mother-in-law.

After the confusion that followed, with Madam screaming for Hastings, and the butler half-carrying Kate out of the room, calling for household staff to clean up the mess, and for Laurie to help Kate back upstairs, Kate ended up back in bed with Laurie giggling about how she wished she'd seen Madam's face, and how it served the old witch right.

Hastings had told Laurie that Ellen should stay until she felt well enough to travel (just keep her out of Madam's way) and that Hastings, himself, would speak to Madam about the delicate matter of money. After all, *he* knew that *she* knew who the father of the baby was, and Madam wouldn't want a scandal just when her only son was about to marry into the wealthy family of Hartford's leading clock manufacturer. Meanwhile, Ellen really should try to eat a little. She hadn't touched her broth. Laurie replaced it with a tray from the kitchen, and told Kate it would be best to have something in her stomach, even if she felt sick again, "To keep from getting the dry heaves, luv."

In fact, Kate was ravenous. The upchuck had made her feel instantly better, and she gratefully scoffed down Mrs. Trundle's chicken in aspic, carrot salad, a milk pudding dessert that Laurie called a blancmange, and a cold popover with a cup of tea. Laurie took the tray away and told Kate to take a nice nap.

Nap. Kate realized that she *was* feeling sleepy, so much so that she could hardly keep her eyes open. Yes, sleep would be good. She felt as if she could sleep for a week. A nap was just what she needed, and then when she woke up, she'd try to sort out the events of the last few hours. Hours? Try seventy years!

Kate lay down and closed her eyes, the kitten beside her. Here they were, Dorothy and Toto in the land of the Wicked Witch. Somehow, in some weird way, they had gone back in time, except that they were now in Mrs. Niemi's time, a time when Elina Niemi was still Elina Saari, a young, unmarried (though pregnant) girl everybody called Ellen — and not a wicked witch at all. Kate couldn't help chuckling. She remembered how Mrs. Niemi liked to brag about *her* mansion by the sea and *her* house filled with servants to anyone who would listen. Kate had heard the story many times. Wouldn't it be funny if this were the way things *really* had been? That Elina Niemi, while she was still Elina Saari, had been nothing more than a *maid* in that huge house by the sea? It hadn't been *her* house at all. She'd only been a servant — a servant of that woman who, oddly enough, sounded a lot like Elina, herself, had sounded when she'd been shouting at Kate back at the Lodge. Had Mrs. Niemi made up all that stuff about being rich and owning a big house? Or was it her memory that was failing? You never knew with Old People. Did she really think the house had been hers? Or was she so befuddled that she actually believed she'd *been* the rich bitch who owned it? The woman in voile.

Voile! That's what her dress was made of. For a moment, Kate wondered how she knew the fabric was called voile, and then she remembered that Mummo, her grandmother, had had one much like it. There was a photo in the Oksa family album of Mummo as a young girl, wearing a gauzy floral dress. She'd been very pretty then. Her hair had been crimped too, although not as stiffly as Madam's. Mummo had told Kate the dress was made of *voili*, adding a vowel to the end of an English word, as Finns did when they spoke "Fingliska," the informal hybrid language of Finns in North America. Voile must have been popular fabric back then. *Poor Madam. I wonder if* voili *is washable!*

Kate felt sorry for Ellen, but realized that Ellen must have done all right with her life if she eventually managed to become Elina Niemi. Kate yawned. *If I go to sleep, I wonder if I'll dream. Can you dream in a dream? No wonder I'm sleepy. I haven't slept in seventy years.* Eyes closed, she tried picturing Ellen's life. Kate's grandmother had been in service before she married, and had often talked about what it was like. None of it had meant much to Kate at the time, but now she could begin to feel a kinship with Mummo and her era. She'd had to work long hours for a pittance. If she wanted time off she had to get special permission from her employer. No union protected her from being fired or exploited. She had very little time for herself. Her behavior was closely watched, and she was expected to go to church services where servants were admonished to be *dutiful*. There were endless rules to follow. In one house, Mummo had told Kate that if a maid accidentally met a member of the family on the staircase, the maid had to stop in her tracks and turn her face to the wall while the personage walked by. Kate had asked why. Mummo explained that servants were supposed to be invisible, and if they faced the wall, the family could pretend they weren't there and didn't have to acknowledge their presence. It must have been like slavery.

Still, many of Mummo's stories had been funny. There had been a couple of other Finnish immigrant maids in the house, and none of them spoke English. Mummo, with glee, told how her mistress — her name was Mrs. Shipley and she was wicked awful fat — kept insisting they call her "ma'am." Finns are hardworking people, but they're not into servility. The poorest Finns consider themselves equal to anyone, and working for someone does not make you their inferior. Since it's *the employer* who needs *you*, therefore *you're* the one who's superior. To the ears of the maids, "ma'am" sounded suspiciously like kowtowing, so they all mischievously called their plump employer "Ham." "Yes, Ham." "No, Ham." After this had happened a few times in front of her friends, poor Mrs. Shipley gave up in frustration, resigned herself to their not being able to pronounce the word. From then on she was content to be called Mrs. Shipley, or "Seeply" which was as close as they could come.

Kate became aware of a soft, sputtering sound. She partly opened her eyes to see that the kitten had crawled onto her pillow and was trying to purr. "Hey, fellow traveler. Sorry you had to get mixed up in this, but maybe we'll both wake up back in our own time." She closed her eyes and allowed herself to drift off into welcome sleep.

...

Kate woke with a start. Something was wrong. The first thing she sensed was the furry head of the kitten inches from her own. It had crawled on her chest and was breathing cold little cat breaths into her face. She was also aware of an odor. Kate sat up. It was dark. There was a lightbulb with a pull chain on the ceiling above her bed. Kate fumbled for the piece of hanging string, gave it a yank, and the bulb lit up.

How long had she been asleep? A sudden cramping spasm gripped her and she cried out. Then she saw the blood. Her clothes were soaked with it and so was the bed. What was happening? The pain came again — the worst menstrual cramps she'd ever had. Kate hiked up her skirts to reveal sodden underclothing. Another agonizing cramp. Her hands shaking, she pulled off blood-soaked cotton underpants. This was no ordinary menstrual period. There was too much blood — and clotted matter. Ellen was having a miscarriage. Kate panicked. Now she was experiencing fear, and it welled up inside her like a tidal wave that threatened to engulf and destroy. *What do I do? What do I do?* She was gasping and crying and moaning. *Am I dying? Bleeding to death?* Kate wanted to scream. She filled her lungs with air but the scream never came. Just as the fear had washed over her, it now subsided and was replaced by an icy calm. *Should I call for help? Who would hear me? If this is still a nightmare, all I want is to wake up. Just wake up, that's all. Wake up now!*

But Kate didn't awaken. Dream or no dream she was in it for the duration. Both her mother and grandmother had been midwives. Mummo, in Finland, had been an apprentice traveling midwife before she immigrated to America and went into service. Finnish women of her generation knew about midwifery the way a lady of the castle, in King Arthur's time, knew about patching up axe and sword wounds.

Kate, herself, had witnessed a birth and even assisted her mother. When a neighbor's wife went into labor unexpectedly, Helvi had been summoned. Kate had been too young to be left alone so her mother had taken her along. "Women have been having babies long before doctors were invented," Helvi had said. Then, later as the birth progressed, "Remember this when you start going out with boys." Unlike some children, Kate had not grown up with myths of how babies were found under cabbage leaves or (the Finnish version) under the floorboards of the family sauna.

There had also been that time at the Dump when a girl had had a miscarriage. The woman had drifted in from somewhere and had stayed the night with the local outcasts. Kate never knew her name. She, Barry, and Sumo, had all been there; and when the woman started cramping and bleeding, Kate, as the only other female, found herself in charge. It had been messy in that filthy building with no utilities. She remembered sending the guys out for buckets of water and telling them to call a doctor, at which the woman started freaking out, saying she didn't want to go to a hospital. Kate never knew why. Maybe she was running from something, or someone. At any rate, the next day she was gone, nobody knew where.

Gradually, the cramping subsided, and Kate was lying in a pool of gore. She felt weak and shaky, but she also knew she'd live. She lay, waiting for another cramp. When none came, and when she felt she might be strong enough to do so, she made an effort to get up. It reminded Kate of the time, at the Dump, when she'd awakened after lying in her own filth for god knows how long. Now she was soaked in blood and the thought of it was so revolting that her first instinct was to get herself cleaned up.

Kate tested her strength; decided she wasn't going to faint or keel over. *Women have been having miscarriages since before doctors were invented.* Her mother had once told her that many first pregnancies end up aborting, and that often, in the early stages, a woman can expel a fetus without even knowing she'd been pregnant. Kate didn't know how long Ellen had been pregnant, but guessed it couldn't have been more than a few weeks. Kate also knew that there could be complications. If the bleeding didn't stop, a woman could die of a miscarriage. She also shrewdly concluded that she, Kate, was not about to die, because if Ellen had died as a young girl, she couldn't have gone on to become Mrs. Niemi, could she? If Ellen had died of a miscarriage, then in Kate's time, there couldn't have *been* a Mrs. Niemi, could there? If Elina Niemi were Ellen Saari in old age, then Ellen would have to live to *reach* old age, wouldn't she? It made perfect sense to Kate at the time in an *Alice in Wonderland* sort of way.

Kate then did what women always do at the sight of blood: began cleaning it up. She'd once read a story in which a woman had to give up studying to be a doctor because she fainted at the sight of blood. Kate had hooted with laughter. The story had to be written by a man. Any woman who faints at the sight of blood would be out cold three days a month for, oh, forty years of her life!

There was a pitcher of water and bowl on the dresser and a couple of towels in the dresser drawer. Kate stripped off the rest of her clothing and wiped herself off with a wet towel as best she could. Without examining them, she rolled her bed linens into a ball, saw that the mattress was soaked, but there was nothing she could do about that. Her knees were still wobbly, and she sat, for a moment, on a clean part of the bed. *I've got to get out of here. I can't stay here another minute.*

But where will you go? *It doesn't matter.* Kate picked out fresh clothing, this time one of the outfits that looked like something Ellen would wear on her day off. She quietly made her way down the dimly lit hallway to the bathroom, where she washed herself off more thoroughly at the sink. (Where did these people bathe?) She sat on the toilet. She was still bleeding, but now the flow was much lighter. She wadded up toilet paper and packed it in place. Oh, for a high-tech nineties sanitary pad with enough absorbency to pick up an oil spill! She got dressed.

Back in her room, thankful that no one had seen her, Kate moved with cold resolve. She closed the door and would have locked it except that the door *had* no lock. Servants, apparently, had no privacy whatsoever. Madam had been big on morality, but there was nothing to keep the son of the rich from coming into her room at night, was there? She pulled out the suitcase and packed Ellen's things. As long as she was in Ellen's body, she might need her life-support system as well. She put on Ellen's coat and hat, a cheap straw, but quite becoming. Ellen, even pale and weak, had been a pretty girl. *Probably that's what got her in trouble.* Then, the kitten cradled in one arm, suitcase in hand, Kate opened the door and stepped into the hallway — and nearly collided with a man.

Kate gasped. The man laid a hand gently on her mouth. "Shh, Ellen, it's me. Can we go in?" She detected a whiff of alcohol.

Kate stood her ground. She knew this man, and for just a moment, she experienced a wave of feeling for him. Frederick! So this was the son-of-the-rich! He was young, looked to be maybe three or four years older than Kate, and was rather short in stature. Not the picture of a leering seducer of young girls, but more the spoiled, horny, scion of the house — one who'd been to a party, it seemed. Kate saw he was wearing a slightly rumpled tuxedo with a wilting pink carnation in his buttonhole. From her own — Ellen's — emotions, Kate gathered that Ellen had been in love with him and had made him the hero of her romantic dreams. Kate stood firm. Wordlessly, she shook off his hand, and started down the hall.

"Please, Ellen, can't we go into your room and talk?" Frederick was following her, speaking in whispers. "Look, Ellen, I just wanted to say I'm sorry. I never meant for this to happen. If it were up to me . . . well, you know how I feel about you." He was slurring his words a bit.

Kate started down the stairs, clutching the kitten, her suitcase bumping against walls. Frederick followed a bit unsteadily. "Where are you going in the middle of the night, Ellen? Why don't you stay at least till morning? We'll sort all this out. I want to help you, but I'll have to talk to Mother." Unused to the narrow stairs, Frederick tripped and nearly fell into Kate. "For God's sake, Ellen, if you're going to fly in the night, at least use the other stairs. You'll kill us both on these!"

Not a bad idea. They had reached the door to the floor below, and Kate unerringly headed for the larger staircase that was used by the family and generally forbidden to the help. She didn't plan to say a word to Frederick. She planned to walk across the gallery, down the stairs and out the front door to whatever awaited on the other side, but Frederick didn't allow that. He grasped her arm and stopped her. "Ellen, please. I want to be with you. I need to be with you tonight."

Kate wheeled and fixed Frederick with angry eyeballs. "Aren't you the guy who just got engaged to be married to someone else?"

Frederick looked down at his polished black oxfords. "I had no choice. You know how Mummy is. But it won't make any difference to us. I'll look after you. We'll work it out."

Yeah, right, Kate thought. *Ellen, my friend, this one's for you.* Kate put down the suitcase and squared off to face Frederick. "And what about your baby?"

Frederick was squirming. "We can work that out too. You don't *have* to have it, you know. There are ways. I mean, I know of someone who takes care of things like that. It's nothing, Ellen. People do it all the time. And don't you see, once I'm married I'll have money of my own and then you and I can — "

It was then the rage came, and once again Kate could feel herself being hurled headlong into a scorching fury, like bungee-jumping into a volcano. "You scumbag," she murmured. "You miserable lying bastard," she articulated. "You dickfaced, shit-eating little *snot.*"

Frederick's jaw dropped. He'd never heard such talk from a woman — or a man either — and certainly didn't expect it from Ellen who spoke English haltingly. Had she suddenly gone crazy?

There was no tenderness now, just fury. Kate had practically learned to read from the walls of the women's room in the Stastas Woolworth's.

Armed with vocabulary, Kate advanced on Frederick. "You festering pool of puke! You spineless blood-sucking leech!" Her voice had risen to a shrill shriek. "You brainless, knuckle-dragging prick!" Frederick was backing up against the railing, looking around in mute panic.

Kate suddenly felt wonderful — exhilarated, jubilant in her fury. "You gutless limp erection of a palsied rhesus monkey! You trail of *sliiiime* dribbling from the asshole of a maggot-infested hyena!" she shouted, then lunged at Frederick, pushing him back over the railing. Frederick screamed, and as he started to fall, his hands clawed frantically and grabbed hold of the lapels of Kate's coat. She could feel herself being pulled over the rail, and as they both plummeted to the floor below, Kate didn't even notice the needle sharp prick of tiny kitten nails digging themselves into the flesh of her throat.

CHAPTER 4

KATE OPENED her eyes. She was lying on her stomach on asphalt tile. She pushed herself up to a kneeling position and saw that she was in Mrs. Niemi's room at the Lodge. *What the bejeezis happened?* She must have fainted. She'd been lying on Mrs. Norland's yarn bag in a scatter of kittens. Kate got to her feet, and found herself looking into the faded blue eyes of a wispy-haired little old lady who was sitting on the edge of Mrs. Niemi's bed. The woman was regarding her with the serenity of one who has no idea of what's going on, exhibiting only the mildest interest in the girl who'd been sprawled at her feet. *This must be Mrs. Niemi's roommate. I guess she came in while I was out. That means Mrs. Niemi is probably down at Administration right now, rounding up paramedics. If I don't get out of here pronto, they'll have a Denver boot on my ass.*

"Excuse me, I gotta go," Kate mumbled, as she gathered up bag, the length of crochet, and kittens — dead and alive — then fled down the hall, expecting to be waylaid at any moment. She saw no one. The Lodge was quiet. Nobody was in the lobby. Kate gratefully slipped out the door into the familiar air of a cloudy Stastas afternoon. Again Kate saw no one. She walked around to the back of the Lodge where the service entrance was, took the two dead kittens out of the bag and tossed them into a dumpster. "Sorry, guys, no time for a wake." Then, for want of a better plan, Kate went home.

...

Home was an aging, ugly little house in an area that was rapidly undergoing changes. Years ago it had stood shoulder to shoulder with others of the same size and value at the edge of town. With time, Stastas had grown and swallowed the houses like a macrophage to make them part of the urban sprawl. The road had been widened, the roadbed raised, and concrete sidewalks put in. As result, many of the front yards had been pared down to tiny strips of lawn, and the houses looked to be sunken, their windows peering forlornly through sidewalk railing.

You couldn't park a car along the highway anymore, and the road construction had put the driveways out of reach. To get to the Oksa house by car, you had to turn off onto a side street and jockey your way along a back alley. Life went on in ghetto mode in the backyards and alleyways, cluttered with vehicles, bicycles, toys, and overflowing trash cans: the litter of living that heaps up where there are too many people in too small a space to live in grace and harmony.

The Oksa house stood in the middle of the block, looking like an owl. From under its asphalt shingled, pyramidal "four-winds" roof, two front windows, like eyes, flanked a door with a beak-like metal awning. A small flight of cement steps led from the highway sidewalk down to the front entrance, but the Oksas never used it. As Kate biked past it, she noticed that the curtains of one of the windows had been pulled farther apart; so the "owl" today had unequally dilated pupils that seemed to stare out balefully as if from a cage. Kate made the turnoff, then backtracked to the Oksa yard by way of the alley.

The house was quiet, pretty much as it had been all week. Kate's father was not at home. Her mother was in the kitchen, cooking a pot of beets, and didn't greet Kate when she came in. She said nothing when Kate opened the wool bag and lifted out a tiny, thin, black kitten with encrusted eyes. She said nothing when Kate got a saucer out of the cupboard, poured in a bit of milk from a bottle from the refrigerator, and set it in front of the animal. The beets, unpeeled and bristling with roots, boiled truculently on the stove, sending up clouds of steam.

"It's got distemper."

Kate looked up. "Huh?"

Helvi Oksa gave a jerk of her head, indicating the kitten. "I said it's got distemper. Won't live long." She picked up a toasting fork and jabbed it into a beet to test it for tenderness, then took the pot off the stove and drained the blood-red liquid into the sink, the steam rising to briefly fog up her eyeglasses. She refilled the pot with cold water to cool off the vegetables, then with her hands, began to bark off the outer skins, stacking the emasculated satiny globes into a plastic bowl to await their fate. They would become Helvi's beet and salt-herring salad, with which Kate had always had a love-hate relationship. As a child, Kate had disliked it because she hated the feel of the hairlike fish bones tickling her throat. Over time, she had acquired a taste for it. She still didn't like the bones, but found the combination of sweet beets, onions, and mayonnaise combining with the salty tang of the fish delicious.

Kate looked closely at the baby cat. It was indeed a pitiful sight — weak, skinny, barely able to stand as it made a feeble effort to lap up a drop of milk from the tip of Kate's finger. There was thick, pus-like matter oozing out of its eyes — one barely open, the other glued shut. Kate took a wet paper towel and tried cleaning them off, but it didn't seem to help much. The lids were so swollen that the eyes were barely visible.

Kate made no comment, but was surprised by her mother's reaction. Her "old" mother would've commanded her to get that dirty, diseased creature out of her kitchen. Now, the woman was content merely to make a medical diagnosis; she hadn't even yelled at Kate for using one of her saucers. *She's one of those pod creatures in* Invasion of the Body Snatchers. *There'll be a mark on the back of her neck.*

"That kitten's too young to be separated from its mother. No point in you trying to feed it. Where did it come from?"

"Mrs. Norland gave it to me. She couldn't keep it at the Lodge."

"*Mrs. Norland?* What on earth would Mrs. Norland be doing with . . . *that?*

"Oh, it's a long story. The Lodge cat had kittens in Mrs. Norland's room. And I think old Mrs. Norland must have been nipping on her lava lamp. She's been talking about somebody wanting to kill her, and today, she just pushed the kittens on me. Two of them were dead already. She shoved me out the door and I dropped my bag with Mrs. Niemi's embroidery floss — "

"Mrs. Niemi does embroidery? I didn't think she could do anything like that."

"She's got one of those big magnifying glasses that lights up. Anyway, she's even crazier than Mrs. Norland. You should've heard her yelling at me. Last week, when I didn't have the floss she wanted, she called me stupid. Today she called me a thief and a slut just because I was carrying Mrs. Norland's bag. The woman's a crazoid!"

Helvi shrugged. "Well, it that's true, then it would *have* to be a miracle. Far as I know, the woman hasn't spoken a word in years."

Kate looked long at her mother. *Now I* know *she's one of the pod people!*

Before Kate could pursue the matter, she heard the clatter of metal, the sound of a garbage can being knocked over. *Oh Christ, Daddy's home.* In one fluid movement, she scooped up the kitten, put the saucer in the sink, and darted out of the room.

Kate's room was a tiny one down the hall, next to the front room, which was now used only for television viewing. At first the Oksas had made jokes about their "sunken living room; " then, later, the incessant sound of traffic had made them mostly abandon it, although its presence did serve to insulate Kate's little bedroom somewhat from the *whoosh* of cars on the highway. Now, even with her door closed, Kate could clearly hear her father in the kitchen. He sounded drunk. The week of sobriety must be over. In fact, he sounded drunker than usual, which was *good*. Kate had become good at assessing the degrees of her father's inebriation. If Heikki Oksa was loud but coherent, there'd be a fight. If he was loud and *in*coherent, he'd probably stumble around, yell, and break something before passing out. Tonight, her father's weepy ululation told Kate that her mother would be leading him straight to bed, where he'd be out cold within minutes. Usually this would be accompanied by the shrill scolding of her mother, but tonight, yet again, Mother was not performing as usual.

Kate didn't have time to wonder about it now. She was preoccupied by her own situation. What exactly had happened back at the Lodge? Had she passed out and had some kind of nightmare? Kate couldn't remember anything except that it had been scary. Should she go back and ask Mrs. Niemi about the particulars? Had she just fallen flat on her face? How long had she been unconscious? Kate vowed she would try to get answers out of Mrs. Niemi no matter how much she disliked the old woman.

And Kate's mother was probably right about the kitten. She should take it back and find Moonrise to feed it. The way it looked, it might die in the night and save Kate the trouble. She put the animal on her bed while she decided what to do with it. He didn't even have a name. *Let's see, what'll I call you? Survivor? No, you'll go belly-up and make a liar out of me. Poor little dude. Dude? – no*, Jude. "Sure. Hey, Jude!" The newly christened Jude raised its head as if to say, "whatever," and deposited a watery brown puddle of feces on Kate's pillow.

...

Once again the house was quiet. Kate could smell supper cooking. Dear Old Dad must have passed out. So had Jude. Kate had done a cleanup job, changed her pillowcase and cover, then put the kitten on an old terrycloth towel into a cardboard box she'd found in the back of her closet. She'd emptied out the contents, memorabilia of Stastas High: schoolbooks; her gym suit *(God!)*; and a copy of *High-Fi*, the yearbook. She leafed through it now, looking all the dorky pictures of herself and her friends in their uncool haircuts. She came upon a photo of Barry Harwood: "The boy most likely to be abducted by aliens." He was wearing a checkered shirt and had his hair cut short. He looked a lot different now. She hadn't seen much of Barry since that time at the Dump, and come to think of it, Barry had been awfully zip-mouthed about what had happened that night. Before she spoke with Mrs. Niemi, maybe Kate should have another talk with Barry.

Kate studied Barry's photo and idly wondered what he was doing now. She and Barry had connected because they were both artists and misfits. Barry had been the best-looking kid in her class, but since he wasn't interested in sports, he hadn't buddied up with the guys. Girls liked him but didn't take him seriously. Barry could tell you which lightener to use to get blond streaks in your hair and what color looked best on you. He also made wildly dramatic jewelry — heavy pendants and large metal bracelets encrusted with onyx and turquoise. He and Kate, who never used makeup or wore jewelry, had seemed like the Odd Couple.

Kate remembered how they'd sometimes spend hours in Barry's basement, Kate drawing cartoons, Barry painting or working with metal. They didn't mix much with the other kids and nether felt comfortable in the social pecking order of Stastas High.

So what had happened to break up Kate and Barry? Drugs.

Kate put the book down, went into the kitchen and picked up her jacket. Her mother called to ask where she was going; supper was almost ready, but Kate was already halfway out the door. "I'll eat it cold later."

Days were getting shorter. As the Dump was several blocks away, in the industrial part of town, Kate decided to ride her bike, a Salvation Army fixer-upper she'd had since she was twelve. It had been a bit too big for her then, but she'd grown into it. It was a green, five-speed boy's touring bike with fenders and a wire carrier basket. The words "Free Spirit" were emblazoned on its crossbar, but after toiling up the many hills in Stastas, Kate had christened it Hercules.

The sky had cleared and the evening was mild. As she rode through the streets of the town, the smell of dinners cooking and shouts of children reminded Kate of when she'd been a little kid herself, playing stickball in the twilight until her mom called "Ka-a-tri-i-i! Supperti-i-ime."

Her tires *thwupped* across the railroad tracks, and she came to a squat building that had once been Ellery Shine's garage. It looked empty, but she saw Sumo's motorcycle parked outside. Nobody lived in the Dump on a permanent basis (water and power had been turned off) but outcasts and derelicts and homeless youth used it as a shelter. Local police came by every now and then to shoo out squatters, and many of the townsfolk said the place should be torn down. Others felt that they'd rather have the "hippies" there, out of sight, rather than lounging on the courthouse steps the way they used to do.

Kate leaned Hercules against a wall and went in through a side door. At first it looked as though no one was there, but then Kate heard the murmur of voices and followed the sound to the unmistakable smell of pot, beer, and unwashed bodies. The odor was sickening to her, and her biggest reason for avoiding the place. It choked, it cloyed, it clung to her hair and clothing for days afterwards.

They were all huddled in the room that had been Ellery's office, sitting on the floor around a battery lamp. Nobody paid any particular attention as Kate came in, but a voice called, "Yo, Kate. Pull up a cockroach and sit down." Kate saw it was Sumo — three hundred pounds of paunch and Willie Nelson braids.

If the group had a leader, Sumo was the one. Sumo dominated by his size alone, and because he was old enough to legally buy beer and cigarettes, he was also the gatekeeper to the Land of Drugs. Sumo had been born Herman Cadwallader, but nobody ever called him that; the name was as much of an embarrassment to Sumo as "Sumo" was to Judge Ivor Cadwallader, his father, who sat on the Town Council. The uneasy relationship between Sumo and his dad nevertheless assured Sumo that he would always be able to afford to buy gas for his Harley, even while he rebelled against the "system" that paid for it. Politics and public image dictated that Judge Cadwallader's son not be a penniless derelict. Sumo accepted the financial safety net, even tried to convince himself that it was his fair due, though with a nagging feeling that his tower of ideals perhaps lacked a few reinforcing rods.

"Hey, Kate, how ya been?" This came from Cherry, a hollow-eyed, hollow-voiced girl-woman with tangled hair.

Kate nodded a greeting, squatted down and peered through the haze. There were a couple of people there she'd never met, but nobody seemed to be making introductions. Whatever the conversation had been, it had stopped when Kate walked in. "What's going on?"

"You may be just the person we need, Kate. We were talking about the Labor Day picnic, and we thought we should put up a booth of our own. You know, to legalize cannabis? Shake up the good citizens of Stastas. Make em see where it's at." Sumo said.

"I don't even smoke pot, Sumo."

"Yeah, but you're for freedom, right?"

"Freedom, sure. Getting arrested sounds like the opposite of freedom to me."

"They can't arrest all of us, and if they do, they can't hold us. Anyway, they won't."

Kate sighed. *With Judge Cadwallader on the bench, she guessed not.* Out loud she said, "But why bother? It won't work. It's just going to piss of the hardasses, and we'll have townspeople with flaming torches heading for the Dump to burn it down — again. Besides, what makes you think they'd even let us put up a booth?"

"Maybe you could get your boyfriend to paint us some signs and a big banner with a leaf on it. We could put it up at night, and there it would be in the morning. We'd make the six o'clock news for sure."

"I haven't even seen Barry in ages. That's why I'm here. I was hoping to find him."

Sumo grinned and leaned towards Kate who tried to avoid the blast of his breath. "Barry hasn't been around lately. If you haven't seen him, then I guess you haven't heard. Barry's left home. He dropped out of school and he's got a place of his own now."

"Since when?"

Sumo took a swig from his beer can. "Since he tested HIV positive."

"Oh *God!* Where *is* he? *How* is he?"

"Scared shitless, I guess. His parents didn't want him at home, so they set him up in the attic of that old theater on Main Street. I hear he's got it fixed up as an art studio and I guess he's into painting."

In Stastas High, Barry had painted scenery for school plays, designed the *High-Fi* cover, and had even won a five-hundred-dollar prize in an art contest back in 1990 BD. Before Drugs. Now Barry was HIV positive. How was that possible? Needles? The Barry she'd known hadn't been into . . . or maybe he had. How could Kate really know?

It was getting dark. Glad of the fresh air, Kate biked along Main Street to the Midtown Theater that had closed during the recession. She recognized Barry's Mazda pickup truck outside and took the narrow wooden staircase to the top floor that had been divided up and rented out as apartments. Barry was HIV positive. She had lost her virginity to Barry Harwood, and she and Barry had continued to have sex when they were going together, although that was some time ago, and it had never really worked out all that well. Was there a chance that she, too, might end up on the AIDS diet plan?

The Barry who opened the door looked fine. In fact, he was the picture of health, and Kate saw that the loft was not only an apartment and paint studio, but also a gym of sorts. Barry had always been good-looking, proud of his physique, and even while he was into drugs, he used to work out regularly and keep a suntan. Drugs hadn't zombified Barry so much as turned him into a fuzzy-minded Peter Pan.

"Oh, wow! Kate! This is gre-e-a-a-at! C'mon in. I want to show you my place and all my stuff. Hey, you need a place to stay? I got lots of room." Barry spoke in a whispery voice in the cadences of a kindergarten teacher addressing a five-year-old — or was this a five-year-old, himself, speaking?

"Look, Barry, I heard, and I'm sorry."

"Oh, you mean about the HIV. Yeah, well, it's kinda . . . you know. But lemme show you what — " Barry pulled out canvases and leaned them against walls and furniture. "Ta-daa!"

Kate looked at the artwork. She didn't know anything about art except what little she'd learned in Stastas High. But this stuff! Okay, it might even really be good — except it was very weird. The colors were all dark and muddy and spooky, and the shapes were scary enough to give you nightmares, even though Kate couldn't make out what they were supposed to be. "Uh, yeah, Barry. You must've really been working hard. It's . . . it's great. Very — uh — impressionist."

"Really? Ya think?"

"Oh sure. I mean — what do *I* know — but look at what's out there. Wasn't that long ago I saw on TV that somebody paid millions for Andy Warhol's picture of Marilyn Monroe. Dead woman's head wallpaper. And that guy who used to paint eyes on chins and noses on cheeks.

His models must've all looked like Mr. Potato Head. You were always a good artist, Barry. But I have to ask you about something."

"Get yourself tested, Kate."

"That wasn't what I wanted to talk to you about. Barry, you remember that time at the Dump when we smoked pot and I passed out?"

Barry looked uncomfortable. "Yeah, I guess. . . ."

"What do *you* remember about it?"

"Oh, I dunno. You must've been coming down with something, because I've never seen anybody freak out like that on pot. I think you must've been sick."

"What do you mean freak out? Did I say anything? Did I scream or cry or what?"

"Well, I didn't want to tell you . . . didn't want to spook you . . . but you went into convulsions. You know, had a fit. We all figured it was a freak thing, and that's right, isn't it? Hasn't happened since, has it?"

"I'm not sure."

"Anyway, it lasted maybe just a minute or so, and then you fell asleep. We didn't leave you alone, Kate. There was always somebody there to look in on you. And when you woke up you seemed to be okay, just scared, that's all."

"Sure, Barry. I was fine." Kate remembered how she'd felt. Terrified. Disoriented. So weak she could barely walk. Soiled by her own urine and feces. Some things were fuzzy. How had she gotten home? Who'd helped clean her up, if anyone? Had anyone thought to get her to a doctor? She didn't think so. There was a big black hole in her memory.

Barry was avoiding eye contact. "We wouldn't have let you die, Kate. Okay, so maybe there *was* something more than just pot in that joint, but we thought you'd be all right. Look, stuff like that happens all the time. Bad trips. ODs. Sometimes people die, but most times you just sleep it off. So we just let you sleep. But we didn't leave you alone. There was always somebody there."

"Okay, then, when I was passed out, did I have any more

convulsions? Was I just out cold? Did I wake up at all?"

"Mostly you just slept. I think you moved around, made some noises like you might have been having a nightmare. We put you in Sumo's sleeping bag to keep you warm. But no, I don't think you had any more convulsions. You're not mad, are you Kate?"

Kate sighed. "No, Barry. You done good." Barry was sounding like the guy in *Of Mice and Men*. Kate had done a book report on it in English class, like a hundred years ago. *Jeez, George, tell me about the rabbits!* She looked long at Barry Harwood. If a man could be beautiful, Barry was. His skin was smooth and flawless with a golden tan. His long blond hair came to his shoulders and was held in place with a beaded Indian headband. He was wearing a leather vest that showed off the muscle definition of his biceps, and a leather belt with a silver and turquoise buckle accented his slim waist. Kate thought he could have been a model or a movie star.

"So, Barry. You're here now. And how are you, really?"

"I'm okay, Kate. Really. I'm not sick or anything. Anyway, not so far."

"HIV. How did you get it?"

"Oh, I don't know. Could have been any number of ways. You know I'm bi."

"Yeah. What about your folks? Where are they in all this?"

"My mom says she loves me. My dad doesn't want to know me. Neither of them wants me in the house."

Kate nodded, then tried to smile. "Hey, Barry, you've got it nice here. And just having HIV doesn't mean you'll automatically get AIDS, does it?"

"Nobody seems to know much about it. It scares people. They don't want to come near you."

Kate had heard of the "AIDS funeral," where a lawn and leaf bagged dead body would be found dumped off in a hospital parking lot. "Look, Barry, I'm sure you'll be fine. And I gotta go."

She turned to leave, then stopped. "And Barry? If you *do* need help. If you need somebody, hey, I'm here. Okay?"

"Okay. Thanks, Kate."

Kate pedaled her bike homeward. It had been quite a day. She'd acquired a pet, passed out at the Lodge, discovered she might be an epileptic, and learned she'd been exposed to HIV. The "Sesame Street" jingle kept running through her head: "*Three of these things all go together, three of these things are kind of the same. . . .*"

CHAPTER 5

Morning. Kate woke to the sound of her father's heavy snoring and the noise of dishes rattling in the kitchen. She'd slept well, felt refreshed, and had no memory of dreams. A faint scratching sound came from the cardboard box, and Kate jumped out of bed to see Jude, still alive, moving around unsteadily. He'd soiled the towel during the night. One of his eyes seemed to be open a little bit wider, although both were still runny. "Let's get you cleaned up and then we'll try milk again," Kate said, "and later we'll see if we can find your mother."

Remembering something, Kate went to her closet, pushed hangers and clothing to one side. Tucked in back, she found a carton of old toys and junk she'd meant to throw out a long time ago. The box had become a catchall for childhood discards; and, like an archaeological dig, each layer represented an era. Kate took out *Nancy Drew Mysteries* and *The Hobbit*, a few preteen magazines, a baseball and a catcher's mitt, a Kermit the Frog puppet, a Rubik's cube, an Etch-a-Sketch, a Slinky, and a battered bunch of Doctor Seuss books: *One Fish, Two Fish, Red Fish, Blue Fish; The Cat in the Hat; On Beyond Zebra*. At the bottom of the box was an old doll — a pink baby with a hole in its mouth and a corresponding hole in its bottom — a doll that drinks and wets. *Ugh!* Kate had never been much for dolls. There was something obscene about their staring eyes and rigid limbs, like a permanent state of *rigor mortis*. But that wasn't important now. Ah, there it was, the tiny feeding bottle with a rubber nipple. She tested it. Seemed okay. Might work for Jude. She pulled on jeans and a sweatshirt and padded barefoot into the kitchen.

Her mother was just leaving for work. Saturday, while government offices were closed, was Helvi's day to do cleaning at the Stastas courthouse. "There's hot oatmeal on the stove and coffee in the pot, Katri. And put on some shoes, for goodness' sake, and some decent clothes for a change, and *try* to do something with your hair. And don't leave the kitchen in a mess. I don't want to see dishes in the sink when I get home. It wouldn't hurt you to give the floor a mopping too, if that isn't too much to ask. I mean as long as you've seen fit to quit school and it's not like you've got a job. You might as well try to make yourself useful somehow."

Nice try, old woman, but you don't fool me. You're still one of those pod people trying to act like my mother.

Helvi Oksa left to catch her bus. Kate warmed a bit of milk and funneled it into the doll's bottle and attached the rubber nipple. She brought the kitten into the kitchen, box and all, and tried to get him to drink. It didn't work. Instead of sucking, all Jude did was mouth the rubber and gag. Kate couldn't squeeze the glass bottle to regulate the flow, and the hole in the nipple was too large. The kitten ended up coughing. Kate went back to her old method of putting a drop of milk on her finger, and letting the kitten lick it as best he could. "Looks like we'll have to try to find Moonrise."

Kate poured herself a cup of coffee. She took a bowl from the cabinet and plopped in a scoop of oatmeal, hesitated a moment, deciding whether she wanted to eat it with an "eye" of butter or with milk and sugar. The milk and sugar won. Kate was ravenous. She hadn't been in the mood to eat the night before, although her mother had kept a plate of stew hot for her. She drank the coffee. Kate was the only one in her age group who drank coffee, had been brought up on it, the way Italian kids grow up drinking wine. As soon as Kate had learned to handle a spoon, her mother had made a mix of coffee with lots of milk in it and dropped in bits of *pulla*, the sweet, braided Finnish coffee bread, to make a delicious mush.

Kate did the dishes, looked at the floor and decided it could wait. Her dad was still sleeping and probably would be till late afternoon. After having been gone most of the week, he'd picked Friday to come home. There was nothing unusual about Heikki's absences, but ordinarily they *began* on the weekend. Sometimes he'd be off on a binge with his drinking buddies, sometimes in the drunk tank, when the cops locked him up to dry. Heikki's driver's license had been taken away long ago, but that hadn't stopped him from driving his ancient Ford station wagon. Luckily the wagon had died of an internal hemorrhage before Heikki could kill himself or anyone else. It still stood, a rusting hulk, in the Oksa backyard along with old tires and scavenged car parts. Kate called it the Oksa Museum of Automotive History.

Somehow, Kate didn't want to go to the Lodge that day. She found excuses to put it off. She ended up sweeping and damp mopping the floor after all, then did a load of her own laundry in the wheezy old Kenmore. As she stripped her bed and balled up the linens (along with the soiled pillowcase and towel, thanks to Jude) to make a second load, she experienced a moment of *déjà vu* and a pang of terror. It only lasted a second, and left Kate's heart racing. What was it she'd almost remembered? Something in a dream? Kate had a vivid dream life. She didn't always recall her dreams, but sometimes, while doing some daily task, she would suddenly remember that she'd already done it — in a dream. Kate tried repeating her actions, regathering the bed linens into a ball to see if it would bring back the picture, but no.

This must be what it's like if you're abducted by aliens. You can't remember it, but you keep getting flashbacks. Then, too, did she *really* want to know what had happened yesterday in Elina Niemi's room? If Mrs. Niemi told her she'd had a seizure, that would make *two.* There was a young man in ECU who suffered from seizures. He'd had brain scans and been on all kinds of medications and still had seizures that completely incapacitated him. Kate didn't want to think about it. *Poor bastard. Nobody should have to live like that.*

Kate made a fresh pot of coffee, in case her father should wake up, and was trying to persuade herself that she didn't really have to go to the Lodge — except for Jude, who was looking reproachful and pathetic. Well, okay then, she'd take her bike and make it a quick trip.

With the kitten in Mrs. Norland's yarn bag in the carrier, Kate pedaled toward her destination. "You know, Jude, I should just keep right on going, all the way to the Humane Society, and then pretend we've never met." No movement from the kitten. "Yeah, and you know what they do to kittens with distemper? They call in a specialist from Switzerland and fly in the latest miracle drugs. Mrs. Norland, you old nutcase, you owe me one for this."

Kate left her bike in the parking lot and went in through a side door. The atmosphere in the Lodge lobby seemed subdued. A couple of Old People sat talking in low tones and paid no attention to Kate as she passed through. Moonrise was nowhere in sight, but Kate expected to find her in Mrs. Norland's room. To her surprise she found the door to Room 15 open and a maintenance crew at work.

"Where's Mrs. N?"

Two men in painter's whites were in the act of applying a coat of beige acrylic to the walls. All traces of Mrs. Norland had vanished — her chair, her lamp, her books, her pictures, her crochet. "Oh, the old girl passed away yesterday. They say she went in her sleep."

"Uh . . . well . . . I guess she *was* kinda old." It always seemed unreal to Kate that a person could *be* one day and simply *not be* the next. Being born took nine months of preparation and waiting. Then, after maybe seventy or eighty years of living, it all just snuffed out in a minute. It happened all the time at the Lodge, but Kate still had trouble grasping the concept that people just suddenly *died*. And nobody ever came back to tell what *really* happened. Kate had a mental picture of Mrs. Norland in her topknot hairdo, crocheting a neverending rug runner throughout eternity. "Uh — I have her bag. I was going to return it to her."

"Leave it at the desk. It'll be sent on with the rest of her things."

"I left a brown paper shopping bag here yesterday. Anybody seen it?"

"It'll probably be in the storeroom. Ask at the desk."

The desk seemed to be the place to go, but, hey, it was just a cheap shopping bag with Mrs. Niemi's embroidery floss in it. She'd check on it later. Kate had been hoping to reunite Jude with Moonrise, return Mrs. Norland's bag (so Mrs. Niemi wouldn't see it and have another meltdown), and exchange it for her own. Then she could deliver the floss to Mrs. Niemi and ask her what had happened the day before. As it was, she still had the kitten in Mrs. Norland's bag, and the floss could be anywhere. Kate decided that right now, before she lost her courage, she would seek out Mrs. Niemi and try to get some answers. It would be safer, however, to leave the kitten in-a-yarn-bag with someone else. She thought of Anthony Reed. Maybe the doc would be willing to kitty-sit.

Anthony Reed was, as usual, in his room, and immersed in a book. "Hey, Kit-Kat, how's it goin'? Wheeled any big deals lately?"

"Be fine if my customers didn't keep dying off. I heard about Mrs. Norland."

"Oh yeah. She was somethin', wasn't she? Place won't seem the same without the Queen Bee."

"I hear she died in her sleep."

"They always say that. Actually, I hear it happened yesterday afternoon, and they had one hard time getting into her room because her body was jammin' the door."

Kate felt a chill, remembering how she, herself, had tried the door and couldn't open it. "S-so what happened? Did she have a heart attack or something?"

"Maybe. When you get that old, the ticker just sometimes stops like a clock."

"I just saw her yesterday. She seemed kind of strange, and she'd been talking about somebody trying to kill her. I thought she was just going nutso, but you don't suppose . . . "

Anthony Reed smiled. "No, Kit-Kat. And I don't think she was 'nutso' either. Old age is an interesting time, and we don't know much about it, simply because nobody considers old people worth studying. We hate the idea of growing old so much that we don't even want to think about it, let alone research it."

"Well, she was going on about somebody wanting to kill her like they killed President Kennedy, and leaving rocks as a sign and stuff like that. It sounded like she'd lost a few of her mah-jongg tiles."

"Dementia of the aged. Old people have lived their lives and are getting ready for the next world. Just like very young children, they tend to drift in and out of their bodies. They are, in fact, living in more than one reality, so it can be confusing to people around them, and to themselves as well. Like sometimes when you wake up from a dream but you're still partly in it and feel like you're in two different places."

"Yeah, that's happened to me. But once I wake up, I don't keep dreaming."

"It may sound strange, Kit, but we dream all the time. The subconscious mind keeps on functioning, and *it* never sleeps. It's like the stars in the sky. We don't see them in the daytime because the sun is too bright, but they're still there. We all have a life in the dream world that's every bit as real, and often more important, than what we do when we're awake."

"So I could be dreaming right now?"

"We both are."

"Okay, then, how come it's so hard to remember dreams?"

"Don't you ever remember yours?"

"Yeah, sometimes, but mostly I don't."

"You won't remember them all, but you can learn a lot from dreams. Try giving yourself a suggestion just before you fall asleep at night. Tell yourself you'll remember what you dream about. Then keep a dream diary. Write down what you remember while it's still fresh in your mind."

"Do you do that, Doc? Keep a diary?"

"Oh yes, Kit-Kat. I've kept one for years." Anthony Reed's face had suddenly become clouded, as if he'd remembered something troubling. Kate studied his face thoughtfully. There was something heavy about Mr. Reed. Something dark and sad and deep. Maybe his dream world wasn't such a good place.

"Say, Doc, would you do me a favor?"

Anthony Reed tilted his head to the side and smiled at Kate, shaking off any shadowy memories. "Sure, if I can."

Kate placed the yarn bag on the table and opened it to display Jude. Anthony Reed looked at the bleary, frowzy kitten and laughed. "Well, Kit-Kat, looks like you got yourself one fine animal there. Has it got a name?"

"Jude."

"Jude. The patron saint of lost causes, huh?"

"I was thinking of the Beatles song, 'Hey Jude.'"

"Well, Jude, don't make it bad. Where'd he come from?"

"It's a long story, Doc, but could I leave him with you for a few minutes? I've got to go see Mrs. Niemi and I don't want her to go ballistic."

"Not much chance of that, but you're welcome to leave him. I'm sure Jude and I are gonna get along just fine."

"Thanks, Doc. And if Moonrise comes around, the kitten's hers. Maybe she'll feed him."

Walking down the hall, Kate almost changed her mind about talking with Elina Niemi. The woman would probably start yelling about how it was all God's punishment for her sinful ways. And maybe it was. She was about to turn back when Mrs. Niemi's door opened and a friendly-faced old woman stepped into the hall. Mrs. Niemi's roommate? No, this wasn't the wispy-haired woman Kate had seen yesterday. The woman smiled kindly at Kate. "Are you looking for someone, dear? I was just on my way down to the recreation room. Can I help you find your way?"

"I was coming to see Mrs. Niemi."

"She's inside, poor thing. Maybe I'd better go in with you. She doesn't speak, and I'm not sure can even hear. Are you a relative?"

What's going on? Am I at the right room? And who is this strange woman telling me something's happened to Mrs. Niemi?

"I'm — I'm Kate Oksa, and I just wanted to ask Mrs. Niemi about — uh — tell her about her — uh — embroidery floss."

"I'm Sylvia Winter. I haven't been here long, but I think Mrs. Niemi is past doing embroidery!" She gave Kate a significant look as she opened the door.

Inside, on what had been Mrs. Niemi's bed, sat the same wispy-haired old lady Kate had seen the day before, the one Kate had thought was Mrs. Niemi's roommate. There was no sign of Elina Niemi or Mrs. Niemi's embroidery or the magnifying glass that had been clamped to her table. The woman on the bed sat silent, her eyes vacant and unfocused.

"But that's . . . that's *not* Elina Niemi!"

"Oh, I *see*, dear. You must have the wrong person," Mrs. Winter said. "This *is* Mrs. Niemi, but her name is *Anna*. I'm afraid I don't know the lady you're looking for, but maybe she's new. I'm sure if you ask Jane at the desk — "

Mumbling apologies, Kate fled. It *had* been Mrs. Niemi's room. Room 13. Next to Mrs. Norland's. But what had happened to the Mrs. Niemi Kate knew? *Elina* Niemi. The one who had called her a thief and a slut. The one who was always yelling about sin and degradation. *Did she pack up her cross-shaped luggage and check out?*

Kate had always lived by her wits, and if she'd had a motto, it would have been: Always question everyone else's sanity before you question your own. Right now, nothing was making sense, but there had to be some solid thing to hold on to. The embroidery floss! She'd bought it for Mrs. Niemi and it was still in her shopping bag. Kate headed for the desk in the lobby.

Jane Clark, the receptionist, looked up from her file cards and smiled brightly, "Hi, girl, how are you?"

You'd never believe it if I told you. "I hear Mrs. Norland passed away."

Jane's voice dropped to a lower key. "Oh yes. We'll all miss her. She was a dear old thing."

"Yeah. It must've been sudden. I just saw her yesterday."

"With these people it's a blessing when it's quick. I understand she just slipped away in her sleep."

Yeah, dozed off leaning against her door again. "I left a brown paper shopping bag with some embroidery floss in her room, and I'm wondering what happened to it."

Jane looked around. "It's not here. It's probably in the storeroom with the rest of her things. I'll buzz for Mike. He can take you down there."

"I was also wondering about Mrs. Niemi. Are there *two* Mrs. Niemis at the Lodge now?"

Jane flipped her Rolodex cards. "I'll just take a look; we have people coming in all the time. Nope. Just one. Anna Niemi. Room 13. And she's been here for five years."

"But what about Elina Niemi? Don't you remember her? Old

woman. Does embroidery. Walks with a cane. Always talking about how she used to be rich and live in a big house. Yells a lot."

Jane looked puzzled. "Really? I don't remember her. Of course I don't know *all* the residents that well personally. Maybe you have her name confused with someone else."

"Her name is Elina Niemi. Her husband was a lawyer. He's dead now. She's only been in the Lodge a short time."

Jane shook her head. "I don't know what to tell you. I've never heard of her. The only Mrs. Niemi I know about is Anna Niemi. She's married to a lawyer too, but he's still very much alive. He put her in the Lodge five years ago, and as far as I know, she hasn't spoken in all that time. Are you *sure* you have the name right?"

"I dunno. Right now I'm not sure of anything, but something's very weird. If I could just find my shopping bag. . . ."

Mike, the head maintenance man, arrived at the desk in answer to Jane's call. Tall, slightly balding with a good-natured face etched with laugh lines, Mike had been a fixture at the Lodge for a number of years. If the air-conditioning malfunctioned or someone dropped a spoon in the Garburator, Mike would be called, day or night. He also served as a discreet and unobtrusive escort to nurses whenever they had to deal with a difficult patient, and had a calming way about him that made him valuable in the ECU when a patient exhibited dementia. Mike was, by nature, cheery and chatty, a reassuring presence throughout the complex, privy to confidences and gossip. Kate thought he'd be a good person to pump for information.

"Mike, Katie is looking for a bag she left in Mrs. Norland's room. We think it must be down in storage with the rest of her things. Would you take her down so she can have a look?"

Mike grinned. "Sure thing, Katydid, follow me." Mike led her down the hall, into the elevator, down to the basement. "Bit of a mess down here, but maybe we'll find what you're looking for. Nobody's come to collect any of Mrs. Norland's things yet."

The storage room was filled with unused hospital paraphernalia: beds, wheelchairs, obsolete equipment, and sundry surplus items. There, under cold fluorescent lights, stood Mrs. Norland's chair, looking bleached and forlorn. Its crocheted cover had been neatly folded along with her other crocheted items and piled on a table. There lay also boxes of her clothing, books, and personal possessions: the remains of Mrs. Norland's life, ready for transit. Her lava lamp stood unplugged, a motionless red blob in mourning. The sight of these things out of context, stacked in this impersonal way, was more affecting than the sight of Mrs. Norland's body might have been. Kate had seen lots of dead bodies at funerals. In the Finnish community of Stastas, everyone went to funerals whether you knew the deceased or not, and Helvi Oksa had always been big on funerals. But the bodies had never seemed like anything but slabs of meat to Kate. Whatever made the person a person was gone. She fingered a piece of Mrs. Norland's crochet, looked around for her shopping bag — and found it! It was empty, but then, someone *could've* taken the floss. . . .

"Mike, what's going to happen to all her stuff?"

"Oh, if her relatives don't want it, it'll go to Goodwill or Sally Ann."

Kate was looking around. "Is this the only storeroom for stuff that's left behind?"

"This is it."

"Do you remember seeing a magnifying glass — one of those round ones with a fluorescent light, about the size of a dinner plate, the kind that clamps to a table and has an arm that extends out?"

"Mrs. Norland had one of those?"

"No, but Mrs. Niemi, in Room 13, used one for her embroidery." Kate kept her eyes fixed on Mike's face. If this was some sort of hoax or cover-up, or government plot to substitute another woman for Elina Niemi, would *everyone* be in on it?

"Can't say I've ever seen one here. Are you sure it was Mrs. Niemi? That old biddy hasn't been in touch for years. She's gone deaf, you know, and I don't think I've ever heard her say a word. She's only in the Lodge because she can still more or less feed herself and go to the bathroom. She'll end up in ECU before long. Her husband never comes to see her anymore."

"Who's her husband?"

"Oskar Niemi. You must know him. Used to be a big-shot lawyer. Retired now." Mike smiled a bit wickedly and raised his eyebrows. "They say he had her put away so he could get his hands on her money."

It *had* to be some kind of plot. Elina Niemi's husband's name was Oskar. Oskar Niemi had died of a heart attack three years ago. Kate and her mother had gone to his funeral. He was buried in the Stastas Cemetery, and his wife had only been in the Lodge for a few months! What *was* this, the witness protection program from the *Twilight Zone?*

Kate took her bag, thanked Mike, and took the elevator back to the main floor. All this was entirely too bizarre, but she'd have to ride it out. If she said too much, she'd sound like a lunatic, and the Lodge was not the place to do that! Not now. She needed to talk, but she needed to talk to someone whose first reaction wouldn't be to put her in a rubber room, someone who might help her sort out what was happening in her head, if it *was* all in her head, that is. Anthony Reed. The Doc was always reading books about how the mind works. He knew about dreams and the subconscious and stuff like that. And right now he was Jude-sitting.

Anthony Reed's door was open as usual and Kate looked in on a strange sight. Jude was on the table, sitting up — or trying to sit up — like an adult cat. His weepy eyes were fixed on Mr. Reed who had wheeled his chair backwards, as far away from the kitten as possible, and sat staring at the animal in what looked to be shock and horror. The words "What's up, Doc?" froze on Kate's lips when she realized that something really *was* wrong with Mr. Reed. Was he having a heart attack or a stroke? "Hey, Doc, are you okay?"

Anthony Reed turned his head and looked at Kate. *"Where did you get that creature?"*

"Jude? I told you. It's Moonrise's kitten. She had kittens in Mrs. Norland's room. The other two died. This one will too, if I can't find Moonrise to feed him."

"Get rid of it. Get rid of it right away!"

"Why . . . what's the matter?"

"I don't know for sure, but this thing isn't what it looks to be."

"I don't understand. It's just a kitten."

Anthony Reed reached over and took hold of Kate's wrist, squeezing so hard it hurt. "Listen to me, Kit-Kat. *Put the cat in the bag and don't look at it. Take it to the dump, throw it in a lake, take it to the Humane Society. Take it* anywhere *as far away from you as possible! Do* not *look at it. Just get rid of it."* Under his breath he added, *"If you can."*

...

Well, so much for a meaningful conversation with the Doc. Has everybody *suddenly gone batshit?* Kate didn't hang around. She scooped up Jude, both bags, and got out of there. The Doc was beginning to scare her and, with these Old People, you never knew what was up. One day they could be telling you knock-knock jokes, and the next day they wouldn't recognize you. Or worse, they'd think you were one of their long-dead relatives. But the Doc had always been normal. And smart. What he said made sense, although he was into a lot of stuff that was out of Kate's depth. *Why would he suddenly do a double axel over a cat? Of course, Mrs. Norland was smart too, and* she's *gone frisbeeing off the edge.*

Kate was still carrying Jude in her arms. "Don't worry, babycakes. I'm not going to stuff you in the garbage disposal." She was about to put him back into Mrs. Norland's bag, but as she entered the lobby, she saw that there was some kind of commotion going on. Jock Ostriker, the meanest man in town, was having some sort of trouble with his wheelchair and was raising hell about it, swearing, whacking the wheel with his cane, and yelling loudly. Other residents were keeping their distance.

Kate didn't want to go anywhere near him, but in order to leave, she had to get past him. She edged close to the wall to give Ostriker as wide a berth as possible. *Someone should take that cane away from him before he hurts somebody.* Ostriker, by now red in the face and screaming incoherencies, looked as though he might explode. Kate wanted to flee, but at that moment, a particularly loud bellow from Ostriker frightened Jude. The kitten squirmed free and fell from Kate's grip to the carpet.

Then everything happened with lightning speed. The kitten, who up till now had barely been able to stand, arched its tiny back, spat, and, with the hair on its back in a stiff ridge, *ran* – ran directly *toward* Jock Ostriker, who stopped yelling and stared, as if stupefied. Moving like a black streak, Jude leapt up and onto Mr. Ostriker's good leg, then clawed his way upward, digging nails into skin through the fabric of his trousers. Ostriker found his voice and screamed. He raised his stick and would've crushed the animal with one blow. By reflex, Kate made a dive to grab the kitten, and as her hands closed around Jude, the cane came crashing down on the back of her head.

CHAPTER 6

"Jock! Jo-o-o-ck!" Someone was calling. "Where are you, Jock?" It was a male voice. "Come *on*, Jock, time to go. It's getting late."

Kate opened her eyes and saw grass. A black ant was crawling up a blade, inches from her eyes. The call came again: "Jock!" *For chrissakes, Jock, whoever you are, can't you hear that someone's calling you?* She seemed to be lying on a patch of greenery. Where? In the woods? *What happened? Did I hit my head on a branch or something?* She tried getting up but fell over, not so much because she felt dizzy, but because her body felt alien, as if her center of gravity had shifted.

Oh God, it's happened again. I'm in a dream again! Kate's body may have been unfamiliar, but her mind and memory were clear — *super* clear. She remembered everything including the nightmare she'd had about being Elina Saari, and the memory helped her to process this new information more quickly. She took stock of her situation and got her first jolt. She was a man! She sat on the grass and stretched out her legs. Tan trousers. Sneakers? Well, maybe some ancestor of sneakers: rubber-soled canvas shoes with laces. Long legs. Long arms.

Lots more shoulder. Kate touched her face. Bit of stubble on the chin — unfamiliar lump on the neck — Adam's apple? Hair — short, shaved back and sides. And a bump on the back of the head. *Ouch!* Cautiously, Kate got to her feet and found she could move easily and with a certain grace.

There had to be some sort of pattern to this! Had she had another seizure? Is this what happened when she had one? Did she go back in time? Well, she wasn't sure that she *had* gone back in time, but that's what had happened before. She'd been standing next to Mrs. Niemi and ended up in the body of Elina Niemi. Only it had been the body of Elina Niemi when she was a young girl, Kate's age. *This time — oh, Jesus! — I was in the lobby of the Lodge. Am I lying there right now, thrashing around in front of everybody?*

At the thought, Kate was struck by an acute feeling of embarrassment and humiliation, which brought back memory of the marauding emotions that had been part of her last "trip." That one had ended badly with Kate as Ellen/Elina falling to her death. She and Frederick, her lover, had nose-dived off the upper story gallery, although Kate didn't remember the landing. Nor did she remember anything afterwards, so she assumed she must have died. Whatever else was going on, emotions were something to be careful of in this place. Right now, however, she was *in* this place and would have to operate by whatever its rules were. Who was she? She'd been in the lobby with a bunch of Old People. Jude had gone berserk and run up Mr. Ostriker's leg. Ostriker took a swing at the kitten and — Jock! Someone had been calling for Jock. *Oh great. I must be Jock! Jock Ostriker, the biggest craphead in town. Mr. Macho, killer of animals!*

"There you are. You must've heard me calling you. Why didn't you answer?" Kate turned. In front of her stood a tall, thin, dark-haired young man wearing slacks and shirt. He was carrying something in his arms. "I've been looking all over for you. Look what I found." Kate saw that it was a small animal — a kitten with weepy eyes — Jude!

Kate felt a xylophone scale of emotions sweep over her: a pang of terror (where did that come from?) then relief at seeing a familiar face, even if it was only Jude's, and then a strange mixture of feelings — what exactly? — for the young man. She tried "being" Ostriker, hoping to find out who this person might be, but it didn't work. She was too agitated to be able to concentrate.

The man was gently stroking Jude's back. "I found him lost in the woods, poor little fellow. Probably followed its mother and got left behind. Cats do that, you know. They'll take their kittens into the woods and leave them to find their way back. Horrid creatures. Well, let's get back to the cabin. We can do more exploring tomorrow."

Exploring? Exploring what? What were these guys doing in the woods? Hunting? Yeah, that would've made sense in Ostriker's case, but nobody was carrying a gun. Nobody was carrying anything. No cameras, no metal detectors, not so much as a berry basket! What were they looking for? Some *thing* or some *place?* Cabin. He'd said cabin. Play it cool now: "Okay, you lead the way."

Kate followed the man who was carrying Jude, and did some mental calculations. If the pattern were the same, she would be Ostriker at about age seventeen. Ostriker was what? Seventysomething? If he'd been born in the early 1920s, this could now be the late 1930s. Close enough on when, now *where?* They were speaking English, so Kate narrowed it down to North America.

Kate saw they were walking through woods of maple and aspen (those trees with the quaking leaves). Not many evergreens. All quite different from the towering Douglas firs and cedars on the West Coast.

The country seemed to be more hilly than mountainous. They were climbing now, and had taken a footpath upward toward a small log cabin on a cleared little hilltop. It was really very beautiful here, if Kate could just figure out where "here" was. Dreams can be fun because they *are* dreams. If you realize you're dreaming, you can do things you wouldn't dare try in real life, knowing you'll wake up safe in your own bed. Except that Kate would more likely wake up on the floor of the Lodge lobby, with a bunch of people gawking at her.

"Here we are again, home sweet home." The young man opened the rough wooden door and Kate followed him inside. It must've been a hunting cabin. There were only two rooms. The main one was sparsely furnished with a wooden table, a couple of chairs, and a rough wooden bench along one wall. There was a wood stove, a small counter with a sink and a couple of cabinets for dishes. A kerosene lamp sat on the table. A bucket stood under the sink drain, and another, with water and a dipper, sat on the bench. The other room was (Kate peered behind the curtain tacked up to act as a door) a bedroom with one bed that was somewhere in between a single and double in width. *Oh swell, I guess we share. Glad I'm not in my old body.* She glanced at her companion. *Or maybe not.*

Kate saw backpacking gear — a couple of canvas knapsacks, boots, jackets, binoculars — and a rifle. Maybe they were hunting after all. In any case, this wasn't just an overnighter; they were here for some purpose, with food to last for several days, judging by the stock of canned goods. There was no sign of a vehicle, so they must have hiked in or been dropped off.

Her companion had busied himself with the kitten, taken a can of Carnation milk off the shelf and poured some in a chipped saucer. Somewhere he'd found a bit of cheesecloth which he now dipped in the milk and gave to Jude to suck. It seemed to be working. "Poor little devil, he doesn't look well, does he? What'll we name him?"

"Jude. We'll call him Jude." Kate said, a bit absently.

"Jude, huh? Jude the Obscure. Suits him, somehow. The Three Musketeers: Jeremy, Jock and Jude."

Thank you, God of Small Things. Now how do I pump Jeremy *for information without sounding like I've been nibbling on the local mushrooms?* "So, Jeremy, did you find anything?"

Jeremy looked at Kate and compressed his lips. "If you mean did *we* find anything, you know perfectly well neither of us did. If *anything* even exists, which I doubt. I don't even know what *anything* is or how I'd recognize it if I saw it. We could, at this very moment, be lying on a beach instead of slogging all over the mosquito-infested woods of Pennsylvania looking for — oh, watch out, kitty — I mean Jude — you're walking in the milk!"

What? Looking for what, *you twit!* "Uh, yes, well, it seemed like a good idea at the time." Kate said carefully.

Jeremy leveled his brown eyes at Kate. "Does this have anything to do with those nightmares you've been having? Why would you feel the need to go looking for some long-dead place that probably crumbled to dust years ago? If all you want to do is make rubbings of old gravestones, every state in New England is full of old cemeteries. So what *is* this? What is it you're *really* looking for?"

"Ah, well, I . . . I really don't know myself."

"Well, it would be nice if you had some idea, since I've given up perfectly good vacation time to go traipsing through these woods with you."

"Uh — maybe it's just because history interests me?"

"Well, it doesn't interest *me.* I don't even think there *is* a burial site here from the Civil War period. God knows the state is *fertilized* with the dead of the Civil War, but they don't have markers. And it's not like it was your family that was buried there, is it?"

Kate's brain was busy probing a possible connection between the Civil War and burial sites and nightmares. "Maybe not, but it's beautiful out here, don't you think? I like being out in the woods." Obviously Jeremy wasn't going to be much help in explaining their hereabouts, and Jock, who would certainly have known all, was not coming through.

Jeremy gave an exasperated sigh. "Then go out and commune with nature while you bring in some wood so I can get dinner started."

Kate was rather grateful to be by herself for a while. It *was* beautiful. The late afternoon sun cast long shadows and filtered through leaves, making them translucent as stained glass. The air was warm and smelled clean and sweet with the scent of plants and flowers of late summer, their oils unlocked by a day in the hot sun. Kate noticed that there was a small brook at the bottom of the hill and wondered if that was their water supply. Would it be drinkable? If this was the 1930s, there was probably less pollution back then and it might be okay. She walked down to it, cupped water in her hand and tasted it. It was delicious. A tiny lobster-like crustacean scuttled under a rock in the water, and Kate could smell the tangy odor of wild mint growing along the stream edge.

Pennsylvania. That's what Jeremy had said. Kate walked to the edge of the woods to look at a shrub with flame-shaped, fist-sized clusters of berries. They were the color of red wine and formed a tight, velvety mass on the tip of each branch. Scarlet sumac. You could make a drink from those berries. Kate wouldn't have known that, but Jock must have! She was rather enjoying all this, testing the feel of her male body. Then, with a mischievous grin, she unzipped her trousers, pulled out her penis, and directed a stream of urine in an arc as far as she could, then laughed out loud. She'd seen someone on *Oprah* or was it *Joan Rivers* say that penis envy was any woman on a camping trip.

"Hey, where's that bloody wood?"

"Coming."

Kate ran up the hill, grabbed an armful of split logs from the pile along the wall and went into the cabin. Jeremy was standing, hands on hips, regarding the potbellied iron stove. "What took you so long? Oh, never mind now. It's too hot for a fire. We light that monster and it'll be like an oven in here all night. I suppose we can open a can of beans. And we'll have to eat the hot dogs or they'll spoil in this heat."

Kate set the wood down. "Why can't we build a campfire outside? We can toast weenies on sticks. We have rolls and mustard."

"Well, I guess we could. The beer will be warm. I hate warm beer."

"We can put it in the creek to cool," Kate said. We could keep other stuff cold in there too. Have we got any plastic bags?"

"*What* kind of bags?"

Oh damn. "I mean *elastic* – no, rubber – something the water won't get into. Never mind. The bottles are capped; they'll be okay. *What did they do before plastic was invented?* We'll tie them in a towel and let them cool while I'm making the fire."

Kate had never camped, nor had she built a fire, but apparently Jock had. She found she knew just what to do. She gathered dry grass and sticks for kindling, set the wood teepee style, lit a match and soon had a blaze going. She felt at home in the woods but obviously Jeremy didn't. Kate watched him as he sat on a stump, looking sulky, gently stroking Jude who appeared to be asleep. Who *was* Jeremy? Was he a relative? A brother? A friend? In that case he must be a *good* one to come out here when he clearly would rather be someplace else. Kate tried to fit puzzle pieces together: two young men in the woods in Pennsylvania in the 1930s. Jeremy had said that Jock was looking for a Civil War graveyard? And Jeremy had asked if it had anything to do with nightmares Jock had been having. So Jock must have told Jeremy *something* about his dreams (or nightmares) and they might be a clue as to what was going on. Maybe after they'd eaten and relaxed over a couple of beers, Jeremy might give out more information.

Nightfall in a forest clearing is magical and spooky. The light fades, stars begin to appear. There are cries and whispers and rustling sounds. *What was that?* Shadows creep up through the trunks of trees until all that's left is the small circle of light around the fire. Kate couldn't remember having been at a campfire, at least not like this one. She watched the wood sizzle and pop, sparks flying into the night sky, while the flame burrowed deep inside a log to turn it red, like lava. Then the color began to fade as the wood darkened and shrank to a slab of segmented charcoal, and finally to a ghostly patch of ash. *It's like we're the only people on earth — or maybe it's like we're the first people on earth. And this is the first fire and we've just discovered it. And from now on we'll always be connected somehow.*

Kate and Jeremy had eaten hot dogs roasted on sticks cut from a soft maple tree. Slightly scorched, slathered with mustard, and tucked into rolls, the wieners had tasted delicious out in the open air. Jude had been offered remnants of the feast (which he'd merely licked), and more canned milk by Jeremy's cheesecloth method. Now, with the fire slowly dying, the two sat on the grass, each sipping a cool beer. Kate felt wonderful. This dream was more like it! She hoped she'd remember this one. She mused that she wouldn't mind very much if she could *stay* in this one.

Kate tossed aside the empty bottle and stretched out on the grass. She could feel the warmth from the fire through the rubber soles of her shoes as she lay looking at the night sky. A shooting star streaked across the heavens, then another — a golden ball of fire that left a smoky trail. "Wow, did you see that?"

"Meteors," Jeremy said. "It's the Perseids meteor shower, or what's left of it. It happens every August, but sometimes you can't see it for cloud cover. Tiny bits of comet debris traveling at 40,000 miles per hour, burning up in the earth's atmosphere."

Kate became aware that Jeremy had moved closer to her. Now he raised himself on one elbow, leaned over her face, and to Kate's astonishment, kissed her, first softly, then passionately, forcing his tongue into her mouth while his hand explored — oh God! For a moment, Kate had forgotten her male body, which was now responding with a very male erection. *Holy Jesus! This guy's gay. Jeremy's gay! And maybe I'm gay too. I mean Ostriker's gay. Mr. Macho is a fag?* Some devilish part of Kate was saying, never mind, it's only a dream — and not a bad one either — so why not just relax and enjoy it? Another part of her was shocked at the strangeness of being in a man's body and making love to a man — a man Kate would've found attractive, had she been in her *own* body. But then, of course, he wouldn't have been attracted to *her. Holy identity crisis, Batman!* Kate pulled herself free and sat up. "I'm sorry, Jeremy. I can't."

"You mean you *won't.* You never want to make love anymore."

"I — I don't know what I mean. It's just — "

"Let me hazard a guess. It's just that little Jock Ostriker doesn't want to face the fact that he's a homosexual. He thinks he can have it both ways. What are you going to do, Jock, marry some boring little twat and hold your nose while you sire a brood of brats to make your ham-handed father happy? Are you going to become a pillar of society and then spend your nights telling the little woman you're going out for cigarettes, while you cruise the seedy district, picking up boys?"

"It's not that. At least, I don't *think* it's that."

Jeremy sighed. His tone turned from angry to weary. "Jock, don't you think I *know?* Do you think I haven't *been* there? When I first found out, I wanted to kill myself. I'd heard all the jokes, the names — fairy, faggot, queer — and those are the *good* ones! It's like finding out that you're a leper. Unclean! Unclean! And then you think, I'll bury it. I won't admit it even to myself. I'll change. I'll be — or pretend to be — just like everybody else. It doesn't work, Jock. Trust me."

Kate's emotions were churning again. Sorrow, pity, compassion, a flash of anger. *I don't* need *this. I have troubles enough of my own!* "Look, Jeremy, I don't know what's going to happen. I just need some time to sort things out."

"Right," Jeremy said coldly and got up.

"Where are you going?"

"I'm going to bed." He went in the cabin and slammed the ill-fitting door which gave only a half-hearted *thunk,* then sprang partly open and hung ajar.

Terrific. Here I am stuck in the woods with a fag with an attitude. Or maybe I'm *the fag with the attitude.* Only now it wasn't so easy to dismiss — what should the word be? Faghood? Gayety? At seventeen, Kate felt suddenly old and tired, tired of all the *shit* about homosexuality. Growing up, Kate had known very little about gays. She'd never heard them mentioned in the Finnish community. They either didn't exist or were so deep underground you never saw a sprout. In high school, there had been a few kids who were *whispered* to be gay, the subject of sniggering jokes, treated with wary belligerence — in case it might be catching? As with the Finnish community, there *were* no lesbians in Stastas High. No, no! In fact, you never even heard the term. It wasn't a word anyone wanted to utter, like "cancer" used to be.

Jeremy had said he thought of killing himself. Well, things hadn't changed all that much. One kid in Stastas High had done just that — hanged himself from the metal basketball backboard support in the gym. Kate tried to picture being gay. What must it be like to find out you're an outcast? You have this big secret you can't tell anyone. Not your parents. Not your best friend. You live in a world of fag jokes, and you can't say a word. You try so hard to be like everyone else. In Stastas High there were all sorts of rules you followed just to fit in with the *cool* kids. You wore the wrong sneakers or the wrong jacket and you were *out*. Kate, of course, had never been *in*. She'd never had the money to buy the cool stuff, and she knew how it was to be whispered about and not be invited to parties. The cool did not socialize with the uncool, at least openly, since coolness was a fugitive quality, easily lost through wrong association.

If Kate had belonged to any group in Stastas High, it was the misfit fringe. They were the geeks, the rebels, and the outlaws. In the fabric of High School life there was a place for them. They were the ones you went to for help when your grades were going south, the ones you tapped for jobs like decorating the gym, the ones who might lend you their homework when you hadn't done yours, and who might even be grateful for the chance to bask, for an instant, in the glory of your brief, though contemptuous, gratitude. Some of them could also get you drugs; settle a few scores (for a price);

or provide dangerous, wrong-side-of-the-tracks sex to the spoiled daughters of Stastas's finer families, the girls who always seemed to be looking for new thrills to brag about to their friends. Like Merry Lee Peckinpaugh, damn her eyes!

In this society, with its rigid pecking order, no wonder a gay kid might kill himself. He didn't know yet that high school wasn't the world. He also didn't have a clue what the real world would do to him. When Kate left high school, she remembered that it had been an amputating experience. School had been her life. She'd hated the system, the hypocrisy, the unfairness, but it had still been her life. The day she walked out, it was almost as if Stastas High had shrunk, as if the building, itself, got smaller and became just a pile of bricks. The students, kids she knew, rushing to classes and worrying about their grades and their pimples and their futures seemed like a bunch of ants. The world hardly noticed they were there. They, in turn never noticed Kate had left. Kate had never gone back into the building.

Later, Kate's friends at the Dump had been more hard-edged. There, nobody seemed to care if you were gay, straight, or bisexual. They all had other issues, the main one being drugs, which they seemed to have in common. Some were rebels; some were runaways; some drifters; some had really creepy quirks, like Cherry, who would go into a fit of hysteria and hyperventilation at the mention of the word *astrakhan*. Nobody knew why, and Kate at first had thought it was a joke. Something like the old "Slowly I turn" routine she'd seen on TV. Or like a Monty Python skit: "Other than that, she's *perfectly* all right." And then one night someone, somehow, out of the blue, had said it and Cherry had gone into a scary fit of trembling and gasping for breath. Kate didn't even know what the word meant or how the sound of it could wield such power.

Such was the Dump, and if Kate had not had an aversion to drugs, she'd have hung out there more. The people there were the only ones who ever got her name right.

Nobody at the Dump worried about your sexual orientation, nor should it have mattered. "What the hell difference does it make who you have sex with? Right, Your Scrawniness?" The kitten was sitting on a log. His eyes seemed to be a bit better; at least they were open enough to reflect the red of the embers. It was getting a bit chilly. Kate put the fire out, doused it carefully, like a seasoned woodsman, picked up Jude and went into the cabin.

Jeremy had lit the kerosene lamp. In its glow, Kate rummaged through camp gear and found a cotton sleeping bag. She laid it on the floor, blew out the light, and crawled inside with the kitten next to her, but sleep would not immediately come. She lay, eyes wide open, staring into the darkness and replaying the day. Was this the dream world the Doc had been talking about? As real and as important as her waking world? When she woke up, would she remember? He'd told her to give herself a suggestion to remember her dreams, but how would that work when she was *already* in a dream? *If* that's what this was. It certainly felt real. The hard floor under her sleeping bag was real. The kitten curled up next to her was real. The body she was in felt real.

That last time, when she'd been in the body of Elina/Ellen, *that* had been real enough too. And she remembered how she'd pushed Frederick over the edge of the railing and gone over with him. *That* had been a dumb thing to do, but she didn't think she could have stopped herself. Whatever emotion gripped her, it was violent and out-of-control. She didn't remember hitting the ground, but hey, that might explain the Mrs. Niemi thing. If Ellen/Elina did die as a young girl, then she couldn't have ever married Oskar Niemi. She could never even have met him. But how come Kate, herself, had survived? She'd ended up back in her own time. *Or was it?* It *wasn't* exactly the same, was it? There was a Mrs. Niemi there, but she was a different woman. Different name. So what had happened? Oskar Niemi married someone else? As far as Kate knew, Oskar Niemi was dead. But not anymore. According to Mike, he was alive, retired, and never came to see his wife, Anna, the zombie woman at the Lodge.

And here it was happening again. Kate wondered if she'd ever get back and, if so, how? Would she just wake up on the floor like the last time? And then would she remember any of this? When Ostriker whacked her with his cane, he must have knocked her all way into the 1930s, but it was like coming in in the middle of a movie.

She tried an experiment: She let her mind wander back to where she'd found herself in the woods, then tried to remember what had happened before that. How had she and Jeremy gotten here? When had they arrived? Where had they come from? If she could just catch a glimpse, maybe she could expand the memory, make Jock Ostriker's past open up. Maybe she could find out what Jock Ostriker was doing here, what he was looking for, and for what reason. Kate willed herself to remember, but all she did was drift off to sleep.

She dreamt she was walking through a graveyard overgrown with weeds. She was holding Jude in her arms, and she was looking for something or someone. She saw a figure in the distance. It looked familiar, but as she approached, the figure moved farther away. She broke into a run, but the weeds grew thick and held her back, and brambles were scratching her arm.

Kate woke with a gasp. It was daylight. She identified the source of her pain: Jude had nuzzled up to her forearm and was trying to nurse. As he sucked on a flap of skin, he was digging sharp little claws into her epidermis. Kate batted him away. "Stop that, you little vampire. What are you trying to do, give me a hickey?"

"I see you're awake." It had turned cool, and Jeremy had lit a fire in the stove. "You *could've* come to bed last night. I wouldn't have attacked you."

"I . . . I guess I didn't want to wake you." Kate stumbled out of her sleeping bag. "I need coffee. Do we have any instant?"

"If you mean, do we have any *this* instant, the answer is no. But

I'll make a pot as soon as the water boils. And you wouldn't have awakened me. I didn't sleep much."

Just what I need – to be in the middle of a lovers' quarrel when I'm in the body of one of the lovers. Kate went out to empty her bladder, amazed at the male capacity. She noted the absence of an outhouse. *Guess we'll be doing what the bears do. I just hope we don't collide with one when Mother Nature calls.*

"You should wear boots instead of those running shoes. There might be snakes." In near silence, they'd eaten a hearty breakfast of hotcakes and syrup, which Jeremy had managed to provide along with excellent coffee, some of which Jeremy was pouring into a thermos bottle.

"Good idea. It's cooler today." Kate pulled on a pair of rubber boots with lace-up leather uppers and was amused to see that they were from L.L. Bean, just like her Dad's old farm boots.

"I don't know why you brought that rifle. It's not hunting season."

Well, I don't know either, dude. That part of the computer program hasn't come through yet. "Just a safety-in-the-woods thing, I guess. In case we get attacked."

"Attacked? By what?"

"I dunno. A bigfoot. A grizzly bear. The Loch Ness monster. A band of roving muppets. I just brought it, okay?" *Jeez!* "But don't worry, Jeremy, I'm not taking it with me."

"Good. I have no wish to be in front of you if you stumble and the thing goes off. You want your pad and charcoal?"

"No, let's find the site first. I can go back and do a rubbing if there's anything to rub. I have a feeling we should go farther east." *(I do?)* "The old man said it was in a hollow, and the ground slopes that way." *Old man? What old man?*

"The old geezer was probably senile," Jeremy said petulantly. "I've packed a lunch since we'll no doubt waste the day walking around in circles."

"Well, you *don't* have to come if you don't want to. In fact, we could just call this whole thing off and get the hell out of here."

"You're only saying that because you know perfectly well that Maurice won't be here with the truck till Thursday."

That might have been a useful bit of information if Kate had known what day it was. Anyway, it explained the provisions and how they got there. "You still don't have to come. You could stay here and babysit the cat."

"And let you go off by yourself and get lost or break a leg? Anyway, I fed Jude and he's asleep. If we prop the door shut, he won't be able to get out."

Jude, in fact, lay curled on Kate's folded-up sleeping bag on the bench. As if sensing that he was being talked about, he opened one eye then closed it. The other seemed to be swollen shut again. Jeremy carefully lifted the bag and set it on the floor. "There, now you won't have far to fall." He set the saucer of canned milk nearby, but removed the bit of cheesecloth "so you won't choke on it without me to hold it for you." He surveyed the arrangements with the look of a worried parent while he put on his knapsack, then simply picked up the kitten and dropped it in his coat pocket. "All right, let's go."

CHAPTER 7

This is like a Disney movie, Kate thought, as she and Jeremy made their way toward the woods. On the edge of the clearing blackberries were ripening on brambles, and chokecherry bushes hung heavy with clusters of red fruit. Kate recognized frothy white field flowers as Queen Anne's lace, each flat white umbel with a central spot of purple. *It's also called wild carrot, and eating the purple centers was supposed to cure epilepsy. How did I know that?*

They waded through brown-eyed Susans, goldenrod and blue vervain, then entered the woods themselves, now sun-flecked and fresh, the grasses underfoot still wet with dew. Looking around, Kate found she could identify many plants and trees — pokeweed, elecampane, sassafras, fox grape — and felt a new-sprung surge of affection for old man Ostriker who had once been a kid with an interest in woods lore and botany. What had happened to turn him into the meanest man in town? When he went hunting, who was he really trying to kill? Or was it that, in this dream, Kate painted her own picture of Jock Ostriker, who was very likely in the Lodge lobby right now, staring at Kate's twitching form. She saw a stray patch of Queen Anne's lace and absently plucked the purple center from a bloom and put it into her mouth.

"With all this undergrowth, just how do you expect to find anything?" Jeremy sounded edgy.

"Let's go a little farther down this slope." In fact, Kate didn't care whether they found anything or not. She liked the experience of walking in woods, but had little interest in the quest, since she didn't know what to look for or what to do if she found it. She tried allowing her mind to float, hoping that some part of Jock would emerge.

"Are you sure we're not lost? I think we're lost."

"Oh, for chrissakes, we are *not* lost. Notice how the ground slopes. We're traveling downhill. To get back, all we have to do is go *up*hill and follow the same trail."

"Trail? I don't see any trail?"

"Oh jeez, Jeremy, we're leaving a track a blind man could follow." Kate stopped and motioned for Jeremy to be quiet. In the stillness she'd heard a soft rustling sound, a stealthy footfall. She stood frozen, then entranced, as a white-tailed deer emerged from behind a stand of small aspen trees. The animal, a young doe, at first seemed unaware of their presence, then pricked up its large ears and turned to look directly at Kate. For a moment they made eye contact, she and the wild creature. Then, in a sudden flurry of motion and sound, the deer gave a snort — a cross between a whistle and a sneeze — stamped its hoof and was gone in a flash of white. Kate, who had been holding her breath, exhaled. "Did you see that? Just like *Bambi!*"

"Like what?"

"Bambi. The deer. Walt Disney. The movie." *Or when did that come out?*

"Never heard of it. You want to stop for coffee?"

They sat on the trunk of a fallen tree and drank coffee sweetened with sugar and lightened with canned milk. Kate was amused to see

Jeremy take Jude out of his pocket and feed him some of the milk, using his handkerchief as a wick, the way he'd used cheesecloth. Something about the kitten kept nagging at Kate's mind. What was it doing here in her dream? Why had it shown up in *both* her dreams? Why had Anthony Reed reacted to it the way he had? It was such a puny little thing; Kate was surprised that it was still alive. It never seemed to eat much, and it didn't seem to be getting any better — or worse either. Of course, things didn't have to change in dreams. In dreams time could stand still, *real* time, that is. *If I woke up now, I'd be on the floor of the lobby. I could spend a month out here and still wake up on the Lodge carpet.*

Jeremy produced a flask of water and used a bit of it to rinse out the cups, dried them with a tea towel from his knapsack, then screwed them, nested, back in place on top of the thermos bottle. Kate wondered idly if he'd come up with silverware and candelabra at lunchtime. She left Jeremy to gather his gear and started down the slope, noticing that the grade was decreasing and that she was entering the flat plain of a valley. The area was overgrown with shrubs and trees — wild cherry, maple, aspen, hawthorn — and there seemed to be a stand of large maple trees towering above the rest of the vegetation.

Then, as she stood looking around, Kate felt herself overcome by an emotion that almost brought her to her knees — a searing longing, a sense of choking homesickness. And grief — utter despairing grief at some loss so great that it was out of all proportion to anything she'd ever felt! *It was here. The house was here. And that's where the barn stood. And the well. And those big maple trees — that was the sugar bush where we boiled sap. And on behind that . . .*

"What in God's name is the matter with *you?*" Jeremy had come up behind her and was standing at Kate's elbow, staring. "Are you *crying?*"

Kate dabbed at her eyes. The wave of emotion was subsiding and she realized how strange she must look. "I think I must've brushed up against something. I'm probably allergic."

"Well, thank God. Maybe we can get out of these perishing woods. We can always spend a couple of days getting a tan till Maurice gets here. Can't we, pussy?" Kate saw that Jeremy was carrying Jude in his arms. "We can stop all this business of looking for a will-o'-the-wisp."

"We've found it."

Jeremy blinked, then looked around. "*This* is what we were looking for?"

"This is it. It used to be a farm. This area was all cleared for crops." Kate pointed, "There was a house and a barn. And the family burial plot will be over there, on the other side of the maple grove."

"I don't see any sign of anything ever having been here. How do you know all this?"

"Trust me, Jeremy. I know."

With Jeremy stumbling along behind her, Kate strode through shrubs and undergrowth toward the grove of maple trees. There were about thirty of them — giants — the trunks of larger ones over two feet thick. A few had toppled, and a couple hung leaning, caught in the act of falling in the fork of a neighboring tree. One looked as though it had been struck by lightning, the tree split and splintered so that part of it hung down as if raked by a claw.

Kate stepped over fallen branches, made her way to the other side of the maples, then stopped. Something familiar was up ahead — a silvery twisted object about the size of a satellite dish — partly visible through greenery. As Kate drew near, she saw another, a bit smaller, a tangle of roots writhed into a mass, their ends trimmed, weathered to pale gray. "Look, Jeremy, it's the old stump fence. Or what's left of it."

"Amazing! It looks like a sculpture!"

"Yeah, and it made a damn good fence. I used to like to climb on it. It's like a jungle gym."

"What do you mean *you* used to climb on it? You've never been here before, have you?"

"No, of course not. I only meant that when they cut down trees to clear the land, they used to pry up the stumps and turn them on their sides so the roots formed a fence. I've seen one before, when I was a kid. They're great to climb on. The family burial plot should be alongside."

Jeremy sighed. "Ours not to wonder why; ours but to trip over roots and get poison ivy, eh, Jude? What are we looking for anyway? Headstones? Wooden markers? They'd be rotted away by now. Or maybe we should just follow that ghost over there."

Kate stopped in her tracks. There *was* someone up ahead. The figure seemed to be a man, but it was hard to tell through the misty haze that now hung over the valley. Kate felt a pang of annoyance. No one was supposed to be here! *Damn.* She quickened her pace and called, "Hello!" The figure didn't respond. *Some local yokel.* "Helloooo!" She broke into a run. The figure didn't appear to be moving, but she didn't seem to be getting any closer to it either. Kate squinted. It looked like an old person — a man with gray or white hair. Short in stature, or hunched over, he looked to be wearing a dark coat. A coat in the woods on a day in August? A farmer in his Sunday-go-meeting clothes? But there was something oddly familiar about the man. Was this someone Jock Ostriker knew? As Kate watched, the figure was becoming less and less distinct, swallowed up by thickening fog.

She was about to call out again, but was startled into silence by an eerie sound. Jeremy was standing next to her, holding Jude. The kitten now had both eyes wide open, and was staring intently into the mist, and *howling* — a long, unearthly, warbling wail, loud and harsh and chilling as a death cry!

...

"We should've named you Banshee, you little beggar. Who'd have thought a tiny creature like that could make such blood-curdling sounds. Have you ever heard anything like it?" They were back in the cabin, and Jeremy was busying himself with lunch.

"No, and it scared the shit out of me. I don't know why he can't just say *meow* like other cats." Kate was looking out the small paned window at rain splattering against it. "Boy, we got back just in time. It's starting to pour."

"When I saw that cloud come up, I knew we'd be in for it. I expect we'll get a thunder boomer. I hope this Taj Mahal doesn't leak."

Kate saw no lightning, but she did hear a low growl of thunder. "I wonder who he was. That guy we saw."

"Probably some farmer out picking berries."

"Didn't seem to be dressed for it. He didn't seem to hear me either."

"Deaf as a post, most likely. Or just doesn't cotton to strangers. These people aren't the type to throw you a housewarming. You remember that character at the gas station?"

Kate didn't, of course, although Jock eventually might. She nodded, realizing it must have been some rube-versus-city-slicker encounter. "I wish we'd had time to check the place out a bit more."

"We'd have gotten soaked. I'll bet your farmer friend is wringing out his socks, consoling himself with a cuppa, and telling the missus about being chased by a couple of nosey parkers." Jeremy laid out the sandwiches from his knapsack and opened two bottles of beer. "At least this is more civilized than eating in the bush and swatting mosquitoes. Anyway, we have to talk."

Uh-oh! When anyone says we have to talk, it usually means you have to do something you don't want to do. "Yeah, well, sure, Jeremy, spill your guts."

"We've known each other a long time, right?"

"Yeah, so?"

"So just what the hell is happening to you?"

"I don't know what you mean."

Jeremy looked pained. "You know, I was hoping we could cut through all this shit and talk to each other. Really *talk* to each other.

Look, Jock, it's me, Jeremy. It's a little late to pretend we're a couple of kids at Camp Wetabed."

"I really am sorry, Jeremy, but there's . . . there's stuff about me that I can't explain right now. I'm not really myself these days."

"I'm glad to hear you've noticed it too! For God's sake, you've been acting like a bwana on safari and I'm your faithful manservant! I can't get close to you. We don't talk. We don't touch. Every time I try to get near you, you dance around like Astaire. You don't even sound like your old self. And that was no allergy in the woods today. You were bawling your eyes out. Why?"

"I honestly don't know. Something just came over me."

"There you go again! *Why* don't you know? What are we doing in this place? You never cared about Civil War stuff, at least not until you started having those nightmares. And you're still having them, aren't you?"

Kate didn't know, so she just nodded, hoping Jeremy would get on with it.

"You've been moody and strange ever since they started. I worry about you. Maybe you should be seeing a doctor."

"You mean a shrink, don't you?"

"I mean that maybe you should be seeing a *psychiatrist.* I also mean that half the time I don't know what you're talking about. Like now."

Kate wondered if anyone called a psychiatrist a shrink in the 1930s. She borrowed a phrase from her own time: "I just think I need time to find myself."

Jeremy gave an exasperated sigh. "I wish you would. *I* certainly can't find you these days. Why have you suddenly become this whole different person? You sound different. You act different. You talk about things I've never heard you talk about. What kind of game are you playing?"

Kate laughed ruefully. "What would you say if I told you all this is nothing but a dream I'm having, and you're just a person in it?"

"I'd say you're faking insanity to avoid the issue."

"Okay, Jeremy, I'm going to be as honest with you as I can. *I can't remember anything.*"

Jeremy rolled his eyes. "Oh sure, tell me another!"

"I really mean it. I seem to have lost my memory. I don't remember anything about my past. I think I hit my head on something that knocked me flat. When I saw you in the woods yesterday — when you found Jude — I didn't know who you were. Hell, I didn't know who *I* was. I just tried going along with everything, hoping it would all come back. Some things *have* come back. I know how to do stuff like build a fire and find my way in the woods. But I don't know where I live. I don't know who my people are. I don't know why we're here and I don't know how we got here. *I just simply don't remember!*"

Jeremy was staring at Kate intently. She could see suspicion struggling with acceptance. *Welcome to my nightmare, Jeremy, old sod. And I think that's all the honesty you can handle right now.*

"Are you telling me the God's truth?"

"I swear."

"You sonofabitch! You cowardly little bastard!"

"Huh?"

"Oh, yeah. It's the perfect solution for you, isn't it? Blot it all out. None of it ever happened. You and I were never lovers. Hell, you don't even *know* me. We don't have to make any decisions about a life together in a world that hates us. Okay, okay. I understand. I really *do* understand. Better than *you* do. I *know* the family pressures. You don't. You haven't told your family yet, and of course you're frightened. I was scared too, and my family didn't take it well either, but it's better than living a lie. But we could've worked it out, you and I. We *still* could work it out. This isn't the only place in the world. We don't have to stay here. We could go to Europe — France or Germany. There are wonderful schools there, and people are much more liberal. And you wouldn't have to depend on your parents for money. Believe me, my parents will be only too happy to finance anything I want as long as it's far, far away from the old hometown. We could live together, go on with our studies, and make something of our lives! I'm not saying it'll be easy, but we could do it." Something he saw in Kate's eyes stopped him. "But of course if you don't remember, it doesn't really matter, does it?"

Christ. I feel like Rambo at a Sunday school picnic. Jock, where are you? Am I supposed to get engaged to this guy? Or should I tell him you just stepped out of your body for a few minutes and will get back to him later? Or should I just tell him to forget Germany; the timing is lousy.

"Look, Jeremy, you're obviously a nice guy and a good friend — okay, *more* than friend, but I wasn't jerking your — I mean I wasn't lying to you. This is all very weird to me, and I don't know how long it's going to last. Maybe I'll just snap out of it, but until I do, I'm flying blind here, and I'm hoping you'll just hang in." Jeremy said nothing, and Kate had to look away from the hurt in his eyes. "And Jeremy?"

"Yes?"

"There *is* something else. Something about that place today. The farm. It made me remember things and feel things, stuff that Jock — I — couldn't possibly remember. Long-ago stuff. It was like pictures flashing and it just knocked the wind out of me." Jeremy was looking at Kate thoughtfully and with a touch of wariness. "No, Jeremy, I'm not crazy. At least I don't *think* I am. But I do know one thing. *I've got to go back there.*"

...

It had stopped raining, and the sun was sending pale, tentative beams through a break in the clouds. Lunch dishes had been washed, although neither of them had been able to eat anything. Kate was on her way to the creek to refill the water bucket; and the air, polished by rain, was clean and sweet, filled with the sounds of songbirds, insects, and the raucous screaming of a flock of crows somewhere in the distance.

Kate approached the stream and realized that filling a bucket in a shallow creek was not a simple task if you don't have a dipper. Hoping to find a spot deep enough to immerse the bucket, she followed the creek upstream until she came to a small pool where water tumbled into it over rocks. She carefully edged down the embankment, then nearly slipped and fell in, as a young bullfrog, startled by her approach, screeched a high-pitched *eep!* and arced past her into the water with a splash. *Madre de Jesus!* Kate laid a hand over her heart. *So much for the quiet of the country!* She scooped up a bucket of water and scrambled up the bank and set the pail down. She would've sat too, but the ground was still wet. Studying the terrain, she saw that the brook flowed from between hills down toward the valley. Only it wasn't called a valley, but a hollow, and it had a name! Something Hollow. Swamp Hollow? Sumac Hollow? Something with an "S." A family name, perhaps. *Damn! I almost had it.*

Kate picked up the bucket and headed back. There was still plenty of daylight, but it was hard to tell from the sky whether it would remain clear. She needed to go back and take another look at the old farm site, but this time she wanted to go alone.

...

As Kate put the bucket of water on the bench, she sensed a change in the atmosphere in the cabin. Jeremy sat brooding at the table. Jude, who was normally in Jeremy's lap or at least within petting reach, was curled up in a far corner, one eye closed again, the other staring morosely into the middle distance.

Kate glanced from one to the other. "You two have a fight?"

Jeremy glanced at her but said nothing. The fingers of his right hand were nervously drumming the tabletop.

Kate could feel another "we have to talk" coming on. She hastily picked up her jacket. "I think I'll take a quick hike down into the hollow and see if I can get a better fix on that place."

Jeremy looked up, startled. "You don't want to go *now*, do you? We'll only get caught in the rain again. And even if it doesn't rain we'll get soaked. We can go tomorrow, give the woods a chance to dry out. And we'll have all day to do whatever you want."

"I didn't mean for both of us to go. I'm just going to nose around a little. I'll be back long before it gets dark."

"This is crazy, Jock. Look, you told me that you haven't been yourself lately, and I'm beginning to think there's something very odd about this place. It's . . . I don't know what. It may be affecting you in some way. In your present state of mind, I'm not going to let you go tramping off into the woods alone. What if you get lost?"

"I'm the one who *doesn't* get lost, remember?"

"Well, what if you get attacked by a bear, or fall and break a leg? I'd never hear you calling for help. And how would I know where to look for you? And how would I find you in the dark?"

"Jeremy, if there are any bears in these woods, they'll leave me alone as long as I don't bother them. And I don't plan to break any legs any more than I plan to kiss a bear on the lips. But I'll tell you what. If it'll make you feel any better, I'll take the rifle with me. If — *if* — on the wildest, remotest chance I need your help, I'll fire the thing as a signal. You'll have no trouble hearing it. And I'll be back before it gets dark."

Jeremy's face clearly said that he didn't like the idea. He sat looking long at Kate, who returned his gaze with what she hoped was one of reassurance. Jude, meanwhile, got to his feet, unsteadily made his way to Jeremy, and began bump-rubbing against his ankle. To Kate's surprise, Jeremy gave him a look of repugnance and rather roughly pushed the kitten away with his foot. He looked back at Kate, his expression serious, his eyes grave and troubled. "Don't go, Jock.

Please. There's something very wrong about all this. *Don't go."*

...

Damn him anyway. Kate was seething with guilt and defiance and anger. They were familiar emotions to Kate in her old world. They were the same emotions that plagued her whenever she found herself acting at odds with the wishes of someone she cared about, usually her mother. Some perceived injustice or unfair constraint triggered mutiny, then guilt, which she tried to wash away with righteous anger, only to end up feeling miserable. Once, at thirteen, Kate had crossed a farmer's field and become entangled in an electric fence that had shocked her over and over again until she'd managed to break free. To Kate, emotional relationships were like that fence. If they couldn't be avoided, then they should be approached with caution and bypassed with little or no direct contact.

Why should I give a rat's ass about what Jeremy thinks? But she did. Jeremy might be nothing more than a dream figment she had created but — or perhaps because of it — she felt somehow responsible for him. He was like the puppy that falls in love with you and follows you home, a sticky web of involvement that Kate didn't want, but had somehow blundered into. Jeremy had begged her not to go, but Kate had gone anyway. It was just something she had to do, and she hated having to justify her actions when she couldn't understand them herself. Maybe, just maybe, if she followed her impulses, she might learn something more about her own situation. *Why* was all this happening to her? *Why* was she suddenly being thrust into somebody else's life, then tossed around like a dinghy on the waves of their emotions? She really didn't need the distraction of Jeremy's problems. She needed to be able to *think.*

The late afternoon woods were wet but beautiful, bejeweled by drops of water, although Kate was too preoccupied to notice. She walked with long, masculine strides with the rifle slung over her right shoulder. Kate had never handled a rifle but the burden felt easy and familiar. It was loaded although there was no bullet in the chamber. The *Sako* was a Finnish hunting rifle with a hinged clip that held five 30.06 soft-nosed bullets, each of which, at the pull of the bolt, could be spring-loaded into the chamber. The safety catch was on. No need to worry about the gun going off accidentally if she tripped over a root.

As Kate drew farther from the cabin and closer to the floor of the hollow, Jeremy-guilt diminished as the sense of *déjà vu* grew stronger. Once again she could feel intrusive emotions and memories crowding in, and she was glad to be alone with no need to explain or conceal. This time she really *was* alone. Even Jude, her dream companion, was back at the cabin. And, come to think of it, Jeremy's treatment of the kitten had certainly turned strange. She'd have to ask about that later.

Kate could now see the old stump fence. This time there were no shadowy figures in the distance, but there was a sense of utter familiarity in the path she took. Kate also became aware that every one of her senses had been magnified. Every rustle, the snapping of every twig, seemed to carry immense significance, as did the patterns formed by grass and pebbles, the texture of leaves and the bark on trees. Everything seemed heightened, enlarged, as if camcorded with a macro lens and shown on a big screen. Such was her awareness that every bit of sensory input seemed thickened and stretched, as if every object were now a symbol of every such object everywhere. A leaf was not just a leaf; it was every leaf ever grown. It made Kate feel a little lightheaded. Then she had the sense of being multiple, as if a number of Kates were striding through the brush, and that she wasn't just one of them, she was *all* of them. And she also fancied that if she changed her direction the tiniest bit, stepped a little to the left or to the right, she'd be, somehow, different. Would she be a different Kate? Another version of Kate? Or somebody else entirely?

She also had the sense that time was overlapping in the same fashion. Was she marching along in a number of time periods? It was as though she, at that point, might step from one reality to another very easily. Could she take a step to the left or right and walk into a future Kate or a past Kate? Perhaps not a Kate at all. Maybe a cave-person Kate or a Kate not yet born? Even her name seemed phony. No, not fake exactly, but irrelevant. Any name might do, because she was everybody. She was Kate. She was Jock Ostriker. She was Elina Saari, and more, so many more. Names echoed in her mind, all being murmured at once so she could no longer make out any of them. They just became a chorus or chant like the sound of the sea or wind blowing through trees. And all the names and all the lives, all the births and all the deaths, Kate felt part of them all, yet she knew that she could single out any person, and view them as easily as zooming in with a camera. It was exhilarating. Was this Jock Ostriker's world or her own?

As soon as Jock Ostriker came into her mind, he was there — there with an immediacy that was almost like a blow. She had zeroed in on him and isolated him like a germ under a microscope. He surfaced in her consciousness and Kate, briefly, had a sense of him. She felt his terror, his confusion, and his fury. Because he was gay? No, not entirely. There was something else about Jock Ostriker. He was, Kate realized, with an icy shock, insane!

Kate was in the body of a man experiencing a psychotic episode — a man obsessed, convinced he was possessed by some ancestor, some long-ago personality, fixated by some ancient event that held him in thrall. And Kate could feel that Jock Ostriker was trying to take over her mind.

She fought for control. She started to run, ran until she was out of breath, then fell to her knees, and saw that she had found Jock's graveyard. It looked to be a tiny family plot overgrown with weeds, the kind of burial place that was found in early America, when death arrived suddenly and inconveniently, and burial in an established cemetery wasn't an option.

Kate saw that there appeared to be three graves. The stones that marked them could have been nothing but rocks in a field, except for the way they'd been placed. There were two small ones and one slab that had been raised on end, but now tilted on its side like a sinking ship. If the scratches on the stone had once been an inscription, Kate couldn't read what it said. But as Kate ran her fingers over the weathered rock, she discovered, at the bottom, letters cut more deeply into the surface. She clawed back grass and weeds and dirt to expose the faint markings. The first letter was "S."

She felt emotions hit her like a pyroclastic flow. They engulfed, choked and scorched. She was a soul in torment. If there was a hell, she was falling into it. All hope was gone. She keened. She howled. Deep sobs wracked her body. She dug with bare hands, fingers bloody, to expose more of the inscription until she could read the name: four letters, crudely cut, "Susi."

CHAPTER 8

THE FIRST thing Kate noticed was the metallic taste in her mouth, as if she'd been chewing tinfoil. Her body felt heavy, immovable. Everything hurt. Her arms and legs felt as if they'd been pulled off and reattached incorrectly, like those of a plastic doll that a child had ripped apart, then reassembled, putting limbs into wrong sockets. There were strange sounds in her ears — a buzzing and a switchboard of chattering voices like a faulty telephone connection merging with a Hispanic radio station somewhere far away. The inside of her head fizzed and sputtered like an electrical circuit shorting out. It felt as if someone had reached into her ears and was trying to pull out her brain — the hard way — left side through right, melting it to mush in the process: *I'm sorry, your call cannot go through . . . sizzle, sizzle . . . that number has been disconnected . . . pop, crackle. . . .*

Kate tried to sit up, but found she couldn't lift her arms more than a few inches. She heard the clink of metal and saw that large black rubber handcuffs equipped with padlocks were cutting into her wrists whenever she tried to move. Like a bug caught in a spider's web, she was chained to a bed. Her left arm and hand had been tied down to what looked like a cricket bat. Duct tape fastened the board to her arm, and a clear tube ran from an IV to a large hollow needle which had been inserted into the back of her hand and taped in place. Around it, gauze pads were stained yellow and red.

Kate fought down a spasm of nausea at the sight of the dripping IV, then experienced an attack of giddy, hysterical fear as a surge of adrenaline coursed through her system. *Why am I locked to a hospital bed? What happened? What did I do? Did I kill somebody? Are the police outside, waiting to take me to jail? Why else would I be chained like an animal?* Kate saw that her legs had also been tied in a spread-eagle fashion, and her feeling of vulnerability fueled more panic. *Where am I? What the hell are they doing to me? Have I been in an accident? But why am I tied up?*

Kate felt as though she could well have been in an accident. The muscles in her arms and legs felt as if they'd been wrung, like wet towels, all their vital fluids squeezed out, and left to uncurl. She could barely move, but her right hand, the one not anchored to the IV, seemed to have a life of its own. Kate watched, fascinated, as it kept convulsively spreading its fingers apart, then the two middle fingers would curl inward in a "come here" gesture. As the fingers curled in, the wrist would bend inward, the gesture repeating and repeating as if sparked by some electrical impulse.

Emotional impulses were running through Kate in a similar way. She'd clench her teeth and pucker her brow as if deeply worried; the next instant she'd be walleyed with panic. Her heart raced, then seemed to stop beating, only to explode again at a racing pace. Kate wanted to cry — scream — laugh, as if programmed by some hellish remote control in the hands of a crazed channel switcher. Then suddenly she seemed to be living just outside of her own body, like a shoe that's not quite on your foot, and existing twenty or thirty seconds ahead in time. The smallest incident was accompanied by a sense of *déjà vu.* Everything — a squeaky wheel on an orderly's cart, a nurse walking by — was accompanied by a sense of "ah yes, I knew this was going to happen!" She was enough in the future to disconnect her from the present, and had no memory of the past, only a dawning feeling of dread. She kept having a physical compulsion to turn her head and look over her left shoulder. She felt terrified. She didn't know of what, but she kept looking for it over her shoulder.

"Well, young lady, you certainly did give us a scare!" A crisp nurse with a bedside smile was looking at Kate through plastic-rimmed glasses. "And how are you feeling?"

Kate tried to answer, but her throat was dry and all she could manage was a croaking cough. She feebly raised her hand and turned her head to indicate the restraints. Her head was pounding. *If my head were my elbow, my brain would be the funny bone.*

The nurse gave her a hard look of appraisal, then smiled brightly. "There's someone here to see you." She ushered in a woman Kate at first didn't recognize, then realized it was her mother.

Helvi Oksa approached slowly with a look of disbelief. "Katri? Katri, are you all right?"

"Hi, Mom." Kate's voice sounded strange to her own ears, and she wasn't quite sure that the words were coming out right. "Can you . . . can you get these matches . . . uh . . ." she *knew* matches wasn't the right word but couldn't seem to form the correct one. "Cha . . . cha . . ." Kate tried raising her hands.

Her mother understood. "Nurse, can you please take off the straps. I'm sure Katri doesn't need them now." It was an order, not a request. The nurse looked hesitant, but then proceeded to undo the cuffs.

"What . . . what . . ." Kate groped for a word.

"You had a fit. The doctor told me you had a fit."

Kate almost wanted to laugh. She'd used the word herself many times, as in "I nearly had a fit," or "She'd have a fit if she knew."

"Have you been taking drugs, Katri?"

"No."

"Are you sure? Drugs cause fits."

"I. . . I . . . no. No drugs." Kate's mind was confused enough but her speech was worse.

"Nobody in our family ever had fits."

Nobody in our family has any sensitivity either. I'm sorry if my nearly dying puts a blot on the illustrious name of Oksa. "Can I . . . have a sla . . . sla. . . *glass* . . . of . . ." Kate inwardly cursed the strange inability to speak that would, to gradually lessening degree, plague her for several days. Her *mind* was working, but her *brain* was acting like a computer with a virus, letters detaching themselves and reforming into a jumble.

Helvi poured water from a carafe into a clear plastic cup, put in a straw, and held it for Kate. Kate managed a sip through the bent straw, then her hand jerked, jarring the cup and throwing water into the air and all over the bed.

"Just lay down and rest, Katri, I'll be back later."

"Mom? When can I . . . get out . . . here?"

"Dr. Bakkaran said not till tomorrow at least. They done all kinds of tests. Heaven only knows what it's all going to cost. But don't worry about that now. Just stay quiet and get better." Helvi left, leaving Kate feeling depressed.

...

The doctor turned out to be a portly man with an accent and an overbearing manner. He peered down at his clipboard, studying Kate's chart, without making eye contact. "Do you know where you are?"

"Hospital." Kate murmured.

"Do you know what month it is?"

"Au . . . August?" Seemed a safe bet according to a calendar on the wall.

"What's the last thing you remember?"

"I can't ber . . . mem*ber* . . . anything."

"How long have you had this condition?"

"I . . . I don't know."

"Had you gone *off* your medication?"

Kate was becoming increasingly annoyed at the man's officious manner. "I . . . don't . . . ta . . . take medi . . .dication."

For the first time, Dr. Bakkaran looked at Kate. "You have a seizure disorder and you've just had multiple clonic seizures, and you tell me you've never taken medication? That's very stupid of you, young woman. If you don't care about yourself, at least consider what you're putting your family through." Dr. Bakkaran hung Kate's chart on the foot of her bed and muttered something to the nurse about discontinuing the diphenylhydantoin, and was gone.

Kate might have burst into tears if she hadn't been so angry. *Thanks a lot, Dr. Shitty Bedside Manner. I'd love to give you a piece of my mind . . . if I could find it. What school for assholes did you graduate from? Everybody's acting like I really screwed up their day!* Her fury, however, seemed to help mobilize her healing forces. She began to feel less fragile, more in control. There was a huge black hole in her memory, but data about her life in Stastas was beginning to trickle through, even as the stiffness and soreness in her muscles began to ease.

Kate's next visitor was brighter and sunnier, but brought news that was equally devastating. Jane (at the desk) Clark came in with a cheery, "How're you doin' girl? Everybody's been asking about you so I told them I'd look in."

Kate was so glad to see a happy, familiar face she almost did burst into tears. "I feel like . . . hit by . . . tr . . . train, but . . . guess I'll live."

"No wonder, after what you went through!"

"Did you see . . . what hap . . . happened? I woke up trussed . . . like a ta . . . t-turkey."

"Well," Jane glanced around and dropped her voice. "You really gave us some excitement yesterday."

"What . . . cupp . . . *damn* . . . hup . . . *happ*ened? What did I do?" Kate was trying to force her tongue to get the words right.

"I didn't notice just what was going on at first, but you must've fallen somehow. You were having convulsions. I called the orderlies, but when they came, you — uh — resisted."

"Re . . . res . . . issted?"

"Ah . . . well . . . of course, you understand, you didn't know what you were doing."

"Ju . . . just tell me what I duh . . . did!"

"First of all, you kicked Phil Cruikshank in the stomach, and then you punched Dave Potts in the face." Jane suppressed a giggle. "He's got a shiner now."

Kate closed her eyes in mortification. "Was that . . . all?"

"Well, you remember that fish tank we used to have in the lobby? You pushed Ben McEvoy into it and it fell over and broke. Glass and fish and water all over the place!"

"Oh, my God! No wonder they t . . . tied me down." Kate didn't know who Dave was, but she'd known Phil and Ben for years. "Are they . . . all right? Was Ben hu . . . hurt?"

"Oh, they'll be fine. Ben needed a couple of stitches but he'll be right as rain in no time. You sure surprised us, though. Nobody would've guessed you'd be so strong! Girl, you were one mean mama!"

"I don't . . . member . . . ann . . . any of it. Last thing . . . Mr. O . . . Ostriker in his walk . . . wh . . . wheelchair . . . and he was sing . . . swinging a cane."

"Mr. Who?"

"O . . . Ostriker. You know, Jock . . . Ostriker."

"I don't think I've met him."

"You must . . . have. Mmm . . . mean old guy. Always yel . . . yelling. He just checked in a few duh . . . days ago."

"Nobody in the Lodge by that name. I think I'd remember. You must've dreamed him up. Your memory's all confused right now. That often happens with seizures. I guess Dr. Bakkaran did a lot of tests."

"Dr. Macar . . . Bakkaran is a j . . . juh . . . *jerk.*"

"Oh, but he's supposed to *very* good. I suppose they did a CAT scan."

"Cat! Yesss . . . there was a cat. A little nett . . . uh . . . *shit . . . kitten.* What happened to him?"

"I don't remember seeing any kitten. Things were kind of crazy. Was it a pet of yours? Somebody may have picked it up. I'll ask around."

"Yeah, thanks." *Maybe there wasn't a kitten either if there wasn't a Jock Ostriker.* Kate just wanted to sleep. Her mind was in no shape to deal with any of this right now. She'd think about it later and try to make the pieces fit. Now she just needed to rest. She dozed off for awhile, but hospital noises and hospital routine kept awakening her. As the day wore on, she found she rather enjoyed the pampering — a wonderful backrub from a male physiotherapist — and lunch on a tray, with tapioca for dessert.

...

Kate was released the next morning. The drug tests had been negative, and the results of her CAT scan showed a peaked brainwave pattern consistent with epilepsy. The test should be repeated later, and she should come back and have an MRI. Meanwhile, she'd been given a prescription for Dilantin.

Kate looked at her medication, white capsules, like timed-release cold medicine, but smaller, each with an orange band around the middle, like a belt: 100 milligrams each; take 3 a day. Kate felt better, better in the sense that her thought processes seemed to be operating clockwise again, and her movements, though slow and deliberate, were a little less stiff. Her spastic hand still sometimes caused her to drop things. She felt shaken and physically assaulted, strange in her own body. Side effects of the medication? She'd been told there might be some, but that she would adjust to them in time.

Kate's mother had come to take her home in a cab — one of the two blue SpeedySure taxis in Stastas — and she'd been wheelchaired to it according to Hospital Law. At home, in the kitchen, she was given the Helvi Oksa brand of TLC: weak tea and toast, poached egg on rice, castor oil rubbed into her bruises, and a dissertation on the Helvi Oksa world view.

"Doctors. What do they know anyway, except how to charge an arm and a leg for doing absolutely nothing. I don't care what anybody says, there's got to be a reason why a healthy young girl should suddenly have fits. Are you *sure* you're not taking drugs, Katri?"

"The tests were negative, remember?"

"Yes, yes, that's what they *say* but I'm not so sure. Nobody in our family — "

" — ever had fits. So call Ripley's."

"Go ahead, make jokes, but it's a serious business. You haven't been drinking alcohol, have you? Alcohol can cause fits."

Kate studied the back of her hand which was black and blue from the IV. "Mom, I *know* it's a serious business. I'm the one with the buh . . . bruises to prove it. No, I don't drink, and if alcohol caused fits, then dear old Dad would spend his life doing an 8.5 on the ruh . . . Richter. Where is he, anyway?"

"He said he was going fishing."

Fishing? Heikki Oksa fishing? Must be another euphemism for drinking. Kate sipped her tea. Funny how the experience of almost dying gives you a different view of things, or maybe it's just that it makes you see more clearly. She looked at her mother who was busying herself with the dishes, and wondered why she'd never noticed that she was putting on weight. Her mother had always been thin, rangy even, but now she seemed to be heavier, thicker through the waist, which actually made her look shorter. She also observed that Helvi's hair looked lighter, and realized, with a bit of a shock, that it was shot with gray. When did she start getting old? It was like seeing an actress in a current film after viewing her early movies. Maybe it was just a trick of Kate's discombobulated brain, or maybe that trick your mind plays when you look hard at something familiar. Kate had done that in boring classes in Stastas High — written her own name, and then stared at it until it began to look strange.

"I wonder what happened to Jude."

"Who's Jude?"

"Remember that sick little kitten I brought home, the one Mrs. Norland gave me? You said it had dus . . . diss . . . temper."

"Probably dead by now and good riddance. I don't want no more animals in this house."

Well, I don't know about Mr. Ostriker, but at least that tells me there really was a Jude!

CHAPTER 9

I⠀T WAS almost like being a little kid again, at home sick. Growing up, Kate had sneezed and sniffled and hacked her way through many a bout with the common cold, and she remembered the misery, yet the oasis, of being able to spend a day with her coloring books and TV, while kids went through their daily routine at Stastas Elementary. A fever of a hundred or more had been the ticket, although the price of admission almost always included having her chest slathered with Vicks VapoRub, and being made to drink tar water.

Tar water had been one of Kate's grandmother's (Mummo's) home remedies, and nobody knew whether it actually cured a cold or merely scared it out of you. Finns have a saying that anything that can't be cured by *sauna, viina* (liquor), or *terva* (tar) is terminal. Tar water was a two-parter: Mummo would set a big pot of water boiling on the stove, drizzle pine tar on top, then fold a newspaper into a cone. Kate would stand on a kitchen chair and inhale the vapor through the cone to break up chest congestion. Afterwards, the water was allowed to cool, and Mummo would filter it through several thicknesses of cheesecloth to remove the tar. At this point it was cloudy — like dishwater — bitter as an accusation, and had to be sweetened to make it drinkable. Dosage: one glassful whenever your cough began to annoy anyone.

Kate wondered what Mummo would prescribe for seizures if she were still alive. The Finns had called it *kaatuva tauti* (falling sickness). The term had stuck in Kate's mind because grownups had uttered it in hushed tones, the same way they whispered the word, *syöpä* (cancer); as if somehow saying the word out loud would visit it upon them. Kate had visualized people falling over like pins in a bowling alley, and when she'd started asking questions, she'd been told to go out and play.

Times hadn't changed much. In the two days that Kate had been home, she'd noticed her mother watching her out of the corner of her eye, as if expecting her to explode. Her father's behavior was even more clandestine. He'd returned from his "fishing trip" without fish, and oddly enough, *sober.* Now he seemed to slink around the house like a cat looking for an exit. A "Hi, Dad," as he walked by, would startle him into a quick wave and a grunt without slowing his pace. If Kate were on the couch, watching TV, Heikki would veer off in another direction — like the White Rabbit, always in the act of leaving, always late for a very important date.

Kate was beginning to feel more like her old self as the physical symptoms subsided. The occasional glitch in her speech and involuntary hand movement were happening less and less often now. Her memory still contained blanks; she remembered absolutely nothing between Mr. Ostriker in the lobby and awakening in hospital. Yet, the memory of Mr. Ostriker was very clear. Why hadn't Jane Clark remembered him? Had he disappeared the same way Elina Niemi had vanished? If Kate went back to the Lodge, would she find someone else in his place? More likely, Jane had made a mistake and Kate would find Jock Ostriker very much alive and causing his usual ruckus. Still, the mystery was exquisitely tantalizing, and Kate knew she'd have to solve it, or at least try.

Kate was also curious about what had happened to Jude. She didn't really expect ever to see the kitten again. He'd probably died and some staff member had disposed of the remains. *Maybe they'll tell me he passed away in his sleep.* She'd have to go back there in any case; her bike, Hercules, was still in the parking lot, if it hadn't been stolen by now.

She pictured, with embarrassment, the awful scene in the lobby: The Old People, Ben McEvoy, Phil Cruikshank, and Dave, whoever he was. *How can I go back and face them?* She pictured herself transformed into a crazy woman, and then reduced to the most abject humiliation of all, that of being "incontinent" — the silky little term her nurse had used to describe runaway bodily functions. In a place like the Lodge, the tale of it would have been told and retold by now, probably set to music as the "Ballad of Kate Oksa." *I'll have to go in there with a bag over my head.*

After two days of staring at soap operas, talk shows, and TV commercials, Kate was beginning to experience cabin fever. She had to get on with her life, such as it might be. She would go to the Lodge. It was a beautiful day, and a walk in the fresh air (depending on which way the wind was blowing from the pulp mill) might be just what she needed. Her father was off on yet another of his mysterious errands, and her mother had gone to the grocery store. It was a good time to leave without having to give explanations or assurances.

It wasn't quite as sunny or as warm as Kate had thought, and there was the unmistakable smell of StasCo in the air. Kate hated StasCo impotently, as did many in Stastas. The pulp mill was the chief employer in town, and so much in control that until recently nobody had dared speak against it. An occasional scientific study had timidly noted the high incidence of cancer in the area, but such was StasCo's power, that even those not directly employed there depended, for their livelihood, on those who were. Recently, targeted by Greenpeace for failure to meet the new government pollution standards, StasCo made much in the local newspaper of how, at *enormous* cost, they had installed a new system that reduced emissions by 75%. But it still smelled the same to Kate (the so-called "smell of money") a sickening stench that reminded her of burnt rutabagas. Kate pictured StasCo as the proverbial eight-hundred-pound flatulent gorilla that could fart wherever it wanted.

Kate cut through the Lodge parking lot but didn't see her bicycle. *I can probably kiss ol' Hercules good-bye.* Then she spotted Mike, the maintenance man, who appeared to be studying the back door as if planning to paint it. "Hey there, Katydid, you're lookin' a lot better than the last time I saw you!"

"Hi, Mike. Yeah, I'm okay now. Say, you didn't happen to see my bike, did you?"

"Somebody left one in the lot on the weekend. It was still here Saturday night so I put it inside. Was that yours?"

"Great! I thought someone had taken it."

"You'll find it inside, leaning against the wall. You know you should get a lock for it and a chain, if you're going to leave it outdoors."

"Yeah, thanks, Mike." She left him examining the lock on the door and went inside. Her bicycle was there, just as Mike had said, and she gave Hercules Unchained a pat, then headed for the lobby, hoping it would be empty. It wasn't; it was full of Old People. Even Mrs. Trachtenberg, who seldom left her room, was there. It looked like some sort of geriatric summit meeting. They were all talking at once, their faces a doodle of worry lines.

"Hello, Katie dollink. You're lookin' better. Come by my room later. I got somethin' for you." Mrs. Trachtenberg gave her a hasty wave and went back to addressing Ed Mingus, who was smiling blandly and nodding in his usual vague manner. Lauralee Beatty shot Kate a quick smile and a "Nice to see you up and around, dear," then resumed talking with Fanni and Martti Hartikainen, the couple who lived in the room next to Lauralee and her roommate, Wilhelmiina Hill. Wilhelmiina, meanwhile, was deep in frowning conversation with the new Mrs. Neimi's roommate, Sylvia Winter.

Well, I seem to be yesterday's news! Mr. Ostriker definitely was not there, but then neither was Anthony Reed or Mrs. Niemi, The Sequel, who was probably in her room doing her impression of a houseplant.

Kate decided the best source of information would be, as always, Jane Clark, who greeted her with "Hey, girl, you're looking *good*. Everybody's been so concerned. I was about to call your house."

"What's going on? Looks like most of the First Floor is here."

Jane dropped her voice the way she always did when she had something juicy to impart: "We had a burglary here last night." She watched as her news sank in, then waited to be asked for details.

"Oh, my God! You mean somebody came in and ripped off the Old People?"

"It was last night at dinnertime. Somebody went into six of the rooms and forced open all the drawers. The residents came back from the dining room to find their property missing."

Kate knew that the doors to the rooms had no locks, but that each bedside table had a lockable drawer in which the residents kept money and valuables. The locks were flimsy at best, and anyone with a screwdriver could have wandered in and made off with the contents. "I guess the cops came. Do they have an idea who did it?"

"Not really, but there's talk."

"Oh?"

"Well, you know old Mr. Goheen and his rotten grandson who's always in trouble with the law. That kid was hanging around here yesterday. I think he badgers Mr. Goheen for money. The word is *he* probably did it."

Mr. Goheen? Grandson? "I'm not sure I've ever met Mr. Goheen."

"Oh, sure you have. The kid's name is Randy. Randy Goheen? You must've gone to school with him. I'm sure you'd know him if you saw him. Maybe your memory's still playing tricks."

Kate wondered why she could remember Ostriker and Jane Clark couldn't, and now here was Jane telling her about the Goheens of whom Kate had no memory at all. And yet everything else seemed normal. She ruefully noted the absence of the fish tank.

"Oh hey, I almost forgot. You were asking about a kitten? It seems there *was* a little black kitten in the lobby the night you had your — uh — accident. One of the residents picked it up, said it was yours, and that he'd take care of it."

"Really? Who?"

"Mr. Reed."

A smoke alarm went off in Kate's head. Anthony Reed and Jude were a bad mix! "I better go see him."

"Oh, you won't find him in his room. Mr. Reed was moved into the hospital wing on Saturday afternoon. Heart attack, I think. He's much better now. Should be able to have visitors."

Kate was already running down the hall.

...

To Kate, seeing Anthony Reed in a hospital bed was like seeing King Kong in chains. To her, Mr. Reed symbolized something elemental, and her teasing him about being a witch doctor wasn't entirely a joke. Arthritis may have crippled him, but he was too *big* to be thought of as powerless. He was a thunderhead of a man, benign, certainly, but looming.

Kate approached quietly. "Hey, Doc, are you awake?"

Anthony Reed opened his eyes and smiled. "Kit-Kat! You're lookin' fine."

"So what are you doing here, Doc? Did one of your spells backfire?"

"You guessed it. Just like my daddy's old Ford. Are you okay now, Kit-Kat?"

"Yeah, I think so. But what about you?"

Anthony Reed smiled. "I'm fixin' to die, Kit, it's getting to be time."

Kate saw that beneath the smile Mr. Reed's eyes were serious. "No, Doc, you *can't*. You're gonna be okay. It was just a mild heart attack. Lots of people have them. Look around you, Doc. Everybody in here is popping nitros. It was just a *little* heart kickup, that's all."

"That's what they think. And I'm not gonna tell them any different. Dying, Kit, is something I kind of look forward to." The man put a large black hand over Kate's small white one and gave it a reassuring pat. "Everybody dies, Kit-Kat. Everybody is *supposed* to."

"But there's no rush, is there? Anyway, you've got to stick around for the first frost. Mrs. Murguia's sister is going to cook you up a batch of collard greens with ham hocks and sweet potato pie. You wouldn't want to miss that, would you, Doc?"

Anthony Reed chuckled. "Well, of course I'll have to stay around for that, won't I? Listen, Kit, I left a note for you in my room. I want you to go get it and keep it. After I'm gone — no, wait — just let me finish, Kit. After I'm gone, and of course, as you say, it could be a *long* time, I want you to read it. It explains a few things. I don't have much — a little bit of money, my mother's wedding ring and my father's gold watch — but I'd like you to have them. And I'd like you to take them out of my room right now and keep them for me. They'll be safer with you."

Kate, to her exasperation found herself grubbing away tears. "Sure, Doc. I'll keep your stuff for you. You're gonna be needing it." *Didn't Mr. Reed have any family? He never talked seriously about them. He was always joking about his first wife's cooking, but had he ever really been married? Did he have any kids? Maybe not. As far as I know, nobody ever comes to see him.*

"Thanks, Kit. The key's inside a book called *Mansions of the Soul*." Anthony Reed closed his eyes, as if suddenly very tired. Kate touched his hand lightly and left.

...

It wasn't until Kate had almost reached Mr. Reed's room that she remembered she'd forgotten to ask about Jude. First things first. She opened the door, went in, and saw immediately that Mr. Reed's was one of the rooms that had been burglarized. The drawer in the nightstand gaped open and empty, the edge splintered. Whatever valuables had been in it were gone. *Oh great! Guess nobody told the Doc. Just as well. Not the sort of thing you tell a heart patient: By the way, all your worldly goods have just been stolen by some punk with fecal matter for brains.*

Nothing else seemed to have been disturbed. The burglar obviously had known that the only valuables would be in the locked drawer. *Randy Whozis? Geehan? No, it was Goheen. Randy Goheen, whoever you are, may you brown eternally in the convection oven of hell.*

The room seemed much larger without Anthony Reed in it. His wheelchair was there, next to his worktable on which sat a rickety old typewriter. Kate tried to picture what must have happened. She hadn't known Mr. Reed had a bad heart. It was his arthritis that had kept him an invalid. What had he been doing when it happened? She knew that Anthony Reed wasn't entirely disabled. He could and did, with pain and effort, get in and out of bed, use the toilet, and even the shower with the help of an attendant. Kate also knew that these things were becoming more and more difficult for him. Perhaps the effort had been too much.

The bathroom door was open and Kate saw something on the floor. She went over and picked it up. It was plastic bag — a plain white bag, the kind that fits kitchen garbage pails, probably the liner from the small wastebasket that stood between Anthony Reed's bed and table. Except this one had been knotted shut. Kate noticed that one side was torn open, and that the inside was wet. What had the Doc been doing, making a water balloon? She crumpled up the bag and tossed it into the trash can. Nothing more she could do here. If Anthony Reed had typed a note for her on his old Smith-Corona there was no sign of it.

The meeting in the lobby had broken up and the residents were back in their rooms. Kate saw that Mrs. Norland's room was now occupied, but wasn't in the mood to go in and meet the new resident. Mrs. Trachtenberg was back too, and as Kate passed her door, she called out, "Come on in, Katie."

"How ya doin', Mrs. T?"

"Oy, the stomach troubles I have! Everything I eat makes me nauseous. Don't get old, Katie." She lit a cigarette, which somehow looked incongruous in her grandmotherly face. "I got a little surprise for you."

"Oh, what's that, Mrs. T?"

"Take a look in that box over there."

Kate saw a cardboard box sitting on a chair. She went over, looked inside, and found herself looking into the bleary eyes of Jude. "Oh, my *God!*" It seemed unreal. "Where . . . *how* did he get here?"

"I don't know where it come from, but it just walked in my door a couple days ago. Poor little thing. Looked half dead and soakin' wet. I asked around and somebody told me it was your kitten. You was in the hospital so I kept it for you. Mike found a box to put it in. It don't look so good, Katie. I'm surprised it's still alive. I tried giving it a little milk but it don't eat enough to feed a housefly."

Something about this was all wrong. Kate found herself backing away from the animal. How could it keep turning up like this? How could it still be alive? Somehow the kitten seemed to be involved in all the strange things that had been happening to her, and the very sight of it made Kate feel queasy. She swallowed, thinking it was like the time she'd gotten sick after eating caramel creams. She'd never been able to look at a caramel cream again. *I feel like I'm about to hurl chunks.*

"You'll have to take it with you, Katie. I can't keep it here."

Reluctantly, Kate reached into the box. Jude tottered over and began rubbing up against her knuckles. *Yeah, sure, act friendly, you little hellcat.* She picked up the kitten, wishing she had Mrs. Norland's yarn bag to put him into. She'd have to take him, of course, but where? Her mother didn't want him in the house — but then, her mother wouldn't want to upset Kate and trigger a possible seizure either. Maybe she could get away with taking the animal home, at least until she'd figured out what do with him. She thanked Mrs. Trachtenberg, tucked the kitten inside her jacket, and headed for the lobby, intending to go out the back way and ride her bike home. On the way she was hailed by Jane Clark.

"Girl, I'm glad you're still here. Mr. Reed wants to see you."

"I just saw him a few minutes ago. I thought I left him asleep."

"It's something about a letter. He seemed to think it was important."

"Okay, I'll swing by." *Maybe he heard about the break-in and wants to know what happened to his stuff. And, lucky me, I get to tell him.*

Kate found Anthony Reed looking solemn, his bed cranked up so that he was in a semi-sitting position. "You wanted to see me, Doc?"

"Yes, Kit. Thanks for coming. I heard about the burglary. I suppose they got everything."

"Just the stuff in the drawer, Doc. All your books are still there. They didn't touch the important stuff."

Anthony Reed smiled. "That's right, Kit. The stuff in the drawer wasn't really important at all. I just wanted to know if you found my letter."

"Sorry, Doc. There was no sign of it. Maybe the cops picked it up. Or maybe housekeeping tossed it."

Mr. Reed sighed. "I was afraid of that. No matter. You're here, and I feel I owe you an explanation, even though it will sound strange. First let me say that I did a terrible thing, but I felt it had to be done, and I hope you're free now." Anthony Reed studied Kate's puzzled face, then continued, choosing his words carefully. "There are things in this world, Kit, that are not what they seem to be. They cloak themselves in other forms and sometimes enter our lives. And if they attach themselves to us, it's possible that they can destroy us. Do you understand?"

"Uh . . . no."

"These creatures — entities — come from distant places, other dimensions. I can't begin to guess *why* they come, but they do have great power, and you might say they have their own agenda. They use our thoughts and attitudes and emotions like a beacon, and if one becomes attracted to you, it can enslave you. They're like a cancer of the soul, Kit, and they can take on any form." Anthony Reed's gaze had locked on to Kate's as if willing her to comprehend and believe. *"Even the form of a tiny sickly kitten."*

Kate felt Jude squirm against her chest, under her jacket. She swallowed hard. "Doc, are you talking about Jude?"

"You named him well, Kit. Jude. Judas. The betrayer. Please don't think I'm out of my mind, Kit. Or if you do, then remember me as a crazy old man who did a very ugly thing, but only because he thought he was protecting you. I had to kill it, Kit, to banish it . . . and I think it also killed me. The event just hasn't quite caught up yet."

The pieces fit. Kate realized that, whatever the reason, Mr. Reed must have tried killing Jude, probably by drowning him in the toilet. He'd put the dead body in the plastic bag, but somehow the cat had lived through it and escaped to Mrs. Trachtenberg's room. And somehow Anthony Reed had had a heart attack.

It was all so crazy! Mr. Reed must be out of his — but Kate couldn't dismiss it so easily. What if he *wasn't* crazy? That helpless little feline had managed to come back to life after being drowned, rip its way out of a plastic bag, find a safe place in which to wait for Kate, and was even now digging its claws into her ribs!

Kate clutched her jacket. She just wanted to get out of there. She didn't want Mr. Reed to see the kitten. Suddenly Kate felt the hot thrust of teeth into her skin. She cried out in pain and, by reflex, let go. Jude dropped from Kate's jacket onto the edge of the bed, scrambled for a foothold, then began crawling upward toward Anthony Reed. Kate saw his look of surprise, then horror and fury as Anthony Reed reached out his large crippled hand as if to grasp and crush the animal. Kate made a lightning grab.

CHAPTER 10

SOMEWHERE SOMEONE was playing Leroy Anderson's "Blue Tango." Kate recognized it from a scratchy phonograph record the Oksas had at home. She opened her eyes and looked around. She seemed to be in a closet, or maybe it was a storeroom. There was a naked lightbulb above her head, and she was sitting on an old wooden kitchen chair. The space was small; there were shelves on two walls around her, shelves stacked with boxes, cleaning materials, bundles of paper towels and toilet paper. She saw a metal lunch box and a tool belt. A stepladder leaned against a wall next to a mop and pail. *Holy shit, it's happened again!* Kate shut her eyes and took a deep breath. *Mustn't panic. This wasn't supposed to happen anymore. The Dilantin was supposed to work. Why is this still happening?*

Slowly, Kate opened her eyes and looked down at her body. Male again. Dressed in a work uniform: brown pants and shirt. She looked at her hands. They were large and well-shaped, and the backs of them were very dark brown. One of them was holding the remains of a sandwich. *Sweet Jesus, now I'm the Doc!* She set the sandwich scrap into the lunch box on the shelf and stood up — easily. No arthritis pain! Kate wished she had a mirror, glanced around for one, but saw only a calendar tacked to the wall. The page was August, 1954, and the calendar had been issued by the Pan American Bank of Miami, with a scene of coconut palms along a sandy beach. The caption said "Sun and surf in Crandon Park, Key Biscayne, Fla."

Florida, 1954. There was something off-center here. Something different. According to her old pattern, she should be Anthony Reed at age seventeen — but that couldn't be right. If the Doc had been seventeen in 1954, he'd be in his mid-fifties now. It was hard to tell Mr. Reed's age, but Kate had always thought of him as being older, and she sensed that the man whose body she now occupied was not a young kid.

She reached into her pocket and took out a wallet. *You're getting better at this, Kate.* Driver's license: Anthony Reed — no photographs in those days — date of birth, October 18, 1927. Not too much else in the wallet: a Social Security card, a standard "who to notify in case of emergency" was not filled in except for a street address written in pencil and smudged enough to be illegible. A bad black-and-white snapshot of a woman with a little girl; twenty dollars in cash; a phone number scribbled on a scrap of grocer's tape from a Publix super-market, and there was also a bunch of keys in the pants pocket, no way of knowing to what.

Kate eased herself onto the chair. *Okay, I'm Anthony Reed, age twenty-six. This must be where I work. Maybe I'm the janitor. I'm in here having my lunch, I guess, but right now I haven't a clue as to what's on the other side of that door.*

As if in reply, she heard a woman's voice say, "Go find Tony the Porter." This was immediately followed by a sharp knock on the door, and a male voice with a southern accent called, "Tony, are you in there?"

Kate opened the door a crack. An immaculate young man in a dark blue suit stood there looking exasperated. "Oh, Tony, thank God. We need you in the front ballroom. The cover on the air-conditioning duct is about to fall down and bean somebody."

A stunningly beautiful but heavily made-up young woman in a strapless dress had come up behind the young man. "Did you find Tony? Tell him to bring a ladder and a screwdriver. Mr. Harttung says it looks like the screws are coming loose."

Kate realized that she was expected to deal with the situation. She buckled on the tool belt, picked up the stepladder, and followed the two flawless people down a wide hallway, through a reception area, down yet another hall, and into a glittering large room ablaze with lights and filled with music.

No shortage of mirrors here! The walls were lined with them. Supporting posts were faced with them. There was even a large, mirrored ball hung from the ceiling. Kate caught sight of herself — a tall, handsome black man who looked incredibly out of place in the all-white milieu.

The room was sparsely studded with couples. Some of them had already resumed dancing, while others stood watching, the way people watch anything that affords a momentary diversion. A balding, elderly man was pointing to a grid that covered an air duct above the entrance. "Seems to be coming loose. Probably from all the vibration. Might fall and hurt somebody." The young woman, obviously his teacher, steered him back onto the floor and they tangoed off, Mr. Harttung's eyes still on the grid.

Kate set up the ladder and climbed up to see that the grid, indeed, was missing one screw while the other seven were working themselves out of their settings. She didn't have a replacement, but set about tightening the rest, noticing the strength in Mr. Reed's hands. Kate wondered if she was being convincing in her role as janitor, but then, nobody seemed to be paying the least attention. She was Tony the Porter, and she was invisible — and an Untouchable: a black in what must still be the segregated South. Kate tried to remember what she'd studied about segregation in history class. Wasn't it about the mid-fifties that it all started to change?

The repair job was a minor one, but Kate took her time doing it, fascinated by this scene from the past that looked like an old movie. It was easy to pick out the dance teachers. The women all wore ankle-length skirts buoyed up by huge crinolines, and their bodies looked to be pinched and molded by a stiff undergarment that nipped in the waist and pushed up the breasts. (And breasts were certainly a lot bigger in those days!) They wore high heels and large hoop earrings, and everyone seemed to have a dark tan, although under their heavy makeup their skin could have been any color. Kate marveled at the perfection of their hairdos. Whether short or long or knotted in back or tied in a ponytail, nobody had bad hair; in fact it looked glued into place. The men were all turned out in dark suits, white shirts and ties. Their shoes were polished, and each had a pocket handkerchief neatly folded to display three starched points.

Kate saw that there were more men teachers than women, and that each was paired with a partner who was considerably older. A young man with a bored expression glanced at the clock on the wall as he danced by with a short, plump matron with blue-white hair. The face of a young woman over her pupil's shoulder appeared tired and haggard beneath its mask of makeup, and somehow Kate knew that when she got off work at ten tonight, she'd have to pick up her small son at a seedy child care center before going home to a tiny apartment in the north end of town.

The scene seemed to slide into a minor key. The pupils appeared as the lonely and the old, doomed to dance or die, as if in some way the cha-cha could keep them out of the clutches of the Grim Reaper who hung around waiting — Kate thought, with black humor — to cut in. Kate shook off the rising feeling of melancholy. *So things are tough all over. Big deal. I can think of worse ways of making a buck than dancing for a living, even if it means pushing old people around the floor.*

Kate collected her gear and made her way back to her cubbyhole. She'd also seen that it was evening, nearly eight o'clock. The sandwich had been dinner, not lunch. This was a dance studio, and her job — the Doc's job — was to be on call and stay out of sight during the busy evening hours. Right now she'd kill for a cup of coffee, and wondered if there might be a machine in back.

To the strains of "Cuban Mambo" *(olé, olé)*, Kate explored the layout. The studio was on a second floor. From the reception area, a long hallway led to washrooms and a back door that opened onto a landing on which stood two galvanized garbage cans. From it, a flight of cement steps led down to an alley. No coffee machine in sight. Kate retraced her steps back up the hall, noticing a series of small rooms on her right. She peered into one of them through a round glass panel in the door, and saw that it, too, was a small studio. There was a record player, a little desk with two straight-backed chairs, a hardwood floor; one wall, of course, was completely mirrored.

On her left, there were doors with no windows. The first was ajar and Kate saw that it was an office, equipped with desks and filing cabinets. It was empty. The business staff probably quit at five while the teachers worked on into the evening. The next door had a nameplate: Alfred Calucci. The manager? The door next to it was the one to Mr. Reed's closet, and beyond that, just around the corner from the reception room, was yet another door. Kate opened it cautiously, and was met by a suffocating fog of smoke. Inside, seemingly unconcerned, people were talking. Kate walked around a partition and saw a half-dozen of the staff laughing, smoking, and drinking coffee. Nobody seemed surprised to see Kate who, thinking quickly, set about emptying overflowing ashtrays into a wastebasket.

A beautiful young man with bleached hair and delicate features was regarding himself in a wall mirror. "My God, I look like I've been dragged through a knothole backwards."

"What's the matter, Rodney, couldn't you afford to get your hair done this week?" That from a swarthy young man with dark curls who looked like a Greek statue come to life.

Rodney sighed theatrically. "I just wish I could afford to get my *shirts* out of the cleaner's. If I could just find a *stable* job that *pays* sixty bucks a week!"

A chorus of voices: "Rodney's looking for a stable job." "How about the Coral Gables Riding Academy?" "He'll be needing a shovel." "Oh no, he'd need a pedigree just to shovel shit there."

"Go ahead and make fun, but we're all throwing our lives away in *this* place!" Rodney said crossly.

"Yeah, garbage-canically speaking. Maybe we should all become beachcombers. With your tan, you look the part already," the Greek god remarked.

Rodney, still studying his mirror image, ran fingers along his cheekbone. "It's fading. I need to get some sun."

"If you get any darker, you could go to Virginia Beach, couldn't he, Tony?" The man speaking had a slight Spanish accent and the posture of a bullfighter.

Kate looked up, startled. She'd almost forgotten her own presence in the room.

"Leave Tony alone." A red-haired woman sipped coffee from a paper cup. "Don't pay any attention to these guys, Tony. They've all been lobotomized."

The curly-haired man took a drag on his cigarette. "Speaking of the beach, who wants to go spearfishing on the weekend?"

"Where are you going, Mario? Boat or offshore?" The man who spoke had a smooth, boyish face, prematurely gray hair and a British accent.

"Boat, if I can get the motor fixed. You got equipment?"

"I don't have a spear gun."

"Doesn't matter, Harry. You can use my other one. Just bring beer."

"Right, and I'll bring a box lunch."

"Well, if you have a date, that's your business."

Everybody laughed and Kate wondered why that was funny.

"Ooh, she's only a wrestler's daughter, but you oughta see her box!" The man who had just come in was atypical — short, rather heavy, with thinning hair and a raspy voice.

"Barbarelli, get your mind out of the gutter." A thin blonde had followed him in. She flopped onto the couch and lit a cigarette.

"Don't pick on me, Stacy," Barbarelli said. "Have a little respect for your elders."

Stacy shook her head and looked heavenward. "Oh, tell us about the old days, Barbarelli."

"You mock, but I'll have you know that I used to be a great lover in my youth." (He pronounced it "yout.") "Ah, when I think of those days and all the women I kissed! But now, you know, the lip is gone."

"Poor old Barbarelli."

"Yeah, now all I have left is the Palmer method."

"What the hell is *that*?"

"Handwriting, girl, handwriting. I told you, the lip is gone."

Stacy rolled her eyes. "Hey, that reminds me, I've got Mahalek this hour. Would one of you guys be willing to diplomatically tell Mr. Mahalek that he needs a jockstrap?"

Mario burst out laughing. "You mean the old guy can still get it up. Did you hear that, Barbarelli?"

"Laugh, you guys, but it's embarrassing as hell. I don't think he wears any underwear, and, well, I can't get in dance position with him. I've had him doing school figures for two weeks."

A buzzer sounded and the room instantly emptied as the teachers rushed off to pick up their eight o'clock pupils. Kate carried out the wastebasket, emptied it into the garbage can on the landing, and then brought it back into the now deserted teachers' room. In contrast to the glittering public areas, the teachers' room was small and shabby.

There was one window that overlooked an alley. Next to it a small desk was pushed up against the wall. Over it hung a cheap wood-framed mirror and a black wall telephone. A sagging divan served as a couch, and, across from it, a low bench along the wall provided additional seating. A room divider, with open compartments for the teachers' personal items, presented its back to the door and screened the interior from public view when the door was opened. Every surface, Kate noted — desk, windowsill, floor, couch, bench — was scarred with cigarette burns, and in the air, stale smoke hung like mist in a Frankenstein movie. But Kate realized that there was absolutely no evidence of pot — marijuana — or any other drug! *Probably hadn't been invented yet.*

Kate ventured out into the reception room. Now that the teaching hour had begun, it was empty except for the receptionist — a middle-aged, trying-to-look-younger woman with thick mascara and lots of clanking costume jewelry.

"There you are, Tony. I was hoping you'd come by. I'm just dying for a cup of coffee. Would you be a livin' doll and go down and get me a light, no sugar." She handed Kate a dollar bill. "And get one for yourself, too."

Kate started for the front stairs, half expecting to be told to use the back way. No such command came, and Kate went down to street level. She opened the heavy glass door and stepped into the humid Miami night.

The dampness was like being hit by a warm spray from a plant mister. Inside, all was air-conditioned and cool, where men in suits could dance all night without sweating or rumpling. Outside was life on Flagler Street, such as it was in a town that, in those days, practically closed down for the summer.

Kate looked around. There was a Walgreens across the street; it seemed to be open. Next to it stood a photography studio and a luggage shop; both were closed for the season. Still, there seemed to be activity on the street — people, traffic, lights — a sense that Miami was beginning, tentatively, to consider itself not just a resort town. It was like a baby, delightedly taking its first steps, unaware of what a giant it was destined to become.

Kate looked for a place to buy coffee and saw, wedged between an orange juice stand and a gift shop (closed for the season), a small hamburger shop with one counter and a half-dozen stools. There seemed to be only one patron; an elderly man in dark clothes sat sipping coffee at the far end. At first Kate thought she knew him, then realized she didn't. He seemed grossly overdressed for the climate. The man caught her eye, gave her a friendly smile. Kate, not wanting to be caught staring, hastily looked away.

"What'll it be, boy? Oh, it's you, Tony." A sweaty short-order cook in a soiled apron was scraping the grill with a metal spatula.

Kate stood at the till, wondered for a moment if she should, *could*, sit down at the counter, then decided against it. "Two coffees to go — one regular, one light, no sugar." Kate, who had so far not uttered a word, was surprised once again by the timber of her voice. *I sound like James Earl Jones!*

The cook filled cardboard cups, attached lids, put the containers in a paper bag, took Kate's dollar and handed her change. "Muggy night. Wish the hell it would cool off. Not much business either. Don't know why the boss bothers to stay open in summer. Guess *you're* okay, though. What with all them rich old ladies who live here year-round, you got a steady job at that dance place."

Kate glanced around. The room was empty now; the man at the counter was gone. "Yeah, so far, so good. Better than when I used to work at the beach. They still close the Miami Beach studio for the summer." *(They do?)*

"Hell, they close *everything* there. Some of them big hotels, if they're open at all, you can get a room for two bucks a night! They got big signs out. Two friggin' bucks a night. My old lady says we oughta check in there, like millionaires, but what the hell, the place is like a tomb!"

Kate took the coffee and left. She was tempted to walk around, look the town over. But that might get her into trouble. How was she, as a black man, supposed to act? *What am I expecting, a bunch of hooded Ku Kluxers to come rollerblading down the sidewalk?* So far Kate hadn't even seen a washroom or drinking fountain marked "colored." There were none in the studio. But then, there weren't any blacks in there except for her. She wondered if *she'd* be allowed to use the washroom. More important, when she did, would she remember to use the men's?

Kate found herself, nevertheless, walking a short way up Flagler Street, trying to pick up impressions of Anthony Reed's life. She'd better get some feedback soon. Here she was, in a strange city, with no idea of where she lived, or where to go when the studio closed for the night. She turned a corner and saw a bus stop. Did Mr. Reed ride a bus? He had a driver's license and car keys, but who knew where the car was? *C'mon, Doc. I know you're in there someplace. Wouldn't you just like to go back to the good old nineties? No, maybe you wouldn't.*

It was sobering to Kate to remember that her two previous dream trips had ended in getting killed. The last time was when she'd blown her brains out in the Pennsylvania woods. *That,* even in a series of weird experiences, had been *the weirdest.* She'd have to sort that out later, try to find out what emotional overload had caused her to kill herself, or more accurately, young Jock Ostriker. There was more to that incident than Kate could grok at this moment. The best she could do was sense that the happening had been *layered* in some way. It had been somehow *multiple.* She hadn't killed herself as Kate, and she didn't even think that Jock Ostriker had just simply come back, taken over the body, and committed suicide. There was something else there. Some other connection to a totally different time. She'd have to give that some thought.

Right now, all Kate wanted to do was try to get back to her *own* time. And how was that going to happen? Was Anthony Reed going to have to die in order for Kate to get back to Stastas? And even so, what made her think she'd survive the trip? She'd come close to losing her life that last time, and she didn't want to have to go through *that* again!

Kate turned back and headed for the studio, passing shops and businesses with "Will reopen in September" signs. They gave Miami the look of a town "on hold." There was a narrow alley next to the studio entrance, and as Kate walked past its dark mouth, she saw a figure in the shadows and a voice called, "'Ey, Tono!"

Kate froze, then remembered she was a big black man. She glared into the darkness and snapped, "You call me?"

"It's me, Noah. Been waitin' for you. Come round to the back do'."

Kate saw it was a young black man. "What do you want?"

"Jus' meet me on the back steps. Don' want the man to see us talkin'." He vanished into the shadows, and Kate was certainly not about to follow, no matter how big Mr. Reed was. But this was a new problem. *The Doc must know this dude.*

Kate went in the front door, up the stairs, past the ballroom where everyone now seemed to be fox-trotting to elevator music, and delivered a cup of coffee to the receptionist who merely said, "What did you have to do, stand in line? I didn't think they'd be that busy this time of night."

Kate laid thirty cents change on the counter and mumbled that she hadn't thought so either, and then went back to Mr. Reed's little room where she felt less vulnerable. Noah, whoever he was, was expecting her on the back steps. That must mean the back entrance. Kate felt uneasy. *Why don't I just let him wait? But then, he obviously knows the Doc. Maybe he's a relative. Maybe he knows where Mr. Reed lives. I may need his help before all this is over.* She took a swig of her now lukewarm coffee and left to confer with Noah.

Kate was just about to go out the back door when the door to the women's washroom opened, and a woman stepped out. Kate stopped, her hand on the knob, almost as though she'd been caught doing something illegal. The woman saw her, smiled, and said "Tony, I'm glad I caught you. There's a light out over the vanity in the ladies'."

"I'll change the bulb."

"Thanks, Tony. We women need all the help we can get!"

The woman was blond, green-eyed, and not very tall, even in her high heels. She was dressed in a black, form-fitting sheath, wore no jewelry except for clip-on earrings, and didn't seem to be as heavily made-up as the teachers in the ballroom. It was difficult to judge her age; she could've been in her early twenties or thirties. The styles of the day made young women look older.

But Kate hadn't been prepared for the shock of recognition. Something about the woman touched off the roller coaster of emotions that were part of her dream trips. She sensed that the woman and Anthony Reed had a history but she didn't know what it was. She tried to zero in on her feelings which were powerful but not exactly negative. She might have expected Mr. Reed to resent white people, but so far, no. In fact, with this woman of the chic black dress and stiffly lacquered hair, was it a feeling of sorrow? regret? protectiveness? guilt? Yes, there was a *tremendous* sense of guilt, as if Kate would've liked to throw herself at the woman's feet and beg her forgiveness — but for *what*?

The feeling eased when the focus of it uttered a cheery banality about there being no rest for the wicked, and teetered off down the hall in her black suede pumps. Kate saw her go into one of the small studios. *Ay caramba!* Who *was* that? *And what just happened here?*

CHAPTER 11

WITH HER hand on the doorknob, Kate waited to regain her composure. *Whoo!* This was something she'd never get used to! These dreams were — what? weird? dangerous? terrifying? Yes, all those things, but they were also exciting — exciting in the way an amusement park ride is exciting. Kate felt she now knew what it was like to die in violent ways. And while she wouldn't care to repeat any of it, there was a — how could she describe it? — a freedom — a feeling that she had, in some way, broken through the surface tension of life. She could look at death as just another event, one that left her own inner self a little wiser but undamaged. It took the finality out of dying, made it seem almost irrelevant. Kate's monkey-curious mind had always asked the question, "What must it be like?" This exploration was not only fascinating but, to some part of her being, addictive. *So whoever you are, Noah, here I come.*

"'Bout time you got here, man! What took you so long?"

So this was Noah. Kate studied the wiry black man leaning on the painted cinder block wall at the bottom of the steps. In the glow of the 40-watt outdoor light they were both surrounded by flying insects. Noah was wearing blue jeans and a T-shirt. He looked fidgety, nervous, his eyes darting around as if he were ready to flee if anyone else showed up.

Kate tried an opening gambit: "So what do you want, Noah?"

"What do I want? What do *I* want? I will *tell* you what I want. I want to make sure *you* know what to do, and I want to make sure ain't *nothin'* gonna screw this up. That's what *I* want."

What's all this about? Drug deal? Robbery? "Okay, explain it to me again."

"You screwin' with me, man? 'Cause I don't *see* the humor, Tono. But just in case, let me spell it out. Tonight is *the night.*"

"Yeah?"

The kid looked at Kate through narrowed eyes. "Tonight you leave the back do' open. That's all you gotta do — just make sure it ain't locked. Think you can do that To'?"

"I don't know. I'm not in charge of the keys to this place."

"Don't gimme none of that crap, man. Look, you *owe* me. Don't you go forgettin' that."

Kate tried to fathom the situation. This guy looked to be in his late teens or early twenties, and Kate was wondering if he was under the influence of something. There'd been no sign of drugs so far, at least in the smoke-pickled teachers' room, but Noah might be something else again. Kate would have to be careful, but she needed more information. He'd said the Doc owed him. What did Anthony Reed owe this man?

"Hey, we're friends, right?"

"Don't screw with me," Noah said.

"We've known each other a long time?"

"I said don't fuck with me."

"And you've done me some favors?"

"Now you see, Tono, *that's* how it *bees.* I does you a favor, you does *me* a favor, cause we *blood.*"

Oh, for chrissakes! Is this rat-faced little snot a relative? And I thought my family was the shits. What would Mr. Reed do? I guess he'd try to talk Noah out of whatever he was planning. "What good will it do, Noah? There's no money. They always make a night bank deposit. So what's the point? Just run the risk of getting caught and ending up in jail."

"Ain't *nobody* gettin' caught, Tono. Just leave the back do' open then *get yo' ass home.* Nobody gets hurt. All we want is a few things to fence, man. No big deal. All *you* do is forget to lock up and then forget we had this conversation."

"And if I don't?"

"Hey, *nobody* fucks with the Rays, bro. Not even you."

Rays? What do we have here, the Sharks and the Jets? Noah's T-shirt had picture of a stingray on it, its tail raised menacingly. Gang insignia? Kate didn't know whether Noah was to be taken seriously. Was Noah really part of a big bad street gang or just a bunch of kids acting out? In any case, who *was* he? Could it be the Doc had a brother?

"So now you does *me* favors when I need favors done." Noah hissed. "You do like I *tells* you, leave the do' open, then get yo' black ass out of here or I might just forget you married to my sister."

Noah melted away into the darkness, leaving Kate standing in the alley. She stood, for a moment, thoughtfully staring after him. Kate didn't even know the Doc was married, probably wasn't, anymore. She reached in her pocket and took out Anthony Reed's wallet, opened it to the picture of the woman with the child and studied it more closely. *That must be her and it looks like they have a kid.* It wasn't a very good photo, but Kate could see that the woman was young and pretty with a Whitney Houston smile and softly curling hair, and that the little girl looked to be maybe five years old. *Nice family, Doc. Too bad it comes with the brother-in-law from hell. And I guess they have a home somewhere around here. Well, I know one thing; I couldn't show up there even if I knew how to find it. Not if there's a wife and a kid. It was bad enough trying to be Jock Ostriker with Jeremy!*

Then Kate, as Anthony Reed, screamed — screamed like *Kate* — and ducked — as a huge flying insect missed her head by a couple of inches. The bug flew by with a loud rattling buzz, hit the wall, fell to the cement with an audible crack. Horrified, Kate stared at the creature as it lay on its back. It was three to four inches long and *gray* — an ugly, textured, hairy gray — dried-looking, desiccated, hideous with its long legs writhing in the air. If Frankenstein had created a cockroach, this would be it. Kate shuddered and hurried up the stairs, back inside.

To her relief, Noah's caper sounded like nothing more than a small-time burglary. If his street gang had any real clout, would they be planning such a lame crime? What could they get? A couple of record players, maybe a typewriter or two? Nobody had computers yet. She hoped she'd been right about the night deposit, and felt reasonably sure she had been. Mr. Reed would have known about that, and the information had popped out the same way that the stuff about Miami Beach had surfaced while she was talking to the fry cook.

So, there were three ways she could handle it: She could blow the whistle and become the focus of attention. *Like forget that.* She could ignore Noah and face whatever the consequences. That idea was at first attractive. But then she had no way of knowing how long she'd be dwelling in Mr. Reed's body, and Kate was very much aware that her other two hosts had come to a violent end. Might Noah be the instrument? She didn't think Noah would be acting alone; it takes more than one to carry out a bunch of office equipment. Would she be setting up Mr. Reed *and herself* as the target of a bunch of street punks?"

The third option was to leave the back door open and let history take its course. What was it to Kate, anyway? The studio would have insurance to cover theft, and as Noah had said, nobody gets hurt. She wondered what Mr. Reed would've done. She didn't think that the Anthony Reed she knew would have anything to do with a B&E. But this was a young Mr. Reed in a different place and a different time, a Mr. Reed with family pressures.

More to the point, Kate really didn't know who did the locking up. She'd have to find out what the procedure was. For want of a better place to begin, she went to the reception desk. To her surprise the room was empty. Kate saw that it was a little after nine. The last teaching hour had begun.

As she passed the teachers' room, she heard voices and squeals of laughter. *What the hell, I'm the janitor.* She pushed open the door and went in. The receptionist was standing by the partition, smoking a cigarette, poised as if ready to run to the desk if she heard the phone ring. Inside, a small group of teachers, who apparently had no nine o'clock bookings, were clustered around some focal point. As Kate approached, she saw that the center of attention was a small, black kitten with rheumy eyes. *Jude!*

"He'd be cute if he weren't so skinny."

"I think he's sick. Something's wrong with his eyes. Where'd he come from anyway?"

"How'd he get in here, and whose is he?"

"Hey, Tony, is this your cat?"

Oh great. I'd forgotten about him. I wonder where he's been hiding all this time. At least his cat genes don't seem to get tangled with mine like that fly's in the movie! Kate was wondering whether to affirm or deny ownership when the door opened and a big man shouldered his way into the room. The receptionist shot him a look and fled so fast she seemed to vanish. Conversation stopped.

"Nobody's booked this hour?" To Kate, the man in the blue pin-stripe looked like he belonged to the mob.

"No, Mr. Calucci," someone braved a reply.

"Then *go home.*" He spotted Jude. "Whose animal is that?"
Silence.

"Animals aren't allowed in here. Where'd he come from?"
Silence.

"Well, if he doesn't belong to anybody, I want him out of here. Tony, take care of it. And Tony, I'd like you to come in early and wax the floor in the front ballroom. Get the key from Miss Milbourne."

Kate found her voice. "Yessir."

The man, obviously an authority figure, either the studio owner or manager, left. The teachers, now subdued, began to straggle out as well. Kate picked up Jude and went out to the desk. The receptionist had lit another cigarette and was blowing smoke expansively, her pack of Pall Malls in plain view, as if to say, "It's okay, he's gone."

When the last of the teachers had come by to check their next day's schedule and departed, she turned to Kate. "Tony, there's only a couple of pupils left in the ballroom, and one interview. As long as you're going to have the key, how would you like to lock up at ten so I can go make the night deposit and catch my nine-thirty bus? If the phone rings, pretend we're closed. The teachers and Miss Tammy will take care of any appointments." She handed Kate a bunch of keys. "Make sure the office is locked. Be sure to turn off the air conditioner and lights in the ballrooms, but leave the overheads on in here." She gave Jude a rub between the ears with her index finger. "Poor little guy."

This was working out okay. Since Kate had no place to go, maybe she could spend the night in the studio — and try to stay out of Noah's way.

...

Back in Mr. Reed's little room Kate formulated a plan. While the strains of Glenn Miller's "*Moonlight Serenade*" played in the background, and Jude licked a bit of pastrami left over from Mr. Reed's sandwich, Kate waited for the nine o'clock hour to end and the staff to leave. She would then lock the street level door, the door to the main ballroom, and the double doors leading into the reception room, thus triple securing the front entrance. She'd lock the office, as instructed. Maybe that way the office equipment would be safe unless Noah and his gang decided to break the door down. At most, all Noah would get would be a few portable record players from the small studios. Not much of a haul, but maybe it would satisfy him. She'd leave the back door open. It was easy. No key was needed. All Kate had to do was turn the button on the knob so the door wouldn't lock automatically. She would then spend the night on the couch in the teachers' room, and "discover" the break-in, if it happened at all, when she "came in early to wax the floor."

Kate took a mouthful of coffee, which by now was cold. She poured a few drops out for Jude into the lid of the carton, and wondered if the burger place was still open. Perhaps she could get a fresh cup and maybe a burger and fries. If they stayed open till ten, she might still be able to make it. She left Jude to deal with feeding himself as best he could, and arrived just as the cook was getting ready to close up shop.

"Sorry, Tony. Fryer's turned off. Just cleaned the grill. But there's still hot coffee and a couple of prune Danish if you want 'em. How come you're workin' so late? Thought you'd be on the bus to Overtown by now."

Bus? Overtown? The Doc lived in a place called Overtown? Kate had no clue as to where it might be. "Oh, I've gotta wax floors in the morning, and I wanted to get it all set up ahead of time. Might even get some of it done tonight when I have the place to myself."

The cook handed Tony a white paper bag. "No charge. I was gonna dump the coffee and the Danish has gotta be dry by now." He hung up his apron, walked around the counter to the entrance to his shop and pulled shut the collapsible metal security gate. In the process, he almost stepped on a large insect on the sidewalk, like the one that had scared Kate earlier. "Damn palmetto bugs." He gave it a kick.

"Up in West Palm Beach I've seen 'em banked up like fallen leaves under street lights."

The studio was strangely quiet when Kate came up the stairs. She realized that the music system had been turned off, and saw, through the window, that the main ballroom was empty. The woman in the strapless dress, Mr. Harttung's teacher, was at the desk making an appointment for a tall thin man with thick glasses.

Kate ducked into the storeroom to wait. The coffee was hot and tasted great; so did the dry Danish. Kate wolfed down both of them and wished she'd had a couple more. Jude was asleep, a tiny bedraggled curl with his head on the mop. Beside him was the lid that still held the cold coffee. It didn't look as though he'd touched it. What was it Mr. Reed had called him? An entity from a distant place. Did he mean planet? A cancer of the soul that could attach itself and enslave her? *Strong words for a, scrawny, no-count, poor excuse for a mousetrap!* Inside Anthony Reed's body, Kate tried probing for a link with Mr. Reed's mind, but found nothing about entities or demonic cats. The 1954 version of Mr. Reed probably wouldn't be into all that yet, although, she saw, with mild interest, that there were books on the shelf in the cubbyhole. Apparently even the younger Mr. Reed spent his spare time reading — stuck in a closet, waiting for quitting time, poring through big fat books. Kate picked one of them up. *Necromancy and the Black Arts: A Manual.* There was also a loose-leaf binder full of hand-scribbled notes and diagrams. What was this? Some kind of a mail-order course on witchcraft? Voodoo? Kate smiled. When she'd kidded Anthony Reed about being a witch doctor, she'd been right on the money, hadn't she?

But if Anthony Reed had any inside information on Jude, there seemed no way she could access it now. All the same, Kate knew that her own feelings toward the kitten had changed. While it was hard to look at the frail little thing without feeling sorry for it, there was something repulsive about the animal. Kate found herself wishing he *would* die — die and get it over with. The other two of Moonrise's kittens had died easily enough. How, then, did this tiny, tottering, fur-covered skeleton with yellow pus oozing out of its eyes manage not only to hang on to life, but to *Kate's* life as well? She couldn't seem to rid herself of it, waking or dreaming. *Maybe it* is *demonic. Maybe it* can't *die!* Kate allowed her mind to picture a lifetime with the feeble little animal, the kitten never growing any older, while Kate, herself, became a bent, dried-up, gray-haired old woman whose life had been spent ministering to its every need. What was that quote? "Dogs have owners; cats have staff." And when she, Kate, died of old age, would the kitten then find someone else to care for it? As if in answer, Jude opened slitty eyes and regarded Kate coldly. Kate stared back. "Don't count on it, hellbait. Ever see the inside of a Cuisinart?"

...

The studio was quiet. Pupils and teachers were gone. What had the receptionist said? Something about a Miss Tammy and an "interview." Surely they, too, would be gone by now. Kate went into the hall and looked around. No one was in the reception room — no sound of anything but the hum of the air conditioner. She checked the length of the corridor and, seeing that there was still a light on in the first of the small private studios, tiptoed over and peered in through the glass panel. Someone was inside. It was the woman in black, sitting at a desk. So *that* was Miss Tammy! Across from her, with his back to Kate, sat a man in a dark coat. Kate couldn't see his face, but he looked to be elderly, with silver hair, and looked vaguely familiar. The man and Miss Tammy seemed engaged in animated conversation, although Kate couldn't make out what they were saying. The private studios, though not entirely sound proofed, were insulated enough to keep the reception area free of the mixture of music. Kate glanced at the clock on the wall; it was a quarter to eleven. The interview was obviously running late.

Kate found she knew the procedure used to enroll a new pupil. Miss Tammy would have given him an introductory lesson, mapped out a beginning course of instruction, and enrolled him as a student. By the look of things, Miss Tammy and Mr. X were hitting it off very well. Maybe she'd sold him a big course of lessons, or maybe they were both just relaxing after a long day. Mr. X appeared to be telling a funny story and Miss Tammy was convulsed with laughter. *Nice to see someone enjoying her work, but doesn't the woman have a home to go to?* Kate was just wondering if she should go lock the back door in case Noah showed up too soon, when she saw Miss Tammy and Mr. X rise from their chairs. She ducked into Mr. Reed's hideaway.

When Kate came out again, all was quiet. She was reasonably sure that the studio was deserted, and set about closing up the place. She turned off the air conditioner (relieved to find she knew how to do that), then the lights, and locked the door to the main ballroom. She started to lock the front entrance, but decided she'd first better make sure that Miss Tammy had gone. *She could still be in the can, and if she is, I can't just go barging in there to see. I'll give her a few more minutes.* In fact, Kate had no wish to encounter Miss Tammy. Ever.

Meanwhile, Kate retrieved Jude and carried the kitten into the teachers' room where she could keep an eye on him. She tested the divan. It sagged in the middle and there wasn't a pillow, but it would do. She wouldn't need a blanket; with the air conditioning turned off, the atmosphere was already becoming warm and muggy. She opened the window to let in some air, switched off the fluorescent ceiling light, then lay, stretched out in the darkness, listening to traffic noises and the soft sputtering purr of Jude on the floor.

Suddenly she was wide-awake and disoriented. Had she been asleep? Where was she? Something had awakened her. She heard it again — a woman's scream! Kate tried to get her bearings. *Right! I'm in the Doc's body.* She groped in the darkness. Where had the scream come from? Outside? Someone being mugged in the alley? Or had it come from *in*side?

She felt her way to the door and opened it. The reception room lights were on, just as she'd left them. Miss Tammy's room still had a light in it and Kate saw that *the door was ajar.* Quietly, Kate tiptoed over to it and threw it open — and froze.

There, in front of Kate, stood Miss Tammy, her eyes wide with terror. Clutching her, with one hand over her mouth stood Noah. His other hand held a knife to her throat. *Holy shit!* Kate stood very still. Noah's eyes were rolling wildly and his breathing sounded oddly irregular. *He's terrified. Or he's on some drug. Maybe both.*

Kate held up her palms. "Take it easy, Noah. Real easy. *You don't want to hurt anybody.*"

"You ain't supposed to be here, man. Ain't *nobody* supposed to be here." Noah sounded near hysterical.

"It's okay, Noah. Just be cool, man. Just *let go of the girl.*"

"Can't let her go now, she's seen us!" Noah tightened his grip. The woman struggled to back away from the knife's edge.

"Listen to me, Noah. Just let Miss Tammy go. There's no need to hurt her. All she's gonna do is walk out of here and go home, isn't that right?" The woman nodded convulsively. "And all *you* gotta do, Noah, is go home. Nobody gets hurt. No harm done. Nothing happened. You got that? *Nothing happened here tonight.*"

"No man, you see, that ain't the way it is, Tono." Noah was half-sobbing. "She's gonna tell the cops, you *know* that. Ain't no way she's not gonna tell. I gotta kill this bitch, man. I gotta kill her."

Kate, very slowly, edged a little closer. "No. You don't want to do that, Noah, because that would only *make it worse.* Right now, all they can get you on is petty theft. But if they catch you when you're wanted for *murder* — "

"Ain't nobody gonna catch me! You just get on out of here, Tono. This ain't none of your business."

Kate glanced around, as if for help. On Miss Tammy's desk Kate saw a bunch of papers, charts. Paperwork. Noah must've surprised her; she'd certainly surprised *him*. Was this the friend the Doc had told her about? The one who got killed? Why the hell was the woman still in the building? Wasn't she worried about being locked in? Or maybe she has a key.

And maybe Noah had an accomplice. "Who came with you, Noah? You're not alone, are you?"

"None of your business, To'!" Noah yelled, and, as if in answer, a pudgy boy of about fifteen appeared in the doorway. He was carrying a record player. At the sight of Kate, Noah, and Miss Tammy, his eyes widened. *Christ, it's just a kid!* Simultaneously, both Kate and Noah turned to the kid and yelled, *"Get the fuck out of here!"* The kid looked from one to the other, dropped the machine with a crash, and bolted down the hall for the back door.

The diversion had been just enough to allow Kate to move in closer. *I'm bigger and stronger than he is. If I can just get hold of the knife I can make him let go of the girl. It's now or never!* Kate lunged and grabbed Noah's wrist and jerked it back. Noah, taken by surprise, loosened his grip on Miss Tammy. "Get out of here!" Kate yelled, "Run! Front door's open! *Get out now!*" Miss Tammy hesitated for just a beat, then dashed out, her heels clicking a frantic tattoo as she ran through the reception room and on down the stairs.

Noah and Kate were face to face, locked in a struggle. Noah's eyes were wild and his voice strangled. "You're one dead nigger, Tono!" Kate's right hand encircled Noah's wrist. Noah was surprisingly strong despite his slight build and Kate had to use both hands to push his arm upward, squeezing his wrist to make him let go of the knife. Suddenly, Noah's face twisted into a tortured smile and he let the knife drop — then Kate felt it rip into her body. Noah had caught the knife with his left hand and thrust it up into her chest.

Kate looked down in surprise and disbelief. There was the handle of a knife sticking out of her solar plexus. She wasn't conscious of pain, as such, but her knees gave way and she slumped to the floor. She looked up through what seemed to be a red mist. Noah was gone. She fell backwards against the wall. Dully she looked at the knife handle. She should try to pull it out, but her arms felt so heavy that she couldn't lift them. *I'm dying ...*

And then she saw Jude. The kitten had made its way into the room and was crawling up her leg toward the wound. The last thing Kate saw was Jude standing on her abdomen, rubbing his head against the knife handle — and licking up her warm blood.

CHAPTER 12

KATE AWOKE slowly, as from a long sleep. She had a dull headache and she felt cold. She saw that she was lying on a checkered asphalt tile floor among metal legs of furniture. Puzzled, she tried to make sense of her surroundings. Her clothing felt damp and her body was clammy with perspiration. Stiffly, she got to her feet and saw that she was in an empty hospital room. Two beds were neatly made. At the foot of each, a bed table with wheels stood at the ready. The room was unoccupied, so what was she doing in it? Oh yes, she'd been visiting Mr. Reed. Kate looked at the empty bed. Mr. Reed was gone; Kate knew that somehow Mr. Reed would turn up as never having existed, and felt a sense of loss. Of all the people she knew, the Doc had been the one person she'd considered a friend. She also felt a sense of guilt. If it hadn't been for her, Anthony Reed would still be around instead of wherever he might be now.

She remembered nothing beyond the part where Jude had fallen out of her jacket. Jude! She looked around for the animal but didn't see him. *Good riddance.* Kate realized she had to get out of there. So far no one had seen her and, thank God, the seizure, if that's what she'd had, hadn't been as severe as the last one. Maybe the Dilantin *was* helping after all. Right now all Kate wanted was to go home, get into some dry clothes and lie down on a real bed. First, maybe, she'd take a couple of aspirin to relieve her pounding headache.

As she made her way down the connecting corridor to the Lodge lobby, Kate's legs were so shaky that she found she had to steady herself by keeping a hand on the wide wooden railing bolted to the wall. *Better hang on to the geezer guide. Don't know if I'll be able to ride Hercules. Maybe if I just sit in the lobby for a little while. . . .*

Fortunately the lobby was empty. Kate thought it must be lunchtime. Even Jane-at-the-desk was absent. Kate eased herself into a chair and slowly closed her eyes — only to open them again with a start. What had she just seen? A pair of eyes looked back at her from under an armchair opposite. *Oh, crap, it's Jude! The demonic hairball!* Kate was in no mood to deal with the animal. She would pretend she hadn't seen him. She would get to her feet and go home. And then she would stay as far away from the Lodge as she could. Let Jude be someone else's problem. She never wanted to see him again.

Kate started to get up, then stopped. Some movement caught her attention, something she saw out of the corner of her eye. She turned to look and saw, of all things, Moonrise. The black cat had come down the corridor and was standing in the doorway. "Well, thank you, Ms. God! Hey, Moonrise, come here." The cat hesitated. "Come on, Moonrise, This Is Your Life. Have I got a surprise for you!" The cat took a tentative step forward. "Here kitty, kitty. Look who's over there. Your hungry offspring. It's tearful reunion time!"

Moonrise, as if sensing something threatening, turned and slowly began to circle the room. Jude, still under the chair, watched her with narrowed eyes. Kate expected the kitten to run directly to its mother, but instead Jude began to move like an animal stalking. Moonrise similarly seemed to be on her guard, creeping low to the ground. As Kate watched, surprised and puzzled, the two felines made eye contact, then slowly, ever so slowly, began inching toward each other. Each moved in a crouch at the pace of a tree-climbing sloth, tail twitching, ears flattened, until they were inches apart, eyeball to eyeball. Then all hell broke loose.

Kate, shocked, wasn't quite sure what happened next. There was a horrible scream from one or both of the cats, then a flurry of fur and fangs and nails as the two locked in combat. It lasted only a moment, then the two stood frozen, eyeing each other, ears back, tails lashing, fangs bared. Kate saw that Jude's ear was bleeding. Moonrise looked murderous; Jude looked equally enraged — small, yes, but dangerous as a piranha. "Hey!" Kate shouted, but before she could intervene, the cats engaged in Round Two. This time Kate saw a bloody gash in Jude's shoulder and a scratch across Moonrise's nose.

"*Knock it off!*" Kate yelled as she leapt up and grabbed Moonrise by the scruff of the neck and threw her bodily across the room. She scooped up Jude and stuffed him under her jacket. Moonrise stared at her defiantly. "You can forget about that Mother-of-the-Year award, shithead!"

The encounter with the cats had gotten Kate's adrenaline pumping, and she had no trouble pedaling her bike home. With Jude in the basket, wrapped in her denim jacket, Kate didn't even feel chilly. She did feel furious and manipulated. *Dammit, I was that close to getting rid of this little bad luck charm. So why don't I just dump him someplace? Or maybe I could put an ad in the* Stastas Buy Sell & Trade: *Free to a good home. No: Free to* anybody. *No: Free sexual favors to* anyone, male or female who — oh Christ, *now* what! Glancing into the bike basket, Kate was dismayed to see a large stain of blood seeping through the denim of her coat.

...

When she got home, luckily, no one was there, although Kate's mother might be expected at any moment. Her father's whereabouts didn't worry her. He'd been staying far away from her ever since she'd had the seizure, so if he were to arrive and see her, Kate felt sure he'd quickly leave.

Kate laid the bundle that was Jude onto the kitchen table and unwrapped the sodden coat. The kitten was alive, but just barely. The cut on its shoulder was nasty enough, but Kate saw that there was another, deeper and wider, on its back. (Why hadn't she noticed it at the time?) The skin gaped open, exposing muscles underneath, and the surrounding hair was matted with blood. The kitten lay, limp and comatose, barely breathing, its back arched backwards, mouth open.

Kate didn't know how to deal with it. The animal needed a vet. But even if she took it to a vet, it would probably die before she could get it there. And wouldn't it be just as well? She didn't know how Jude had managed to make it this far, but he was a gutsy little guy, she had to give him that. *I don't know what you are — probably just a kitten born under Murphy's sign of the zodiac.* Kate sighed. Her life with Jude had certainly been bizarre, but a lot of that may have been due to her own seizure disorder. Jude just happened to be there, and hell, maybe there had never even *been* a Mrs. Niemi, or Mr. Ostriker, or Anthony Reed — any more than there'd been a Cowardly Lion, a Scarecrow, or the Tin Man.

Kate put Jude on layered paper towels in the cardboard box in which he'd spent his first night. She picked up her bloodstained jacket, wondering how so small a kitten could've lost so much blood. Handling the bloody coat, Kate experienced another passing flash of *déjà vu: blood on a jacket; blood on sheets?* She rinsed the jacket in cold water in the sink, then put it in the washer with a cup of powdered detergent. She stripped off the rest of her clothing that, though dry by now, felt stiff and stale. She tossed her clothes in the washer as well, but didn't turn it on until she'd taken a shower and put on fresh jeans and sweatshirt. Thirsty and dehydrated, she downed a can of

A&W Root Beer, turned on the Kenmore, went into her bedroom, took one last look at Jude, then lay down on her bed and fell asleep to the soft *chug-chug* of the washing machine.

...

She woke to the murmur of voices. In her half-asleep state, she identified one as her mother's. But who was she talking to? It sounded like a man's voice. Her father's? Could be. Or maybe not. At any rate, it wasn't drunken screaming or even quarrelsome palaver. The voice sounded sober and civilized. Did Mother have company? Not likely. Kate strained to hear.

"You and your husband . . . very fortunate . . . carries great financial rewards." Nope, not Heikki Oksa's voice. Must be a salesman. He sounded like a salesman. The voices were coming from the front room, so whoever it was must have come in through the front door. Only solicitors did that.

"I don't know nothin' about rewards, Mister, but we're poor people." The loud flat tone was definitely Helvi Oksa's.

"Which is precisely why I'm here, my dear madam." *Had* to be a salesman. Encyclopedias? "Anyone . . . in this program . . . economically sound." Insurance. That's it. Or investments. But why would anyone bother to try to sell anything to the Oksas? *Everyone knows we're flatass broke.*

"Your husband has taken steps . . . secure your future and provide your daughter with . . . can't possibly fail. All we need . . . both your signatures."

Helvi's laugh was a loud, harsh bark, and Kate had no trouble hearing her part of the conversation. "Listen, Mister, that's what my husband does best — *fail!* Look, whatever you're selling, Mister, we don't want any. And I'm not signing my name to anything."

Kate had to find out what was going on. She got up and quietly eased into the hall. Standing in the bathroom doorway, she could peek into the living room without being noticed. She saw that the mystery guest was an elderly man with white hair and a briefcase. He was dressed in a dark suit and coat (in Stastas in August?) and was just getting up to leave. With his back to Kate, he offered Helvi his hand. "I understand, Madam. You wish to discuss it with your husband first. I'm sorry I missed him today, but I'll be in touch." With a nod and an old-fashioned bow he was gone.

Kate padded barefoot into the living room. "Who was *that?*"

"Oh, God knows. Somebody selling something. I told him we don't want any."

"What did he mean about Dad taking steps? And where *is* Dad, anyway?"

"Your guess is as good as mine, on both counts. Funny old coot. Looked old enough to be retired. Maybe he's trying his hand at selling to make a little extra. But he's not very good at it. I never did understand what it was he was trying to peddle."

Kate wondered, too, as she went to put her wash in the dryer. What dealings could the old man have with her dad? Or was there some connection between him and Heikki's unexplained behavior lately? Had her dad gotten himself involved in something shady? Something that had to do with men who wear black suits? The old guy had seemed friendly enough, but. . . .

...

There were no immediate answers. Evening came but there was no sign of Heikki. Kate helped her mother do the supper dishes without making any mention of the kitten, but from time to time went into her room to look in on Jude. She was feeling depressed. It was a deathwatch, but why didn't death come? The kitten continued to lie inert. The bleeding had stopped, and at one point, Kate had even tried to patch up the cut by pulling the edges of the wound together and fastening them with a strip of adhesive tape.

The animal lay, eyes shut, its rib cage moving slightly with every rapid, shallow breath, and the whole thing was getting on Kate's nerves. She wanted it to be over. She wanted the kitten out of her life. She even thought of killing it, but how? She couldn't take it outdoors and smash its head with a rock, nor could she bring herself to just take it somewhere and abandon it. If only it would just *die!* Death with dignity. She wondered if people eventually began to feel the same way when a vegged-out family member was being kept alive on a respirator. Wouldn't they just want to pull the plug? She wished there'd been a plug to pull with Jude to put him out of his misery — and hers.

Helvi had gone to bed. Kate sat staring morosely at the TV screen, watching an old movie: Irene Dunne and Barbara Bel Geddes in *I Remember Mama*. It was a black-and-white print, not the colorized version, and on the second hand 24-inch Zenith console, the picture tonight was fairly sharp. Kate wished they could afford cable. As it was, they only got one channel reliably, three if the gods were smiling, and lately the picture had begun to show signs of schizophrenia. The antenna probably needed a new wire. It hadn't been replaced since that autumn day Barry Harwood had climbed up to attach it so they could watch *The Simpsons*. That was *ages* ago! Kate's eyelids were beginning to droop. Time to go to bed. She'd seen the movie, knew how it came out. She turned off the set, went to her room, put on the number 86 football jersey she slept in; and resisting the urge to look in on Jude, climbed into bed. "Good night, John-Boy. Hope I'll see your stiff and lifeless form in the morning." She dozed off, the movie plot still playing in her brain: something about Mama chloroforming a cat.

CHAPTER 13

ONCE MORE Kate awakened to voices, but this time the sun was streaming in the window and the voices were unmistakably those of her parents. Her father had come home last night after all. There was the familiar smell of coffee, and Kate, longing for a cup, thought it best to first make sure it was safe to go into the kitchen. It sounded as though her parents were having an argument, although Heikki Oksa's morning voice wasn't his usual hungover wheeze.

"And I'm telling *you* that you better not be getting us into another one of your harebrained schemes." Helvi had the floor.

"Shut up, woman, you don't know what you're talking about."

"Oh, don't I? *When* did you do anything that wasn't a disaster? You have no judgment. Anybody can talk you into anything. You're like a little kid."

"Hey, who's the head of this house? Who puts food on the table? Who's supported you all these years — and listened to your nagging? *Women don't understand business!*"

"Business? Your business is the bottle. And if I didn't go out and scrub up other people's dirt, we'd all be out on the street. So don't tell *me* how *you* support this family! If you'd been a *real* man, we'd still have the farm. We could've made a go of it. No, *booze* was too important. You couldn't even keep the job at the Brickworks."

"Jesus Christ, that was because I hurt my back. What do you expect from me? I hurt my goddam back!"

"Sure, accidents happen — to drunks."

(So far, the argument was a rerun.)

"Listen, woman, you've made me feel like shit for the last time. From now on things are going to be different. *I'm* the man of this house, and from now on, what I say *goes*. So *don't* tell me what to do anymore, because *I have the power.*"

"What are you talking about?" Helvi managed to sound both bored and exasperated.

"Aha! Wouldn't you like to know? You think I'm going to tell you everything?" Heikki was getting louder.

"You're raving. You should be certified."

"Is that so? Well, you might be surprised to know that there are people who think Heikki Oksa is a man to be reckoned with. In fact, I may be going into partnership with one of them."

Kate pricked up her ears.

"If you mean that old codger who was here yesterday, wanting me to sign something, you better get a smarter partner."

"Here? Yesterday?" Heikki sounded as if someone had let the air out of his balloon.

"White-haired old coot in a black coat. Didn't get his name. *Or* his sales pitch. But he certainly mentioned *you*. I told him whatever it was we didn't want any."

"You told him. . . ?"

Helvi's voice was now reasonable, almost friendly. "What did he want, Heikki? Is he trying to get you to sell household cleaners? *Amway?* You remember what happened when you tried selling plastic greenhouses? And the mail order *shoe* business? And *my* favorite, the rent-a-used-formal-gown business! Just what any girl would want for her prom or her wedding day! We've still got the six 'designer originals' that you paid three hundred dollars for, moldering in the cellar. You *know* those things are frauds. Or they're pyramid clubs where they don't want you to sell the product. They only want you to sell other suckers like yourself. *And they always want money up front.*"

"This time it's different."

"Oh, Heikki, Heikki. You've no idea of how much I want things to be *different*. But you always do the *same dumb thing* over and over. The only thing age teaches you is how to walk more slowly."

"And if things don't go right, whose fault is it? *Yours!* You're the one who's always working against me. I could have made something of myself long ago if it weren't for you and your big mouth. You never show me any respect. You never show me any support. But I'm telling you, woman, once and for all, you've stood in my way for the last time. I'm not going to forget this. I'm putting it right here, behind my right ear."

Kate couldn't help laughing. Although she couldn't see him, she could picture her father's gesture of tapping the spot behind his earlobe. It was a Finn thing. Mummo had done it too — the Finnish version of the "chip on the shoulder." Whenever one wanted to dramatize that an insult or injury would not be forgotten, and would one day be repaid, it was figuratively put "behind the right ear" or "in a hole in a tooth."

"I don't care if you stick it up your ass with your longest finger. The truth is the truth."

"You watch your mouth, woman. And you better watch your step from now on because, like it or not, *I'm the one in control now. You understand?*"

"And whatever stupid thing you've got yourself into, *I don't want any part of it.* And I'm not cosigning anything. We have a kid who has fits. We may have to take care of her for the rest of our lives. We can't afford any gambles. And we're not paying one red cent to any smooth-talking salesman. Do *you* understand?"

"*Saatanan perkeleen akka!*" Heikki, as usual, when his agitation circuit breaker blew, defaulting to cursing in Finnish.

Kate heard the kitchen door open and slam shut, and thought it safe to enter. "So, Mom, where *are* you and Dad going on your second honeymoon?"

Helvi gave her a sideways look. "Don't need any of your smart remarks, miss."

Kate poured a cup of coffee from the pot on the stove, stirred in milk and sugar. "You don't have to worry about me being a burden, you know."

"Don't I? How do I know that? How do *you* know that?"

"I just do."

"That's all very well, but people who have fits can't predict the future."

"Seizures, Mom, *seizures.*"

"Fits are fits even if you fry them in butter. You never know. They could get worse. And even if they don't, you'll be on drugs for the rest of your life. You'll always be an invalid. Better get used to it."

Kate wondered if she could read that to mean something like, "Sweetheart, you could never be a burden to us, but I'm terribly worried about the quality of your life. I'm only putting up a front to hide my anguish." *Well, maybe not. Still, with my mother, you always know where you stand.*

"Is there any *pulla?*"

"In the bread box."

Kate cut herself a slice of the sweet golden braided loaf flavored with cardamom. "So, what do you think Dad is up to?"

"Nothing good."

"He doesn't seem to be drinking as much these days."

"He's all excited about another one of his get-rich-quick schemes, but it won't amount to anything. He'll always be just a drunk."

Like I'll always be an invalid. Kate pictured herself and her father with the words "invalid" and "drunk" tattooed on their foreheads, and felt a little sorry that that was all her mother could see.

Of course, her mother might well be right. Kate remembered several of her father's abortive business ventures. They always involved an initial outlay of money that the Oksas couldn't afford. The pattern was that Heikki, in a flush of boozy bravado, would announce that he was reinstating himself as head of the house and going into partnership with some tycoon. Helvi would unsuccessfully try to talk him out of it. Heikki would then be parted from whatever cash he could beg borrow or wheedle, and the so-called partner would vanish, leaving Heikki with some sort of kit with which to start his new enterprise. In the Oksa cellar, along with the mildewing formal gowns, were also several boxes of shoes (men's white wingtips and women's high-heeled ankle-straps) and a geodesic dome greenhouse that Heikki had never even been able to assemble, let alone sell.

Perhaps her mother had been right about Kate too. Maybe she *would* become a lifelong burden. *Nope, I'd sooner off myself.* Kate pictured leaping to her death off the railroad bridge or committing ceremonial *hara-kiri* with a Ginsu knife. No, somehow she knew that violent death was not the answer, and why should she, of all people, have to worry about committing suicide? All she'd have to do is go off her medication and wait for the Big One!

". . . And for goodness sake, go put some clothes on!"

Kate realized that her mother had been talking to her, and that yes, she was still barefoot in her football jersey. She went into her room — *oh jeez, I forgot all about Jude!* She looked in the box.

The kitten had died during the night. There was no sign of life. The animal was cold and limp, the paper towels stained with body fluids. *Poor little sod.* Well, she'd have to get the corpse out of the house without her mother seeing it, or Helvi would go into cleaning mode and Kate's room would smell of Lysol for a month! How to do that? Kate put on her jeans, sweatshirt and sneakers. She picked up the kitten along with the soiled paper towels and looked for something to wrap it in. She didn't want to go through the house carrying a suspicious looking bundle so she decided to use her jacket again, the one she'd washed the day before.

Helvi was busy at the sink as Kate sauntered in, trying to look casual. "And where do you think *you're* going?"

Kate tucked the rolled-up jacket under her arm. "Oh, I thought I'd go out to the Lodge and befuddle a few geriatrics — you know, walk in on Ed Mingus and say, 'Hi, Dad.'"

"I think you spend too much time over there."

"What's the harm? I run a few errands. They pay me a few bucks."

"You never had fits till you started going there."

"They're not *catching*, Mom!"

"How do you know that? Nobody seems to know *what* causes them."

Impossible to argue with Helvi's logic. Kate decided breeziness was the best tactic. She gave her mother a smacking kiss on the cheek, something she hadn't done in years, and sprinted out the door. Helvi, dazed, recovered herself enough to call after her, "And put your jacket on!"

So far, so good. Now, where can I dump this cat? Not around home, that's for sure. Besides, Mom could be looking out the window. Kate made a show of strolling leisurely to her bike, tossed the bundled jacket into the basket, and mounted up. How was she going to get rid of a dead kitten? She couldn't just put it in somebody's garbage can. Trash wouldn't be picked up again till next week. She couldn't throw it in the bushes. It would smell and draw flies and some dog would be bound to drag it out. Gross! She couldn't bury it in somebody's yard. Kate regretted that she hadn't thought to seal it in a Ziploc bag at least. *What do I have to do, pedal all the way out past the edge of town to the city dump? Old Jude here is as hard to get rid of dead as he was alive.*

It didn't take Kate very long to come to the obvious conclusion. She needed to find a dumpster, and the nearest one was behind the Lodge. Kate had tossed in two other dead kittens, and Jude could go the way of his siblings. It seemed fitting, somehow.

Kate felt almost lighthearted as she guided Hercules through the parking lot to the back entrance. She hoped that her luck would hold, and that neither Mike, the maintenance man, nor anyone else would be taking a shortcut through the back way. She saw no one.

Kate leaned Hercules against the side of the Dumpster, then carefully unrolled her jacket. She took the kitten, still encased in paper towels, and was reaching for the lid of the container.

"Katri Oksa, is that you?"

Oh shit! Kate turned to see who had called her name and found herself looking into the smiling eyes of Wilhelmiina Hill, the former schoolteacher, the new resident who had just moved in with Lauralee Beatty.

"I thought I recognized you. How are you feeling, dear? I was very concerned when I heard about your illness." She noticed Kate's look of consternation. "Oh, I'm sorry, dear, did I startle you?"

"Oh, hi, Mrs. Hill. I . . . I'm okay, I guess." Kate tried to look as though she *weren't* holding a dead animal in a fold of paper towels.

"Katri, is something wrong?"

There are times when all you have left is the truth, and Mrs. Hill seemed to be a kindly woman, not one to be afraid of. "Well, actually, Mrs. Hill, my kitten died, and I was just about to put it in the dumpster. I couldn't think of what else to do with it." Kate held up her bundle and unfolded the paper towels.

Mrs. Hill looked at Jude. "Oh, what a shame, dear. Such a poor tiny thing. Yes, why not? What harm can it do? Although maybe we should put it in a bag or something. Wait a minute. I was just coming from the drugstore. Yes, here's a plastic bag." Mrs. Hill opened wide her canvas carryall, lifted out a Value-Mart bag and upturned it to dump the contents inside. "It might be better if we put the poor little thing in here. It gets pretty hot in that dumpster with the sun shining on it, and I don't know when they're scheduled to empty it. We don't want it to smell and draw flies." She held the bag open as Kate reached over to deposit the earthly remains of Jude. As she did, her hand made contact with Wilhelmiina Hill's and. . . .

CHAPTER 14

KATE LOOKED around. Her first thought was, how peaceful! The sky was a clear, fathomless blue, and she could hear the susurrus of little waves lapping on a pebble shore. The sun was warm, but a cool puff of wind carried the fragrance of flowers and evergreens and the scent of the ocean. The breeze felt like a caress on Kate's skin, and she breathed deeply, drinking the air in great gulps. Not a hint of pulp mill in it! Into her mind flashed on old poem she'd had to memorize in Miss McLennan's English class:

I will arise and go now, and go to Innisfree,
And a small cabin build there of clay and wattles made.

Kate had never been clear on exactly what "wattles" were, but it sounded nice, and she'd always liked the poem.

Kate knew that she'd "flashbacked" again. She didn't know to where, but here she was, once more, on some odyssey, which meant she must have had another seizure in the Lodge parking lot; and would be lying there, next to the dumpster, waiting for someone to find her — at least so she hoped. Better that than punching out paramedics and smashing fish tanks.

Kate saw that she was sitting on grass, *holding Jude.* But the kitten, far from being dead, had never looked so good! There were no signs of wounds or sickness. The animal was lying peacefully in Kate's lap, gazing with the clear eyes of a healthy young feline at the world around him. His coat was a soft, glossy black, his very being aglow with vitality, and he seemed to have grown bigger. Kate lifted him up and impulsively nuzzled her face into his luxurious fur; he smelled vaguely of cloves.

Maybe I'm dead too. Maybe I had a seizure and died, and here we are, Jude and I, in heaven. It was beautiful enough, but somehow Kate didn't think so. For one thing, Kate saw that she was in a cemetery, and didn't think cemeteries would be needed beyond the Pearly Gates. Streets of gold — maybe, but even that was a stretch. Cemeteries? *Nah!*

Cemetery wasn't quite the right word either. Cemetery made you think of mown grass and perpetual care. This was more of a graveyard, and a neglected one at that. The location was lovely, right next to the sea and surrounded by towering trees; but the area itself was uncared for, overgrown with weeds. Yet the place didn't look abandoned. In fact, some of the graves seemed recent — tended plots among neglected ones. Rather than having a groundskeeper, it looked as if it were up to each family to maintain its own. Older plots, perhaps because the family had either died out or moved away, lay swallowed up by wild growth that fettered and obscured crumbling markers.

Still holding Jude, Kate got up to explore. The cemetery was sizeable enough to contain a number of graves, and the overall design was a hodgepodge of styles, some rather bizarre. One family plot, containing a single stone and a few flat concrete markers, was surrounded by a wiggly wire loop fence similar to ones seen surrounding houses in old photos. Kate tried to read the inscription on the stone but couldn't make it out. Another grave was covered by a concrete slab with an anchor partially embedded in it. The inscription indicated that it was the last resting-place of one Kristo Hautamäki who had drowned in a storm in 1902.

There was a corner where the graves were all of children (some epidemic, perhaps?) and Kate noted that many adults had been young — women who may have died in childbirth, and young men lost at sea. The dates went back to the early 1900s. Kate smiled as she noticed two horizontal slabs, side by side of a married couple. Frost or heaving earth had caused one of the slabs to shift so it looked, to Kate, as though the husband had turned over in bed, with his back to his wife.

The overall effect was gothic — the silent graves, the towering trees, and ravens. As Kate walked about, a number of ravens wheeled in, lit on the grass and stones, lifted off in a flock to circle the area, then swooped back down again in a ballet of black wings. Another sound made Kate look up. She saw an eagle — a solitary bald eagle perched high in a Douglas fir. With wings slightly spread, its head abristle with white feathers, it fixed a merciless eye upon Kate and began to chatter, as if delivering a high-pitched sermon.

What place is this? To Kate it looked familiar enough; it had to be the Pacific Northwest, but where was she? On one of the islands? Kate felt quite normal, but then realized that she might not be Kate at all. She checked her clothing. The sneakers, jeans and sweatshirt, of course, were gone — replaced by sandals, a dress, and a sweater. Kate noted that the sweater, a cardigan, was made of thick warm natural wool, and was patterned with geometric designs knit into it in darker shades. She'd never owned one, but Kate recognized it as one of the Cowichan sweaters hand made by native women on Vancouver Island. The were very expensive to buy, and had been a bit of a status symbol in Stastas High, where some of the rich kids had brought them back from visits to Canada. Kate saw that hers had wooden buttons and hummingbird figures worked into the front panels.

This time at least Kate was a woman — a girl. Probably Wilhelmiina Hill. Who else? Kate wished she had a mirror. *And I'll be Mrs. Hill until*

I — she — gets killed off, and ends up as never having existed. Sorry about that, Mrs. H. You were a nice lady.

What happens now? For the moment Kate was content just to *be* in that tranquil place. The eagle had stopped its vocalizing and stood gripping a branch with powerful talons while it preened its feathers. To Kate, the bird looked resentful, ill-tempered, as if impatient with the task. Finally it spread wide wings and lifted off to fly toward the ocean. Even the ravens had departed. Except for Jude, Kate was alone.

Around her, nature was rampant. A wind stirred the branches of the towering evergreens. Somewhere a gull called. Grass was soft under her feet. The sun felt warm on her shoulders, but the wind was brisk enough now so that Kate was grateful for the sweater. She listened to the *lap, hiss, lap, hiss* of waves on shore as they slid onto the beach and drained back, combing through the pebbles — and fancied that she was stranded like Robinson Crusoe on a deserted island — except for the dead. She was, after all, surrounded by graves. That alone was a pretty good indication that the island was inhabited, and soon enough she would have to deal with the confusion of who she was and where she was. But for the moment, she was rather enjoying a feeling of being detached, and a little giddy. She felt almost as though she were viewing herself from a distance or from a great height. Here she was again, having been moved like a chess piece. What purpose could there be to all this? Perhaps that's what life was — a chess game some higher entity was playing, although it was probably being played only in her own head while she lay unconscious, maybe even dead, next to a dumpster in the parking lot of an old-people's home, in a little nowhere town named Stastas. Kate stroked Jude. "And you're the one that started it all, aren't you?" The kitten ducked its head, raised it to rub against her hand, then stretched its legs and arched its back to made sliding contact with her palm. "I guess you and I will have to try to find out where we are. We can't very well stay here."

It was then that Kate realized that she wasn't alone. There, by the cemetery gate, on a stone bench, sat a solitary figure. It was a man — a white-haired man in dark clothing — and he was looking intently at Kate. There was something familiar about him. Kate knew that she'd seen him before, somewhere. She started to walk toward him. The man sat waiting, smiling. When she reached him, the old man held out his hands. His pale blue eyes twinkled. "Thank you for bringing back my cat."

...

Kate stared. Jude was squirming in her arms and Kate almost mechanically handed the kitten to the old man who received it and placed it gently on his knee. He proceeded to stroke it idly, while Jude twined against his hand, humping his back as he rubbed his chops, flanks and tail lovingly against the man's fingers.

"I don't blame you for being confused, my dear. You and Pussykins here, have had quite a journey!"

To Kate, as when one sees someone out of context, recognition came slowly. Of course! Kate had seen the man in her own living room, talking with her mother! She'd also seen him in the front hall of the big house in Connecticut where Elina Saari had worked, and again, sitting on a stool in a diner in Miami — and later, that night in the studio, hadn't *he* been Miss Tammy's late night interview? And wasn't this the same figure she and Jeremy had followed in Pennsylvania — when the mist came up just before the rain?

"I . . . I *know* you, don't I?"

"Oh yes, we've seen each other several times. You see, I've been following your progress from a distance."

To Kate this was all very *Alice in Wonderland*, and she was now convinced beyond all doubt that she had to be dead or dreaming. She did feel a little like Alice, trying to maintain her aplomb while talking to a caterpillar. Or maybe she was more like Dorothy in Oz. Only this wasn't Glinda, the good witch. Just as well. Kate disliked Glinda, considered her an airhead. Anyway, here was this bozo thanking her for bringing back the demonic fuzzball. "Who *are* you?"

"Sit down, my dear, we'll have a chat." The old man patted the bench. "For now, let's just say that I'm S.P. Perkele, at your service."

Kate tried to stifle a giggle. *I just hope I can remember all this when I wake up!*

"I see you find my name amusing. I gather you've heard it before."

Damn straight, I've heard it! Perkele was one of her father's favorite swear words. Heikki, an American-born Finn, clung to his culture through invective. Anything that displeased him, any malfunctioning tool, became Perkeleen this or Perkeleen that (the possessive form), thus adding it to an ever-growing inventory of things that belonged to the devil.

"Perkele is a name for the devil, isn't it?"

"Quite right, my dear Kate, it's one of the Finnish words for devil, and you see, you *do* have some knowledge of your mother — ah — in this case, your father's tongue."

"And you're going to tell me that *you're* the devil?" *Should I humor this nutcase?*

"Well, yes, but I'd have to qualify that by saying that I'm one of many." The old man chuckled. "For this particular job, let's just say that I'm the *Finnish* devil."

"I thought there was only one devil."

"Now there, you see, *God* has Jesus Christ and the Holy Mother as well as guardian angels and saints galore, but the poor old devil is expected to do everything by himself with only few clumsy imps for a workforce. Actually, I'm one of the minor devils, not nearly as important or powerful as, say, the *American* devil.

"In fact, you might say my followers are the children of a lesser devil; they're impassioned, to be sure, but much less sophisticated. You've heard Finns use words such as *Saatana, Piru, Perkele, Paholainen.* They always sound thunderous when pronounced by a man who's just hit his thumb with a hammer, but they're only proper names for *me*. They pale compared with the graffiti on any American wall!"

"Okay, Mr. Perkele," Kate tried to say the name with a straight face. "What do you want with me?"

"Ah, now we come to the interesting part. But *do* sit down, my dear." Kate, who had been standing, finally sat. "How can I explain this simply? Maybe I should ask what *you* want of *me* — because it was your own adventurous spirit that brought me to you. It was your desire for change, your curiosity about other realities, that attracted, actually *created*, the opportunity to travel as you have. You wanted to leave Stastas. You were never happy there."

"No, I guess not."

"Interesting little town, Stastas. Did you know that the name means 'maggots on a corpse?' No, I thought not. I don't think the town fathers did either. It was named after a tribe of Indians. Back then that's what they were called. Now they'd be Native Americans. They bred so prolifically that they became a bit of a joke, and got the name because there were so many of them. You know, Kate, Stastas isn't a bad little town. One of my favorite places, really." To Kate's surprise, the smiling old man began to hum, then to sing softly:

Dear old Stastas, Stastas High
Guide our hearts as years go by
Truth and justice
Pride to last as
Time goes past us, Stastas High
The Stastas school song! The old fart knows my school song!

"But you, Kate, felt stifled in Stastas. You wanted out. You weren't happy at home. You'd dropped out of school, unwisely, I fear, but you felt you had your reasons."

The old man was sounding like *This Is Your Life*. Kate wondered just how much he knew about why she'd dropped out of Stastas High. She hadn't been a bad student. In fact, Kate had been a very *good* student, but she'd also been rebellious, irreverent, and *not* from one of Stastas's leading families. Her wicked sense of humor and puncturing of hypocrisy had combined to make her *persona non grata* among the more anal of the teaching staff. There'd been that cartoon she drew of the principal (a man given to drinking and wearing colorful leisure suits) as a two-hundred-pound tipsy canary. No one had failed to recognize the subject of the drawing. And there'd been the time that the obese guidance counselor, Mrs. Butkus, had tried to convince Kate that being a librarian was just as good, and *very much like*, being an archaeologist, and *much* more suitable for a girl. The next day, on the blackboard, there'd been a large drawing of a hippo sitting on four folding chairs. The caption read, "Being a guidance counselor is very much like being Miss America." Kate had not claimed responsibility, but her style had given her away.

The deciding factor had been the Student-of-the-Year award that Kate had worked very hard to get. The award had always gone to the tenth grader with the highest marks, and that year it had been Kate. She'd studied, and she'd gotten extra credits by doing extra assignments. She'd single-mindedly devoted herself to winning the award, and knew that she'd aced it — handily. Then, at the last minute, it was announced that the basis for the award was being *changed*. No longer was it go to the student with the best grades, but was now to be awarded to the *best-rounded* student, one who excelled not only scholastically, but in athletics and extracurricular activities as well. Kate saw the award go to Merry Lee Peckinpaugh, the daughter of the head of the school board. Merry Lee was a pale blonde who giggled a lot and whose extracurricular activities included being sexually active with the football team. As soon as Kate turned sixteen, she dropped out of school.

"When you left school, Kate, you felt you had no place to go. You didn't want to stay in Stastas, but you had no way of leaving it. You were too young. You had no job, no money. Yet you wanted, passionately, to change things, and it was your powerful desire that attracted a guide — Pussykins, here."

"A kitten? A sick kitten?"

"Oh yes! Never underestimate the power of the weak and the helpless. Of course, Pussy was on a quest of his own, a mission given him as a form of discipline. Pussykins had been a bit naughty, you see, and needed a learning experience for his own good, didn't you, Pussy?"

The old man had been affectionately rubbing Jude's nose with his index finger. Now Jude opened his mouth and gave the finger a hard bite, drawing a drop of blood. The old man, still smiling affably, placed the nail of his middle finger against the thumb and released it, giving Pussykins a *twhack* on the side of the head.

"So what are you trying to tell me, grandpa? That I've sold my soul to the devil?"

The old man laughed. "Oh no, Kate. We devils don't need to *buy* souls. We might *rent* them for a while, to provide experience when it's requested. Selling of souls is a fiction we haven't bothered to dispel because it serves a purpose. You might be amused to know that your father is half convinced that *he* sold *your* soul to the devil! Had you noticed him acting strangely? Particularly after you experienced that seizure that put you in the hospital? Part of him believes that he's responsible for that. Eventually, of course, he'll come to realize that selling a soul is like selling the Brooklyn Bridge.

"By the way, Kate, don't *you* sell your father short. He's gone to great sacrifice to give you exactly the background you needed in order to be where you are today."

Kate looked puzzled. "Sacrifice?"

"Certainly. Do you think it's *easy* being a drunk and a failure?

"Anyway, as long as you people insist on putting negative and positive values on experience, dividing it into neat little piles labeled 'good' and 'evil,' then you'll have to have gods and devils. And we, the facilitators, if you please, will have to play the roles. But I see I'm not really addressing your questions, am I, Kate?"

"All I want to know is, what's going on? I know I'm dreaming. At least I *think* I'm dreaming, but why are these dreams so weird?"

"All of life *is* a grand dream, Kate, and your experiences have taught you a great deal. Let's start at the beginning. Your first journey was back into the life of Elina Niemi. In that one, you learned what a powerful force anger can be."

"Yes, and I got killed."

"Correction, Kate. It was Mrs. Niemi — or rather, the girl who *might have become* Mrs. Niemi, who died, remember? Elina Saari, the girl they called Ellen, was working for a wealthy family in Connecticut. She fell in love with Frederick, their son, and she became pregnant. Elina wanted to marry Frederick. She wanted to be mistress of that big house with all the servants.

"Originally, Elina had the miscarriage but she didn't die, nor, of course, did she marry Frederick. In that reality, Frederick never had any intention of marrying her. To him she was just a servant girl. Elina was sent away and eventually she met Oskar Niemi and married him.

"But Elina was never able to let go of the past. She continued to fantasize about being the wealthy mistress of that house. I think she was more in love with the house than with Frederick. As she grew older, and after her husband Oskar died, she harked back more and more to that time, until she began to believe she really *had* been the rich mistress of a large house by the sea. She even began to sound like the woman she'd worked for, all those years ago. Elina Niemi wanted to go back. You and Pussykins, here, gave her the opportunity to do that."

"You mean Mrs. Niemi *wanted* to get killed?"

"A part of her *did*. It's a bit complicated. She wanted to experience a different version of what happened. She wanted closure, as they say these days. You, Kate, merely experienced the event and then returned to your own time, or should I say, a *version* of your own time.

You noticed that there were differences. In that version, of course, *Oskar* Niemi had married another woman — the speechless old lady you saw at the Lodge."

"But why me? Why did *I* become Mrs. Niemi? And Jock Ostriker? And Mr. Reed? Why them?"

"More about that later. One of the connections, of course, hinges on your nationality (and mine, *ha-ha*). Another connection was the Lodge. All those people lived at the Lodge, and whenever any group of people come together, there are always strong underlying uniting forces, even if it's only a crowd at a baseball game. If you've ever wondered why a certain group of passengers crashes in a plane, or gets trapped in a hotel fire, think of what exquisite timing and logistical planning it took to orchestrate the event."

"But wouldn't that just be an accident? They were just in the wrong place at the wrong time?"

"No. Any earthly event takes much behind-the-scenes planning and cooperation. Your experiences took place on several levels, Kate, and were designed to let you explore the power of emotions and their function in creation. You're a natural. You may not know it, but you're a mystic. You always will be, and your powers will grow stronger. Each of 'your people' took you back to a crisis point in their lives, and allowed you — and themselves *through* you — to take part in an *alternative outcome*. And, in each case, there *was* a Finnish connection, but that was just our way of making the game more fun."

"Jock Ostriker wasn't Finnish. Neither was Anthony Reed."

"Jock Ostriker, in fact, *did* have Finnish roots but in a slightly different way. Someday you will uncover more information about how and why he died. As for Anthony Reed, his situation was different. He had let the young Finnish woman die the night of the robbery in the dance studio. You remember Miss Tammy? Her name was really Tammi. He felt responsible for her death, because, of course, he'd left the door open for Noah, and in the original version of the event, he hadn't stopped Noah from killing her. Anthony Reed had always been haunted by that night, and was glad to be given the opportunity to go back and change the ending."

"He told me once that a friend of his died because of him," Kate said.

"That was Karen Tammy. She was the head interviewer at the dance studio. It was her job to enroll new students, and she often worked late at night. If an interview ran late, Anthony Reed would usually stay late himself just to walk her to her car and make sure she got to it safely. The night that Karen Tammy was killed, Anthony Reed had left the door open for Noah and gone home early. He didn't know Karen was still in the studio, in fact, he didn't know she had a late interview because he'd left to avoid any chance of meeting up with Noah."

Kate felt a swell of emotion, a rising tide of feeling that seemed to cause all her nerves to ache. "But I'm the one who caused them all to die. Mrs. Niemi, Mr. Ostriker, and Mr. Reed!"

"You've had the unique opportunity to actually experience *their* feelings — fury, grief, guilt, love, fear — just as you're experiencing strong emotions right now. Emotions are the most powerful building blocks of reality, Kate. Learn that. Know that. *Use* that. On your plane of existence, that's one of the great lessons. You're taught to mistrust your emotions, yet they are your most valuable tools for living. You are told that they are dangerous, that they come from some wild and primitive source and that they must either be denied, or tightly controlled, or they'll sweep you away. You even misunderstand love. Heinous acts are committed in its name only because you see yourself as vulnerable when you love. Anger is a wonderfully creative force, properly applied. Fear can be a grand motivator; so can guilt. These emotions can cleanse us and realign our goals. They should never be suppressed. If human emotions were allowed healthy expression, your society would not be the violent one it is today."

"You mean if I feel like whacking somebody I should just go ahead and do it?"

Mr. Perkele smiled faintly. "I doubt that it would come to that. Before you got the point of wanting to whack, there must have been a series of events that might have been dealt with in such a way that whacking would never even come up as an option. You are walking down the street. You see a large and threatening person approach you. You think, this fellow might do you harm. You run away, but you still share the planet with this fellow, and you keep seeing him. Each time you become more frightened, more insecure. Your fear builds. You picture the violence he might do you. You build such a case against this fellow, that one day you bring a gun and you shoot him because you're just so desperate to end your terror of him."

Kate couldn't keep from giggling, because as Mr. Perkele delivered his speech, he'd been acting out the part of both bully and victim with comic gestures.

"But!" Mr. Perkele paused, index finger raised, "What would have happened if, when you first saw this threatening person, you had instead given him a big smile and wished him good day? Chances are the fellow would have smiled back and you might have even become friends. Or, if the fellow *were* a threatening person, chances are he would never have been a threat to *you* because now he might not consider you a victim. If, indeed, he *were* an aggressive bully, you would at least have gained more knowledge of him, and possibly formulated a better way of dealing with him — whether that meant learning how to avoid him or how to quell him. At least you'd have an honest assessment of the threat rather than the imagined one you'd been harboring.

"When we allow our fear to go outward to seek knowledge, the fear dissipates. It turns in action. Action is creative. If we bottle up fear it grows within us, distorts our ability to function creatively, and works against us. This is a lesson humans must learn, individually and collectively. Nations often behave the same way. They go to war because they imagine it will bring peace. What could be more absurd!"

Kate took a moment to consider this. "Yes, but there *are* scary things in the world. There are murderers and muggers and wars and bombs and people who break into your house to rob you and people who drive around shooting at other people."

"Indeed there are, Kate. And I say that if natural aggression and the nature of emotions were better understood, there would be less crime, possibly none at all." Mr. Perkele raised his eyebrows. "Do you know that in your world, nothing is impossible? Anything you want or need or concentrate on will materialize in your life! You've heard the saying, be careful what you wish because you'll get it? It's true. The material is all around you. There is no shortage of anything. Nobody *needs* to commit crime. The universe is abundant and most people fail to take advantage of that."

Now he's sounding like Auntie Mame. "Then why are so many of us poor?"

"Each of you chooses the circumstances of your birth. That's your starting point. From it you can go anywhere. You see, Kate, it's not only your emotions that you need to mobilize; it's also your thoughts. If you go around thinking I'm poor, or I'm fat, or I'm sick, or I'm ugly, or I'm doomed to failure, then that's what you are materializing in your life."

Hadn't Anthony Reed said something like that? Could that really be the case? Kate would have to think about that later. "If we can get anything we want, then why do we *have* crime?"

"Because at this point in your development, it's not understood that one cannot benefit from violation. It may even *seem* that crime pays, but the cost to the criminal is ultimately enormous. Life is short; existence is eternal."

"You mean criminals will burn in hell? Well, I guess *you* would know."

"Let's pretend for a moment that we have a world in which everything is made of the same stuff — let's say it's made of beans. Now these are interesting beans in that they can be put together to look like anything. If you look around you'll see people, cars, houses, trees, flowers, dogs, and cats — all made of beans. Now these beans aren't permanently glued together. The beans can come apart and then be recombined to become something else. That house over there can fall apart and the beans may recombine to become a streetcar or a group of people.

"Now let's say that your mind controls what the beans do. You might want to build a bunch of beans into a beautiful ten-speed bicycle. And there it is! Suppose another entity who hasn't learned to use his beans sees your bicycle and decides to take it. If he does, he will find that because the bike was not his own construction, it will not work for him. Maybe when he tries to ride it, he'll crash. Or someone steals it from *him*. Somehow, because it's someone else's rightful materialization, it will not ever bring him pleasure or satisfaction. Or he'll find himself experiencing other difficulties, like poor health, what he perceives as bad luck or lack of success. He may come to correct his behavior. Otherwise he will probably have to learn that lesson more than once, and a sharper lesson will be given each time, because each time he commits a crime, he deals a wound to his own psyche. It will be that much harder for him to realize that he could have been using his own beans all along."

"If it were that simple, then everybody could just have a perfect life. Nobody would be sick or poor. Everybody could have everything they want just by thinking about it."

"Next time you watch Olympic figure skaters, notice how effortlessly they seem to move. It looks *so* easy, doesn't it? Flawless and beautiful. Yet, to get to that point, that skater had to fall down many times, and to train many hours a day for many years. Nothing comes to us without challenge because life on Earth is a *school*. It's the same with every achievement worth pursuing. You have to learn *how*. The bigger the goal, the more effort it takes. Some materializations are easy. Others can take a lifetime or more than one lifetime. Simple wishing won't do it. You must concentrate on your goal and then you must also do whatever is necessary. The combination of thought and emotion and determination to follow the path you want *will* materialize success. But, if you want to play the cello like Yo-Yo Ma, you must start by learning to play the cello. And then you use your beans."

"Okay, I know that the beans are just an illustration. But if you're saying that there *is* stuff like that, why can't we see it?"

"You can and you do. It's everywhere."

"You're talking atoms and molecules?"

"Something like that. The same particles that formed the dinosaurs and rocks and water also form *you*. They've always been around and they just keep recycling."

"And I can make it work by using my mind? My thoughts?"

"And emotions. Make friends with your emotions and don't fear them."

"Not even after they made me kill Frederick?"

"That was a good example of how an emotion, if suppressed, will eventually explode into an act of violence. You experienced Ellen's conflicting emotions. She was fixated on Frederick, but as you noticed, a part of her also harbored a hatred. Love and hate are closely allied. She was unable to express either emotion and reached a level of desperation. She was not able to interact with Frederick on an even footing. She was, after all, a servant who barely spoke the language. She became a seething mass of psychic energy, not unlike ball lightning. Had she been able to more clearly communicate with Frederick, the relationship might have been different. The pregnancy may not have happened. There are numerous other possible ways for that situation to have gone."

"And Noah killed Mr. Reed because he hated him?"

"Noah was another good example. Noah hated and feared every-one. He was a young man at war with his own environment. Can you imagine how frightening that would be? Everyone is your enemy or potential enemy. The only ones who will protect you are those you can dominate. You fear everyone; hence you hate everyone, most of all yourself because of your own wretchedness. We see Noahs all the time: petty tyrants and fanatical leaders who demand mindless support, terrified of being overthrown or killed. They always — what was that odd term in the old TV show? Self-destruct! Yes, that's what happens. They self-destruct. Their fear continues to fill them like an overinflated balloon and finally they just pop. If their natural aggres-sion were understood and channeled outward into creative energy, imagine how much good such people could do with their lives."

Kate had been listening thoughtfully, looking a little puzzled. Mr. Perkele smiled at her. "I don't know how much of this you'll understand, but *you really didn't cause the death of anyone.* You've been traveling through your own psyche, and in that context, Elina Niemi, Jock Ostriker, Anthony Reed, *and Wilhelmiina Hill* are all parts of your own greater entity. In a sense, they are all alternate selves of your own. All you did, with Pussykins, here, as a *cat*alyst (forgive me, I couldn't resist that one) was experience *one version of each event that took place!*" Mr. Perkele paused to let that sink in, then continued.

"There are *many* versions, all equally valid. By being there, you added *one more possible version*, and by doing so, you altered all of them. Be assured, that in another reality, Mrs. Niemi is still doing cross-stitch tablecloths, Jock Ostriker is still raising Cain, and Anthony Reed will be sitting down to his dinner of collards and sweet potato pie. In some versions, Moonrise never had a litter of kittens at all. Animals also have their alternate realities!

"What you did though, is ping the cosmic web. If you could see Mrs. Niemi now, you'd find a kinder, happier woman in place of the enraged, embittered one you knew. And she no longer talks about her house by the sea. Elina's death in that reality allowed all other versions of Mrs. Niemi to stop obsessing on her. You see, there *is* a reality in which Elina Saari actually married Frederick and *had* his baby. With all the emotions Elina had invested in it, it *had* to become a possible version of her life. In that one, she really did become the mistress of the house by the sea, and that's the bleedthrough that *your* Mrs. Niemi was picking up on.

Mrs. Niemi never owned such a house, but the other version, the Elina who married Frederick, *did*. But that reality turned out badly. It was so disastrous that its effects have been impacting negatively on *all* of Elina's realities. Killing both of them early on — Elina and Frederick — didn't wipe out the negative reality, but it did dilute it enough, by adding another, that now its impact isn't as harmful.

"It's not generally realized, but you *can* alter the past. The way you live your life today affects your past as well as your future. It's because there really is no such thing as chronological time. Time, in *my* reality, manifests differently. You only see your own version of it. It has many more properties than you would imagine. Think of it this way. You wouldn't have an accurate picture of water, if you'd only seen it as ice. The past is no more fixed than the future.

"So, as for Mr. Reed, you'd be surprised to find he's having his collards and pie at the home of his daughter, in Chuluota, Florida, with grandchildren all around him. And while he still has a few aches and pains, he regularly goes fishing with his grandsons. He doesn't need to punish himself with arthritis or loneliness."

"And what about Mr. Ostriker?"

The old man frowned, then sighed. "There's no version of Jock Ostriker at the Lodge anymore. I'm afraid he's in the psychiatric ward at the Stastas Hospital. We can't win 'em all."

"Okay, then, if there are lots of versions of everything, is there a version where *I'm* still in Stastas? And when I go back, will I meet *myself*?"

"There are a number of versions in which you remain in Stastas, but you won't be aware of those. In one of your lives, you died when you had that seizure that put you in the hospital. In another, you didn't leave school and will go on to higher education. In another, you're the daughter of a wealthy family; your dad did rather well in that one — and there's yet another in which you have a brother and two sisters. You see, anything that *can* happen, *does*, in some dimension or other. Any choice we make opens up a whole different future — call it a *possible* future.

"You're walking down a street and you decide to turn left instead of right. You've just altered your future. But there's another future that's been left behind, the one you would have had if you'd turned *right.* That becomes *another possible version* of your life, one that may be followed *by another version of you.* Of course my example is an oversimplification. There would have to be emotions involved. If you're torn between two courses of action, and enough emotion is generated, you will in fact create two versions of the event, and an alternate self will follow the one you didn't choose.

"And speaking of living in different realities, I have a little good news and bad news, as they say. It's *all* good news, really. The good news is that you, Kate, will live a long and healthy life, free of seizures and any other physical disorders. The other part is that while you may go back to Stastas — and there's a good chance that you will — *it won't be as Kate Oksa.*"

Kate stared at the old man, unsure of how to interpret what she'd just heard. *Oh no, he couldn't possibly mean. . . !* "You're *not* going to leave me here in someone else's body!"

"I think you'll find it for the best, Kate."

Kate fought back rising panic. "But how? What? I — I don't know who I am! You can't just *leave* me here. What about my parents?"

"Not to worry. This is, after all, just one version of the event. Your parents are about to start an interesting new adventure. I've spoken with each of them and taken their measure. Your father will find the success he wanted. Your mother will have the husband who can provide. They'll have the means to go on to productive lives, and their luck — both good and bad, I'm afraid — will be reflected in all their realities.

"Your father, as I said, had been trying to contact me for years, but his focus was fuzzy. He didn't have your laser-like mystic qualities. Through you, he was finally able to connect with me. And I played the part he expected. He was all too eager to sell his soul to the devil — *ha-ha* — but when I told him I wanted *yours* as well he *did* hesitate at first, but agreed when I made him an offer he couldn't refuse. Now he can either grow in understanding and come to realize that he *never* had any power to deal in souls, or he can ricochet between success and failure, triumph and guilt, until he does. We literally have all the time in the cosmic realm to learn our lessons, Kate, and you, my dear, will go on to an alternate future that will be a good one. In the version *you're* about to enter, Heikki and Helvi Oksa didn't *have* any children. You didn't like your old life. You're getting a new one. Your wish is coming true."

Kate felt herself hyperventilating. Somehow she had to make this man — this *devil* — understand that you don't just walk into someone else's life and expect to live it! She knew nothing about Mrs. Hill's early years. If she tried to pass herself off as Wilhelmiina Whatever-her-maiden-name-was, everyone would be bound to think she was crazy. She felt like leaping on the old man's chest and screaming at him to send her back to Stastas.

"Oh, and by the way, Kate. You, as Wilhelmiina *Haapala*, won't remember any of this. It would be too much to expect you to function in *this* life with memories from the future, so the future will expand for you in the fullness of time. You'll be Wilhelmiina, at least for the present, but, as Kate Oksa, you will alter *her* future for the better as well. For one thing, *your* version of Wilhelmiina will never end her days in Stastas Lodge!"

Stunned, Kate got to her feet and turned and stared at the old man and Jude. Already she was having trouble remembering what it was that was so important. The old devil smiled, a smile of surprising sweetness, his mild blue eyes fixed on Kate, as he stroked the head of the kitten.

Jude's eyes were fixed on her too, in an enigmatic look of appraisal. It was then that Kate saw what Anthony Reed had seen, and what Jeremy, that long-ago night in the cabin in Pennsylvania had seen: Jude — or Pussykins — or whatever the name of the creature really was, ducked its head forward, innocently, as a kitten might do to lick its own chest. As Kate watched, she felt the hairs on the back of her own neck rise, and a chill creep up from the base of her spine. There, on top of the kitten's head, in the space between its ears, opening slowly, was *a second pair of eyes*. The eyes were red as the coals of a campfire, and projected such wild and alien glee that Kate felt hyp-notized — and paralyzed. She stared, unblinking, not even aware that she was holding her breath, and as she did, the eyes began to fade, as if dissolving in mist, as the cat and the old man slowly vanished, and Kate, in the last moment of her Kateness, realized that she was alone in the cemetery.

CHAPTER 15

WILLIE HAAPALA guided her rental car through town, noticing that traffic in Nanaimo was becoming a nightmare of congestion. There had long been talk of a bypass, but it was still in the limbo of bureaucratic planning. The Island Highway was being four-laned, and the flowering plums along Nicol Street had been ripped out in the name of progress, replaced by some twiggy mix of varieties which would eventually afford a nice avenue of trees. For now, however, spring would not bring that solid drift of pink that had lifted spirits and carpeted the roadway with fallen petals.

Willie was used to seeing changes. She'd lived long enough to witness many. As she braked hastily to avoid a white station wagon that cut in front of her without signaling, Willie found herself thinking kindly of a time when cars had been a novelty, something you took out for a Sunday drive. If a car passed your house, everyone looked out the window to see who was driving by. Technology: It gave with one hand but took away with the other. Willie could remember growing up without television, without radio, without telephones, without electricity. Somehow they'd managed. Life had been harder, but it had been simpler and less assaulting.

I guess this launches my career as a curmudgeon! My God, I'll be seventy-nine on my next birthday! A woman my age has no business gallivanting around the country. I should be home knitting sweaters for my grandchildren and thinking up suitable epitaphs for my tombstone. Something terminal, like Time Expired *or maybe something continental, like* Occupado. *Of course I don't have any grandchildren, and I plan to be cremated.* "What's the matter, mister, don't you have any signal lights?"

The traffic seemed more nerve-racking than usual, perhaps because Willie had been driving for several hours, and perhaps because she'd spent the last ten days on Broom Island; and that was always like going back in time. There were still very few cars on the island where Willie had been born. She'd grown up there in a tiny village – a Hans Christian Andersen village – an ethnic village composed of Finnish people who lived Finnish lives. That is to say that they worked hard and conscientiously, but under all that Nordic stoicism, lay high drama, rife with convoluted relationships and seething emotions. If you were to say that Finns are stolid, you'd be right. If you called them volatile, you'd be right too. They were also friendly and distant, gregarious and reclusive, cooperative and quarrelsome, fiercely independent, yet clinging to their own kind. They were also highly suspicious, yet so honest that no one on the island had ever needed to lock a door.

Willie had loved and hated the place. The settlement had been founded back in the early 1900s, when many Finnish immigrants had come to North America to escape tsarist rule. As with other settlements that had preceded it and failed, things had gone badly. The golden dream of Utopia had foundered on the rocks of poverty, tragedy, disagreement, and mismanagement. All this happened long before Willie was born. The descendants of the early settlers, those who had remained, had gone on to make livelihoods by fishing, farming, and cutting timber.

Born in 1914, Willie's childhood (she later realized) had been idyllic in the small, family-like community. She'd gone to a *Little House on the Prairie* two-room school that had been enlarged in 1928 to a three-room schoolhouse, with four more grades added, just in time for Willie to get her high school education.

There had been an oddly pivotal incident in her last year of schooling, when Willie had been found, dazed and feverish, wandering around in the island cemetery. From that time, to the puzzlement of her parents, Willie, or Wilhelmiina, as she had then been called (usually shortened to "Miina") had become focused on leaving Broom Island. "She's changed, somehow," her mother had mused. "There's something different about her."

"She's just growing up, and there's nothing here for young people," her father had said. "Young people need to get out into the world."

Willie had never told her parents that she found their Finnishness stifling. She felt she needed to escape being swallowed up by the community. The thrust of youth compelled her to seek the world outside, the world of the English-speaking people — the *toiskieliset* (people who spoke a different language), shortened to *kieliset*. She wasn't ashamed of her heritage, but she found it too limiting, and when a young Finnish immigrant boy asked her to marry him, she said no.

Willie had married, many years later — and divorced. There had been no children. Willie rarely even thought about it anymore; it was almost as if the experience had happened to someone else. She felt a bit smug at having reached an age at which the fires of passion weren't likely to flare up again. Like menopause, it was liberating. At any rate, the relationships that she'd developed throughout her life had never been allowed to compromise what she prized most: her freedom and independence.

A retired schoolteacher, Willie had made a bit of a name for herself as an authority on the early Pacific Northwest, and was familiar with the history of both native tribes and white inhabitants of the area. She could pinpoint the degree of cousinhood and the number of "times removed" one might be in relation to an early settler.

But it was on a different sort of journey that Willie found herself tooling along the Island Highway on an August afternoon in 1993. And a beautiful day it was — warm and clear, with white puffs of cloud hanging motionless. Willie had always loved Vancouver Island for its beauty, but noted sadly how much of the forests had been cut down to make room for industrial growth and runaway housing development.

Willie passed Johnson's Farm Market, started to turn, then remembered she needed to gas up her rental car before turning it in. *Damn!* She should have filled her tank in Nanaimo. Now she'd have to find a station on the highway. She headed toward Ladysmith, spotted a gas station on her left, made an impatient U-turn, and pulled into a Mohawk: "Mother's Nature's gas station," run by First Nations.

A young native boy in a ponytail came over to fill the tank and clean the windshield. It was a pleasure for Willie not to have to get out and pump gas herself. Self-serves were taking over the world, and Mohawk, at least this one, still provided courteous, swift, and efficient service with a bit of a "down-home" touch.

The station had a convenience store; on its wall was posted a First Nations bulletin board, decorated with pictures of war canoes and cluttered with notices. In front of it was a table covered with handcrafted items for sale, including several of the Cowichan knit garments done in traditional thick, water-resistant wool yarn in natural colors, with patterns of deer, eagle, whale, or raven. Behind the table sat an impassive native woman. She seemed to be in a world of her own, detached from the hubbub of cars pulling in and out, oblivious to the young people as they rushed forth to pump gas, squeegee windshields, process credit cards, and wish everyone a good day.

Willie pulled out and backtracked to the airport. The airport in Nanaimo had been recently rebuilt, replacing what had been a series of little shacks with a new building — small, as airports go, but *skookum*, with an avenue of trees planted along the approach.

Willie returned her rental car and took a seat in the terminal to await the small plane that would take her to Vancouver. She was feeling a bit nostalgic, wondering if she'd ever be going back to her old home on Broom Island again. It wasn't going to be all that easy to sever ties with the house — or with Broom Island. Why? It wasn't as if she'd spent a lot of time there lately. Her mother had died in 1985, and Willie had only visited the old house three or four times in the past few years, just long enough to look in on the place where she and her mother had spent time every summer since the death of her father.

As she waited, Willie's thoughts kept harking back to the village of Satama. It was no longer a predominantly Finnish community. Islanders still talked of the influx of "the hippies" in the sixties, and still used that term to designate all newcomers. Indeed, on the other end of the island, Willie had seen some rather grand homes being built. "Big city people bring big city ways," an island grocer had said. "You can't leave your doors unlocked anymore."

Willie's house — The Haapala house — stood on Kaunio Road, on a hillside facing the sea. It had come very close to being sold in 1967, when Willie's father had suffered a heart attack, and the Haapalas had moved to Nanaimo in order to have better access to medical care. It had almost been sold again in 1970, when Willie's father died, and her mother, at age 74, considered herself too old to go back and cope with the house alone. Willie had rescued it by buying it from her as a summer place for them both.

Now, perhaps, it *was* time to sell. The decision wasn't as cut and dried as she'd thought it would be. There had been an inquiry about buying the property made by some professor who had visited Broom Island and fallen in love with the place. Willie had agreed to meet with him, but first she'd wanted to go look the house over with an eye to establishing a selling price. It had turned into a sentimental journey.

She'd flown in on a Sunday night, ten days ago, rented a car, spent a couple of days in Nanaimo, looking up old friends and visiting the graves of her parents. She had then driven north along the Island Highway, through Courtenay, Campbell River, past Port McNeill, and on north to Port Casper where she'd caught the Island Empress, the ferry to Broom.

Willie had always loved the half-hour ferry ride, and whenever the wind wasn't blowing too hard, she liked to stand on deck and watch the waves, the snow-capped mountains, and the familiar picture postcard view of the approaching land mass, with the village of Satama snuggled on shore.

The scene hadn't changed much through the years. The Broom Island Inn still stood, rickety now, but dominant, at water's edge. Behind it was the Broom Island Co-op, the only general store in town. Satama had a gift shop, a small convenience store in the Inn, and the Ship Out, a tiny outlet owned by old Kusti Rönkkö, where he sold a few groceries (mostly canned goods), fishing gear and bait. It was a place for fishermen to stock up before they went to sea. Sports fishermen could leave their catch to be smoked or canned by Kusti and his two sons, then shipped to them later.

The area by the ferry dock was the heart of Satama village. There were no speed limit signs, no parking meters, and no parking lots. The only traffic light on the island hung over the outdoor entrance to The Sea Hole, the bar in the basement of the Inn, and the light was always green. The strip of road was blacktopped, other areas were either dirt or gravel, and cars jockeyed around each other, nosing out parking spots in front of the Inn and the Co-op.

As Willie drove her rented Camry off the ferry, she waved, as always, to the knot of people on the steps of Danielle's gift shop, which was perched right next to the ferry terminal as if waiting to catch disembarking tourists. Danielle, a short, plump woman with bleached blond hair, was standing outside, sipping coffee out of a styrofoam cup. She smiled and waved back. Willie wasn't sure Danielle even recognized her, but people on Broom Island always waved at cars coming off the ferry.

Willie made a right turn onto Kaunio Road and drove out of the village. On her left, she passed houses and farms, comfortably settled, with enough land around them to assure privacy. Most of the buildings were old. Looking only to her left, Willie fancied that she could have been driving through a countryside in Finland. Homes were made of squared-off logs or of lumber, neat but unadorned, functional, and built to last by early Finns. Outbuildings were either painted (the ubiquitous red with white trim) or a natural weathered gray. All the homes along Kaunio road had some sign of the sea — fishnets piled up or spread to dry; a boat anchored or pulled up on shore; or at the very least, fish-float fences. The fences were all over the island: colorful cork floats threaded onto fence wires to form a pattern. A tug on a wire or a brisk wind could set the whole fence into motion.

In between the well-tended properties, stood others where the vegetation grew rampant, and the buildings looked to have been thrown together from scrap. These were the "hippie" houses of the sixties, a legacy of the Vietnam War, when draft evaders from the States had invaded Broom Island. Most were empty now, tumbledown shacks, some with "For Sale" signs. Willie noted that some had been recently sold, with evidence of new construction going on.

On Willie's right was the sea. Through a greenbelt of Douglas firs she could see the familiar rocky shoreline curving gracefully with its jumbled buildup of logs washed up on the beach. One had to be sure-footed to navigate the barrier; either climb over or jump from log to log, in order to get to the water. Island children developed the balance and agility of mountain goats. The shore was treacherous as well, the rounded stones slick with algae and seaweed. And the water was always *cold*. Broom Island wasn't a place for swimming or lying on the beach. It *was* perfect for picnics and bonfires and salmon barbecues — no shortage of firewood! It was also becoming a tourist attraction. When there wasn't a "salmon wind" to churn up sand, the waters were clear and beautiful for scuba diving. Whale Point, where orcas came to rub their bellies on the pebbly shore, was becoming a magnet for whale watchers and photographers.

Had Willie continued up Kaunio Road to its end, she would have come to Tranquil Bay, an area posh with homes of the rich and famous. More were being built all the time as the wealthy discovered Broom Island as a good place to get away from whatever had produced their wealth. Some of the houses were, indeed, already up for sale, the inhabitants having discovered that, though idyllic, the island had little by way of social life or excitement; and that Tranquil Bay wasn't all that tranquil when winter storms blew in. Most homes with decks that faced the water had heavy, see-through plastic panels mounted along the railing to minimize the blast of the wind, while still preserving the view.

The Haapala house was located about halfway between Satama and Tranquil Bay. Willie stopped at her own familiar fish-float fence, got out of the car and opened the gate. It wasn't locked, just wired shut so it wouldn't blow open in a gale. It swung with a creak. Willie picked up the familiar rock she always used to brace the gate open, then got back in the car, drove up the curved driveway and parked.

Memories! She could almost hear the voices of her parents, see their ghosts: *Isä* carrying in an armload of wood from the shed; *Äiti* going out to feed the flock of chickens. Willie could see her in the pink checkered dress that she'd sewed from the cloth of chicken feed bags. In those days, feed, flour and sugar came in cotton bags with colorful printed designs, so farmers' wives could use the fabric for clothing, curtains, or hand-made quilts. Willie, herself, had worn "chicken linen" dresses to school, as had other island children back in the 1920s and '30s. It took four bags to make a housedress.

The Haapala house was a departure from the typical Finnish architectural style. It had three stories and a railed walkway on the topmost — a widow's walk — from which her father had liked to keep a weather eye on the sea. Originally, the house had been painted red (with the usual white trim) but the paint had long since faded, worn, and weathered to a silvery, antique rust-gray. It made the house look timeless, dreamy, even a little sinister, and reminded Willie of an evocative poem by Walter de la Mare. She stood for a moment, fancying the silent old house to be crowded with "listeners" — a host of phantoms from her own past, phantoms that she, from the "world of men" might disturb, startle or dismay. Should she be intruding at all? Can anyone really go back home?

She took out her keys and opened the door and entered a large room. It was an adaptation of a typical Finnish *pirtti*. In Finland, the *pirtti* was the heart of a farmhouse — dining room, kitchen, living area, entertainment center, and temporary sleeping quarters for perhaps a dozen or more hands at harvest time. It was large enough to allow a sledge or wagon to be brought inside in winter for repairs, and was heated by a series of wood stoves. Depending on the size of the house, there could be a half-dozen of them, bricked and mortared, standing shoulder to shoulder, with iron stovetops for cooking. Each unit had its own fire box. Each had a chimney that connected to one main one. Each could be fired up as needed for cooking, baking, and heating. The *takka uuni* complex was designed for efficient use of wood, and to provide heat even in the coldest, most bitter Finnish winter.

The Haapala *pirtti* wasn't that large, nor did it have an entrance big enough to drive wagon through. The island climate was mild, compared with the one in Kajaani, where Willie's parents had come from. It did have an expanse of hardwood floor, and there was a *takka uuni*, a single unit, that her mother had liked to use for baking bread and *pulla*, even after they'd modernized the kitchen. The long wooden dining room table was still there, but the benches were gone, replaced by more comfortable chairs. It was rarely used in any case, as the house now had a large, cheery, well-equipped kitchen, and that's where Willie and her mother had taken their meals, and hosted the occasional dinner party.

There were a couple of other rooms off the *pirtti* — a small one that had once been a bedroom, later converted to a comfortable little den with a small TV set they rarely watched. (Reception was dreadful. They only got one fuzzy channel.) Willie noted that the room would be perfect for an office. All she would need to do was put in a desk and filing cabinets. She could put her Macintosh computer in there. Next to it was another small room that had been, over the years, a library, a sewing room, and a bedroom, but now was just used for storage. It had its own bathroom, as Willie's father had occupied the room briefly after his heart attack; the bath had been installed so that he wouldn't have to climb stairs.

A staircase led to the second floor where the rest of the bedrooms were. The topmost story of the house was empty. If Willie, say, wanted to convert the place into a bed and breakfast, there'd be no shortage of space. She'd have to install one or two more bathrooms, but it might be doable. Still, did she want to take on something like this in her old age? People of her age were selling their houses and moving into retirement villages.

The house smelled musty, needed airing — and probably a lot more than that, Willie mused. How much of the infrastructure could still be counted upon? Would it need a new roof, for instance? No doubt it would; a carpet of bright green moss had formed on the old shingles. Floors could use sanding and refinishing, and a lot of the old furniture would need to be replaced, although there were some nice pieces, some handmade by her father who had been a skilled carpenter. But what about the plumbing and the wiring? And the septic field? They were putting in sewers in town, but Willie doubted they'd extend beyond Satama limits. And she'd have to do something with the yard and property. Were the outbuildings still usable or were they dangerously close to collapsing — the sheds, the *sauna*, the garage, her father's workshop?

In the back of Willie's mind had been the thought that she might want to retire to Broom Island one day to do some serious writing. The prospect of returning to this, her childhood home, seemed less inviting now that she'd seen it again. Perhaps it *would be better* to unload it. It had always been much too large, built to house a family with many children — children that had never been born. It was costing her money just to keep it: property taxes, utilities, and the stipend she'd paid to a neighbor to keep an eye on the place in her absence. It would cost a lot more to refurbish it. Could she even afford it? Willie had been frugal during her working years, and had invested her earnings. She had also been the only beneficiary when her mother died. If she sold her house, she calculated that she'd probably be able to take this one on. But was it wise at her age? Her mother had moved away when she was younger than Willie was now, feeling she couldn't cope with the place. Besides, wouldn't she be lonely here all by herself? Wouldn't she feel cut off from the world, people she'd known for years? Wasn't coming back to Broom Island to live a *really dumb idea?*

On the other hand, what a great place it would be for guests — her friends from all over the world — to come visit! The house she lived in now was so small, and the guestroom so tiny, that if she had more than one visitor she had to situate them in a motel.

She'd think about it later. Now she intended to get settled, open a few windows, then later light a fire in the *takka uuni* to dry out the dampness.

Willie had ended up staying ten days and discovering that the root system that connected her to the island was still very much alive. There had been changes, and Willie, in her solitude, now had a chance to discover them. For one thing, many of the people she'd known had died. She visited the cemetery and paid silent respect as she wandered among tombstones. A new section had been annexed and added, with crisp new polished granite slabs contrasting sharply with the weathered, dissolving markers in the old section with their near-illegible lettering.

The Broom Island cemetery was located next to the sea on a gentle slope so that the dead, presumably, had a nice view—mountains and water. On one side stood a woods of huge Douglas firs; on the other, along the road, a tall, thick hedge of laurel afforded privacy to those visiting graves of loved ones. The setting was charming, and one could wander leisurely accompanied by nothing more than an occasional chattering bald eagle or a flock of ravens that seemed to like the spot. The grass was beautifully mown now, and not as it had been in Willie's youth, a tangle of weeds and brush. Many of the markers had built-in wells in the rock into which a little vase of flowers could be situated. Willie noted, with mild distaste, that some of them contained faded plastic flowers. She preferred the more organic method of remembrance, the custom of adorning graves with seashells, either scattered on top or laid out in pretty little patterns. She rather wished that the graves of her parents had been on Broom Island, but they'd died in Nanaimo and lay buried in Cedar Valley Memorial Gardens.

Willie had always liked visiting the cemetery, and it had been there that she'd had a strange experience when she was seventeen. She didn't remember much about it. She didn't even remember how she'd gotten there, but obviously she'd been ill. People didn't visit the cemetery much back then, and it was lucky that the father of one of her classmates had happened to come by. Something about her demeanor had caught his attention, and he'd asked her if everything was all right. She'd been dazed and disoriented, and the kindly neighbor had taken her in tow and deposited her at her home. There, her mother had laid a hand on her forehead, and declared that she was burning up with fever. Willie had been put to bed and given a couple of aspirin. The next day she'd been fine. Nobody knew what had happened; everyone assumed she'd had a touch of the flu.

Willie had often thought about that day. It nagged at her consciousness. To her, there had always been something more to it, but she'd never been able to remember *what*. It had been a significant time for her, in any case. Well, of course, age seventeen, for any kid, is a significant time. You're just emerging from childhood, about to come of age with the need to deal with the adult world. You've been sheltered by your family, but now you have to come up with plans as to what to do with the rest of your life. A scary time! Willie, as a schoolteacher, knew how daunting such decisions could be, when it seemed as though your entire future hinged on your SAT scores.

But Willie remembered that her own state of mind had undergone a more drastic change. For one thing, she'd dumped her boyfriend, a nice young man whose family had emigrated from Finland. His dreams were to get married and later take over his father's farm. Suddenly Willie had lost interest in him, turned down his proposal. There again, girls of seventeen dump boyfriends all the time, but it had been more than just that. Now she couldn't stand the thought of living on the island anymore. She wanted *off*. There was a new energy and determination at work within her, the sort of restlessness of spirit that makes young men run off to sea. Not unusual in the island young, but *most* unusual in Wilhelmiina Haapala who hadn't been planning anything of the kind. And what *had* young Miina been planning? Or better, what *had* young Miina been *like* as a child? Fun-loving kid with a serious side. Liked to read. Liked school. She had always thought she'd like to become a teacher and teach on the island. Then, suddenly, that's not what Miina wanted at all, in fact that's when she decided she didn't want to be called Miina anymore, nor Wilhelmiina. That's when she'd announced that she wanted to be called Willie. She still wanted to be teacher, but somewhere else, far away.

Willie mused that if she'd stayed on the island, she might have married that young man, Albin Hill. The family name had been Uusihautamäki, but they had shortened the name to Mäki, then anglicized it when they came to British Columbia, as Finnish people often did. Many family plots in the cemetery had not only Finnish and English versions of the family name, but often variations in spellings as well, as people chopped off awkward prefixes, suffixes, and eliminated double consonants and vowels. The Pikkusaarinen plot, for instance, also had the names Pikkusaari, Saari, Sari, and Little, a translation of the word *pikku.*

Willie stood looking thoughtfully at an inscription on a stone: Albin Hill, b. March 2, 1912, died April 11, 1962. Beloved husband and father. *The road not taken*! Had Willie married Albin, she'd have been a widow long ago. What would her life have become? Would she ever have left the island? Would she have become a schoolteacher? Would she have made her way to the United States? Perhaps, perhaps not. At any rate, Albin Hill died of a heart attack and was survived by his wife, Hilkka, and his son, Niilo. Willie remembered Hilkka as a sweet-faced, earnest young girl who would have been content to stay on the Hill farm and raise children. As it turned out, they'd only had the one son. Willie didn't know where Niilo had gone, but his mother, Hilkka, had sold the farm and was still living in the village.

Willie had no regrets. She'd lived a good life. She *had* become a teacher and had loved her job. She'd traveled widely, and had moved freely with few encumbrances, gathering experiences the way a bee gathers pollen. Now, if she chose, she could bring it all back to her hive here on the island, and use it in the books she hoped to write.

It wouldn't be *all* that difficult. All she really had to do was sell her house, pack her belongings, and move away from the small American town in which she'd lived and taught school. Move away from Stastas.

CHAPTER 16

It was drizzling when Willie's plane landed in Seattle. It had been an annoying flight. Usually when she visited Vancouver Island, she preferred the Victoria airport as her point of arrival and departure. This last trip, however, she'd opted for Vancouver to avoid having to make the two-hour drive to Nanaimo late at night. By day, the drive over the Malahat offered one of the loveliest views on the planet, but driving an unfamiliar rental car over the mountains through what might be heavy rain was not her cup of Earl Grey. That decision meant a return trip through Vancouver as well, and Willie hated the Vancouver International Airport with its annoying airport tax and its interminable line through Customs. On top of everything else, the plane had been late — some trouble with an auxiliary power unit — and Willie would be getting home later than she'd hoped.

Grateful to be back in her own aging white Volvo, Willie drove into the town of Stastas. She sighed as she passed the town dump, redolent yet again with the mephitis of rotting garbage, and strident with the screech of seagulls; gulls that made a daily trip inland from the ocean, then returned to the sea in the evening. Willie rather enjoyed seeing the gulls, but she wished someone would do something to control the stench and at least screen the dump with shrubbery.

Proceeding through the industrial section, she saw that they were finally tearing down Ellery Shine's old garage to make room for — *what?* The Oksa Farm Equipment dealership! Willie was not a close friend of the Oksas, but knew them as part of the Finnish community, and had always felt a bit sorry for them, particularly Helvi. The Oksas were what an Australian friend of hers would've called "battlers," making their way through life via trouble and strife. Lately, the Oksas seemed to have been buffeted by winds of fate, blown from one extreme to the other. About a year ago, their house had burned down, and they'd had to move into a mobile home park. Then, like the proverbial bolt out of the blue, Heikki Oksa had hit a lucky number on the lottery and used his winnings to open a dealership in farm equipment. Willie suspected that his wife, Helvi, had been the moving force behind that decision. Now it looked as though their fortunes must be growing, why else would they be changing to a roomier location?

The Oksas should have been one of the area's first families. As a mental exercise, Willie began a genealogical calculation: Heikki's father was Olavi Oksa, who immigrated to America in the late 1920s and shortened his name from Oksaniemi. He, in turn, was the son of Karhu Oksaniemi of Oulu, Finland who was, if Willie remembered right, the seventh cousin of Aksel Oksaniemi, who came to America in the late 1800s and became a traveling minister of the gospel. That would make Heikki his seventh cousin, twice removed. Aksel's son, Pentti was the father of Oskar who went to law school and shortened his name to Niemi. That made Heikki a ninth cousin to Oskar — an unwelcome kinship to retired big-shot society lawyer Oskar Niemi, but kinship nonetheless. With that background, if Heikki could just shun the curse of drink, he might even become respectable. *Ha! You've still got it, old girl, if you can keep all that in your head at your age.*

Of course, you can't always remember where you left your car keys.

She took a right turn and headed for her house on Cottonwood Street, on her way passing Stastas High, the school where she had taught for many years. The building hadn't changed much since she retired, except for the paint job. Lately, there had been a flurry of mural painting on public buildings, something that hadn't existed in her day. Now any blank wall in or around town could be expected to blossom out in huge, bold, colorful designs, or larger than life pictures showing town history and early geography. Stastas High, a rather unimaginative boxy building, now had walls emblazoned with scenes of the school's sporting events — football, basketball and soccer. The paintings had been conceived and executed by a talented pupil (there'd been a contest) with help from fellow students.

Willie pulled into her driveway, noticing that the grass needed cutting, and that there were a couple of weathered grocery store flyers on the lawn. She'd have to call the post office — or better yet, she might be able to make it to the post office before they closed, to pick up her mail. She hoped that the little John Deere mower/trimmer she'd left to be repaired was ready to be picked up as well. First she'd check her taped messages. There were a few: an I'll-call-back-later from a friend in Miami; a notification from the Rexall drug store that the photos she'd left to be developed were ready; a request from her bank to call back (that would be about reinvesting a maturing CD); and a message from Helvi at Oksa Farm Equipment that the lawnmower was ready to be picked up. Excellent! Willie could go get both the mower and the inside dirt on the Oksas' relocation at the same time. Nothing from the professor who was interested in the house on Broom Island. *Maybe it's just as well.*

Willie did a quick walkabout through her house and found everything as she'd left it. Her cyclamen, even though she'd moved it from the window to a cooler spot on the table, lay in a coma. She gave it a drink, knowing it would revive. If she were to sell this house and move back to Canada, how much would she miss her old life in Stastas? *Not a hell of a lot!*

Willie lived modestly. She tended to be a minimalist and had not gathered a hoard of treasures, although she could well have afforded a more luxurious lifestyle. She preferred to live lightly, to be free to travel, and her closest friendships were with people far away. Her house was small and practical, comfortable, but not lavish enough to be a target for burglars while she was off on her jaunts.

No, she wouldn't be leaving *Tara!* In fact, retirement on Broom Island would afford, if anything, a much better setting to entertain visiting friends. The house was large, the view was of sea and mountains, and even with new development going on, there was still a Shangri-La quality about the place. And if she lived another ten years, how much could they mess it up in that length of time? Sounded good, but Willie flipped the coin in her mind. She *was* nearly 80. Okay, so she was in good health — for now. But supposing, like her father, she later needed medical care? And how was she going to be able to handle keeping up that house by herself? It was *big* – built in anticipation of a family that had never materialized. Her mother hadn't thought she could cope with it at age seventy-four. Wouldn't it be more practical to sell it as well as her house in Stastas, and buy a condo in some high security building, with enough services to coddle the Queen Mum? Willie sighed. One thing that always depressed her was being practical. She didn't feel she had to decide that right away. Maybe she'd never even hear from Professor Whozis.

But Willie did. She made a quick trip to pick up her mail so as not to be gone too long in case the professor called after all. The lawnmower could wait till morning. Back from the post office, she leafed through the stack — catalogs, bills, a card from a friend traveling in Scotland, and — there it was, a letter from J. F. Banks, 706 Brighton Street, Portland, Maine. It was dated August 17th — ten days ago:

Dear Miss Haapala:

I plan to be in Stastas on the 27th of this month, and would be grateful if you could take the time to meet with me regarding your property on Broom Island. As you know, I'm looking for a house with acreage as a retirement home for myself. If you have made the decision to sell your house on Kaunio Road, I would be most interested in buying it.

There is also another matter upon which I would very much like to confer with you. I am doing genealogical research on one of the Broom Island families, and was told that you were the person to contact. Possibly we could have dinner together. I am eagerly looking forward to meeting you. I'll be staying at the Stastas Inn and will call you from there.

Cordially,

J.F. Banks

Hmmm. The 27th. Why, that's today! Willie felt caught off guard, and a little annoyed. She realized that she simply wasn't ready to make a decision about selling her house yet. The professor would just have to hold his water. She wondered what sort of professor he'd been. He must be retired now. She glanced at the clock. He might be calling at any moment. Willie laughed ironically, thinking it had been a long time since she'd been on a blind date. She wondered what she should wear. Something stuffy and conservative, she thought. He sounded old-fashioned — old-fashioned enough to actually write a letter when he could have called and left a message on her machine.

Willie took a quick shower, then looked at herself in the bathroom mirror, wishing she had time to get her hair done. As a little girl, Willie's hair had been white. *Liina tukka*, they'd called her — towhead. In the early sixties, on her first trip to Finland, Willie had been amused to see replicas of herself everywhere in the white-blond Finnish kids. She'd been reminded of a movie, *The Village of the Damned*, in which the children had all been aliens with glowing eyes and white hair. As she'd grown older, her hair color had deepened to golden blond. Now it had returned to white again. Not gray, she adamantly maintained, but just about the same color that it had been in childhood. She liked to wear it short, a halo of curls, easy style, low-maintenance. Now the curls needed trimming, and she could also use a perm. Exposed to ten days of salt sea air on Broom Island, her old permanent had lost its will to live. Well, there wasn't much she could do about it now, except give it a quick blow-dry. Willie made a mental note to call Rose, her hairdresser, to see if she could fit her in the next day. Morning would be good. Willie could pick up her lawnmower, then get her hair done.

...

And so it was that at seven, on Friday evening, August 27th, Willie Haapala, smartly dressed in a blue and white, two-piece, polka-dot jersey knit that set off her freshly shampooed white locks, stepped into the dining room of the Stastas Inn. The professor had sounded pleasant on the phone, and she recognized him immediately, although she hardly needed ESP to do so; his was one of the three occupied tables in the room. The other two were taken up respectively by an elderly couple, and another that looked to be a family birthday celebration complete with party hats and cake with candles.

The professor had iron-gray hair and was a bit of a cliché in his Harris Tweed jacket with elbow patches. When he spotted Willie, he stood up, and Willie saw he was quite tall. *Good-looking in a dusty sort of way. Wonder if he's married. It didn't sound like it. He didn't say he wanted a retirement home for him* and *his wife.*

Professor Banks extended his hand. "Miss Haapala." Like most non-Finns he pronounced it "Huppalluh," making the soft, Finnish "p" into a "puh" instead of the sound somewhere between a "b" and a "p." The Finnish "p" and "t" confound the English tongue, just as the English "th" is frustrating to Finns who flatten it to a "t" or "d" or even try to fake it with an "f." rendering the town of Ladysmith to

Ladysmiff. "I've been looking forward to this. I'd planned to come a few weeks earlier, but there was a family emergency and I'm afraid it took precedence over everything else."

Willie shook hands. Family emergency? Maybe he *was* married after all. "I'm so sorry. I hope everything is all right with your family now."

"Yes, well, I guess you might say that everything is resolved now. But please sit down, Miss Haapala." He helped her get seated, and Willie mentally acknowledged how *nice* old-fashioned manners were. They lent a grace to living, and only the elderly observed them anymore. These days feminists make a business of resenting it if a man opens a door for them; and many men, particularly those of Willie's generation, still insisted on doing it regardless. Willie called it the "ERA ballet:" when a woman pushes open a door and the man behind her can't bring himself to just walk through, so he reaches past her shoulder to make a show of holding that door open, if it kills him, until she releases *her* hold, leaving him in sole possession, and, goddammit, a gentleman to the last!

"Actually, Professor Banks, this worked out very well. I only just got back from Broom Island and found your note."

Professor Banks smiled a bit sheepishly. "I *did* try calling, but I got your answering machine, and I just can't talk into those things. I'm afraid I'll stutter or say something stupid, and it's so irretrievable!"

"The one *I* hate is 'call waiting.' If I'm on the phone, I don't *want* to know if anyone is trying to get through."

"I guess that's what I like about your Broom Island. It gives the impression of being cut off from all that."

"Not really; not anymore. There are computers and modems and fax machines and satellite television for those who choose to have it. But when I was growing up there, we didn't even have electricity. Everything was gas — gas lamps, gas washing machines, and even gas irons for pressing your shirts. You still see them in the museum. Power didn't come in until long after I'd left in 1951, and telephones not till 1957."

"How did you end up in Stastas, Miss Haapala, if you don't mind my asking?"

"Oh, just lucky, I guess." Willie's laugh always astonished people. It was a hearty guffaw, short, loud, and more suited to a madam in a bordello than to a frail, white-haired schoolteacher. "No, it was *kismet.* As a young girl, I couldn't wait to get off Broom Island. After I finished high school, I went on to become an elementary school teacher. Then, after World War II, I moved to the States — better opportunities, new adventures. I continued my education and went on to teach high school. Stastas had a job opening and I took it. I never dreamt I'd be there for the rest of my life!"

"You never married?"

"Once, briefly. That's how I *really* came across the border. A post-war bride. It didn't work out."

"I'm sorry."

"It was doomed from the start. I wanted Cary Grant and *he* wanted Lizabeth Scott."

Professor Banks grinned, his face breaking out in a pattern of laugh lines that, oddly enough, made him look more boyish. "Lizabeth Scott?"

"You remember her from the 1940s movies? She always played the sultry-voiced blonde stranded in a bus station, waiting for which-ever came along first, a bus or Van Heflin. She had the devotion of a cocker spaniel, if not the intelligence, and desperately needed a man to keep her out of jail."

Professor Banks laughed. "We're the generation that had our youthful dreams shaped by Hollywood."

"Oh, in my case, it wasn't youth, I'm afraid. Just bad judgment. I was in my thirties! You see, I don't marry in haste; I only repent at leisure. But what about you? Are you married, Professor?"

Professor Banks shook his head. "No. I guess I've always been too wrapped up in my work."

"And what sort of professor are you, Professor?"

"Astronomy."

"Well, aren't we a pair! History and astronomy. You have your eye on the stars, I dig up ancient dirt."

...

Willie and Professor Banks had enjoyed a pleasant dinner of steamed prawns in herb sauce and a bottle of sparkling wine. Now, over coffee, it seemed time to get to the heart of their meeting.

"Your house on Broom Island is just what I've been looking for. I probably shouldn't say that, but I'm no good at dickering."

"I'm sorry, Professor Banks. I fear I'm here under false pretenses. I haven't yet decided to sell. I'm sure it would be a practical thing to do, but suddenly I'm having second thoughts."

"I don't blame you. If it were mine, I'd never sell it."

"If I *were* to sell it, it would be comforting to know that someone would continue to love it and care for it. It's just that I'm not sure I wouldn't want to retire there myself, you see."

"Why wouldn't you? It's a beautiful place!"

"Oh, old age and cold feet, I suppose. People my age are moving into places where they don't have to worry about mowing the lawn or re-roofing the house. There, you see, now *I'm* the one who's said too much to a prospective buyer."

Professor Banks laughed. "I guess we're the reason people hire realtors. Anyway, my offer stands, roof or no roof. One expects that an old house is going to need repairs."

"I'm not usually this indecisive and I do promise that I'll give you a definite answer before you leave Stastas. But you also said in your letter that you were researching an island family?"

"Yes, Susi. The name of the family is Susi. It's Finnish, isn't it?"

"Yes. It translates to 'wolf.' There was a family by that name on

Broom Island but not anymore."

"There was a family — a very old family, dating to the Civil War, in rural Pennsylvania. The name Susi was engraved on a tombstone at the site of their farm. The name was all I could make out on the stone marker."

Willie thought back for a moment. "As far as I can remember, the Susi family settled on Broom Island much later, not until the early 1900s. Is it possible that a member of your Pennsylvania Susis might have immigrated to Canada? I seem to remember that there was some sort of tragedy connected with that family."

"A suicide, perhaps?"

"Yes," Willie said, trying to recall, "You may be right, Professor Banks. I do believe there was a suicide, but something else as well."

"Oh, please, call me Jeremy, Miss Haapala."

"Willie, please, by all means. Are you connected in some way with the Susis?"

Jeremy Banks hesitated for a moment. "I wasn't going to go into that, but at the risk of having you think me certifiable, here goes. Many years ago, I lost someone very close to me at the site of the Susi farm. We were boys together, very close friends. His name was Jock Ostriker."

Willie cocked her head. Ostriker? Was that a name she'd heard? For a moment there it sounded almost familiar. No, she guessed not, then shook her head to indicate that the name meant nothing to her.

"I'd known Jock since we were children. It was in the summer of 1937. Jock had insisted on going into the woods to look for a Civil War gravesite. Out of nowhere, he'd developed an interest in old cemeteries, said he wanted to do rubbings of old gravestones — that sort of thing. He'd been acting strangely. Distant. Moody. He was also having nightmares. He'd thrash about in his sleep and wake up screaming. He was never able to explain much of it, but I had a feeling that he was somehow convinced he was experiencing something from another life. Nobody believed in reincarnation in those days, but from what Jock told me, he seemed to be tapping into something like that."

Oh shit. This guy's gay. Ostriker, whoever he was, was his lover. Oh well! "I wouldn't discount reincarnation, Jeremy."

Jeremy looked relieved. "I'm so glad! It's the first hurdle. I was afraid you'd get up and leave."

"I'm not leaving. I'm intrigued."

"We found — well, Jock found — the site he was looking for, and it affected him strongly, emotionally. Then a thunderstorm came up and we had to leave, but later Jock insisted on going back there alone. Willie, he went back to the spot, and at the site of a stone that had the name "Susi" cut into it, he put the barrel of a hunting rifle in his mouth and pulled the trigger."

"Good God!"

"He *could've* wanted to kill himself. There were reasons. He had, as I said, been acting strangely. He was having emotional swings. He talked like someone I didn't know, made references I couldn't follow. And he claimed to have lost his memory. I didn't believe him, but he claimed not to know who he was."

"And you believe that somehow this reincarnational self took over and prompted the suicide? That he'd somehow transformed into a member of the Susi family?"

"I don't *know*. That's what's been haunting me all these years. You realize, of course, that all this was over fifty years ago! I . . . I felt so *guilty*. I never should have let him go back to that place alone. I should've insisted on going with him. Maybe I could've stopped him."

"You say that your friend *could* have wanted to kill himself. You mean the Jock Ostriker you knew had reason to be despondent?"

"Yes. And that's what haunts me. If Jock killed himself, it may not have been because of me, but I certainly contributed. I was putting pressure on him."

"You were lovers."

Jeremy met Willie's gaze. "Yes. I was a little older than Jock. He was at a vulnerable stage in his life. Nobody knew he was gay. I think he was still fighting it himself. His father was a hard man, and Jock was terrified of him. In those days being homosexual, as it was called, was a terrible family disgrace."

"Not that different now," Willie said. "I think the world *is* opening up, growing up, but it's a slow and painful process."

"I wanted us to go away. There was no future for us where we were. I wanted us to go to Europe and study there. I suggested it to him, but he claimed, at that point, to have no memory of anything. I thought he was just making it all up to avoid the issue. And then he insisted on going back to that place. And like an idiot I tried to stop him, told him he might get lost or break a leg. He said he'd take the rifle so he could signal me. He wouldn't have had that gun with him if it hadn't been for me."

"It must have been terrible for you."

"I heard the shot. It was still light when I went looking for him. I'm not a very good woodsman, I'm afraid, but I found my way to where we'd been earlier. I think I knew even before I saw him what I was going to find."

"He was at the Susi farm?"

"Yes, although there was nothing left. No buildings. Everything was overgrown. I didn't see him at first. I called but there was no answer. He'd said the cemetery was on up along the stump fence. Earlier that afternoon, we'd seen an old man going in that direction, so I took the same path. And I found him."

"He'd found the gravesite."

"Yes. Such as it was. It looked like he'd been digging around a stone, trying to uncover the name on it." Jeremy's eyes were so full of pain that Willie dropped her own. She had a feeling that this was something Jeremy had never really talked about, but that he needed to do so now.

"What did you do?"

"I . . . I couldn't leave him there. It would be dark soon. There might be predators. I don't know how I managed it but I got him back to the cabin. It was getting dark by then, and too late to strike out on foot to notify anyone. Maurice . . . Maurice was a friend of ours. He was the one who had driven us to the hunting cabin and left us there. He was coming to pick us up but not for a couple more days. Willie, that was the longest night of my life!"

"However did you get through it?"

"Well, I guess I know why they call it a 'wake.' I didn't sleep, of course. Mostly I just talked to Jock. I guess I tried to make some sort of sense out of what had happened. I cried. I yelled at him. I said awful things. I kept asking him *why*. I reminisced about our boyhood. Do you remember the time, Jock, when we. . . ." Jeremy paused to silently revisit whatever had followed.

"It must have been a nightmare," Willie murmured.

"You know, Willie, I think at one point I'd convinced myself that it *was* a nightmare. That whole experience was dreamlike. It seemed monstrous that in an instant your whole life can be plunged into chaos. It didn't feel as if it could be real. Odd things kept happening. That old man in the cemetery and the kitten howling."

"Kitten?"

"Yes, I'd found it in the woods earlier when were hiking, looking for whatever it was that Jock was trying to find. It was black and tiny and lost — and looked to be sick. I thought perhaps its mother had abandoned it. I couldn't just leave it there, so I brought it back to the cabin. We were trying to take care of it, nurse it along, but then it disappeared. It was gone when I got back. Must have gotten out. At any rate, I don't remember seeing it, although in my state of mind I probably wouldn't have noticed." Jeremy paused. "Yes. The kitten was . . . strange." He seemed to shake off a memory.

"Anyway, after I'd carried Jock back to the cabin, it was too late to do anything but wait till morning. The next day I set out on foot as soon as it got light. I must have been a frightening sight myself, disheveled and covered with blood. I made my way down to the road and had to walk three miles to where there was a gas station and a little store. I got there before they opened and then I had to wait an hour before anyone showed up.

"We'd stopped there for gas on the way up, and the man who ran the place had been barely civil to us. I guess the sight of me waiting for him reinforced his feeling about outsiders. He let me use his phone. He seemed rather eager at that point to let me use it. Anything to get rid of me, I guess. He probably thought I was a mass murderer. I called the police. They came, and I rode back to the cabin with them. Amazing how clearly I still remember it all even though it was so long ago."

"At that point, you must have been at least somewhat relieved that it was over."

"It wasn't, quite. I think they thought I'd killed Jock. I'd moved the body from the scene, you see, and I certainly looked the part. I had to take them to where it had happened."

"You had to go back to the graveyard?"

"Yes. The rifle was still back there. Scene of the crime."

"They didn't seriously think you'd killed him!"

"They asked a lot of questions, of course. There was an investigation, but the nature of the wound made it clear it had been self-inflicted. The worst of it was dealing with Jock's family and my own. It became a major scandal. Jock's family blamed me. They may not have known why, but they blamed me. *I* blamed me."

"Surely no one could have held you responsible."

"No, they couldn't, and maybe it would have been more clear-cut if they *had*. It was just that now our relationship, Jock's and mine, became a *cause célèbre* of speculation and innuendo. My family and I became the target of stares and whispers. It was the proverbial last straw. My father and mother wanted me *out*. Not just out of the house, but out of town, perhaps out of the country. In a perverse way, it gained me my freedom. But I've never been free of the sense of guilt."

"Then it would help to know about the connection with the Susi family," Willie said. "You may not have had anything to do with Jock's suicide. Was there any other name on that tombstone? First name, perhaps, or any other stones with names carved on them?"

"No. It was almost as if someone had it carved it rather hurriedly. Or maybe someone had found the task too difficult and just left it at that, as more of a marker than a memorial stone. Perhaps it had been a hasty burial. Maybe the intention was to do a proper job later. Or maybe nobody was left alive to *do* a proper job."

"Burials weren't as structured then," Willie said. "If, for instance, some ancestor of Jock Ostriker committed suicide at that site, he might not have been found right away. Neighbors could have come upon the remains and buried whatever was left to bury. Someone could have cut the name into a stone, as you say, as a marker. Even if he'd been discovered soon afterwards, it would have been logical to put him in the same ground, specially if there were other Susis already buried there."

"The markers were nothing more than rocks from a field. I tried researching the Susi family on computer through a historical society, but found no burial records, at least so far. The society is in the process of documenting the area, and asking anyone with information about the early settlers to contact them. The name was known, and I found a brief reference to the fact that the area used to be known as Susi Hollow, but that's all."

Willie sat silent. There was something elusively evocative about Jeremy Banks's story — about Jeremy Banks himself. She'd sensed it when she first walked into the room. Willie had, throughout her life, experienced an odd phenomenon at meeting people. Every so often, she'd meet someone for the first time and have, fleetingly, the absolute conviction that this was a person she already knew. So compelling was it, that the first few times it happened to her, she actually greeted the individual as an old friend, only to end up muttering embarrassed apologies when she realized that she didn't know them at all — *couldn't* have met them before. Jeremy Banks was one of those. To Willie's eyes, at first glance, Jeremy's face had been almost as familiar as that of a family member. She'd learned to mask this reaction, but she also knew that anyone who entered her life, and was thus "recognized," would live to play some significant part in it.

"Jeremy, think back on that day. You say Jock was behaving strangely. Was he speaking like someone from the past? Was he taking on the personality of someone from the Civil War period? I'm not saying that's what happened, but he could've been delusional and living out the fantasy."

Jeremy shook his head helplessly. "It's not that simple. Yes, he did behave like a different person, but it wasn't anything I could put my finger on. Actually, if anything, he was *breezy*, rather flip and worldly. I sometimes felt he was laughing at me. *That* was the difference, you see. Jock wasn't like that. Jock was much more subdued. Silent, sometimes even brooding. He was . . . *intense.* Jock wasn't inclined to be a comedian, but that day, when he left to go back to the farm site, he was making jokes and telling me I had nothing to worry about. As I said, he only took the gun because I was concerned about his going alone. At that point I could never have guessed that he'd use it on himself."

"I don't know, Jeremy. People do funny things. He doesn't sound like a man about to commit suicide, but sometimes when a person has made up his mind to kill himself, he can actually become euphoric. His troubles will soon be over, you see. He's found a solution to his problems."

"It was horrible. That whole time was so strange. We followed a figure through the mist, and then the freak rainstorm came up, and there was just an overwhelming sense of doom about all of it. That cabin in the woods — I guess kids today would say that place had 'bad vibes.' I was beginning to hallucinate, myself."

"Oh? How so?"

"Oh, I don't know. I told you we'd found a kitten lost in the woods. It probably had distemper, and I was trying to take care of it. But there was something strange about the animal. It . . ." Jeremy seemed to think better of what he was about to say. "Its presence fed my dark fancies, I guess. It was a stressful time and the mind plays tricks.

"I'm wondering now if there *could* be anything to the reincarnation thing — did some member of the Susi family commit suicide on that site, and could Jock have had some connection to the family? I don't know that any of his ancestors were Finnish."

"Sad to say, Jeremy, we Finns are *always* committing suicide. Scratch any Finnish family, and you'll find someone who's either hanged themselves or shot themselves — the two favorite methods. I don't know why that is. Maybe it's the climate. It either induces dark despair or blind rage. Take the Vikings, for instance, the scourge of their times. I understand that early on they all used to be butterfly collectors." (There, now she'd made him smile.) "Tell you what, I may know of someone who might be able to give you some family history on the Susis. There's a woman in Stastas Lodge. She's in her nineties, and I think she may be wandering a bit, but she *is* a member of the Susi family."

"Here? In Stastas? That's an amazing coincidence!"

"Not really. There was a strong Finnish community in Stastas, and back then Finns always migrated to where there were Finns. During the Depression, everyone migrated to where there might be jobs. Stastas was a mining town back then, and many Finns found work as hard-rock miners. A lot of Finns here have ties to British Columbia. Finnish people are also great travelers. The joke is that there are five million Finns in Finland — and another ten million traveling around the world. And they always seem to find their own kind. Now, of course, second and third generations are being absorbed into mainstream North America but there are still pockets, like Lake Worth, Florida, for instance, where you'll still hear Finnish spoken on the streets.

"Augustina Susi was living on Broom Island as a young girl. She met her husband when he came there on a visit. They married, and as he was connected with the Stastas mining industry, she, of course, ended up here. She's always been a formidable woman, and it's possible that if she likes you and happens to be in the right mood, she may be able to help you. I'll take you there tomorrow and introduce you. Her married name is Norland."

...

Willie had dropped Jeremy at his hotel and returned home, still preoccupied by her encounter with the professor. Nice man. But *why* did she have such a persistent feeling that she knew him? Willie had never met him before, couldn't possibly have! In the past, whenever Willie experienced feelings of recognition, they were usually fleeting, not nagging. When she'd first laid eyes on the man she eventually married, she'd had a strong flash of it when they were first introduced. Romantically, she'd called it love at first sight — that feeling of "I've known you all my life" — that lovers experience. (Later, after disillusionment set in, the memory of it smarted like a paper cut.)

To a greater and lesser degree, Willie had thus recognized people from time to time. Some had become lifelong friends, and Willie sometimes wondered whether there *could be* something to reincarnation, and the meeting of old acquaintances over and over in various lifetimes. There was another evocative element too in these incidents of recognition. Once, she'd had an affair with a man with "Egyptian eyes." The man did not look at all Egyptian, but to Willie, his eyes always did. Just as one school principal had been, to Willie, Syrian. In his case too there was nothing tangible to indicate this, as he was of Scottish ancestry; but whenever she made eye contact with the man, to Willie, he was Syrian. In both cases Willie found it interesting that the man with the Egyptian eyes had a strong interest in Egypt, and confided to Willie that if he ever went to Egypt, he thought he could find the legendary secret chamber between the paws of the Sphinx. She hadn't known the "Syrian" principal all that well (he'd been her boss); but Willie learned that he had traveled extensively throughout the Middle East.

Now here was Professor Jeremy Banks with not one, but two reasons to seek out Willie Haapala. Perhaps she *would* end up selling him her house. And she would at least *try* to set up a meeting with Augustina Norland. She considered calling the Lodge in the morning and making an appointment, then decided against it. Dealing with Augustina Norland was iffy. Willie remember how, a couple of years ago, she'd wanted to interview her for an article she was doing for a magazine. Augustina had been all queenly graciousness, that is, until the day came. Then she suddenly backed out and flatly refused to see her. Willie had realized ruefully that if she'd conducted the interview on the spot, there would have been no problem. She didn't blame Augustina. At her age, she probably had days when some body part was aching, and that alone could turn her cranky and capricious. No, best just to show up at the Lodge with Jeremy in tow. If Mrs. Norland was feeling up to it, her curiosity alone might gain them audience. Calling ahead of time might only give her time to think of a reason to refuse.

Willie got ready for bed. She had a busy day planned: lawnmower at nine; hair appointment at ten; lunch with Jeremy at the Stastas Inn at noon; then possibly a meeting with Mrs. Norland. She got into bed and picked up a novel she'd just started reading, but found she couldn't concentrate. The day's events kept intruding; Jeremy Banks kept intruding. She put the book down, turned out the light, and stared into the darkness. *Who* was *that masked man?* Sometimes when Willie was presented with a problem or a question, she found that by altering her state of consciousness she could "see things." It was an exercise in meditation she'd developed over many years, and used it not only to contact her subconscious mind, but also as a means of getting to sleep on those nights when sleep was hard to come by.

She would lie, staring into the darkness, allowing her body to relax until her mind stopped racing. She would then concentrate on seeing nothing, only blackness, as if she were looking at a large blackboard. If a vision intruded, she pictured herself rubbing it out with a chalkboard eraser. Once she was able to suspend thought and see only darkness, she would begin to deliberately create images. She would start by thinking of something simple, like "apple," then wait until the apple appeared before her eyes. The pictures often surprised and amused her. Instead of her old familiar Volvo, the word "car" might produce an image of a streetcar or just a hood ornament. "Flower" might appear as a bag of flour. As she continued the exercise, moving deeper into an altered state, the images became brighter and more distinct. "Jeremy Banks," she said, then was quickly yanked back into full wakeful alertness, her heart racing. Before her eyes had flashed a picture, but it wasn't Professor Banks, at least, not as she knew him. It was boy. A young man with dark hair and brown eyes. He was holding something in his arms, but the picture flashed by so fast Willie didn't get a good look at what it was. An animal? A pet? Willie tried to bring the picture back but found she couldn't. The experience had unsettled her, and she could no longer induce the relaxed state she needed.

That had certainly been odd . . . and unexpectedly disturbing. Professor Jeremy Banks, man and boy! Where could Willie possibly have met either? Yet *she knew she had*, and she also realized that whatever history they shared had complicated, and perhaps darker, undertones. Willie lay in bed, eyes closed, probing within her mind, trying to focus memories that only eluded, teased, and seemed to mock, until she finally drifted off to sleep.

CHAPTER 17

SATURDAY MORNING was bright and sunny as Willie drove through the industrial section of Stastas, past Cadwallader & Son Lumber, over the railroad tracks, then pulled into the parking lot at Oksa Farm Equipment. Clearly the Oksas needed a bigger place. The parking lot was much too small and the store itself, which previously had been a plumber's supply shop, was crowded with machinery: lawnmowers, weed whips, garden tillers, chipper/shredders, and lawn tractors — all jammed together in a jumble of metal. Chain saws, belts, and spare parts hung from the walls. Helvi Oksa was sitting behind the counter, working at a cluttered desk area behind it, so that only her head was visible. Willie called out a cheery good morning.

Helvi looked up, gave Willie a thin smile and shoved a piece of paper across the counter: the bill. Willie opened her bag and dug out her VISA card from her wallet. Helvi processed the payment. "Your mower's in back. Barry will bring it out and put it in the car."

"I see you're going to be moving to a new location up the road. Business must be good." Willie said conversationally.

"It's been tolerable," Helvi answered, with the caution of one who has been undercut by the Norns so many times that the very acknowledgment of good luck carries the danger of its immediate reversal.

"You could certainly use more space. Farm machinery must take up a lot of room."

"We can't keep any big items in stock here," Helvi agreed. "We have to order nearly everything, and that always takes time, and folks don't like to have to wait." Helvi seemed to be relaxing a bit, letting down her habitual guard. "Got time for a cup of coffee? I just made a fresh pot."

"Sure," Willie said, a bit surprised. She'd known Helvi when she was schoolgirl; both Helvi and her husband, Heikki, had been in her history class in Stastas High back in the early sixties. Helvi had been at an awkward age then— tall, self-conscious, and so terribly shy that Willie had wondered if she had any friends at all. Heikki she remembered mostly for his truancy — the empty seat in the third row — and it had come as a total surprise to Willie to hear that the two had married. Of course, as so often in the Finnish community, there had been the usual malicious little rumor that Helvi must have been pregnant; whether there was any truth to it was never verified. In any case, the Oksas had never had children.

Willie and the Oksas were not close friends by any means, but she'd always been aware of their doings. Any mention of a Finnish name will resound upon a Finnish ear like a Klaxon. Nationality is so ingrained in the Finnish psyche that if one Finn excels, all puff with pride, and if one is disgraced, all squirm under the sting of the humiliation. Any event becomes galvanically interesting to a Finn if it turns out that anyone involved is a *suomalainen.*

"Cream and sugar?"

"Just black, thanks." Willie looked at Helvi and had a momentary surge of affection for the dark-haired, solemn-eyed, careworn woman in front of her. She raised her cup. "Well, here's to your success.

May your business continue to prosper and may you both live long to enjoy it."

"Well, thank you, Miss Haapala." Helvi said, addressing her as she had in high school. "It's been a blessing, this place." She sighed. "We've certainly had our ups and downs. Guess it's no secret that Heikki likes to take a drink now and then. This place is giving him something to do. Of course, he can't pick up anything heavy with his bad back, but we hire young boys to do lifting."

"Too bad you don't have a big strapping son to help you out."

"We weren't blessed. So we just hire local kids though they're not always reliable. They usually don't stay long, but there's no shortage of them either. We have to find a good mechanic though. Barry's turned out to be very handy with machinery, but he won't be with us much longer. If you hear of anybody, let me know."

"I don't know of anyone offhand, but I'll keep it in mind. It would be a good job for someone." Willie sipped her coffee.

"We don't want anyone who's on drugs. Seems like that's all the kids do these days."

"That does seem to be a problem," Willie agreed. "That place you're buying? Ellery Shine's garage? Didn't that used to be a hangout for drug users?"

"You should have seen it!" Helvi said. "You wouldn't *believe* the filth! And the *smell!* How those people could stand it, I don't know. It was disgusting. I said to Heikki, we'll tear the whole building down. We don't want any part of it."

"Were there people still using it? There wouldn't have been any utilities hooked up."

"It was worse than a dump. Power and water been turned off long ago, but I guess them that used it didn't care much about that. Looked like a bunch of filthy animals had been living in it. But not anymore. They'll have to find another headquarters."

Willie put down her coffee cup and glanced at her watch. "I'd best be going. I have an appointment at Rose's to get my hair done."

"I'll get Barry to help you." Helvi turned her head and raised her voice, "Hey, Barry, Miss Haapala is here for her mower." Then, to Willie, "Barry will bring it out the back way and put it in your car."

Willie went out and opened the trunk of her Volvo. The machine, a small trimmer-mower, was fairly light in weight and the handle telescoped for transport. The young man in a tank top (Barry of the bulging muscles, Willie noted) lifted it easily. "I had to put a new recoil spring in it. That's why the pull rope didn't work. Spring was busted."

"You're Barry Harwood, aren't you? You went to Stastas High, didn't you?"

"Yes, ma'am." Barry looked a bit puzzled.

"Oh, you wouldn't remember me. I used to teach there many years ago, but aren't you the one who's responsible for all those beautiful murals on the school wall? I saw your picture in the paper when you won the contest."

Barry grinned, the artist in him pleased to be recognized. "Yes, ma'am."

"I think they're very good. I hope you're continuing with your artwork. You could have a excellent career as an artist."

"Yes, ma'am, I am. I'm working summer jobs so I can save money and go to art school."

"Good for you and best of luck." Willie smiled, gave him a wave as she drove off. *Nice young man. Good-looking boy. Now if I were only a hundred years younger! He seems clean-cut, too. See? Not all young people are aimless or on drugs.*

Next stop was Rose's beauty salon. Rose of the Magic Fingers, was Willie's ironic name for Rose McKinley who had been doing Willie's hair for many years; and Willie kept going back to her, even though there was always some surprise element in Rose's handiwork. Willie had already been through a number of haircuts and styles that she didn't want again, thus having invested time and direction: "Rose, next time do *not* use bluing!" "Rose, the shaved sides are really *not* me." Willie hoped that eventually, just like those theoretical monkeys with typewriters who, by laws of chance, would reproduce all the world's literature, Rose would be bound one day to come up with the perfect cut and style.

Over the years, Rose's business had grown from a single chair to five, and she now had a couple of assistants. She catered mostly to mature women, but the last assistant she'd hired was a girl in her early twenties, intended to attract younger clientele.

Rose had agreed to "do" Willie at ten, a wee bit reluctantly, since she already had several appointments booked for the morning. It was the politics of Hair: Willie had given Rose short notice; Rose was telling Willie that while it was inconvenient, she would accommodate her, as an old customer. Willie had expressed appreciation. Both women knew it had been more of a negotiation. The tip would be larger than usual.

When Willie arrived, no one was there except the staff. "Give me a good, tight perm, Rose, so it'll last a while. No coloring. No streaks. No spikes. Oh, and just keep the length even; that ridge in back last time made me look like Woody Woodpecker."

Rose was using her magic fingers to snip the ends off the old permanent. "You have very fine hair, Willie, but there's still lots of it. If you let it grow longer, we could do more with it."

"I just want hair I don't have to fuss with. Wash and wear."

As they were talking, Willie saw, through the plate glass window, a van drive into the parking lot. The driver opened the door and helped two old women disembark and escorted them into the salon. He then went back and lifted another out bodily, carried her inside, and gently set her into the chair next to Willie. "There you go, sweetheart. See? We don't need the wheelchair. When you're done, Prince Charming will be happy to carry you back again."

The old woman giggled. "Oh, Ben, I feel just like Scarlett O'Hara."

Everyone laughed, including Willie. She knew these women: Lauralee Beatty, Fanni Hartikainen — and "Scarlett O'Hara" was Mamie Schuler. They were all residents of Stastas Lodge.

"Good morning, ladies. What's the latest gossip at Space Command?" Willie asked with a grin.

"Well, let's see. Oh, we're getting a Tai Chi class next week," Fanni said. "I'm going to sign up for it, even if Martti can't." Fanni and Martti Hartikainen had been residents of the Stastas Retirement Village until Martti's Parkinson's disease had confined him to a wheelchair. They'd recently moved into the area referred to as The Lodge and were, at the moment, the only married couple living on the first floor. Fanni was leaning back with her hair in a tray while Penny, the young assistant, gave her a shampoo. "Any exercise that a 90-year-old Chinese woman can do, should be right up my alley."

"Me too," Lauralee Beatty said, her hair worked on by Iris who was dividing her time between Lauralee and Mamie. "And I'm going to sign up for the Wednesday square dance classes as well. You should come, Willie."

"Sounds like fun," Willie said, bleakly picturing herself in flat shoes, a knee-length crinoline skirt, do-si-doing. She wouldn't have minded the dancing, but she *hated* the costume, thought it would make her look silly. *As opposed to sitting here, in front of God and everybody, with a terrycloth towel around my neck with Rose putting perm rods in my hair.* She closed her eyes and listened to the conversation going on around her, while her head was being swabbed, then bagged in plastic, with wads of cotton batting wedged along the edges to keep lotion from running down her face. The smell of the chemicals was making her a bit queasy, and she silently vowed the day would come when she'd no longer be putting herself through this. If it hadn't been for Jeremy Banks, she might not even be here today.

"Yes, you should just move into the Lodge and join us," Lauralee was saying. "A lot of your old friends are there, and we all have *such* a good time. It's nice not to have to worry about cooking or keeping house. Of course, there's always a waiting list, and if I were you I'd get my name on it as soon as possible."

Willie uttered a noncommittal "Hmmm."

"You know, Willie," Lauralee said. "My roommate, Editha Coffey isn't going to be around much longer. She's not that old. She's only 88, but she's *so* frail and sleeps most of the time. I declare, she'll nod off right in the middle of a sentence when I'm talking to her! She'll probably be going into ECU before long. You and I could even end up as roommates!"

Oh, swell. And every month I could look forward to being hauled in here in the fartmobile to get my hair – oh, my God, they're all getting exactly the same hairdo! Willie looked at the three women. Their hair was being combed out in the same bouffant with the ends turned up. *They all look like old Eydie Gormes! What is this, the geriatric flip?* The last time Willie had seen that hairdo was at Bernadeen Chilson's funeral. Bernadeen, alive, had never worn her hair that way, nor had she ever worn makeup. But there she'd been, coiffed and cosmeticized, looking better than she ever had, but totally unrecognizable. It wasn't just the waving lotion that was making Willie feel a little ill. It was the carnival fun-house mirror aspect of the three grinning faces that suddenly seemed grotesque. A hellish future beckoning to her, come join us, come join us. *Aaaaaargh!*

...

When Willie and her short, overly curly, "I'm-gonna-wash-that-man" hairdo arrived at the Stastas Inn, Jeremy was already there. He rose and greeted her with a friendly smile, although Willie noticed the almost subliminal flicker of his eyes to the top of her head, then back again.

"Yes," she said. "It's me. Or should I say it is *I*, since I'm in academic circles. I *did* tell Rose I wanted a short, tight perm."

Jeremy suppressed a laugh. "It's charming. It suits you. You look *absolutely marvelous.*"

"Thank you, *Fernando Lamas.* I look like my mother's Persian lamb coat." Willie slid quickly into a chair before Jeremy could make a ritual of getting her seated. "I think I need a glass of wine. What wine goes well with a BLT?"

"You're having bacon, lettuce, and tomato?" Mmmm, that sounds good. But I think *I'll* have a Heineken's with it." Jeremy said.

"Even better. I'll have one too. We can have a leisurely lunch. If we get to the Lodge around two o'clock, Mrs. Norland will also have eaten, and maybe we'll find her in a receptive mood."

"I really appreciate your help in all this, Willie. I feel guilty imposing on your time, and hope I can make it up to you in some way."

"'Tain't nothin'; just call me 'Good Deed Woman.'"

"Sometimes I ask myself why I'm even bothering with any of this. It was all such a long time ago."

"I *did* wonder about that. Why now?"

"Well, for one thing, I have the time. No, that's not really it. I've been retired since 1982. Of course, when we're caught up in our careers and the business of living, we tend to move along a track. I'm sure there must've been long stretches in my life when I hardly remembered Jock Ostriker. It all came back to me recently, though."

"Something happened?"

"You remember my mentioning a family emergency? It was a family tragedy. A companion of many years. He's dead now."

"I'm so sorry."

"He was a lot younger than I am. He had AIDS."

"That terrible disease!"

"I was hoping — well, we both knew that there *was* no hope of course. But at first, when it was only the HIV, I wanted to take Steven to a peaceful, clean environment. Broom Island. We'd stopped there once when we'd been traveling through British Columbia on vacation.

We rented bikes and rode all over the island. We were exploring the island cemetery. That's when I first saw the name Susi on a tombstone and it rang a bell. It's an interesting place. Beautifully kept."

"Yes, it is now. It used to be neglected, but now they keep the grass mowed and the shrubs trimmed. The town council hires high school kids to do the job."

"Steven loved the outdoors, and he loved the Northwest. He was born in Prince George, grew up near Kamloops. He worked with the forestry service on Vancouver Island for a year while he was going to college. I promised him we'd go back there to live."

"Where did the two of you meet?"

"In Maine. I'd been teaching at Portsmere College. It was a private school for very wealthy young men — at the time. Now I hear it's becoming politically correct and going co-ed."

"Ah, and Steven was a pupil?"

"No, he took a job there as athletic director. Steven was very physical, unlike me. We were a bit of an odd couple. He was too young for me, of course, and although we were together for nearly thirty years, it wasn't continuous. He left me several times, and we each had our interim relationships, but he always came back. That last time, he came back with HIV."

"And you took him back."

"Of course. We were going to retire — I, because of my age, and Steven, because of his illness. We made plans. But then he started developing lesions and . . . he killed himself."

"Good God! You had to go through that horror *again!*"

"Yeah. What are the odds?"

"I am so very sorry. It's — I don't know what to say."

"This time I saw it coming, but I obviously couldn't stop it. He'd talked of suicide ever since he found out he was HIV positive. I got him to see a counselor, and for a while he seemed to accept the situation, and get on with his life. Or maybe he just pretended to for my sake, I don't know. But then when it became full-blown AIDS, I was afraid he would do something desperate. And he did. He used one of the guns in his collection — a German Luger. I'd gone out to pick up groceries. I wasn't there to stop him."

"When someone decides to kill himself there's no way anyone can stop him."

"But it makes one feel so helpless."

"You *still* want to live on Broom Island?"

"Yes. I don't really want to go on living in that house in Portland. Too many memories."

Willie nodded. Her heart went out to this poor, sad, man who bravely wanted to make a fresh start at an age when most cling to the security of old friends and familiar surroundings. How adventurous of him to be willing to make such a drastic change! Or maybe it was actually wise of him.

What security does an old person really have? All those women at the Lodge, for instance, had been vital members of the community. They'd had their families, their jobs, their social lives — and their day. Now they'd been warehoused. Some of them seemed happy enough, at least cheerful enough. Maybe it actually *was* enough. Maybe, after years of work, family responsibilities, involvement in community affairs, it came as a relief to be rid of all that. Could it be that there, in the Lodge, surrounded by contemporaries, they'd found a freedom they hadn't had in years? If so, wouldn't that give new meaning to the term, second childhood? Childhood was a time when you were taken care of. But you had no power either. No autonomy. No *raison d'être*. Would an adult be content with that in old age? Would Willie? You'd have time for yourself. No one to look after. Nobody to cook or clean for. Your own needs would be met. You could devote your years to pursuing whatever interested you. Assuming you still had your faculties, you could take up any hobby or course of study. Or would there be too much *clamor* – too much regimentation? Willie had always been a loner. She couldn't picture having a roommate. She would also hate being *herded* into activities.

And these people *weren't* in their old familiar surroundings either, were they? The Lodge was like a biosphere; it could exist anywhere, insulated from the real world. There was little of their old lives left — a few sticks of furniture, photo albums, and memories — and fewer and fewer visits from either friends or family.

Those who didn't live at the Lodge were ill at ease there. For the middle-aged, it was a place of bad *juju*, a reminder that they, too, could end up there one day. For the young, it was simply depressing. And if you were visiting a parent, even if the parent seemed content, there was always a nagging feeling of guilt. Willie suspected that everyone in Stastas suffered from Lodge guilt, why else were there so many well-intended, but strained and awkward, efforts made to bring cheer to the residents?

She wondered if kids still visited the Lodge on Halloween. While Willie had been teaching, high school students used to go there in costume on Halloween night and roam the halls singing "Pumpkin Bells" to the tune of "Jingle Bells." They'd had to sing something jolly, you see, nothing morbid. Must have been confusing to some of the less mentally connected, and annoying to others. And at least one resident had become hysterical. That was the year the movie *Star Wars* came out and Halloween night was rife with Darth Vaders and Chewbaccas and droids. One kid had dressed as one of the Sand People, made the cloak and hood from burlap bags, used black foam plumber's insulation pipe to mold eye-sockets and mouth, and cut strips of ping pong ball for teeth. It had been brilliantly realistic, but so menacing that it sent one old lady into a screaming fit. After that, there had been a directive that no Halloween costume worn to the Lodge would in any way resemble the Grim Reaper.

You had to either live at the Lodge or work at the Lodge in order to fit in there. And when you entered as a resident, you tended to give up other memberships — like the one in the human race.

Better, in old age, thought Willie, to travel to the Fiji Islands and take whatever you find, or move to Reykjavik or Thailand. Experience another culture before you die. Ah, but old age does beat you down. You don't have the energy, do you? You have medical conditions that umbilical-cord you to your doctor. You want your comfy chair and your slippers. Look at the way *I'm* agonizing over a much lesser decision!

She and Jeremy had finished their lunch, and then, for a bit of fresh air and exercise, decided to take a stroll through the Stastas town park until it was time to go see Mrs. Norland. The park, like the town, was small and devoid of any particular point of interest. There was a bronze statue of a former mayor that served as foothold for pigeons, and in one corner stood a children's playground. Willie and Jeremy stopped to watch a group of kids crawl through a large S-shaped tube.

"Playground equipment was a lot different when I was a kid," Jeremy said.

"It was lethal. Remember the teeter-totters and the Giant Stride?"

"I nearly had my brains bashed out by a wooden swing once."

"I would have liked the monkey bars, but girls in my day had to wear dresses."

"Whenever I climbed up on the slide, I could always count on Angus MacFarland to come up behind me and shove me down." Jeremy was watching the children. "They're all so newly minted, aren't they? Everything is ahead of them. They see the world through unprejudiced eyes until they're taught otherwise."

"Yes, and you and I are supposed to see it through the eyes of wisdom. I wonder if we do. Or do we just continue to blunder and live out our lives as moron jokes?"

Jeremy laughed. "I remember those. Why did the moron tiptoe past the medicine cabinet?"

"He didn't want to wake the sleeping pills. Oh yeah, there were lots of those, but we Finnish people had a different version. We had *hölmöläinen* jokes."

"Hulmo — what?"

"*Hölmö* is the Finnish word for moron. *Hölmöläinen* means, literally, someone from Moronland. Many of the jokes were more in the nature of stories rather than just one-liners."

"Tell me one."

"Well, there was the *hölmöläinen* who built himself a house, but forgot to put in any windows. Outside the sun was shining, but inside it was so dark he couldn't see a thing. Ah, thought the *hölmöläinen*, I need to bring in some sunlight. He got a burlap bag and took it out into the yard, opened it up and let the sun shine into it. He then closed the bag, took it in the house, and opened it to release the light, but nothing happened. I didn't close the bag quickly enough so the sunlight got away, thought the *hölmöläinen*, and tried again. He kept trying and trying and finally the sun went down and it got dark. The *hölmöläinen* then stopped — because he already had enough darkness inside his house."

Jeremy chuckled. "I think every culture has such stories because it's human nature to need to laugh at someone to whom we can feel superior. And the moron jokes, being apocryphal, are totally innocuous." Jeremy paused. "But you know, actually, that thing with the bag and the sunlight? That really should have *worked*."

...

A little before two o'clock Willie pulled into the Stastas Lodge parking lot. "We're here. When you meet Mrs. Norland, you may find her a bit eccentric. She's not your average little old lady. She's heavily into philosophy of all kinds: theosophy, I Ching, Buddhism, Yoga, Rosicrucianism. You name it; she's pursued it. She's the closest thing we have to the Oracle of Delphi. Sometimes she pretends not to speak English, but she's actually fluent in it. In fact, she's multilingual.

That's on her *good* days." Willie raised a cautionary eyebrow. "I must also warn you that there are days when she seems totally deranged. She's so mystical it's sometimes hard to tell if she's with you or not. Just follow my lead. If I sense disaster, I'll organize a hasty exit and we can try again tomorrow. That's if we find her willing to talk to us at all."

Willie led the way through the lobby, smiling and nodding at the residents, saying a word of greeting to each, then stopped at the desk to introduce Jeremy to the receptionist. "We're hoping to see Mrs. Norland, Jane. How *is* she today?"

"I believe she's expecting you," Jane said. Dropping her voice, she added significantly, "She ordered tea."

Willie glanced sideways at Jeremy. "Oh, how lovely. She's still in Room 15, isn't she?"

"Oh yes, go on ahead," Jane said. "I'm sure she's looking forward to your visit."

As they made their way down the hall, a rangy, shorthaired black cat bounded past them and headed in the same direction. "I'm glad you called to set this up," Jeremy said. "I felt a bit uncomfortable just barging in. It's good that Mrs. Norland is expecting us."

"I didn't call."

"But Miss Clark said — "

"We're entering Norland Country. Anything can happen. Get used to it."

To Jeremy, "Norland Country," was clearly a world apart. He entered through Mrs. Norland's open door like a subject seeking audience with a queen, and almost felt he should bow down before the woman in the high-backed chair. The scene, to him, was deliciously mad — the red crochet everywhere; the undulating lava lamp; and the ancient woman with jet-black hair and ring-encrusted fingers working yarn. The black cat, the one they'd seen in the hall, was now sitting on the arm of her chair like an Egyptian carving.

"Come in. Come in. The Double Woman brings the Stargazer,

so we will speak the English tongue."

"Mrs. Norland, you're looking very well." Willie deferentially took Mrs. Norland's outstretched hand. "May I present my good friend Professor Jeremy Banks."

"Ah, the man whose past is in the stars and his future is in the past."

"How do you do, Mrs. Norland? It was good of you to see me." Jeremy now wondered just how he was going to broach the subject of the Susi family.

Willie proved helpful. "Professor Banks is doing genealogical research into some of the leading Broom Island families. I was pleased to be able to tell him that we have a member of the Susi family right here in Stastas."

"Yes, Mrs. Norland. I was hoping you might be willing to help me with some of the family history. There was a Susi family in Pennsylvania, about the time of the Civil War. I wondered if there was a connection."

Mrs. Norland had put down her crochet, and was slowly stroking her cat. "Your inquiry, Stargazer, is like a creeping mist. Better an arrow."

Jeremy glanced at Willie and was reassured by her bland expression. "Yes, quite right, Mrs. Norland. I was interested in what happened to the Susi family in Pennsylvania. I understand there was some tragedy."

"More than one tragedy, isn't it so, Stargazer? Three tragedies sit upon your soul. You seek absolution?"

"I . . . I don't know, Mrs. Norland." The woman was cryptic and disconcerting and Jeremy sensed he'd have to be totally up front with her or she'd spit him out like a plum pit. "I want to know why my friend killed himself in a graveyard at the Susi farm."

"If it is your right to know, you will know. First we'll have tea."

"Oh, how kind of you, Mrs. Norland, but you shouldn't have gone to any trouble," Willie said.

"It saves time, Double Woman. And I have very little time left."

Mrs. Norland rose majestically, and indicated a little table on her right. Willie noticed, for the first time, that it had been neatly set. There were three flowered china cups, saucers, and spoons, a teapot under a cozy, sugar, cream, and one plate with three little cakes.

Mrs. Norland went to the door and closed it. "Moonrise, see that we're not disturbed." The black cat seemed to absorb the instruction, then curled up in front of the sill.

Politely, Jeremy helped Mrs. Norland get seated, then pulled out Willie's chair as well, and finally sat down himself. Mrs. Norland lifted off the tea cozy and proceeded to pour out three steaming cups of tea from an ornate pot, the stones in her rings glinting on her ancient fingers.

"Have a teacake." It was a command. Both Willie and Jeremy reached for one at the same time. Their fingers collided, their eyes met, and both looked quickly away in confusion.

Mrs. Norland took the remaining cake, delicately bit off a corner and swallowed. "You think me odd, Stargazer, but I tell you tragedy is in the eye of the beholder."

Jeremy chewed his teacake. It was dry and clung to his upper palate. He took a sip of tea. "You mean, of course, that a tragedy is more of a tragedy if it involves one directly."

"I mean, Stargazer, that it is drama. It is all just drama. One grand play on a cosmic stage." Mrs. Norland's rings flashed as she made a graceful, languid gesture, infinitely more eloquent when performed by an aged hand.

So far this is all going rather well. Mrs. Norland is being her usual inscrutable self, but I don't think she's wigged out. Jeremy seems to be holding up okay. Willie nibbled her teacake. *That was strange though, when I touched his hand. It was like I was tuned in to two TV stations at once. I think he noticed it too. Wonder where Mrs. Norland got these teacakes — Stastas Sand & Gravel?* She took a swallow of tea. It was hot, strong, and had an undertaste of spices. She needed that. For some reason she was feeling very sleepy.

"You will need a guide," Mrs. Norland was saying.

"A guide? To where?" Jeremy asked.

"To reach your destination, you cannot travel on the surface of matter. You must travel *through* it. You will need a guide and you will need a way."

Jeremy shot Willie a look of inquiry. Was the old woman having one of her "bad" days? Should they be leaving? Willie appeared to be relaxed enough, in fact she looked to be on the verge of nodding off.

Mrs. Norland got up and picked up a shawl made of red ombre yarn. Jeremy, at once on his feet with a mumbled "Oh, please allow me," wrapped it around her shoulders.

Mrs. Norland headed for the door. "Come."

Willie got to her feet too. She was feeling a bit lightheaded, but it was obvious that Mrs. Norland wanted them to follow her. There was something so surreal about it all, that Willie didn't know whether she was asleep or awake. She took Jeremy's arm, either to steady herself or for reassurance, and the two of them watched Mrs. Norland reach for the doorknob and open wide her door. Moonrise bounded through it and was gone.

Willie blinked to clear her eyes. *Okay. Now I know none of this is real. Are we on a psychedelic trip?*

Instead of a view of the Lodge corridor, they were looking at an open field. It looked like a farmer's field of hay, softly blowing in the breeze, waving in the sun, except that it seemed endless.

Mrs. Norland beckoned them to follow; and they did, Willie and Jeremy, hand in hand, like a couple of children, into the sunlight of some unknown time and place, a place outside any law of physics or common sense. So stunned were they by the singularity that they didn't speak. They merely followed, wading through hay that waved softly but afforded no obstruction. They didn't know where they were being led, but they found the experience so spellbinding that they didn't even stop to question.

Mrs. Norland halted and looked toward the horizon. Willie and Jeremy caught up with her.

"We will summon transport, but you must not falter." Mrs. Norland said and raised her hands above her head. Willie's eyes followed hers, and at first she couldn't make out what it was she was seeing. There seemed to be some movement — a black storm cloud? No, it looked more like a *dust* cloud. A twister? A tornado? It was not a tall spout, but low and wide, and Willie could see the whirling dust as it seemed to be coming closer. She could hear the wind now, a howling hiss, and she watched as Mrs. Norland stood facing it, arms still held high. She seemed to be shouting. Was it the shriek of the wind or was it Mrs. Norland, Willie couldn't tell, but surely they needed to find shelt— but what was happening now? Something was coming out of the dust storm. It looked like an animal, and for a split second Willie thought it was Mrs. Norland's cat. But no, it was much larger, more like a panther, black as midnight, and coming straight for the old woman.

The storm was upon them now, and they seemed to be almost in the eye of it, buffeted by swirling dust. Mrs. Norland turned and beckoned. *Are you crazy, old woman? We should be running the other way!* Nevertheless, still holding on to Jeremy, almost dragging him, Willie fought the wind to get through to Mrs. Norland who was standing next to. . . a . . . *beast*. The animal was huge and black and sleek and seemed to pulsate with energy equal to that of the storm that formed a whirling mass around them. It stood as if cast in stone, and Willie saw that its eyes were like deep black holes.

"Climb on!" Mrs. Norland shouted. Then, seeing Willie and Jeremy's look of utter disbelief, "*Hurry. If you value your lives, climb on!*"

Feeling giddy with the craziness of it all, Willie leapt on the back of the animal, surprised by her own agility, and glad that she was wearing slacks! *I'm dreaming. I could perform on a flying trapeze in a dream.* "Come on, Jeremy!" she shouted, burying her hands into the animal's fur. She felt Jeremy behind her, his arms around her waist.

The huge cat's body tensed, and just before it leapt and shot into the dust, it turned its massive head to look back at Willie who gasped at what she saw. She'd have fallen if Jeremy hadn't been holding her. There, in front of her, between the creature's ears, she saw, just for a moment, fixed upon her own, *a second pair of eyes.* They were large and red and flickered like flame, and the message they transmitted hit Willie in the solar plexus like a blow. The communication was instantaneous like a massive download from some alien computer. Later she would sense she had been, in that instant, forever altered. Then the dust swept in and blotted out everything.

CHAPTER 18

WILLIE AWAKENED gasping for breath. She was standing next to a table, and gripping the back of a wooden chair. Looking around, her first impression was that she was back in her own early childhood on Broom Island. She saw that she was in a one-room cabin made of rough-hewn logs, chinked with moss, not unlike some of the houses built by the first settlers. It was evening; there was an oil lamp burning on the table. The room was warm — almost too much so. The warmth was coming not from a fireplace or a stove, but from something she recognized as an early version of the *takka uuni* in Willie's own childhood home — a brick-enclosed firebox set against a wall, with an iron stovetop for cooking. There was a pile of wood neatly stacked next to it and bits of kindling in a bucket. The *uuni* in the cabin must have been fired up to prepare the evening meal.

As Willie tried to get her bearings, she became aware of an eerie noise — an incessant howling. At first she didn't know what it was, but then realized that it had to be the caterwauling of cats — more than one, she judged, coming from somewhere over her head. She looked up and saw that the low ceiling was made of planks laid over beams, and that in the corner, next to the table, a crude ladder built of saplings led up to an opening with a push-up panel. The noise was coming from the attic.

She found the racket of the cats annoying, and her first thought was to thump the ceiling with the handle of a brush broom she saw leaning against a wall. As she moved toward it, she felt her movements to be heavy and awkward. Then she realized that her clothing was wet, and saw that the floor beneath her feet was wet as well, water draining through the cracks between wide floorboards.

She looked down at her own body. *I'm pregnant. I'm about to give birth. My water just broke and I'm about to go into labor. Okay, Willie, don't panic. Remember that you're just hallucinating. This isn't real. Somehow I'm picking up on someone else's life. Maybe this is what a medium does – or a channeler. I seem to be alone here, and –* Willie felt a spasm, not of pain exactly but more like a tightening in her belly, as if all her abdominal muscles were contracting at once. Labor. *I certainly never expected to experience labor pains!* The spasm passed, and Willie made her way across the room to the bed and sat down on the edge, then carefully eased herself down to a lying position. The bed had a rough-hewn frame, with no head or footboard, just a wooden platform pushed into a corner of the room. It was covered by a handmade quilt, and under the bedding, the mattress felt solid, without springs, stuffed with something. Cotton? Probably cattail down, Willie noted absently, drawing from her memory of early American lore. It also felt lumpy. Willie sat back up and swept her hand over it. The mattress bore depressions of bodies; and there seemed to be *three* of them! *Mama Bear, Papa Bear, and Baby Bear?* Beside the bed stood a woven lath basket that had been lined with cloth and had a pillow in it. Willie realized it had been prepared as a bassinet.

Since the cabin had only one room, furniture was arranged to provide maximum space. The table was pushed up against a wall next to a window, with wooden chairs at each end and a bench running the length. The oven had a cast-iron door so you couldn't see the fire unless the door was open, but it was obviously the focal point, the heart of the house. A third wooden chair sat next to it with a woven basket that contained hanks and balls of spun wool, and a piece of knitting on wooden needles.

Benches along the walls provided seating and workspace. Next to one, Willie saw a spinning wheel, a tall hourglass shaped butter churn, and a large wooden tub. The tub was hooped together like a barrel, but with straight sides, with the characteristic two longer staves that stuck up on either side and served as handles. Was that for bathing? No, this one wasn't quite big enough for that. Besides, a Finnish family would have a sauna. Willie remembered seeing similar tubs used for mixing bread dough. There were photos in the Satama museum on Broom Island of early settlers bent over such a tub, women in bib aprons and wearing the traditional *huivi*, the obligatory white kerchief on their heads, not tied *babushka* style under the chin, but knotted in back. The caption had been *emännät leipomapuuhissa*: the women of the house at their baking.

There was a rag mat on the floor. A bench along another wall held a bucket of water with a dipper. There were wooden shelves for provisions and dishes; pegs in the wall for hanging clothing. It was primitive but cozy, particularly in the limited light of the oil lamp that created an island of illumination and cast the corners of the room in soft shadow. It was like being in an early American painting. To Willie, the historian, it was a fascinating dip into the past, and if not for her condition, she would have loved to have the opportunity to explore it at leisure.

Then, to Willie's surprise, the door opened and a blond boy of about age nine or ten came in, carrying a bucket. "I did the milking, *Äiti*. The cow's in the barn."

As the boy put the pail on the bench, next to the water bucket,

Willie experienced a wave of maternal tenderness for the lad. "You're a good boy, Jukka." She realized that they were speaking Finnish. *This is a Finnish family circa the 1860s. It has to be the Susi family – the one Jeremy is researching, but why am I here? Jeremy is the one who should experience this.* Willie had a momentary picture in her mind of Jeremy as a pregnant woman. Well, why not? Equal opportunity. She realized the boy was speaking to her.

"What's the matter, *Äiti?* And why is the floor all wet?"

"Jukka, I want you to help me. Go and fetch Sanni Pihlaja. Tell her it's my time. She'll know what that means."

"You want me to fetch her *now?* It's dark out, and *Isä* has the horse. It's a long way to walk. Can't we wait for *Isä* to come home?"

"No. It's very important. You'll have to go, Jukka. Stay in the middle of the road and don't be afraid. Do you think you can do that?"

The boy nodded a bit uncertainly.

"Oh, and Jukka?"

"Yes, *Äiti?*"

"Don't come back here tonight. Spend the night at the Pihlajas, and come back in the morning."

The boy nodded again, then left. *Well, what do we do now? So this is what it feels like to be two people. Maybe that's why Mrs. Norland always called me Double Woman. I wonder who it is I am. I think I have an idea, and I –* another spasm hit her, and Willie waited it out. *I hope all this ends before I actually have to go through having a baby!*

There seemed to be a sense of urgency aside from the pregnancy. She sensed that her time there *was* limited, and that she had to find out where she was, who she was, and to get as much information as she could. She got up and looked around the cabin for something, anything that might help her. Then, there it was – the documentation in any Finnish Christian home: the family Bible. It was a simple, worn volume written in Gothic script, lying in plain sight on the table next to the lamp. She started to sit down on the bench, then thought better of it and moved to a chair so she could rest her back. She opened the book to the family record, reached over and moved the lamp closer, then began reading the register of the Susi family, each inked entry done in the careful, stylized penmanship of a time when handwriting was an art, even for those with limited education. She ran her finger down to the last few entries: Kalevi Mauno Susi, born January 17, 1786; died April 8, 1859. Aune Amalia Susi, born June 8, 1800; died May 19, 1866. *Must be the boy's grandparents. If grandma died in 1866, the Civil War would be over by now.*

She studied the entries to piece together the genealogical sequence: Mikkeli Otto Susi, their son, was born July 4, 1829. In 1857, he married Stiina Greeta Komulainen born December 8, 1832. Their son, Jukka August Susi, was born October 27, 1859. *I wish I had a pencil and paper so I could write all this down.* Willie then laughed at the absurdity of trying to bring back notes from a hallucination. She was going to have to rely on her memory. There had been two other children born to Stiina and Mikkeli. Both had died in infancy.

Okay, I must be living the life of Stiina Susi who is about to have another Susi to enter into the Good Book. I wonder where her husband is. For that matter, I wonder where Jeremy is. The boy said his father had the horse. Perhaps Stiina's husband has gone to town. Or he could be on a hunting trip. The boy spoke as if he were expecting his father to come home soon. God, I wish those cats would shut the hell up!

Willie was gripped by another contraction and realized she'd have to face the possibility of giving birth before this episode ended. *I don't know nothin' about birthin' babies, Miss Scarlett. . . .* Willie wondered how soon that might happen. Some women, she'd heard, are in labor for hours. Others pop out their babies in taxicabs on the way to the hospital.

Willie went back to the bed, stripped off her wet underthings — cotton pantaloons and petticoat — then lay back down again while she assessed the situation. She'd sent Jukka for the neighbor woman, but had no idea how far away she was, how long it might take her to arrive, or if she even would. The information had just come out of her mouth, so it must have been Stiina coming through. This being a "double woman" was disconcerting. At least the boy was out of the way.

Willie didn't know what was going to happen next. She and Jeremy were supposedly investigating a family tragedy. Was Stiina going to die in childbirth? *If so, get me out of here before it happens!* Another contraction made her tense, then hold her breath. *If this is natural childbirth, I'd rather be in Phila– God, those cats are driving me crazy!*

The cats were howling now as if demented. It wasn't just an ordinary warbling duet as between two rival toms; there seemed to be dozens of them, all mewling and screaming. No doubt a number of felines had given birth in the attic and established a cattery up there. Willie could stand it no longer. Carefully, she inched herself out of bed, heavy and clumsy as she felt. She steadied herself against the wall, groped her way to the broomstick, grasped it by the brush and raised it above her head to give the ceiling a whack with the handle, then another. The wailing stopped, but only for a moment, then started up again. Annoyed, Willie took another swing and struck the ceiling boards repeatedly. Once again, there was a moment of silence, then it resumed: *YOUWLLLLLLgarblewarblewarble HISSSSSS!! MEEEOW-OW-OW-YORTLE-WAHIL!*

Willie looked at the ladder, then at her own protruding bulge of pregnancy. Could she make it? All she had to do was to climb a few rungs until she could push up the panel and look inside to see just what was going on up there. Maybe she could take the broom and shoo the clowder out of the attic. How did they get up there anyway? There must be an opening from the roof or some other entrance from the outside. Another contraction gripped her. They seemed to be coming fairly close together. She remembered something about timing them. She looked at the ladder. *Not a good idea. Don't try it. You might fall and break your neck.* Willie felt she had to concentrate, but how could she do that with that unearthly racket going on? There was no way she could ignore it, and she was becoming angry and frustrated enough to try anything.

Willie picked up the broom with one hand and carefully began inching up the ladder, holding on with the other. *That wasn't so hard. Just take it easy, one rung at a time. Hold on tight and don't lose your balance. Piece of cake. If you start having a contraction, just back down again. Stiina's pregnant, but she's a strong healthy young woman.* Willie had made it up to where she could reach the panel. She pushed against it with the broom handle. It was made of a couple of boards joined together and had been laid across a hole cut in the ceiling planks so it lifted up easily. She went up another rung to where she was close enough to push the panel to one side and cautiously stick her head into the opening.

The cats were quiet now. Willie couldn't see much of anything. *Damn, I wish I had a flashlight.* The space was narrow, and it looked as though there were things stored in it, but Willie couldn't make out what. She could make out the dim shape of the chimney. *No way am I going to try crawling in there.* Willie grasped the end of the handle and thrust the broom inside, swung it from side to side, thumping it against the floor and whatever objects it encountered. "Hey, shoo, get out of there! Scat!"

She smelled a fetid animal odor and heard the scurrying of feet. Then there was a sudden, shrill cry, and Willie lost her grip on the broom. She saw the gleam of eyes in the darkness and caught sight of a large, burly orange cat, just as the animal, panicked into flight, came rushing toward the open hole straight at her head. With a screech, it leapt on Willie's shoulder, then catapulted off and landed at the foot of the ladder and streaked away. Willie felt herself lose her balance, clawed for a handhold on the ladder, failed to get a grip, teetered for a second, then pitched backwards and fell. As she did, her body hit the corner of the table, knocking over the lamp, spilling oil and fire — then her head struck the floorboards.

CHAPTER 19

JEREMY BANKS was no longer holding on to Willie. The storm had passed, and he saw that he was now in a wagon hitched to a horse. Jeremy was holding the reins, and the animal was standing still, as if awaiting orders. The time seemed to be evening, and he was on a rutted dirt road that led through sparse woods. There was a full moon in a clear sky; Jeremy, the astronomer, noticed that even in bright moonlight, he could see stars more clearly when there were no city lights to bleach them.

So where am I and what am I doing here? Hallucinating? Yes, that would be logical — some state of altered consciousness brought on by Mrs. Norland's tea, perhaps. Jeremy Banks was acquainted with the effects of LSD; several of his students had used the then fashionable drug of the day, and he too had experimented with it. But that had been a long time ago. He mused ruefully that all he'd wanted to do is make inquiries about the Susis; he hadn't expected the "Wolf" family would literally bite him on the ass and send him spiraling off on a drug trip. Nevertheless, here he was, and there seemed to be no immediate way to return to normal.

He put down the reins and stood up. He was shorter and stockier. He looked at his hands. They weren't his. He touched his face and felt a beard. His clothing was different. He seemed to be wearing trousers and jacket of some coarse fabric and a hat with a brim. He fought down a feeling of disorientation. *This can't last. Whatever drug I'm on will wear off.*

He looked at the horse. It seemed to be a farm animal, an all-purpose nag for riding, plowing, hauling. The wagon was a box-style farm wagon, light enough for one horse to draw. There was a rifle in a scabbard next to the seat. *Have I been hunting?*

Jeremy found no evidence of game, but could see in the moonlight that there were bags in the wagon, possibly of grain, and boxes of what looked to be supplies. He also saw, on the floor of the wagon, a couple of oil lanterns. Jeremy bent over and looked into one of the boxes and found what looked like purchases made in a store. He was able to make out what they were: brown paper loosely wrapped around a length of cloth; a tin of tar; a can of kerosene; some candles; chewing tobacco; a bag of liquorice; a box of Lucifer matches. He must have been shopping.

He lit one of the Lucifers and held it till it nearly burned his fingers, then lit another in order to light one of the lanterns. *Early American headlights*, he thought. The lantern didn't give off all that much light, and Jeremy wondered how well he'd be able to see if it weren't for the moon. Of course, people probably didn't drive at night except in rare cases, and a horse pulling a wagon wouldn't be careering along at the speed of a car — and the horse could probably see in the dark anyway. A lantern or two might be enough. Life in the 1860s, if that's where he was, did go on at a slower pace.

He saw a leather pouch that looked somewhat official, opened it, and found papers inside. Jeremy brought them closer to the light. It seemed to be a bill of sale for property. Some land transaction involving the Susi family. He couldn't quite make out the entire name; foreign names are difficult to guess if they're not clearly written. He stuffed the papers back into the pouch for the time being, and turned his attention to the rifle.

Jeremy pulled the gun from its scabbard. He didn't have a vast knowledge of firearms, but he saw that it had a wooden stock and an octagonal barrel that looked familiar. He realized that it resembled one of the guns in Steven's collection (only his had been a replica): a muzzle-loading Henry rifle circa 1860, a rifle used in the Civil War, forerunner of the Winchester, but somewhat rare in that not too many had been manufactured. Steven had always had a love of antique firearms and a thorough knowledge of any he owned, whether genuine or reproduction. This would be a collector's item now. Was this something Susi brought back from the war? Or did he buy it later? Perhaps this was a gun he'd bought for himself and carried during the fighting.

Had Susi been to town on some errand, possibly involving the sale of land, and picked up a few things at the general store? And was he now headed for home? Jeremy felt that there seemed to be some urgency about *getting* home. He felt a welling of anxiety. Home, presumably, would be in the direction in which he'd been going — at least the direction in which his horse was pointed. Continuing on seemed a logical next step. There was no point in staying where he was. He blew out the lantern. His eyes would adapt better to the darkness without it, and as in a line of poetry that came to mind, "the road was a ribbon of moonlight." At least some of it was; there were patches of moon shadow cast by trees. Nor would Jeremy cut as romantic a figure as Alfred Noyes' dashing highwayman "riding, riding, riding;" more of a farmer bouncing and jouncing — and for a moment Jeremy felt nonplussed when he remembered that he didn't know *how* to drive a wagon. Ah, but apparently he *did*. He slapped the reins and the horse moved forward. *I don't know who you are, old boy, but you're used to horses and wagons.*

The horse seemed used to the trail. *Probably knows his way home, knows he'll be fed and watered when he gets there.* Jeremy gave the horse its head while he tried to analyze the driver. *I'm a much younger man. Probably in my thirties. I'd guess I'm a family man, married, maybe with children.* (This from the cotton cloth and the bag of candy.) *If this is a valid experience, then I could be living in the time of the Susi family in Pennsylvania in the 1860s. Obviously I'm one of the Susis. And if I am, I could be headed for disaster.*

If indeed disaster were imminent, the warm summer night gave no hint of it. Jeremy took a deep breath of clean air that smelled sweetly of woodland and nighttime. He was coming to a gentle curve in the trail and crossing a shallow creek in which the water was a mere trickle. It was then that he began to sense that he wasn't alone. Thoughts were crowding in on him, thoughts that weren't his own. Or maybe they weren't thoughts at all, but *something* was going on in his head. Was he hearing voices? If so, he couldn't make out what they were saying. Was the personality of the man in the wagon trying to get through? Jeremy rather wished he would; he needed information about who and where he was.

Suddenly he felt a sharp pain in his head, as if he'd been struck. Jeremy grimaced and pressed his temple. Was he having a stroke or just experiencing a terrible headache? He could clearly hear a voice now. It was a male voice, speaking rapidly, with urgency, then crying out as if in pain. But the voice was speaking in another language and Jeremy understood nothing. The ranting continued, and seemed to be getting louder to where Jeremy instinctively tried to shut it out by putting his hands over his ears, but of course that didn't help. The voice was shouting, desperate, with such blind terror in it, now virtually screaming, assaulting Jeremy's senses to where he felt he could no longer bear it. Then it was Jeremy who screamed, screamed to drown out the sound, and then he felt himself falling, falling, sucked into some black vortex.

The next thing Jeremy knew he was lying on the ground, the moon pale, bright, and indifferent above him. *What the hell just happened?*

He'd fallen out of the wagon. The horse was now silently standing to one side of the trail, as if he'd pulled over to park, and looking back at Jeremy, ears pricked up, as if to say, are we ready to go yet? Jeremy picked himself up, realized he'd been unconscious — for how long? He felt bruised and his clothing was clammy. Dew? Sweat? Jeremy rubbed his chin. His mouth was sore and he could taste blood. He suspected he might have had a convulsion — or perhaps he had bitten his tongue when he fell. At any rate, the voice in his head was gone. Susi was gone. Jeremy didn't want him to come back.

What had all that been about? First there had been the crushing headache, and Jeremy now ran his fingers over his (Susi's) left temple. He'd lost his hat, and now could feel a roughness and puckering of the skin. He touched the other temple. It felt smooth and normal. The mark must be a scar from an injury. Had Susi been wounded? Had he been shot? Had he been in the Civil War? Jeremy didn't know what the year was, but Susi had lived in that period of history and could well have been a veteran. He hadn't died in it, because he was *here.* Jeremy hadn't been able to understand what Susi had been saying, but it was clear that something had happened to him. Something traumatic.

Was Susi having the 1860s version of flashbacks experienced by Vietnam vets? Or had his head wound left him damaged? Was the man totally insane or was he subject to random episodes of derangement? And what might Jeremy expect now? More immediately, what should Jeremy *do* right now? He would have liked to return to his own life, but didn't know how. He would have to see the experience through, and wondered where Willie was during all this.

He decided he would have to continue on. Glad that the animal hadn't wandered away, Jeremy patted the horse reassuringly on the neck, then climbed rather painfully back into the wagon, almost falling backwards when he misjudged his stride. His length of leg was different. Shaken by his experience, Jeremy wondered about the life Susi led. Jock Ostriker had spoken of a farm. Was Susi a farmer with a family? Had he returned from the war to pick up his old life, only to find himself scarred in mind as well as body? Or had he suffered some farm or hunting accident? Medical help would have been hard to come by. *Poor old sod.*

It was then that Jeremy's horse turned to the right, onto an even narrower roadway that first led down a gentle slope, the up again, over a rise. As the wagon crested the hill, Jeremy saw a glow on the horizon. His first thought was that it must be a town, then he quickly realized that it was a fire. He urged his horse to a trot. Jeremy felt as if his body had suddenly turned to ice. Panic! Heart pumping he was racing to the scene, and then it was Susi who was suddenly in charge. He leapt off the wagon and ran toward the blazing cabin. Fire was everywhere. Most of the strips of bark that had been the roof had burned away, as had the dried moss between the logs, affording a view of hell through a fence. The leather hinges on the door were gone and the door lay flat. It was clear the walls were about to collapse. Uttering a cry of anguish, Susi ran inside. He was surrounded by flames and scorching heat, but he saw his wife's body on the floor and took hold of her by the arms, tried pulling her outside just as the remaining part of the roof gave way, and a wall caved in, showering him with burning debris and burying the woman. He tried with his bare hands to move the fiery logs but the heat was too much. His lungs were burning. He made a lunge for the door and dived through it just as the rest of the building came crashing down, sending a huge cloud of sparks heavenward.

Susi struggled to his feet and stood watching the blaze. He was badly burned but didn't seem to notice. He screamed then, a cry that racked his damaged chest. He stood a moment, gasping, coughing, his lungs burning from the smoke and heat. Then he turned and walked away, his movements stiff and painful. The horse, spooked, had bolted to the edge of the clearing, running a wagon wheel over a stump so the wagon tilted, its wheels jammed. The animal was neighing and trying to jerk free, its eyes rolling in terror and reflecting the red glow of the flames. There were other witnesses as well — a host of cats. They were sitting scattered, at a safe distance watching the cabin burn down while basking in the warmth.

Deliberately, his face frozen into an impassive mask, Susi walked over to his horse and unhitched it from the wagon. He then reached for the rifle, took it from its scabbard, and walked back to the burning pile of logs. Only the chimney and the brick oven were left standing. He raised the gun and fired it once, as if in salute, over the pyre. Cats, startled into flight, vanished into the darkness. Susi stood for a moment, as if in prayer or contemplation, then turned the gun on himself.

...

By the light of the moon, a lone woman traveled on horseback along the road toward the Susi farm. She was muttering to herself as she hastened along, wondering why it was that babies always seem to be born at night, and, with a good-natured chuckle, answered her own question by saying that they were usually *conceived* at night. Sanni Pihlaja was also wondering whether, at age forty-eight, she wasn't getting a little too old for this sort of thing.

Sanni had made many such journeys by night as well as by day. Twenty years ago, in the Old Country, Sanni had been a midwife and a practical nurse. In the New Land, she was the unofficial medicine woman whom country people called upon in emergencies, particularly the Finns, many of whom couldn't speak English and mistrusted foreign doctors. She was used to traversing much longer distances than this one — on horseback, by canoe, and on foot (often through heavy mud) to reach someone's bedside. At least the Susi family lived within easy distance, their farm less than five kilometers away. A walk over to see Stiina was, for Sanni, just a good stretch of the legs.

When little Jukka Susi had arrived that evening with the news that Stiina had asked for her, Sanni had seen to it that the boy had been reassured, given a glass of milk and a piece of gingerbread, and comfortably bedded down for the night. She had then decided to saddle her horse. It would be faster, easier to carry her medical kit and a few supplies; and the horse probably could see better in the dark than she could. Not that that was a problem; there was a moon. Nor was there was any real hurry. Stiina's babies always took their time about being born. Sanni would probably be there all night, and anticipating that she had tucked a piece of needlework into her bag — a quilt square she might sit and appliqué while Stiina dozed between contractions.

She sighed as she thought of Stiina Susi. Poor little thing. She hoped that this time the baby would live. Jukka, her son, was the only survivor of Stiina's three pregnancies. Two other children that Sanni had helped bring into the world lay buried in the family plot — a little girl, stillborn, whom Sanni had hastily christened Saara, in hopes that baptism would make her little soul acceptable to God in Heaven — and a son, Vilmari, who had only lived six days.

Stiina's life hadn't been an easy one. Her husband, Mikkeli, was another cross for her to bear. Stiina had devoutly prayed that he would come home from the war — a war she felt was none of his business. "It has nothing to do with us. Let the *kieliset* fight their own war. You have a wife and a child and a farm to look after!"

But Mikkeli had gone anyway, saying that it was a man's place to protect his family and to fight for his new country, and that no man should be the slave of another. He'd gone off to serve in the U.S. 100th Pennsylvania Infantry — and Stiina had cried. She'd been pregnant for the third time. And, of course, Mikkeli *had* returned. But he'd never been the same, had he? He'd been injured, shot in the head. The wound had healed, but since that time Mikkeli had suffered from "spells." And you never knew what he would do at such times.

Mikkeli and Stiina had been a loving couple, but now there were times when Stiina was afraid of her husband. She had confided this to Sanni, swearing her to secrecy, as if Mikkeli's illness were a shameful thing. And, of course, many people who showed sympathy to those with other disabilities regarded mental illness as being of the devil. Stiina, mindful of her son, Jukka, wanted Sanni to be aware of the situation. "In case anything ever happens to me," she'd said, underlining her words with a significant look.

Sanni remembered that Mikkeli Susi had been a good, if spirited, young man. Yes, he'd been a little wild, liked to get drunk at weddings and housewarmings. But he'd been determined to make a new life for his wife and family in America. He and Stiina had been happy then, especially when Jukka was born. Mikkeli had been a good father, and for the most part he *still* seemed to be a good husband and father. He loved his family and worked hard. But Stiina had made a chilling confession to Sanni, "Sometimes it's as if somebody else looks out of his eyes. I look at him and something evil looks back at me."

Sanni had seen it only once, a few months earlier that winter, when she had come by to check on Stiina who, in her second month of pregnancy, was bothered by morning sickness. Sanni had been bringing oil of ginger, her own mixture of three or four drops to a tablespoon of olive oil to be rubbed on the abdomen to help control nausea. She'd also brought fresh ginger that Stiina might slice up to brew a stomach-settling tea. Not the wild ginger that grew in the woods and could be used as a contraceptive, but precious homegrown ginger that Sanni had gotten from Mennonite settlers and nurtured with care. Stiina had greeted her at the door, her eyes bright with tears, and ushered her inside. "It's Mikkeli, I don't know what to do!" she'd whispered.

"Where is he?"

"He's out in the snow. He's naked. He won't come in. He'll die out there."

"Give me his coat. I'll go out and talk to him. Why don't you put on the coffeepot. I'll see if I can get him to come inside."

Sanni had gone out behind the barn to find Mikkeli there, totally nude, sitting next to a small fire. He'd laid a short wooden plank upon it, so that one end was burning in the flames, while Mikkeli sat crouching in the snow, resting his bare feet on the other. Sanni called out a greeting as she approached. She didn't want to startle him, nor did she want him to burn himself as result of any sudden movement. "That looks interesting," she said. "Mind telling me what you're doing?"

"I'm burning off benzene."

"There's benzene in the plank?"

"No, benzene in my body. Poisoning me. I have to burn it off. Benzene drains into the wood. Fire burns it away."

"Where did you learn to do that?"

"Voice told me." Mikkeli had looked up then, and Sanni had been shocked by the look in his eyes. She could see what Stiina had meant. They *were* the eyes of a stranger, and they contained such evil cunning that Sanni felt a clutch of fear.

She kept her voice steady. "But don't you think it's time to come inside? It's awfully cold out here."

"Got to burn off the benzene."

"How do you know when it's gone?"

For a moment, Mikkeli looked confused. Sanni took advantage of that. "Benzene burns blue, doesn't it? Look at the fire. Flames are red. I think it's all burned away."

Mikkeli was now staring at the burning plank and blinking, as if he were just waking up. The flames were creeping dangerously close to his bare toes. Sanni went over to him and put the coat over his shoulders. "Let's go in and get a good hot cup of coffee." Mikkeli offered no resistance as she helped him to his feet and gently guided him, violently shivering, inside, where she and Stiina rubbed him down and wrapped him in blankets. He seemed vague and disoriented, but gratefully drank the coffee, after which the women got him to lie down on the bed, where he soon dozed off.

"He'll be all right now," Stiina had said. "For the time being." Stiina later told Sanni that Mikkeli had no memory at all of the incident.

Sanni had turned left at the Susi turnoff, and as she rode over the hill, she could see that something was wrong. The glow in the distance could only be fire. She urged her horse onward, then as she came upon the site, slowed down, stunned. The Susi cabin lay a charred ruin, still burning, logs crackling, sending smoke and sparks into the night sky. She saw the abandoned wagon. There was no sign of the horse. Her heart racing, Sanni dismounted and called out for Stiina, hoping she had taken shelter in the barn or sauna. There was no answer. She ran to the barn. The cow was in a stall, and Stiina shooed her out in case a spark should ignite the building. She checked the sauna but found it empty. An orange cat streaked past her, and she noticed distractedly that there seemed to be a number of the animals slinking around.

Fearfully Sanni approached the cabin. She was met by a blast of heat, and it was then that she saw the body of Mikkeli Susi. She hadn't noticed it immediately because there was nothing to clearly indicate that he wasn't part of the rubble. He was lying near the burning logs, his clothing smoldering, and his skin darkened and charred. But Sanni saw that he was holding a rifle, and that his hand gripping the barrel appeared to be welded to it, roasted by the heat. Half his face had been burned away — no, it looked as though it had been *blown* away.

"*Herran Jestas!* What have you done?"

CHAPTER 20

WILLIE OPENED her eyes and realized, with a start, that she'd been about to fall asleep. *Had* she been asleep? *How embarrassing! Dozing in my tea like a doddering old crone.* She was at the table with Jeremy — *still* at the table, as if they'd never moved from the spot. She looked at Jeremy who seemed to be shaking his head and blinking as if to dispel a fog. Mrs. Norland's place was empty, and Willie saw that she'd returned to her crochet-covered "throne." Willie got to her feet, a bit stiffly, and approached the old woman.

Mrs. Norland was leaning back in her chair, her eyes closed, snoring softly. Moonrise lay curled up in her lap. As Willie drew near, the cat opened one eye just the merest crack, then closed it again.

"Mrs. Norland?" Willie whispered and got no response. "She's asleep, Jeremy. We'd better go."

"I . . . I don't know what just happened here," Jeremy mumbled. "It was a dream, wasn't it? Very odd. Very real."

"Yes, it must've been," Willie answered as she quietly opened the door which, this time, presented quite a normal view of beige asphalt tile corridor flooring. "We'll talk about it outside." She carefully closed the door behind them and didn't see that the old woman's eyes were now wide open, watching them go.

...

"And so, 'Stargazer,' do you think you found the answer to your question?" They were back at the Stastas Inn, in the bar, having a much-needed scotch on the rocks.

"That was the most bizarre experience I've ever had. Have you *ever* in your life been through anything like it?"

Willie frowned. "No, I don't *think* so. Still, there was something familiar about all of it, almost like I'd been on a trip like that before."

Jeremy nodded. "Back in the 1960s, we all tried LSD. I guess we expected some sort of epiphany, some flash of enlightenment, but in my case it was chaotic. I remember a ceiling covered with paper fans that looked to be pulsating with life. They were moving, opening and closing, like the wings of butterflies."

"Don't tell me, let me guess. You were one of them?"

"I was *all* of them. It made me feel nauseated, but it *did* leave me with the nagging feeling that there is life and consciousness in all things. It was as if I'd been shown something I wasn't quite ready to see. I never took LSD again, but now I'm wondering if Mrs. Norland put acid in our tea."

"Or psilocybe mushrooms in the cakes. She'd know where to find them! We must have each had our own hallucination. I didn't see much of you in mine."

"It was all so mythic — the black cat and the whirling storm. People who claim to have had out-of-body experiences sometimes mention a whirling sensation in the solar plexus. I don't have any idea what the cat represented."

"I don't either, but there was something familiar about the animal," Willie said. "And 'familiar' may be the operative word, if Mrs.

Norland is a witch!"

"The husband — I don't even know what his name was — "

"Mikkeli. Mikkeli Susi. His wife's name was Stiina. Augustiina. Mrs. Norland was probably named after her. They had a son, Jukka, who became Mrs. Norland's grandfather. Stiina Susi was pregnant, about to give birth. She sent her son to fetch a neighbor. In my experience, I *was* Stiina — as well as myself."

"Mikkeli Susi had been to town," Jeremy said. "He came home to find his house in flames. He tried to save his wife, ran into the burning building — got badly burned himself — tried to drag out her body, but she was buried when the roof and wall collapsed."

"In that case I — as Stiina — must have set the cabin on fire when I fell off a ladder. I remember falling, hitting the table. There was an oil lamp on it, but I remember nothing after that."

"Mikkeli killed himself. Shot himself with the rifle. You say a boy escaped?"

"Yes, Jukka August Susi. He would have been about nine years old, born in 1859, which would have made it the summer of 1868. Mikkeli wouldn't have known that Jukka escaped."

"Susi was driving home and saw the flames. By time he got to the cabin it was on the verge of collapse. He saw his wife on the floor. She must have been dead by then; the heat was like an inferno. The cabin was going up like a pile of kindling. He thought his son had died too."

"You saw it?"

"I *lived* it. Do you think that's the way it really happened?"

"I don't know, but if *you* experienced Mikkeli's part of it, and I experienced Stiina's, they seem to fit, don't they? Somehow Mrs. Norland sent us both to the same place to *live through* a brief time in the lives of the Susis. I can't *begin* to guess how she did that. Maybe she has hypnotic powers, in which case she *could* have induced a false memory in both of us. I *simply don't know.* Anyway, why would she do it? Everything was so clear, all the way to the howling cats I was trying to quiet when I fell off the ladder."

"The cats survived. They were all over the place. I wonder about the boy? Did he come home and find his house burned and his father dead?"

"I don't know. I told him — that is, Stiina told him — not to come back that night but to spend the night with the neighbor. I hope he followed instructions."

"Well, since it was a hundred and twenty-five years ago, it's too late to be worrying about childhood trauma. I guess they must have buried Mikkeli and Stiina, if there was anything left of *her* to bury, in that plot."

"Mikkeli and Stiina Susi had two other children after Jukka was born. Both died and were buried there."

"Okay, if we really *did* experience a bit of history, I'd love to know how that old woman brought it about."

"You want to go back and ask her?"

"I don't think so. If I never see her and her eldritch cat again, it'll be too soon. I don't think she'd tell us anyway. She'd only say something oracular."

Willie laughed. "It was like being in a dream. You can get distorted images in dreams, but you can also get accurate information cloaked in symbology."

"Yes. The field of hay. The storm. The beast. I'm sure they were symbolic, and probably designed to trigger some neurological spark in us. I've read that medicine men, shamans, use such methods to shock a patient into believing he's being cured."

"When I took you to see Mrs. Norland I thought she might *tell* you something of the Susi family history. I didn't think she'd make it a Saturday night movie. Did it help you understand what was going on with your friend?"

"I'm wondering if Jock could have been a reincarnation of Mikkeli Susi — I mean, as long as we're throwing out conventional wisdom anyway."

"I don't know how we could ever know that, but there *was* an overlapping of experience. Both Mikkeli Susi and Jock Ostriker killed themselves in the same place in the same way, and from what you tell me, it wasn't just an accidental stumbling onto the spot. You know, the sort of situation where a place is said to be haunted and a hapless stranger gets caught up in the vibes and reenacts the violence. Like in the movies: *The Shining,* or *The Amityville Horror.*"

"Yes, Susi and Jock killed themselves in the same way. In Jock's case it had been coming on for some time. He was suffering from sleeplessness *as well as* nightmares. I think he was afraid of going to sleep for fear he'd have one, so he was sleep-deprived as well."

"Did he ever tell you about his dreams? Was it the same one recurring?"

"No, he never really could describe them, but it might have been hard to do. When I, as Mikkeli Susi, was driving home in the wagon, I experienced . . ." Jeremy paused.

"What?"

"I . . . I'm trying to put it into words. First I got this blinding headache, and then I heard voices. No, it was just one voice. Voice of a man who was very agitated, terrified, maybe in pain."

"What was he saying?"

"That's just it, I don't *know.* He was speaking a foreign language. I couldn't understand him."

"Finnish? Was he speaking in Finnish? Mikkeli Susi was Finnish."

"I wouldn't know Finnish from Dutch."

"Can you remember *anything* he said?"

"Sorry. I can't. But I got the impression that the man may not have been in his right mind. I don't mean that he was a raving lunatic. Obviously he lived a normal life at least some of the time, but I think he had some condition that caused him to have psychotic episodes. He may even have been subject to seizures. I might have had one when I fell off the wagon."

"You fell off a wagon?"

"It was the voice. It kept getting louder and more invasive and I was panicking, trying to block it out — and then I blacked out. When I came to I was lying on the ground. Susi had a good-sized scar on his left temple and I wondered if he'd been wounded in the Civil War. He could have been a veteran. He had one of those Henry rifles."

"Oh yes, it was patented in 1860 by Benjamin Tyler Henry. A repeating rifle that made all the difference in the Civil War. It was said you could load it on Sunday and shoot all week long. It had a few bugs, though. It was still a muzzle loader and you could burn your hand on the hot barrel. Interesting that you recognized it." Willie smiled a bit smugly. She loved doing that — pulling out a bit of historical trivia and dropping it like a smart bomb. It was one of her little vanities.

Jeremy slightly raised his eyebrows and gave a nod, subtle tribute to her expertise. "I've seen the replica. Susi may have been suffering from the aftereffects of his war experiences. He seemed to be reliving something horrible."

"And you think Jock was somehow pulled into Susi's experience?"

"Some things seem to fit, don't they? Jock was obsessed with finding that farm. And when he found the place, he reacted to it emotionally." Jeremy's smile was a bit grim. "Maybe Mikkeli Susi's spirit had been contacting Jock and trying to take control of him, if that's at all possible, but *why*?"

"Or it could have been the other way around," Willie said. "It could have been that Jock Ostriker, in *his own* time of stress, had somehow connected with a like-minded ancestor and picked up on *his* world view, rendering himself vulnerable to the same fate."

"You believe in earthbound spirits?"

"I prefer the idea that each of us, throughout our lifetime, develops and records a view of the world from our own vantage point. This becomes archived as part of the cosmic record, much like burning a CD of computer data. Sometimes this view can be accessed. I think all those people who believe they were once Cleopatra or Beethoven may be tapping into the world views of those individuals. Maybe that's what happened to Jock Ostriker. He may have been picking up on Mikkeli Susi's *weltanschauung*."

"Maybe so. Or maybe it's just that I *want* to believe it so I'll feel less guilty about Jock's death."

"There could even be a blood tie, I suppose," Willie said. "It's a reach, I know, but there *are* similarities in the family names, Jock, and the boy, Jukka — Jock, Scottish. Jukka, Finnish. Not that it matters. I remember reading a theory that while some families are literally reincarnations of their own ancestors, it doesn't require a genetic tie."

"Jock was born and raised in rural Pennsylvania. His parents were salt-of-the-earth types, meaning that when salt it mixed with earth, nothing can grow there. His father was a heavy-handed, bloody-minded, bootstraps sort of man with no tolerance of anyone who didn't share his point of view. Jock was his only son, and his father expected him to become a clone of himself."

"What about his mother? Do you know anything about *her* family?"

"She was a religious woman with a literal black-and-white interpretation of the bible. I think she was afraid of her husband and devoted her energies to the church. The few times I visited Jock I noticed that nobody in that house, except the father, dared to talk out loud. The wife always whispered, and so did the children."

"There were other children?"

"Jock had a sister. Shadowy little thing. Her name was Amelia."

"Hmm. I saw that name too when I was going through the Susi family records. Jukka Susi's grandmother was named Amelia. Or Amalia, the way Finns spell it. I think it was her middle name. But that could be nothing more than blind coincidence."

"If you believe in blind coincidence."

Willie smiled. "Well, there you have me. I *don't*. I'm afraid I'm one of those people who looks for life clues everywhere. I've always been fascinated by the idea that we all live many lifetimes simultaneously. And if that's the case, then we all have previous as well as future selves floating around in a timeless present. You say Jock was going through a stressful time."

"Absolutely. It's not easy in today's world to be gay. Picture how it was back then! I think every gay or lesbian at some time considers suicide when faced with the knowledge that they will be hated, feared, and shunned. Jock was facing a major decision. His family would never have accepted him."

"And Mikkeli Susi was also fighting mental demons, possibly as result of his head wound, and was living a tortured existence. He may have been keeping it secret as well. His world ended with the fire in which he lost his family, or thought he had. If he had known that his son survived, things might have been different."

"And if Jock had been a little older, more experienced, he'd have been less vulnerable. If he'd lived, he might have gone on to try to live a so-called normal life, and God only knows where that might have led him."

"At any rate, Jeremy, from what you tell me, some instinct led your friend Jock to the farm where Mikkeli's destiny was played out. Maybe the location itself helped trigger Jock's suicide. And it may also be possible that each of them, Mikkeli and Jock, only experienced *one version* of what happened. Someone once told me that anything that *can* happen *does*, in some dimension or other, and that it's the only way we can really explore all aspects of any event."

"I guess we'll never know, and it probably doesn't matter. We can't change it now."

"There is, too, one other thing. Maybe Mikkeli Susi needed to be heard, and this is something I'll eventually have to talk to Mrs. Norland about. It may even explain why I was involved at all. You see, the tragedy haunting the Susi family wasn't just Mikkeli's suicide, but whether it might have been *he* who killed his wife. Nobody knew what happened that night, but there were dark stories about how Mikkeli had gone mad, killed Stiina, set fire to the cabin, then killed himself.

"Maybe Mrs. Norland wanted to set the family record straight by using us as a couple of witnesses. I speak Finnish, so I could document the events that led to the fire. You experienced Mikkeli Susi's role. He did not kill his wife, he tried to save her.

"But whatever the connection was between Mikkeli Susi and Jock Ostriker, it was a private one, and in my opinion, *that* particular tragedy no longer needs to sit on *your* soul, as Mrs. Norland said."

"Yes, come to think of it, she said I had three tragedies. Two down, one to go?"

"Well, Stargazer, I wouldn't start worrying about it now. I don't know how long we were 'out' but it's nearly five o'clock. I'm going to go home and freshen up, then I will take *you* to dinner. I'll be back to pick you up in a couple of hours. Do you like Spanish food? I know a place that serves a wonderful *paella* and a great *margarita*."

"Sounds good to me, Double Woman. But why does Mrs. Norland call you that?"

"I really don't know. She just always has."

CHAPTER 21

WILLIE LEFT Jeremy at the hotel, glad for the moment to be alone. She needed time to think. There were things she had almost mentioned to Jeremy, then left unsaid. She hadn't told Jeremy about the animal with the two sets of eyes. There was something evocative about that — something familiar — something she should be able to remember. There had been that jolting sense of communication with the big cat. It was as if the animal had dumped on her a vast amount of data that she would eventually have to assimilate — a huge load of information like a bag of unread library books.

Then there had been that sense of recognition when she first met Jeremy Banks. Not only did Willie feel that she had met him before, but she'd also had that flash vision of him as a young man. What was *that* all about? In fact, the entire story of Jock Ostriker had struck some kind of chord. Willie, as she listened, had felt that she could almost see the place — the woods, the cabin, and . . . and . . . a kitten? *Again with the cats!* But Jeremy *had* said there'd been a kitten. . . .

Willie was also bemused by having been caught up in any of it.

What was it that Mrs. Norland had said to Jeremy? "If it is your right to know, you will know." Well, in that case, what right did *Willie* have to know? Was there some other connection she hadn't discovered yet? Willie couldn't answer that . . . yet . . . but she had a nagging feeling that Jeremy might prove to be a key: Stargazer, the man with a flock of tragedies — like vultures — sitting on his soul.

...

Jeremy, too, was glad of a chance to be alone to weigh what had happened. When he'd come to Stastas, he'd expected to find a proper elderly lady who might be willing to sell him her house, someone who might also have knowledge of the Susi family. He hadn't expected to find Mary Poppins. Except he was Jeremy Banks, not Michael Banks, and both he and Willie were a bit old to be wandering around in chalk drawings. He fleetingly wondered just how old Willie might be. Probably about his own age. It was hard to tell. She was also more fun, and had more of an edge than he'd expected. And there *was* something hauntingly familiar about her. He'd enjoyed their easy conversation and had talked more to her than he had to anyone in years — perhaps a bit *too* freely.

Still, there were things he *hadn't* mentioned. He'd deliberately left out the part about the kitten with the second set of eyes. Despite the terrible events of that day, Jeremy had never forgotten the animal. The poor thing looked as though it wouldn't live long, and Jeremy had tried to make its remaining time on earth comfortable. As he'd later tried to do with Steven. As he'd failed to do with his father.

"Three tragedies sit on your soul," Mrs. Norland had said. Yes, that was another thing he hadn't told Willie. There was another, a much older tragedy, the accident that had crippled his father. Jeremy had felt powerless then too. No, that wasn't quite right. Declare yourself powerless and it absolves you of guilt. Jeremy carried the guilt like a bus pass. With both Jock and Steven, Jeremy felt that he *should* have known, *should* have been able to do something. With his father — well, he'd only been nine years old. What could he have done?

What if Jeremy hadn't been in the car with his parents that day? What if Jeremy had been a different type of son — one that his father could have loved and approved of? They'd been arguing, as usual, this time about *him*. His father wanted Jeremy to go to a boarding school where he would "toughen up" and "become a man." His mother refused. His father was shouting, "No son of mine is going to grow up to be a namby-pamby!" And Jeremy heard his mother shout back, "He's not your son!" Nobody remembers exactly what happened after that. Had his father steered the car off the embankment on purpose, or had it really been an accident?

Nobody had been killed. The only one badly injured had been his father who then spent the rest of his life in a wheelchair, forcing both Jeremy and his mother into guilty bondage. Later, his mother had tearfully declared that she'd only said that in the heat of anger, and that *of course* her husband was Jeremy's natural father. The subject had never been discussed again.

Then, in his teens, Jeremy came to the bewildering realization that he was gay. He went through the usual terror, denial, the determination to never let it be known. He endured the teasing of classmates and probing of adults as to why he didn't have a girlfriend. And he did it all by himself. There was no mentor, no older gay man to advise or reassure him. There was no gay community that Jeremy knew of. He was hopelessly alone until he met Jock Ostriker.

One day, in his senior year in high school, after much soul searching and anguish, Jeremy got up the courage to tell his mother. She asked him, *Are you sure?*

It had been a classic scene in the family home: "Mom, I'm gay." Or, back then, it had been "Mother, I'm a homosexual." Jeremy remembered rehearsing the word, not even being quite sure how to pronounce it, until he could actually say it without stuttering, without putting in too many "mo's."

He pictured his mother's initial confusion. All mothers have watched their children go through any number of stages, most of them temporary. Youngsters often have crushes on same-sex teachers and classmates and rock stars. Sexuality is *not* the cut-and-dried issue people pretend it is. Yes, Jeremy could understand her asking if he were *sure*.

He could also now, with hindsight, imagine that his mother would have been standing there, trying not to overreact, while *her son's* future flashed in front of her eyes like a Fellini movie. He would be shunned. He would be hated. He might even be killed. It would be a disgrace upon the family of such monumental proportions that they'd have to flee the country, perhaps the planet. And whatever would his father say? If only all this were just a mistake! Last faint grasp at a straw of hope: "Jeremy, are you *sure?*"

His mother had no way of knowing about the torment of the damned that her son had already been silently enduring. She didn't know about the knife he kept under his pillow, never quite having the courage to use it to plunge into his heart or to open his veins. She didn't know the wrenching effort it took to actually come out and put it into words. *Yes, Mother. I'm sure.*

Then, of course, Mother told Father. And from that time on, Jeremy became invisible. He couldn't remember that his father ever spoke directly to him after that. Jeremy had been well looked after (appearances had to be kept up, of course) and sent off to college in New England. There had been strained homecomings during vacations and holidays.

The summer that Jock died, had been Jeremy's last real visit home. Jeremy went back to school, graduated, and went on to pursue studies in Arizona. When America entered World War II, Jeremy tried to enlist in the army. He was rejected, not because he was gay but because he was underweight. Jeremy's six-foot frame, in those days, never carried more than a hundred and twenty pounds. He'd always been whip thin, to the chagrin of his mother who did her best to fatten him up, and the annoyance of his father, a beefy man of medium height who, once wheelchair-bound, continued to put on poundage. Jeremy could remember how his father's eyes would occasionally follow him wordlessly with a sliding sidelong look of speculation. Once out on his own, Jeremy only went home for the funerals of his parents.

Closure? No. You never do attain closure when it comes to your parents. They continue to walk with you forever, and Jeremy fancied he could still hear his father's voice raised in reprimand, his mother's in rebuke: "You realize you're killing your father!" Tragedy sitting on his soul? Oh, yeah! And somehow old Mrs. Norland had picked up on it. He'd hardly gotten a single sentence out before she'd pinned him like a butterfly specimen.

Are there people from whom nothing can be hidden? Is there, as Willie had suggested, a cosmic record of everything that's ever happened, every word ever spoken? Jeremy had dipped into metaphysics about the same time that he and his friends were trying on LSD for size. He was familiar with the term, "cosmic consciousness." He'd read about the Akashic Records. Is it possible, as Willie had said, that each person makes a log of his life, a chronicle that endures forever? Jeremy pictured a huge library with a book for every individual. Cumbersome. Willie had likened it to a compact disk. Well, why not? Information doesn't require *space*, per se. A tiny seed carries a coded pattern that "tells" it what to become. Why couldn't a human also carry his entire earthly history (and perhaps even beyond) as naturally and easily as DNA? And if we had instruments sophisticated enough, it might even be possible to access such information.

Telepathy, Jeremy mused, existed. We've all experienced it in one way or another. But only since the age of computers have we begun to use instant communication in a practical way. Only now we call it e-mail. We send it into cyberspace. Nobody has to pick up a phone and say hello. It just goes, and then the person for whom it's meant can read at his or her convenience. Jeremy had often thought that the computer was like a rudimentary mock-up of the human brain. Was it invented because people were now ready to seriously explore the workings of the mind, and computers were like toy models? Jeremy tended to reject a lot of what he thought of as metaphysical mumbo jumbo, but this sounded more scientific. Futuristic, certainly, but intriguing.

Why could we not, quite unbeknownst, be weaving a tapestry of all human experience, each adding our own *oeuvre*, with nothing ever lost or inaccessible? Was the human race evolving toward one where motives could not be hidden, deceit would be impossible, and like-minded people could pool their knowledge and effortlessly work together to achieve astonishing things? He thought about Willie Haapala — Double Woman — as someone with whom he might be able to discuss these things without being labeled crazy.

CHAPTER 22

Willie was feeling inexplicably lighthearted, as if some weight had been lifted from her *own* soul, and its absence was making her feel festive. On the way home she stopped at the wine shop, the Stastas Market, then at Gisela's, a place that specialized in imported delicacies. She bought saffron, and couple of tiny Spanish sausages, *chorizos*, made of pork and highly seasoned with chili and garlic. These weren't the big fat ones you normally see, but tiny, compact cylinders packed with flavor. (Gisela ordered them especially for her from a supplier in Ybor City, Florida.) Then there would be one more stop to make, at the Sea Drift, for fresh mussels and prawns.

Willie planned to cook dinner. She knew if she took Jeremy to a restaurant, he'd insist on picking up the check, and she wanted to make a gesture. She was going to disappoint him about the house, and hoped that a nice home cooked meal might soften the blow. As she carried in her bags of groceries, she mentally calculated that she could prepare a pitcher of margaritas ahead of time and — *eek!* Willie caught sight of herself in the hall mirror. She's forgotten about the hairdo. She'd have to do something about that as well.

She busied herself in the kitchen, browned chicken pieces in virgin olive oil, mixed a couple of cupfuls of stock with saffron and seasonings, then cut up the sausage, onion, fresh tomato, and herbs. All she'd have to do later is brown the rice lightly in the pan, put in the other ingredients, pour in the stock, and pop the *paella* pan in the oven. Then, when it was almost done, she would add the prawns and mussels and let them cook till the shells opened.

Now, the wine! Willie opened a bottle of Australian Shiraz and left it to "breathe." She mixed the margaritas, prepared the glasses, and set the table. She then took a shower and shampooed to get rid of the new-perm smell, blow-dried her hair and gave it a vigorous brushing, even though Rose always said not to wash your hair the same day. *That's better.* By a quarter to seven, she was meeting Jeremy in the lobby of the Stastas Inn.

"Oh, Willie, don't *you* look lovely this evening!"

"Why, thank you. I like a man who hasn't forgotten the art of flattery." Actually, Willie felt she *did* look good. She'd changed into a flowing A-line, ankle-length, cotton knit gown she'd found in a quaint little shop in West Palm Beach. With its hand-painted, stylized fish designs done in silver on a sea-green background, the dress was more funky than formal, and set off Willie's hair which was now a halo of short, white, soft curls.

"Am I all right as I am?" Jeremy asked. He stood tall and slim in his tweed jacket. "I'm afraid I wasn't expecting to go anywhere fancy."

"You're fine. Come on."

They pulled into Willie's driveway, Willie got out and Jeremy, a bit puzzled, followed her into the house and on into the kitchen. "But I thought you said . . . "

"Are you kidding! *Where*, in a town like Stastas, would you find a decent *paella?* Or, for that matter, a margarita!" She took out two glasses, the rims of which had been moistened with lime juice then delicately frosted with salt. She put in a couple of ice cubes and poured in the mix from the pitcher she'd had chilling in the refrigerator. "There, just the way my favorite bartender in Puerto Vallarta taught me: real lime juice, *not* concentrate, stirred and poured over ice, not slurpeed in a blender."

"Well, Willie, here's to you." Jeremy took a sip. "That's delicious."

"It'll take me a few minutes to put my *paella* together, so if you'd like to take your drink into the living room and turn on some music — "

"I'd rather stay here and help you."

"Well then, you can start on the salad. You'll find mesclun greens in the salad spinner. How are you at salad dressings?"

"Well, I'll need olive oil, garlic, vinegar, honey and — uh — mustard. *And* salt and pepper."

"No problem. Use my African blue basil vinegar and the *sel gris,*" Willie handed Jeremy a jar filled with gray sea salt. "The metal pepper mill has green peppercorns in it." She took out a head of fresh garlic and a jar of white, satiny, clover honey. "What else did you say? Mustard? Try this stuff from Finland." She handed Jeremy what looked like a tube of toothpaste. "The dressing can marry while the chicken and rice bakes, and meanwhile we can both go sit down and do some serious drinking."

"After today I think we've earned it."

While the house filled with the delicious aroma of spices, Willie and Jeremy, seated comfortably in the small living room, were sipping a second margarita. "Your house is comfortable, Willie. No, what I really mean to say is, *you're* comfortable to be with. And I really don't know how to express my appreciation for your kindness. Somehow a 'thank-you for your hospitality' or 'I've had a lovely time' doesn't seem to cut it. You know, it's odd but I keep having the feeling that we've met before. When we were at Mrs. Norland's, there at the tea table, I had the strangest flash of memory — but it was gone before I could get a grip on it. Something to do with a campfire, of all things!"

Willie smiled. "Yes, I wondered if you noticed it, too. It's as if we had some hidden history. Maybe we do. When I was about seventeen, I began having — well, I guess you'd call them paranormal experiences now. I never told anyone about them because, back then, I'd have been considered either demented or possessed by the devil. One of them is that when I meet someone for the first time, I occasionally recognize them as an old acquaintance. I knew you when I first laid eyes on you. Everything about you was totally familiar to me. The feeling usually lasts only a moment."

"It hit *me* when I first brushed my hand against yours at Mrs. Norland's tea table," Jeremy said. "I took your hand again later in the dream or whatever it was we were having, but the effect wasn't the same." With a smile, Jeremy held out his hand and Willie reached out and took it. They looked at each other, then both shook their heads. "Nothing."

"I guess it's like an Ouija board. Sometimes it works, sometimes it doesn't." Jeremy said.

"I know one thing. Whenever I recognize a person in that way, that person always becomes a player in my life."

"A player?"

"Yes, in the Gospel according to Willie, we're all players, like characters in a play. We have roles to perform. Sometimes they're only bit parts, sometimes supporting, sometimes major. We may appear as villains or heroes or just extras in a crowd scene in other people's lives. In our own, we're the stars. And when you go through life, you never know who will turn out to be a player. Some fleeting incident or contact can sometimes change your life completely. And we never know what ripples are going to fan out from our own smallest acts whether they be kind, cruel, or just incidental."

"You mean like the old man in the peaked cap who drives in front of you at 35 miles per hour and slows you down — and then you pass an accident in which you might have been involved if you'd been going at your usual speed."

"Exactly. The man on the street who accidentally bumps into you and knocks you out of the way of a falling safe? You just met a player! He had a role to play and came in on cue, even if his only line was 'Oops, excuse me!'"

"Sort of like a guardian angel, you mean?"

"Could be, but I don't think players necessarily make a distinction between positive and negative. One player can open a door of opportunity; another may slam it in your face. It's part of the game."

"And the name of the game is?"

"*I* believe the game is called gaining experience. All life is experience. And I also have a suspicion that many who appear in our lives as players have appeared in our lives before. Or should I say they appear in a number of our lives. They may have only a cameo role in this one, but they may have a much bigger one in another. Their presence is supposed to remind us of something. Like Alfred Hitchcock always appearing in his own movies to remind us who the genius was."

"So you think it's possible that we *do* know each other from some other life."

Willie looked a bit pained. "I know how that sounds. It's *so* New Wave. But then, maybe the New Wave is just the first gropings of the human race striving to recapture its heritage. As for you and me, if we were to spend time together, we might be like a couple of old school chums meeting years later, each remembering different things and ending up with combined total recall. Or maybe not. Maybe it's a need-to-know thing. Or maybe it's sometimes better *not* to know that the friendly grocer you chat with, was in another life, your father-in-law, your sister, or your boyfriend."

"I can see how that could be unsettling."

"It's fascinating to speculate on stuff like that, but probably more practical to focus on our own time. And right now, I think it's time for me to add the seafood while you toss the salad."

...

Dinner had been so delicious that it almost halted conversation as they savored the fragrant yellow rice with chicken and seafood. Willie's favorite company dish had once again proven itself a winner. "I'm afraid I didn't have time to make dessert."

"I couldn't possible eat any. I'm stuffed. That was the best *paella* I've ever had."

"Well then, we'll put the dishes in the dishwasher and just relax over a drop of *lakka* liqueur instead. I brought some back from Broom Island."

Back in the living room, Willie poured pale amber liquid into tiny glasses. "It's made from cloudberries. There are so many Finns on Broom Island that the Co-op imports a lot of stuff from the mother country. You can find things like Presidentti coffee, lingonberry jam — which is lovely, by the way, a lot like cranberry. They also have cloudberry preserves, although I find them a bit too bland."

"That's nice," Jeremy tasted the sweet drink with a light, haunting berry flavor, although, in truth, *he* found *it* a bit bland.

"And this is the part where I have some good news and bad news," Willie said.

"Oh, I think I guessed the bad news. You've not going to sell me your house, are you?"

"No. I realized today, after I left you, that I can't sell it, and I just *hope* I'm making the right decision."

"You can usually trust your instincts."

"I don't want to spend my old age in Stastas. I was having my hair done this morning, and in came these women from Stastas Lodge. They're nice ladies, all of them, and they seem to be happy there. But at least one of them is younger than I am, and already packed up for the Pearly Gates. Okay, I'm an old woman, but there's got to be more to the rest of my life than that."

"Staying in Stastas doesn't mean you'd end up at Lodge."

"No, of course not, but I want to completely eliminate any possibility of it. I just have a strong feeling that I should go back, that that's where I'm supposed to be." Willie chuckled. "When I was teaching school, I remember that if you encountered a straggler student in the hallway, you always asked them, 'where are you supposed to be?' Kids used to hate that. And I always half-expected that one of them would give me some existentialist answer. I feel I've been asked that question now, and the answer is Broom Island."

"It's not that different for me either. I have to make a decision as to what to do with *my own* life. Old age is a foreign country, isn't it? You find yourself there, but you're not sure you speak the language."

"It has its perks, though. Nobody expects anything of you anymore, so you can pretty well do what you please." Willie unobtrusively removed the liqueur glasses, replaced them with a couple of snifters, and poured a little St. Rémy Napoleon brandy in each.

"That's true. Society has labeled you a senior citizen and taken its eyes off you. You've run your race. If you're lucky, you no longer have to scrabble around trying to make a living, and you're no longer embroiled in the politics of playing either the academic or the corporate game. Those with children have seen them grow up and go."

"I like to think of it as a whole new beginning. You've done your time for the world, and now your time, whatever you have left, is your own."

"To do all those things you wanted to do but never had time for," Jeremy finished.

"Yes, but it's got to be more than playing golf or shuffleboard or herding with other so-called senior citizens. I don't want to die with my thumbs in the twiddle position. And since I was never a group person when I was young, why would I change when I'm old?"

"Nobody prepares you for old age. We all go in as pioneers."

"It *can* be an exciting time, I think. That experience today, for instance, left me feeling that I came out of it changed, somehow, as if it opened — oh, I don't know — maybe some new pathways in my brain. Something *happened* and the effects of it aren't over. I think this sort of thing is a rightful part of old age, but it's misunderstood by young and old alike."

"And, in your case, it's tied up with your wanting to go back to your old home on Broom Island?"

"Yes. I feel my life has shifted direction. I'll put this house up for sale, and I'll probably have to go through some rigmarole with Immigration again, since I'm an American citizen now, but that shouldn't take too long. '*I will arise and go now, and go to Innisfree.*'"

"'*And a small cabin build there, of clay and wattles made.*' William Butler Yeats. So what's the *good* news?"

"Jeremy, if you really want to bury yourself on an obscure island in the Pacific, I invite you to come and stay with me while you look for a suitable place of your own."

"Seriously?"

"There are always houses going up for sale on Broom Island, and if you're on the spot, you'll have a good chance of finding something you like. I have loads of room in that old house of mine. Of course the place needs repair, and I want to do some remodeling. Set up proper guest quarters. Might even turn it into a B&B. As soon as the major work is done, you're invited."

"Maybe I could make myself useful. Help with the renovation."

"You don't have any pets, do you? I'm allergic to cats."

"Can't abide them. And I don't have HIV either."

"Thank God for that. That settles it then. Come in the spring. The island is spectacular when the Scotch broom blooms and turns it yellow. Or if you can get away earlier, come at Thanksgiving — or even Halloween! With luck, I should be in by then. We can roast hot dogs over a West Coast campfire and tell spooky stories."

"Hey, that reminds me of a good campfire story I'll tell you one day about a really strange kitten I once knew."

Something about the way Jeremy said that made Willie look at him sharply. "Why wait? Tell it to me now."

"You may regret saying that."

"Somehow I don't think so."

"Jock and I had known each other since we were boys."

Willie inwardly wondered what door she'd opened now. This didn't sound like a campfire story to her.

"We met at Camp Wetabagami. It was a Boy Scout camp. We used to call it Camp Wetabed. Jock was eleven, I was thirteen."

Okay, so maybe it was a campfire story.

"I was there as the official camp bugler. In our troop nobody could blow the bugle except for me but I was *terrible* at it. I had no musical talent whatsoever, and when we'd had to choose an instrument in music class, I picked bugle because it only had four notes. I was so bad that my father banished me into the woodshed to practice, although he insisted I learn to play. With my father, if you started something, you didn't quit until you mastered it. But I was hopeless. As they say nowadays, I *sucked*.

"I didn't usually go to camp. But that summer my mother wanted me to get away for a while, take a break from looking after my dad. She convinced him the experience would be good for me, and I guess he thought it would make me into a man."

"Your father was ill?"

"He was in a wheelchair. Car accident when I was nine. Anyway, off I went to Camp Wetabagami in the Pennsylvania mountains. I hated it. I had no skills for making friends. And then there was my awful bugling. I'd blow reveille at sunrise and then go hide so the troop couldn't find me. I'd gotten death threats, and I knew the least they'd do is throw me in the latrine."

Jeremy frowned. "This *is* a tale of great pathos, Willie, so quit laughing; you'll choke on your brandy. Anyway, my ultimate humiliation was yet to come. One day we had an overnight visit from another troop. You guessed it. They, too, had a bugler. Only *he* was *good*! Right after I'd blown taps in my own quavery style, this chap picked up *my* bugle and blew like Louis Armstrong. You can imagine the scene. All the guys ganged up on me and I just grabbed the bugle, ran off into the woods, and threw it down a hillside into the bushes. It was there Jock found me blubbing my eyes out and trying to rehearse what I might say to my parents to get them to let me come home. Here comes this little kid. To a thirteen-year-old, an eleven-year-old is a little kid.

"He didn't say much. He just sat down beside me and looked at me. I told him to go get lost, but he just kept sitting. Finally I yelled at him. Asked what he wanted. And he said, 'You're the best bugler in the troop.'

"I told him he needed his ears cleaned. Hadn't he *heard* the other guy? 'He's not in our troop,' he said. 'You're *here*. You'll be here tomorrow, and the next day. And, anyway, you're better than you used to be.'

"Well, that's how I met Jock. We ended up scrambling down the hill, hunting through the bushes, looking for my bugle. If it hadn't been for him, I wouldn't have lasted the six weeks."

"So you and Jock continued in scouting together."

"No. I dropped out after that, once again proving to be a disappointment to my father who'd wanted me to become an Eagle Scout. Mother won that one. Jock and I didn't see much of each other until we were both in high school. Jock lived in the country; I lived in town, but we'd ride our bikes. When I could get away we'd go to the movies. It cost a dime back then if you got there before six o'clock. Somehow Jock and I just hit it off in spite of our ages. We had a lot in common. Jock's family was . . . odd. And so was mine. And although our relationship was totally innocent back then, I think we both realized we were different.

"I went off to college, and there formed a better idea of just who

I was. And who Jock was. It was a year of discovery for both of us. We spent time together whenever I was home. And if there hadn't been a world out there, we could have been happy. Jock was still going through all the stuff I'd gone through when I was younger. He hadn't yet come to terms, as they say, with his sexual orientation. In my case, I think I always knew I was gay. I wasn't confused. To tell the truth, I doubt that many are. You may be in denial, but you usually *know*. Jock, I think, was in denial, and on that last camping trip, the one *he* insisted on — God, why did I *go?* I *hate* camping. And it seems the people in my life all *love* it. Steven loved camping. Mister Outdoors. Why didn't I just say no? Maybe Jock would still be alive."

"Jeremy," Willie said gently, "I'm sure you've been there many times. Don't go there again. Try to let it go."

"Do you believe in signs and portents, Willie?"

Willie thought for a moment. "Yes. Yes, I do. I believe in precognitive dreams because I've had them. I believe in hunches, ESP. I even believe that it's possible to read a tarot deck or a crystal ball. You see, if your subconscious mind needs to contact you on a conscious level, it will find a way to get your attention. Which is what I think signs and portents are."

"You don't regard them as supernatural?"

"No. Nothing is supernatural. If it happens, it can't be supernatural. These things are simply not yet understood. In another era, television would have been supernatural — big time."

"You don't believe in devils or demons or evil spirits?"

"I believe we can encounter them because we *create* them, the way we can create a nightmare, but — " Willie suddenly stopped, then said slowly, "I have met them and they're not . . . evil." She sat, mouth open, staring at Jeremy. "I've no idea why I said that!"

"You remember my telling you about that kitten at the cabin. I think *it* was a thing of evil. Jock had gone out for water and I was alone with it. Jock and I were both upset over our relationship. I was sitting, brooding, waiting for Jock to come back. I knew we'd have to have it out.

"The kitten had been sleeping across the room. It woke and came over to me, and I rather absentmindedly picked it up and put it on my knee. I was looking at it, but I was thinking of Jock, and suddenly the animal — the *thing* — in my lap looked at *me*. Mind you, the kitten was sick. Its eyes had always been crusted shut. Now, all of a sudden it's looking at me, making eye contact. And then it just bent its head, and right over its eyes, I saw *another pair of eyes*. I blinked. I thought I was having double vision. But the eyes, Willie, were *red*. Like coals. And they just bored right through me. I guess I must have jumped — I threw the animal to the floor. I was startled and stunned. Didn't know what to make of it. But then, just as quickly, it was all over. The kitten was just a kitten again. And I was left wondering if I was losing my mind. Later I came to think of it as some sign or warning of Jock's suicide. I assumed I'd been hallucinating."

Willie had been listening, her expression enigmatic. "You're right, Jeremy. That's one hell of a campfire tale! But I think I can match it."

"Wasn't just a story, Willie," Jeremy mumbled.

"Neither is mine. I don't know who or what your kitten was, but I think I've met him all grown up. You remember my saying that our encounter with Mrs. Norland and her black beast somehow altered my life. When I got on the back of that huge black cat and you were behind me . . ." Willie paused. "Do you *even remember* anything like that? I mean, we were each transported into other areas of reality in which we each seemed to live lives as the Susi couple. But we've never talked about how we got there. Did we each go through the same thing?"

"I remember walking out of Mrs. Norland's room into a field, and I remember an oncoming twister, and the big black panther or whatever it was — and Mrs. Norland commanding us to get on its back."

"Okay then, we each had the same experience. Yours wasn't different from mine up to that point. I remember feeling a little light-headed, and jumping onto the animal and grabbing its fur. And then it turned its head to look at me, and it was then I saw that *it* had another set of fiery red eyes."

Jeremy stared. Nobody spoke. Then Jeremy said, "I . . . I didn't see that."

"I was in front of you, blocking your view. Anyway, it only lasted for a second. It lasted for one second, and for the next twenty years if I live to be a hundred."

"How could any of this possibly *be?*"

"Obviously it *can*, although it defies logic."

"We've only just met. How could I have seen something over fifty years ago, and you . . ."

"I don't know. We share something. Probably the way people who claim to have been abducted by aliens share something. We made contact with something — or something made contact with us. And in that arena, time probably doesn't even compute so the fifty or sixty years means nothing. The other night I had a mental flash of you, a picture of you as a young man. I don't know where that came from either."

"My question would be *why!* Why is any of this happening?"

"Mine too. Okay, you said you thought your kitten was a portent of evil. What did it leave you with? Did you have any sense of having had communication with it?"

"Oh, Willie, I . . . I don't really remember. It was all so *fraught*. But I can tell you this. It left me with the feeling that there's always the unexpected! In those days I may have had my eyes on the stars but my brain was in mathematics. Two and two always made four. Things added up. Astronomy, as you know, *is* mostly math. Very concrete. I never had any use for astrology, for instance. I was not a kid who believed in anything beyond the five senses. Visions, apparitions, clairvoyance — I didn't believe in any of it. After the kitten I wasn't quite so sure. I found it unsettling to think that my own brain could throw me a curve."

"Maybe it was more of a nudge. The long-ago kitten may have served to activate some area in your brain that prepared you for an event that would take place half a century later."

"If that's the case, what are we, as human beings, supposed to be doing? Are we supposed to be becoming aware of other existences?"

"Perhaps. Or maybe what we need to do is bring our conscious mind and our subconscious mind into closer concert. It could result in an enhanced way of living, couldn't it? There may be a subtle and elegant order beneath what seems like random chaos, and if we could tap into it, we might live more civilized lives."

"You think?"

"Wouldn't it be empowering to feel the connection between our conscious selves and the very source of our being? We'd know that we have access to limitless power and creativity, and that we can use it to direct our lives."

"The Bible talks about faith moving mountains."

"And an Eastern sage, living the principle of the Tao, leads a life of serenity and purpose, knowing that there is no need to frantically pursue anything in order to achieve it. We wouldn't be so fearful or desperate, would we, if we knew that we create our own reality and have the power to change it. We'd never feel like victims, and we wouldn't feel we're at the mercy of anyone else's random violence or predation."

"But look around you, Willie. There's violence and predation everywhere! We've always had the great battle between good and evil."

"Yes, we have. But you know, Jeremy, it may be just a roller coaster ride. Why do you suppose *Alice in Wonderland* and *The Wizard of Oz* are so enduringly popular? In each, a young girl experiences wild and wonderful and frightening things, but ends up safely at home, realizing there had never been any real danger. I think these books and others like them remind us that that's exactly what we're doing. We're living rambunctious lives in which all sort of things happen, but we'll wake up safely at home.

"You and I are older, closer to death, and I think we begin to prepare for it. We may not be as firmly entrenched in our bodies anymore. We may be more likely to have out-of-body experiences and contact with people who are no longer *in* earthly form."

"Then we'd all be in danger of being certified insane! You can have paranormal experiences when you're young, but I think, at our ages, we'd be put in a home!"

"Which is why we tend not to discuss these things except, as you and I are doing, with each other."

"Wouldn't such experiences be totally disorienting? If old Uncle Arthur can straddle realities and play chess with a friend long dead, how does *he* know where he really is?"

"He may not. And his kin will dismiss his chess game as senile dementia. But who can say he's not really doing it? Can you? Can I? Our old age will probably be the result of how we've lived life, what beliefs we hold. If we're locked into some organized system of beliefs — or if we have none at all — we will structure our old age accordingly."

Jeremy shook his head. "This is something I'm not sure I'm prepared for. Different realities? Neurological explorations? Multidimensional lives?"

Willie grinned. "I'm trying to keep an open mind. There's just so much *stuff* that's too fascinating to pass up. It's not a new concept. In the old King James Version, Jesus said, 'In my father's house there are many mansions.'"

"*No* kidding!" Jeremy glanced at his watch. "Do you realize it's one-thirty in the morning? I've got to be getting back."

"What time do you have to leave to catch your plane?"

"I'll take a bus at seven for Seattle. My plane leaves at ten, and I should be in Portland by early evening if I don't get hung up at the Newark airport. That place is a zoo."

"It's a good thing we got to see Mrs. Norland today. I had thought you might be staying in Stastas a little longer."

"I would have waited if we hadn't been able to see her, but now I'm eager to get back to Portland. I, too, plan to put my house up for sale. After Steven — well, it would always hold bad memories for me."

"I could to drive you to Seattle. It's not all that far."

"I couldn't possibly ask you to do that. The bus will be fine; I made arrangements this afternoon and I already have my ticket."

Willie stood up and comically crossed her eyes. "What you *can't* ask is me to do is drive you back to the Inn *tonight.* After all that tequila and wine, I'm afraid I'm in no shape to get behind the wheel of a car, and neither are you."

"I'll call a cab." Jeremy was yawning.

"You'll never get one in Stastas at this hour. Good news is I have a guest room. Bad news is it's about the size of a phone booth. Can you sleep standing up?"

"By now I think I could hang like a bat from the closet rod, but this is such an imposition. I should have left hours ago."

"Not at all. I'm an early riser. I'll get you back to the Inn with plenty of time to shower and change and pick up your bags, and then I'll take you to the bus station."

...

With Jeremy duly tucked in for the night in Willie's guest room, in Willie's guest pajamas, Willie found herself wide awake as soon as she lay down. It had been a long time since she'd had a gentleman caller spending the night. Yes, he was obviously a player. It would be interesting to see whether their paths would cross again. Odd the way they'd both been caught up in that thing with Mrs. Norland — and the cat they rode in on! Okay, it had been part of the theatrics, and any hallucination Mrs. Norland orchestrated would be every bit as dramatic as she, herself, was. But the eyes! The eyes of the animal! That second set of glowing eyes! What *was* it about that? It could have been straight out of a horror novel, but it was more than that. It was almost like an electric current flowing from the animal — like an enormous download, although Willie didn't know where, on the hard drive of her brain, it had been stored. Willie tried to replay and recapture the moment, attempting to analyze, yet again, what it might have meant. She realized one thing: she'd been given a sense of purpose. She was sure now that going back to Broom Island was the thing to do. When she got there, would she be getting further orders? Had she been given a mission? And what *was* a mission anyway? Surely not to bring about world peace or a cure for anything! So was a mission simply something that you had to do? Everyone has one. We all have Things To Do. That sounded better, not so grand. At her age, perhaps that was the most precious gift of all — knowing that you still have things to do!

...

And so it was that, at a quarter after six in the morning, a baggy-eyed Willie Haapala drove her frowsy friend, Jeremy Banks to the bus station in Stastas. They were both a little hungover.

Jeremy had slept fitfully, as he always did when he had to be up early the next morning. He never used an alarm clock, claimed not to need one, but his sleep tended to be shallow and he kept waking up to check the time. Jeremy had also found himself mentally going over the conversation with Willie, and looking for loopholes in her theory, which seemed to state that there *is* no such thing as good and evil, only varied experience. What about crime? What about dictators who oppress, torture and kill? What of pedophiles who prey on *children?* What of mass murderers and serial killers and terrorists? What of sadists and rapists and racist groups like the Ku Klux Klan and neo-Nazis? What of satanic cults and their unspeakable rites? Yes, next time he and Willie had a chance to talk, he would have to ask *how* she explains away such things if they're not evil.

This, however, didn't seem to be the appropriate time to get into that. He had a bit of a headache, and Jeremy wasn't really a "morning" person. He wasn't a late sleeper, but preferred to ease into the day with little conversation until he'd had his coffee and read the morning paper. Now he had a long, tiresome, trip ahead and a sad house to return to. He stared rather forlornly out the window as the town of Stastas slid by.

Willie, at the wheel, gave him a sidelong glance. *Old chum, you look like I feel.* Would she ever see him again? Would Jeremy decide after all that a move to Broom Island would be too big a change in lifestyle, and that he would rather remain in Portland? Surely he had other ties there, friendships of long standing. She parked her car in the lot, got out and opened the trunk so Jeremy could take out his suitcase. They went into the bus station and sat down to wait.

"I'll call you when I get to Portland." Willie noticed he didn't refer to it as home.

"I hope you have an uncomplicated trip. May your luggage arrive when you do."

"Ah, the Blessing of the Traveler. There are no atheists at airport carousels. We have time, would you like a cup of coffee?"

"Oh, dear heaven, *yes*. I'd love one."

Jeremy headed for the coffee machine. Willie sat waiting. There weren't many people in the bus station at that hour — a young woman in jeans with torn knees, a middle-aged matron in a floral print dress designed to mask her thirty pounds of excess weight, and an elderly, white-haired man wearing a dark coat and a black felt fedora.

An elderly white-haired man in a dark coat? Willie looked again. Didn't she *know* this man? As if feeling her eyes upon him, the man looked at Willie and smiled, then with a bit of an old-fashioned flourish, raised his hand to his hat brim in a gesture of tipping it. He had something on his knee. Willie looked more closely and saw that it was, of all things, a cat: a small black short-haired cat with a glossy coat. How cute! A kitty-cat. A *kissa*, as cats were called, in Finnish. The old gentleman was gently stroking it as the animal rubbed against his hand, arching its back, allowing its tail to twine around the man's wrist. Willie smiled, then had a sudden flash of *something* and a tiny frisson of fear. She gasped, almost called out — then caught herself as she realized how outlandish that would have been. She didn't know who the man was after all, *couldn't* have known!

"Willie, are you all right?" Jeremy was back with two Styrofoam cups of steaming coffee. "You look as though you've seen a ghost."

"Yes, I'm fine. No, it was just that I thought I saw someone I knew. But I was mistaken."

"Oh? Where?"

Willie looked around, but the old man was gone.